SAVING HIS MATE

ALIENS OF OLUURA: BOOK ONE

IVY KNOX

CONTENTS

CONTENT WARNING

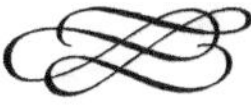

If you don't have any concerns regarding content and how it may affect you, **feel free to skip ahead to avoid spoilers**!

This book contains scenes that either mention or describe abduction, rape, anxiety, and depression which may be triggering for some. If you or someone you know is in need of support, there are places you can go for help. I have listed some resources at the end of this book.

PROLOGUE

CHLOE

"Who is she? How long have you been talking to her? Have you slept together?" I fire off all the questions I don't want the answers to, but I know I need the truth, no matter how awful it is.

Drew stands there, looking between my trembling bottom lip and his phone in my shaking hand. He knows he's been caught.

Our phones have the same black rubber case, so when the screen lit up on the phone sitting on the coffee table, I thought it was mine. Then I read a text from "Lana" that said, "Still wet thinking about last night." Definitely not mine.

At first, remorse fills his gaze. But then he straightens to his full height and his light brown eyes hold something else. Actually, it's nothing at all. That's what guts me. Any humanity that was there before is suddenly gone.

"Lana is Sully's cousin. She just moved here from Texas. And yes, we slept together. I don't know how long it's been going on. Since the summer, I guess, but definitely long enough for me to realize that she makes me happy," he says, his eyes almost defiant with his admission.

According to Drew, he had "no intention of cheating" when they first met. He was at his friend Sully's apartment watching a baseball game and she stopped by to hang out. She and Drew talked; they joked and got to know each other a little. That was it. Then they started texting, and after that, a line was crossed.

It began as an emotional affair when they were simply texting back and forth, and eventually it got physical too. They sent flirty messages to each other pretty much every day, and most of them led to explicit descriptions of what they wanted to do to each other. How much they wished they could be together. And how I was the only thing keeping them apart.

I had no idea she even existed. It's not like he ever said, "Hey, hun, I'll be home late tonight because I'm going to fuck my best friend's cousin, who's fourteen years younger than you and barely of legal age to drink, by the way. Don't wait up."

I wish he had, because this breakup would be far less painful and I wouldn't feel like such an idiot.

"You want me to feel bad about this? I just, I don't. I tried to make this work, but I can't pretend with you anymore, Chloe," Drew says, snatching his phone from my hand.

"Pretending? How long have you been pretending to love me?" I ask, my voice wobbly and panic twisting my insides.

I thought we were happy. I mean, I was happy. Sure, we're no longer in the honeymoon phase, but passion doesn't last forever. Things are comfortable between us after four years together. I'm good with being comfortable. Comfortable feels safe.

"Come on, Chlo. Is this really that surprising to you? We haven't had sex in two months," he says, like that should explain everything.

"Happy couples go through dry spells all the time. It's normal," I try to reason.

"We don't laugh together like we used to," he mutters over his shoulder as he heads into the bedroom and starts pulling his boxers from the dresser and stuffing them into a suitcase.

I follow close behind into the bedroom. "Work has been stressful. I know I've been working too many nights. We just need a weekend away or something. We can get that spark back," I plead. "What about Becca's wedding this spring? I already RSVP'd with a plus-one."

I feel like such a fool trying to convince him to stay with me after what he's done, but it feels like the life we've built is slipping away and I don't know what else to do. Like the more he pulls away, the more I'm inclined to reach for him.

This was my life too. A life I enjoyed.

"That—that's not the only thing." He throws a pair of socks into the suitcase, and his eyes lift to meet mine. "Look, I'm not trying to be a dick…but it's not…you're not—you're just not the same girl I fell in love with," he says, his eyes briefly scanning up and down my body as he says it.

He probably thought that visual assessment was subtle and maybe I didn't notice.

I definitely fucking noticed.

My heart feels like it's falling through my gut and out my ass and crashing through the floor at top speed. It also feels like I'm suddenly naked and on display, even though I'm wearing my favorite oversized cardigan, black leggings, and fuzzy socks ensemble that I'm able to wear daily since I work from home. I'm a graphic designer, so my clients don't need to see me, and I can wear whatever I want. Most days, I feel cozy and cute in this look. Right now, I feel like a frumpy ogre.

It's in that moment that I notice the waistband of my leggings feels tighter than usual. These used to fit perfectly. *When did they get tighter? I wonder. Is he right? Have I become undesirable? Could I have tried a little harder to keep him interested? I could've squeezed in a few more morning workouts, I guess. I didn't need that slice of cheesecake I ordered at dinner last weekend. Are all my clothes tighter? When was the last time I wore actual pants? Do I need to start buying a size up? I bet Lana would never let herself go like this. That's why he chose her over me.*

I take a slow, steadying breath and rub my temples. "Okay. So to be clear, you're dumping me because you've been cheating on me with this Lana person, and now you want to start dating her, and this is my fault because I'm fatter than I used to be? Is that what you're telling me right now?"

The sadness in my chest starts transforming into something else.

Rage. White-hot rage. Almost as if a little concentration is all it would take to unleash a ball of fire from the depths of my throat and melt his stupid face.

His stupid, handsome face. That stupid single dimple in his right cheek and that stupid straight nose and those dumb fucking cheekbones that could cut glass. I hate his stupid jet-black hair that's short on the side but long and mussed on top. I hate those lean arms that are covered in tattoos from shoulder to wrist. I hate thinking about how safe I've always felt inside them.

"I didn't say that, Chlo." He grabs his backpack and shoves his laptop into it. "Don't put words in my mouth."

"You didn't need to say it. I got the message," I throw back as I walk out into the living room.

"I'm just not happy anymore. We're not happy. Not like we used to be," he says, following me now.

A new and endlessly frustrating realization pops into my head.

I quickly turn on my heel and bump into him. "Wait. So you cheat on me and *I* don't even get to dump *you?*"

This is some bullshit.

"You know what? Fine. Whatever. You're moving out, then?" I ask, rushing to get the words out before my voice cracks. I don't want him to see how much he's crushing me.

"Yeah, I'm gonna crash at Sully's place for now while I look for a new apartment. I'll come back next weekend to grab the rest of my stuff. That cool?" He slings his backpack over his shoulders and rolls his suitcase to the door.

"Okay," I say, tears filling my eyes. "I need to start looking for a place too, I guess."

I should start calculating how long I can afford the rent of our apartment on my own. Possibly two months? Maybe three? Chicago is such an expensive place to live, especially when you're alone. But my mind is starting to shut down and I don't have it in me right now. That's a problem for tomorrow.

He cracks open the front door and then turns to face me.

"Listen, Chlo, I know this is sudden," he says as he stares intently at the spot of chipped paint on the doorframe. "You deserve better than me. Good luck and take care, okay?" He holds up his hand and clearly doesn't know what to do with it, so he settles on lightly fist-bumping my shoulder.

I just...*what?* Four years giving my heart and soul to this selfish prick and he wishes me luck? Tells me I deserve better? Really? And he gives me a fist bump, of all things?

"Uh...yeah, thanks," I reply coldly.

"Right. Bye," he says before shutting the door.

I rush to turn the deadbolt behind him and fall into a sobbing heap on the doormat. I clutch my stomach and wail into the cold, tiled floor beneath me. The sounds I'm making will surely have the neighbors wondering if I'm trying to resuscitate a wounded donkey, but I don't care. If I want to ugly cry in the fetal position, who's going to judge me? No one, because I'm all alone.

Completely alone.

CHAPTER 1

CHLOE

"See, Reggie? This is why it's better for me to stay single. Drew would never let you hang around if he was still here," I say to my neighbor's fluffy white Himalayan cat as he stretches lazily on my balcony.

Reggie has become my main source of entertainment, as well as my closest confidant over the last week. He also hasn't judged me for emptying several bottles of wine, leaving takeout containers all over the kitchen counter, and slubbing out in the same coffee-stained hoodie day and night.

I pad over to the wine rack, reveling in the feel of the cold floor against my bare feet, and pull another bottle of white from my stash. It's the last bottle I have, and my heart is still very much broken, so it looks like I'll have to venture out tomorrow to get more. I sigh as I twist off the cap and the wine hits the inside of my glass with that satisfying *glug, glug, glug* sound.

Reggie barely lifts his head as I return, and I find myself admiring his lack of fucks to give. I wish I could be more like that. But since

Drew took a sledgehammer to my heart, it seems my cup of fucks over-floweth. Especially when I stumble onto his new girlfriend's Instagram page every night before bed and see the photos of them together with captions underneath that include an obscene number of heart emojis.

Ugh.

"I'm fully aware that I shouldn't be looking at her Instagram, but apparently I'm actively seeking opportunities to make me hate myself even more," I say to Reggie, taking a sip of the wine and letting the sweet tangy flavor settle on my tongue.

I plop down on the stool by the open sliding glass door and comb through Reggie's downy fur. His tail makes a contented swish back and forth as a loud purr rumbles from his chest.

"I wish I saw it coming, you know? The cheating. The lies. I didn't see him slipping away from me until it was too late." My eyes fill with tears that threaten to spill over onto my cheeks. This would be the fourth time I've cried today. Just today. I can't believe I have any tears left, to be honest.

I rub my eyes and shake my head, trying to avoid going down another rabbit hole of depression. Instead, I'd rather eat my feelings, I decide. I reach for the half-eaten slice of carrot cake I was nibbling on for breakfast and moan as the hardened sugary frosting sticks to my teeth. "Much better," I mumble to Reggie with my mouth full.

He blinks at me and tilts his entire body until he's lying on his side. "Life is easier for you, little man. Look at how cute you are," I say, leaning down to scratch behind his ears.

Three big bites later and my plate is clean, my belly is full, and my sadness has returned. The conversation Drew and I had the day he left replays in my mind, and his hurtful words cut even deeper now.

Thankfully, my memory cloud evaporates at the touch of Reggie's paw kneading into the arm of my sweatshirt. He's purring even louder, and clearly he can tell I need a distraction.

"Reggie, dinner!" my downstairs neighbor Mrs. Schulman hollers through the door on her balcony. Reggie scrambles up in a hurry and hops down over the steel frame of my balcony onto hers.

"Later, Reg!" I yell. Even in my fragile emotional state, I'm not offended by his quick exit. He's a cat, after all, and he's motivated only by the promise of meals and snuggles.

Before the silence of my empty apartment can weigh too heavily on me, my phone lights up with a text.

> Jenn: Girl, this guy said I'd be prettier if I smiled more. When I rolled my eyes, he said he was kidding and told me to stop acting crazy. I almost choked on my lasagna.

> Me: Seriously? Red flags abound. Time to bail.

> Oh and he's also had four gin and tonics already. FOUR.

I laugh. That sounds awful. I'm not looking forward to reentering the dating world at all. Dating apps. Small talk. Rejection. Kill me now.

> Are you texting me all this right in front of him?

> No, he went to the bathroom. But I am MISERABLE. HELLLLLP.

She follows this plea with several crying emojis.

Jenn is five eight, with long, thick blonde hair and legs for days. She goes for a run every morning at six a.m. before heading off to her very stressful and high-paying job as a corporate attorney. Oh, and her hair dries perfectly straight. No frizz. None.

She's brilliant and sweet, and physically, she's an absolute goddess. If Jenn's not finding decent guys out there, what chance do I have? Me, a chubby brunette in my mid-thirties with a soft stomach and spider veins on my thighs.

> Want me to rescue you? We can do the pretend family emergency call.

> Or you can just tell him your best friend is having explosive diarrhea and you need to bring her some extra toilet paper. That'll scare him away for the rest of time.

> I love you.

> Hey, we're still on for a rom-com-a-thon and sleepover tomorrow, yes?

My heart swells at her enthusiasm to watch the same movies we've seen a hundred times.

> Yes, it's a date. I'll get more wine.

> Can't wait!

I walk into my bedroom and plug my phone into the charger on the nightstand. Jenn has stopped by a few times this week to check on me, and even though I hate letting her see me like this, I'm truly grateful to have her.

I look at the lock screen of my phone and part of me is slightly hurt that I haven't heard from Drew since he left. I know he's moved on, but I don't know, part of me hoped that Lana would've realized immediately that Drew's a loser and dumped him by now. Then he'd come crawling back to me. Or maybe, spending more time with Lana would've made Drew realize how much he missed me.

Not that I'd take him back, of course, but it would certainly boost my self-esteem to have someone, *anyone* want me.

Although, remaining single wouldn't be so terrible either. Most days, I'm perfectly content to read or watch TV without any human interaction. I don't mind the quiet. But at the moment, the quiet reminds me of what I've lost.

Or maybe I'll adopt a pet. I've always wanted to rescue a dog of my own. I begged Drew to let me get one. He said he didn't feel like cleaning up after a dog and was worried it would keep us from "enjoying our life together." So much for that.

I head into the bathroom and turn on the shower. I strip down to nothing in front of the bathroom mirror, and I take a step back so I can look at my full reflection.

I sigh. I want to see a woman trying her best. I want to compare the color of my eyes and hair to rich chocolate or whiskey or something else universally loved. I want to appreciate the gap between my front teeth. I want to be kind to myself right now. I'm desperate to have those confident, positive thoughts.

But I just hear Drew's voice in my head as he tells me I'm not the girl he fell in love with while his eyes scan my body. Then I see my skin, too pale. I see my hair and eyes as a plain, uninteresting shade of brown. I see the gap between my teeth as a flaw I should've had corrected with braces as a teenager. I see my full breasts, hanging a bit lower than they did when I was in college. I see every dimple, roll, blemish, and vein that, maybe, if they didn't exist, I would still have a man who loves me.

Placing my hands on either side of the sink, I lean in close as the steam from the shower starts to fog up the corners of the mirror. The dark circles under my eyes are a stark contrast to my pale skin. I feel as emotionally tired as I look physically. I'm so sick of feeling broken.

I pull the elastic from my hair, and my previously messy bun falls in even messier waves down my back. I stand back up, as straight as I can.

"I don't need him, or anyone else," I say as I step into the shower and tug the curtain closed behind me.

Tomorrow is the day I look for a pet to adopt. Pets bring you nothing but joy. They don't judge, or manipulate, or leave you for someone else. They just love you. Maybe I'll adopt a cat *and* a dog, or maybe two dogs, or three.

If my destiny is to become a spinster, I might as well lean into it.

CHAPTER 2

CHLOE

I wake up with a shiver and reach down to yank my comforter over my head. My tongue feels like it's wearing a sweater, and my head feels like a balloon filled with sludge. Whatever time it is now, I want to sleep for at least two more hours. My work emails can wait.

But there are no blankets to grab. When I reach down, I feel the cotton fabric of my ratty nightgown under my fingers, and it's then that I realize I'm not covered at all.

I'm…not in my bed. The cold steel beneath me is unforgiving on my neck, and I'm afraid to open my eyes because this is definitely not where I went to sleep. This isn't even a bed. I slowly crack open one eye and am blinded by the bright light hanging above my head.

What the fuck?

I slowly squint both eyes open and, once my vision adjusts to the light, scan my surroundings without moving my head. If someone else is in here, I don't want them to know I'm awake.

My eyes first land on what looks to be a wall of cinderblocks in front of me. No windows, nothing on the walls, just smooth gray stone from ceiling to floor. There are several machines on either side of me and directly behind my head that are beeping and whirring. My right arm is connected to one through an IV. Behind the IV is another gray stone wall, but on my left side is a thick beige curtain. I hear beeps and whirrs on the other side of the curtain, so I assume some poor soul over there is in the same pickle I'm in. The light above my head is extremely bright and shining on my face and body, but the rest of the room is dimly lit. I'm alone.

For now, at least.

I lift my head slightly and feel a sharp pain behind my eyes that has me immediately lowering my head back down on the table and pinching the bridge of my nose to stop the pain.

Am I hungover? That last bottle of wine was still half full, and I stopped drinking when Reggie left. That was hours before I fell asleep.

No. No, it can't be that.

I quickly run through the rest of the evening in my mind. I showered, applied my serums and antiaging cream, and brushed my teeth. I spent about an hour browsing through pet bios on the local rescue group's website, getting increasingly excited about my furry soon-to-be sidekick. I threw on my favorite old-lady nightgown and turned on reruns of *The Office*. I think I fell asleep within two or three episodes.

Typical nighttime routine. Nothing out of the ordinary.

So again…what in the actual fuck?

My thoughts are interrupted by the sound of something being wheeled into the room I'm in.

The sound is coming from behind me, and when I try to tip my head back to see what or who it is, the pain behind my eyes returns and I struggle to keep them open. The beeping machines are blocking my view, so whoever it is seems to be intentionally staying just outside my eyeline.

Then they speak. "Welcome, human female," says the monotone robotic voice.

"What? Human? Who are you?" I ask, dread pooling in my gut.

"You are currently under medical evaluation. Your heartbeat is increasing. It is recommended that you calm down immediately," the robot warns.

Well, this is a crazy dream I'm having. It's a dream, right? It has to be a dream.

"What the hell is going on?" I shriek while attempting to swing my feet off the table, only to realize my ankles are cuffed to the bottom corners. Looks like I'm not going anywhere.

I lie back down with a frustrated huff.

"How did I get here? Did you drug me?" I ask.

The robot says nothing.

"Are you going to tell me what's happening here or what?" I nag the robot, my panic reaching its peak.

"You are currently under medical evaluation," the robot repeats. "Your patience is appreciated while we complete our examinations."

Oh my god, who programmed this thing to sound like the world's worst customer service rep?

"That didn't answer my questions." I scratch at my scalp nervously and sigh. "Let's try this: Representative. I'd like to speak to a representative!" I shout behind me.

If this thing is programmed like a call center, maybe this will help me get through to someone?

"Your heart rate is increasing. It is recommended that you calm down immediately," the robot warns again.

"Telling someone to calm down always has the opposite intended effect, just FYI."

I pinch the sensitive skin underneath my right bicep because I know it'll hurt like hell and will probably be an effective way to wake me up.

I hear the robot's wheels moving around behind me, and I start to get even more nervous. What's it doing? "Sedation is a necessary part of our evaluation process."

Uh-oh.

"It ensures your safety while we conduct the health scans needed to determine which planets and which species you will be best suited for," it says, my surroundings becoming blurrier by the second.

"Uh, what did you say? Which planets I'm suited for? What does that mean?" My limbs are starting to feel heavy, and the urge to close my eyes is stronger than I've ever felt.

"Did you...did you give me...something? Because I feel weirb. Wait, why can't I say 'weirb'? Is it 'weirb' or 'weird'?" My thoughts are as jumbled as my words as my eyelids give in to the haze and the world around me fades to black.

* * *

THE MOMENT my eyes slowly blink open, it becomes abundantly clear that my situation has gone from "pickle" status to "absolute shitstorm."

I sit up slowly and look around.

The steel table, beeping machines, and mysterious robot are gone, and in their place is a glass cage the size of my bedroom that I appear to be trapped in, with ripped-up shreds of white fabric all over the floor, and two other women lying close together in the fetal position in front of me, their limbs twitching in their sleep.

Then I assess how I feel. I'm still wearing my nightgown, and aside from a slight rip at the bottom, it's mostly intact. My legs and feet are still bare. As I pat my arms, ribs, stomach, and thighs, I don't feel like I was physically violated or hurt anywhere. That's a plus, I suppose. The sharp pain behind my eyes is gone, and I'm not hooked up to anything. At this point, I just feel groggy and confused.

I lean forward, pressing my forehead and nose against the glass. I can't see much of anything beyond the cage we're in, because the room is dark, but I can tell it's in a much larger space based on the occasional creaks I hear and how those creaks echo throughout the room.

I put my hands over my ears and shut my eyes tight, trying to fight back the anxiety that threatens to consume me. How did I get here? Where is *here*? Am I still on Earth?

I realize I'm starting to hyperventilate when I hear movement over my shoulder.

"Ah, you're awake. You were out for so long I thought you might be dead. A dead roommate would've been kind of a drag," the woman says as she leans her back against the opposite glass wall.

Her hair is a brilliant copper red, hanging down past her shoulders in French-braid pigtails. Little hairs stick up and out every which way, like she's had the braids in for days, which she clearly has. Even in the darkened room, I can see freckles dusted over her nose, cheeks, and forearms.

"I'm Kate," she says with a smirk. She's wearing an oversized navy-blue T-shirt with white block letters in the center that say, "It's wine o'clock somewhere!" There's a rip in the neck and left sleeve, and several small holes toward the bottom hem. Her yellow flannel pajama bottoms are covered in blue dinosaurs and are rolled up in cuffs to her pale shins.

"Um, hi. I'm Chloe," I reply, trying not to sound too shaken following her sarcasm. As much as I love deadpan humor, I'm not in the mood for it right now.

The woman to Kate's right sits up next to her with a yawn. "Don't mind her, she's just going through her goth phase later in life than the rest of us." She points to her chest. "Ava."

Even in her dirt-stained pink tank top and satin purple shorts—clothes that she, too, must've gone to bed in when she was taken—she looks surprisingly camera-ready and downright gorgeous. Her brown skin is so clear that she's practically glowing in this dark room. Her black hair is short, just below her ears, and falls in soft, styled waves. Her nose is tiny in comparison to her big eyes and full lips.

I'm amazed that neither of them seems at all scared. Perhaps they've been here a long time and the shock has worn off?

"Do you happen to know where the fuck we are?" I ask, hoping they can provide some answers.

Ava chuckles. "I wish. The only thing I can tell you is that we aren't on Earth anymore."

My eyes widen.

"Yep. Aliens are as real as that shit bucket over there in the corner." She points to a white cylinder slightly raised on a platform and tucked in the back corner of the glass enclosure.

"Are you serious? That's our toilet?" So that's what the pungent stench is in here. That and body odor, which might be coming from me, or Ava, or Kate. Or most likely, all three of us. I can't believe I'm starting to miss that steel table and infuriating robot.

"It's not the worst. Once a day there's a suction sound coming from underneath it, and then it's empty and doesn't reek anymore. Fresh water gets poured into that big bowl behind you, and we get a pile of dusty dog-food-like kibble once a day. It lands on the floor next to the water bowl. So I wouldn't give the place five stars, but maybe a solid three point five?" Ava says dryly.

I chuckle at that. I feel so relieved to have someone I can actually talk to.

"How long have you guys been here? Do you even know?" I whisper, now wanting to ask at least a hundred more questions.

Ava tilts her chin up and closes her eyes. "I think it's been a week, or maybe five or six days. It's hard to tell when the lights are always off. No one ever comes in here. But Kate and I arrived at the same time, as far as we can tell. You were put in here two days ago. We woke up and there you were."

Two days. I lost two whole days. Maybe even more than that, since I don't know how long I was in that other facility.

"What's this all over the floor?" I ask, grabbing some of the shredded fabric in my hand and letting it slip through my fingers.

"Remember how you'd see birds in cages at the pet store and there'd be like, shredded paper on the bottom of the cage? I think this is kind of the same thing. I'm not totally sure of the purpose, but it certainly seems like to them, we're just pets." Kate says the last part in a bitter tone.

Them. Whoever took us in our sleep and brought us here. I hate *them* so much I could scream.

I scan the entire cage slowly and carefully, looking for a latch or a crack in the glass or something, anything, that could maybe get us out of here. Though I have no idea what we'd do after we get out of the cage. I can't see much beyond the glass.

"We've tried pounding on it. Kicking it. Throwing ourselves into it. We've stood on each other's shoulders to reach the top. We've looked for openings in the floor, even locks. There's no way out," Ava says, as if reading my mind.

I put my face in my hands. This is so insane. "What else? Tell me everything. Please," I plead.

Kate blows an errant lock of hair out of her eyes and takes a deep breath. "From what Ava and I can gather, we were kidnapped from Earth in the middle of the night while we slept, hence the pj's. We were taken to a facility with robots and were tested for who knows what."

"Yes, I had a robot too!" I exclaim, somewhat comforted that I didn't imagine the whole thing.

"I don't remember seeing any robots. I was in and out of consciousness the whole time," Ava adds, her face solemn.

"Then we were brought here. I have fuzzy memories of someone wheeling me through a hallway before I was put in this cage. We haven't seen anyone else since, or even what this room looks like with the lights turned on. That"—Kate points to the soft blue glow coming from the top of the waterspout inside our cage—"is the only source of light we've had."

"But how do you know for certain that we're no longer on Earth?" I ask.

"The creature wheeling me through the hallway to this cage wasn't human. He was..." Kate grimaces. "...freaky looking. A little guy with three legs, a giant beak and scales. It was him and someone else talking around me. When they spoke, it was just a series of clicking sounds."

Yeah, that's not a good sign.

I pause, taking in this new information. "So you don't know how long we'll be in here or what we'll be used for when we get out."

"Nope." Kate leans in a bit. "By the way, how old are you, Chloe?"

"I'm thirty-five. Why?" I ask, surprised by the change in subject.

Kate and Ava share a knowing glance.

"What is it?"

"We're both in our thirties too. And clearly we're all on the thick side." Ava gestures at my body and then Kate's. "Those similarities can't be purely coincidental."

She's right. We're all around the same size. I'm probably the biggest out of the three of us, a little softer in the middle with breasts that are slightly bigger, but smaller in the backside. Ava is the opposite —smaller in the chest and waist with wider hips. We haven't compared our heights, but I would guess that Ava and I are both five six, while Kate is probably five feet at best, thick and curvy everywhere.

I scoff. "So is it safe to assume that these aliens have a thing for chubby women just past their prime? Lucky us."

They both laugh.

Apparently, Drew dumping me for a twenty-one-year-old still leaves a bitter taste in my mouth.

Oh my god, Drew.

He dumped me right before I was taken. Could that have played into this?

I sit up straight. "Were both of you in relationships or close to your families back home?"

Kate responds first. "I was in the process of getting a divorce. We were separated for about a month before I was taken. I have three brothers, but I'm not close to any of them or my parents."

"Oh, I'm sorry," I offer, not really knowing what to say.

"What for? The divorce? Don't be. He's a controlling, manipulative asshole, and I was very close to cutting him out of my life forever," Kate says with a wistful sigh.

Ava shares next. "I walked in on my fiancé having sex with my best friend on my birthday. That was a month ago. I was staying in a motel. And my mom died when I was in high school. My dad and I aren't that close anymore, and I can't stand my stepmom."

"Okay. So we were all newly single, living alone, with no close family nearby." My suspicions were correct, it would seem, and for the first time ever, I hate being right.

"Easy targets," Kate adds, nodding.

Ava groans and leans her head back against the glass.

We sit there silently, letting the reality sink in that we were obviously being watched or followed, and chosen for what I can only assume is something truly, truly awful.

* * *

OVER THE NEXT FEW DAYS, we get to know each other. I learn that Ava was living in Los Angeles and Kate was living in Boston. We were all taken from big cities.

They both use the toilet bucket and don't even blink at the lack of privacy. I hold it for as long as I can, but after what I guess is a full day, I use it while begging them not to look. After the second or third time using it, though, I don't care anymore. We're living like animals now, so stressing about lack of privacy doesn't seem worth the energy.

We also discuss potential ways to escape and ultimately come up empty. We brainstorm strategies to stay together, though, and Ava shows us some basic self-defense moves she learned from her fitness trainer. If someone does ever come to check on us and open up this cage, we don't plan to just sit here like docile kittens waiting to be adopted. There's strength in numbers, we remind each other, so we're going to do whatever we can to remain as a group, and attack as a group if needed.

Every night before bed, the crumbly and dusty kibble Kate and Ava mentioned lands in a pile on the floor, and they shove handfuls of it into their mouths.

Upon seeing it the first night, I didn't want anything to do with it. By the third night, though, I'm inhaling the kibble without hesitation. Instead of a crunch, the moment my teeth connect with the kibble, it falls apart in stale flakes. It tastes like dirt and something else. A little salty, and maybe something similar to chicken? I can't put my finger on the flavor, but since it's not making me gag, I keep wolfing it down.

After we finish, the three of us lean against the back wall of the cage in a row, rubbing our full bellies.

"It's not pasta or a cheeseburger, but it does the job," I say.

"Pasta!" Ava bellows dramatically. "I miss pasta so much."

"That, and coffee," I add. "I wonder if I'll ever have coffee again." I would've had an extra cup, or four, on that last morning I was home if I had known I was about to be kidnapped by aliens.

Ava scratches her head and rests her chin on her crossed arms. "The list of things I miss about Earth is fucking endless."

I nod, silently mourning along with her.

Then Kate starts chuckling softly to herself.

When it continues after a few minutes, Ava and I stare at each other, dumbfounded.

Kate wipes her eyes, her face turning red. "I'm sorry. I was just thinking about how we all probably thought we hit rock bottom when we were still on Earth. And then—" She breaks into a much louder giggle fit. "And then we were kidnapped by aliens and thrown into a glass cage *with a poop bucket*." She slaps her leg as she rolls onto the floor, howling with laughter between gasps for breath.

Ava and I exchange eye rolls, both annoyed at first by Kate's callousness regarding our situation. Then that irritation fades into matching smirks, and soon we're laughing too.

"Yeah, I would trade my left tit for that rock bottom right now," I say as the laughter fades.

Kate and Ava nod.

"At least we're not going through this alone though, right?" Ava looks at both of us earnestly. "If I were alone in this cage, I'd lose my damn mind."

"True. Thank god we have eac—" My words are cut off by the sight and sound of several overhead fluorescent lights being turned on at once. I'm suddenly blinded due to the lack of exposure to any light at all. I rub my eyes and squint as quickly as I can, desperate to see what's outside of our cage.

It's…massive. This room is massive. And round. It's a big circle. As my eyes take in the plain wood-paneled walls, the walls themselves begin to change. They start flipping inside themselves, like doors to secret passageways, rectangular panel by rectangular panel until every inch of the walls is covered in what looks like maroon wallpaper with slightly lighter maroon stripes.

The ceiling is domed and looks to be about a mile high, with gold velvet ropes and tapestries draped in every direction toward the center at the highest point. It reminds me of an old-timey theater.

The floor in front of us is all white tiles with a subtle swirly design. But a moment later, the floor flips in on itself, and instead of swirly tiles, it's covered in black velvet carpet with at least twelve tall oval stands that look like podiums.

My mind spins as my eyes continue to scan.

I notice that our cage is raised on a platform, like a stage, almost. We look to be about three feet off the main floor. The back glass wall of our cage is somewhat close to the back wall of the room, with nothing else behind it, making it seem as if we are the main attraction.

"Shit," I mutter before the steel double doors on the opposite side of the room swing open.

CHAPTER 3

VARREK

"Let us make this quick, Ahlvo," I tell him, my patience already wearing thin. My skin crawls as I follow behind my closest friend and second-in-command through the halls of the Nu'Piix Enbalo Post—a hub of sellers, a tavern, and a brothel clustered together at the port on the north side of Nu'Piix.

Nu'Piix is a small, desolate planet that takes me a full day to reach. I keep my visits to this place short and infrequent, and I have not explored beyond the port. I would guess the mass of beings strolling around me at the entrance of the tavern would say the same. We do not come to Nu'Piix to settle down and make a home. We are here to sell and trade our goods and to have a drink and a fuck before we depart.

Not that I have indulged in the latter here, as sharing a bed with a female would require me to remove my jumpsuit and reveal the royal Daaskano band etched into the skin on my bicep. I would not expect many on Nu'Piix to be familiar with my line, but the risk of being exposed is far too great. Someone could find out who and what I am —a former prince who is thought to be dead, a criminal, and a traitor to my father, King Muryk Daaskano of Trovilia, my planet of origin.

So the jumpsuit stays on, and I will tend to my aching cock later with my hand, as usual.

"Patience, brother. You are always in such a hurry to leave here. There is much to explore," Ahlvo says in a jovial tone as we enter the tavern and find a tall table to stand at. We punch in our order for two ales on the table's screen pad. "I reckon our meeting today will be worth the wait."

A moment later, our ales are delivered, and we both take large swigs.

"Who is this meeting with, exactly? And why must I be in attendance?" I ask, concerned that close contact with someone other than Ahlvo will expose my identity. "We come here to trade our wares. Then we leave. That is all I wish to accomplish on these outings."

"Bzzsil Chi contacted me and said he had an item for sale that he thought I would be interested in. He is holding an auction for it and will contact me when it is set to begin. I thought you might want to be present in case it's something we can use," Ahlvo tells me before taking another long sip of his ale.

"Bzzsil Chi? He is filth," I scoff.

Bzzsil Chi is a pvorki, a species that is native to the swamps of Nissth. He's a third of my height and twice as wide. He stands on three legs and is covered in oily yellow scales and hard brown knobs that run down his arms, back, and tail. His wide neck disappears into his black beak, and his matching black eyes are ovals that occupy the entire top half of his face and bug out in opposite directions. He is not pleasant to look at.

He runs the brothel here and holds some of the more exotic product trades. Ahlvo and I were introduced to him on a previous visit when Ahlvo was hoping to acquire some tools to turn the buuf-casi berries that grow wild on our planet, Oluura, into a potent ale.

I have heard many rumors about how Bzzsil acquires and treats his brothel workers. They are all unsavory and leave a sour taste in my mouth. He is quite possibly the least honorable male I have ever met. Or the second least honorable anyway. I want nothing he has to offer.

Ahlvo eyes me skeptically. "You are not even a little curious? What if it is a lush and willing female?"

"How willing could she possibly be if her body is being sold to the highest bidder? You assume she would choose to be part of such an auction? Only a female without any other options would choose this, and at that point, it is hardly a choice. It is survival." I shake my head at his naiveté.

He hangs his head in shame. "You are right. I just..." He rubs his hands down his face. "It has been a while for me yet. What about you? When was your last mating?"

I sigh. "Too long ago."

Admittedly, it has been many, many moons since I have felt a soft female pressed against me. My cock stirs at the distant memory of my last mating. It was long before I left Trovilia, when I still held the title of prince and when I had a loving family, a father I admired, countless medallions earned during my time as general of Trovilia's elite warriors, and a line of eager females to sate my needs.

Then I am reminded of the virus that ravaged Trovilia's population, killing most of our females, including my mother. I wince at the heaviness in my heart. It has been five years since her final breath left her body and my father started sinking into madness, and yet the emotional wound still feels fresh.

It was the beginning of the end.

It is why I fled with my clan and started life anew on Oluura. Keeping them alive is why I must come to this seedy port every three moons.

I am able to sell and trade herbs native to Oluura in large batches here at port to acquire med supplies, screen pads, ship components, furs, and food that I bring back to my clan.

They are all that matters now. I will not prioritize my loneliness over their needs.

"You will need to find a willing female using just your charms, brother," I say with a smirk. "Not our credits."

Ahlvo and I have been friends since we were young warriors in training. We met during a training exercise for newly appointed warriors, and he quickly became one of my most trusted allies. We have saved each other's necks in battle countless times. He was there to grieve with me when my mother's soul left this world. He even helped me plan and execute our escape from Trovilia. His family came with him. I owe him my life four times over. So when he wishes to have me tag along to a secret auction on Nu'Piix, I go.

I might go begrudgingly, but still, I go.

We empty our chilled mugs just as Ahlvo's screen pad buzzes with a new message. Ahlvo's eyes light up as he reads it, and then he grabs my shoulder. "The auction is about to begin."

AHLVO IS GIVEN instructions to enter the large structure next to the brothel. I have never been inside this building, but I have been curious as to what it is used for. It's twice the size of the brothel, and as we follow the winding halls inside according to Bzzsil's directions, I notice that it also seems completely empty and in need of extensive repairs.

The stone walls are chipped, uneven, and heavily dented, and there is straw and dirt covering the floors. It is as dirty as the paths around the brothel outside, so I cannot imagine what this "valuable item" could be. What would he want kept hidden inside these crumbling walls?

We find Bzzsil waiting for us in front of a pair of double doors made of steel at the end of long, dark hallway. When he turns to face us, his mouth opens and a drop of saliva flies from the corner of his beak. "Ah, welcome, my friends. You will enjoy this very much, I suspect. Please do tell others that Bzzsil Chi can secure all kinds of goods from throughout the galaxies." His voice lowers to a whisper. "Even if they are not considered to be legal."

His two-fingered hands curl around the handles and pull open both doors, and I am hit with a blast of flashing lights and loud music. The room is clearly soundproof, as I could hear nothing outside the closed doors.

Bzzsil leads us to an oval stand in the center of the room, complete with a screen pad lit up for our use. He points to it and begins rattling off instructions. "Scan your identification pattern here, and once the auction begins, you can tap the pattern to accept the current bid or go higher. If you should win the auction, your credits will be transferred from your pattern to mine."

"What is this button for?" Ahlvo asks, pointing to the yellow triangle in the top right corner of the screen.

"Ah! That is if the bidding gets so high that you need to use another form of payment instead of credits. I do accept many forms of payment," Bzzsil leans in and says in a slithering tone. "Just press that button and I will come right over to consider your offer."

I have grown tired of his odd, deceitful eyes, partially because they linger a bit too long on mine. I worry, briefly, that he recognizes me and is hinting at the wealth I once had as Prince of Trovilia. But the concern passes when I remember that Bzzsil is not that clever. If he knew of my past, he would have tried to extort me long before now. He is nothing more than port scum trying to make a deal. "We have plenty of credits," I growl. "Begin the auction."

He cackles, unbothered, and shuffles away, his wide tail swinging from side to side. He slips behind a large red curtain that blocks the other half of the room from sight. I scrutinize my surroundings once he disappears as I attempt to drown out the cacophony of horns and drums being played together in a bizarre tune. The air in here smells of stale smoke, and I try not to think about how many crooked dealings have occurred in this space.

There are several other tables like ours in here, with at least one male at each.

After letting my eyes wander around the room, I decide that most of the males in attendance do not seem like potential threats to us. Ahlvo and I are taller, broader, and, I imagine, more experienced fighters than the majority of those around us. There is a male behind us to the left that has been eyeing us warily as he speaks into his screen pad and fiddles with the other screen pad on the table. He is a monjuri, a lean, bipedal creature the width of my leg, with rubbery gray skin; hundreds of small, sharp teeth; and four eyes.

There is also a pair on our far right, next to the wall, that are heavily armed. Ahlvo and I carry weapons as well, but they are all concealed. These two strap their blades and guns on the outside of their clothing as if encouraging attackers to approach. They are slightly shorter than Ahlvo and me, but they are thicker. They are flixiels, which means their tough hides make them harder to injure or kill. But not impossible.

Not that I have any intention of harming the flixiels, or anyone else here, but a good warrior must be prepared for any potential threat each time he or she enters a room. Based on the characters assembled around us, brought together by a scoundrel like Bzzsil Chi, it is clear that Ahlvo and I must remain on high alert until this auction ends.

Ahlvo's eyes meet mine, and he says, "Unmatched," while tapping his fist against his chest. It is a signal we used in battle, when we were in a hostile environment and we were confident that we could take the enemy down with minimal effort.

The curtains open slightly on both sides, leaving an opening just wide enough for several j'takka females to stroll out and line the outer walls of the room. They are dressed in tight gold uniforms that do not cover much of their deep violet skin. They perform a synchronized dance as the music gets louder and picks up tempo. They shake their large breasts and sway their hips to the song that plays, capturing the attention of every male in the room.

Ahlvo gives me a knowing glance and wags his brows in appreciation.

I roll my eyes at him and laugh.

Ahlvo very much appreciates the female form—all of them, in fact. It does not matter the species, size, or shape. And wherever he goes, females are drawn to him like a chirbex beetle to a halu plant on a hot morning.

His mood is always light, and his smiles come easy. He is a constant source of merriment among our clan. Despite the grisly sights he has seen in battle, his shoulders remain loose and he ends each day with hope for the one that follows.

Whereas I seem to become pricklier and more jaded the older I get.

The song fades out and the dancers disappear behind the curtain as Bzzsil marches out onto the floor to his own erratic tune. He slides his wide, round feet across the carpeted floor before stopping in front of the curtain, dead center, grinning at his audience. His chest is puffed and his stance proud.

"Welcome, friends. I have summoned you here because I have acquired something truly unique, something that no other seller in this galaxy has been able to offer, and I wanted you to be the first to lay your eyes upon it," he says, his voice booming.

"In other galaxies, this item is in high demand. It is illegal to own and sell in all galactic regions as its place of origin is too primitive to even communicate outside of its own planet," he scoffs, his tone incredulous. "Can you imagine?

"Lucky for you, I have many connections. I was able to secure this initial order, and more will follow. Because I am certain that one auction will not be enough to sate your desires," he says, as the curtain slowly parts behind him. He steps to the left of the curtain, giving us an unobstructed view of the goods.

It is a large glass cage, and inside the cage are three terrified-looking creatures with soft, flat faces and tattered rags covering their bodies. Their skin is slightly different colors, as well as their manes, but all look smooth to the touch. They huddle close together, their bodies visibly shaking.

"Behold, the human female." Bzzsil gestures to the cage occupants. "This creature is bred on a planet called Earth, and it is said that to spend even a moment sheathed inside a human female's tight, warm cunt is to experience a level of pleasure unknown to most males.

"Today, I have three human females for sale," he says.

"What are the ownership terms?" the monjuri yells, his screen pad still held to his ear.

"Ah yes. You will not get your human female for just one eve. This is not a rental. I am selling each one as a pet, for you to keep and fuck and do what you will, for however long you wish!" he shouts, then lowers his voice to almost a whisper. "There are no refunds."

My attention is pulled from Bzzsil's dubious sales pitch by a sweet scent filling my nose. It is...floral and rich and...extremely pleasant. I am not sure why, but it has a calming effect on my body. My shoulders loosen, and yet my skin begins to prickle with awareness, as if sensing a coming storm before it hits land. I do not know the source, but I am suddenly desperate to keep breathing it in.

My gaze is guided by my nose as I search until my eyes connect with one of the females in the cage, and I suck in a breath. The scent comes from her. It feels as if time is speeding up and slowing down at once. She is standing between the other two females, but just as soon as I notice their presence on either side of her, their features become hazy and nondescript. All I see is her.

Her gaze holds mine with matching intensity, and I wonder if she is experiencing the same dizzying sensations I am.

She is...mine.

I am as sure of that as I am my own name. I feel it in my blood. This delicate, small female, with her captivating dark eyes and long silky mane of the same dazzling color. With skin so light that it looks almost translucent and her soft pink lips, slightly parted in a way that makes my cock throb against my thigh.

Could this be my inara? My anchor to all things good and right? My everything?

I never truly believed the stories told by my mother and the elders about fated mates, and I am humbled and shocked I have been chosen to receive this great honor. It does not happen to everyone and has not happened among my people in many years. I assumed I would spend the rest of my days alone, caring for my clan. Fated mates were part of my past life on Trovilia, before the virus. Before the chaos. Before the pain.

I am then hit with another scent, but this one is sharp and acrid, and I realize it is my inara's fear. It wafts invisibly off her skin and floats directly into my nose. My body responds to it instantly, my fangs sharpening in my mouth and claws extending from my finger-tips. As my muscles contract, I find it difficult to lean on the table in front of me without crushing it under my grip. I straighten my spine and shift my weight back and forth between my feet, trying to conceal the change in my body from onlookers.

As her fear scent continues to take up residence in my lungs, my breathing becomes more ragged. The need to pull her from that cage and take her away from this place courses through my veins like fire. I have never experienced such an intense and primal need before, and yet I know I must not allow anyone here to see how important this female is to me already.

A hand tightens around my elbow and gives me a quick shake. My eyes refuse to leave my inara and her frightened eyes, and when Ahlvo's face pops in front of mine, blocking her from my view, I expose my fangs in a furious snarl.

"Varrek, tell me what is happening," Ahlvo commands, concern and confusion swirling in his eyes. Then a grin spreads across his face. "Are we readying for a scrap?" He cracks his knuckles as he glances around the room. "Point out our target and I will gladly throw the first punch."

I find that I cannot bring myself to tell Ahlvo the truth of what is happening. "It-it is nothing, Ahlvo. Merely a flash of memory. The females on D'Alluk. Our final mission for my father. Their fear." I take deep breaths in an attempt to calm myself. "Their faces, they still linger in my mind. Seeing these females must have triggered it."

The excuse I give for my behavior is not entirely false. These flashes have come and gone many times since we left Trovilia. They began after our final mission. My father had reached the peak of his madness; all rational thought and compassion for others had left him completely.

* * *

IT STARTED WITH THE VIRUS. When an older male Trovilian had returned home from a trip to D'Alluk, a neighboring planet. He had no symptoms of sickness, but his mate died within a few days of his return. The virus spread so quickly, silently, and within one moon there was no way to contain it to protect our people. It did not sicken healthy males. It took the most vulnerable first: the elderly and the young. Then it took females of all ages, sick as well as healthy. So many of them, thousands of them, gone from this world.

When it took my mother, I thought my father would follow her to the final rest. It was not uncommon to see mates who were separated in death choose to reunite for the final rest. But he did not.

Instead, he sought revenge for the pain he suffered. The peaceful farm planet of D'Alluk became the target of his vengeance. He blamed the people of D'Alluk for my mother's death, and for the all the deaths that occurred. He assembled a war council of veteran warriors of Trovilia, most of whom had also lost their mates and daughters to the virus, and their shared rage fueled conspiracy theories about whether it was created in a lab, how our planet was intentionally targeted for the spread, and which planets would be next. There were no facts or data to support these ideas, but the ideas themselves were enough for the war council to decide that attacking D'Alluk was the only course of action to protect the rest of the galaxy.

As general of Trovilia's elite warriors, I tried, and failed, many times to provide rational thought in order to combat the lunacy of their plans. They wanted to drop bombs. They wanted to decimate their places of worship. They wanted to burn entire hillsides of crops to starve the D'Allukans.

I should have been the one with my father's ear during these times. We were both grief-stricken after losing my mother, but only I could see beyond our pain to the pain we'd be inflicting upon others for something they could not control. The D'Allukans did not create this virus to attack our females. It was simply a disease their bodies were naturally immune to and ours were not.

But he was locked in a cycle of hate and fear, so no matter how sound the logic, it could not break through the madness in his mind.

Our mission was to kidnap a large group of the D'Allukan females from their homes under the cover of darkness and bring them to

Trovilia, where they would be forced into a breeding program designed by my father and the war council as a way to preserve our race. In my father's twisted mind, this would also serve justice to D'Alluk for the devastation the virus caused us. Their virus takes the lives of our females, so we take their females in return.

I had to swallow the bile rising in my throat upon hearing these plans in my father's war room. What he was suggesting…it was unheard of. What the females would endure once we brought them to Trovilia twisted my insides. Their bodies would be reduced to nothing more than vessels to carry and deliver our young.

I had never been a squeamish sort. As a Trovilian warrior, I was used to the grisly sights on the battlefield. The blood, the gore, and being covered in both for days on end. Fine. But this? Harming innocent females was so far beyond my scope of brutality that I could not stomach even discussing it as an option.

"This is rape. What you are planning is a program enforcing rape —a crime so heinous that a Trovilian male convicted of such would be sentenced to death. You realize that, yes?" I asked him.

"It is only rape if the female is a Trovilian citizen. That is the way our law is written, my son. We need our race to continue. I have examined all other options. This is the only way to protect our kind from dying out," he said, his tone cold. "Besides, they will be given food and shelter in exchange for their role as breeders. That will be enough to compensate them."

"This…*this* is the only way?" I could not believe the male sitting before me was my father. My blood. "This goes against everything we are. Everything you have taught me. Females, *all females*, are to be revered. They are the life-bringers. They are what anchors us to the good and the true. Without them we are lost."

"And we have been lost!" my father shouted, getting to his feet. "For too long, we have been lost. This will correct our course. You leave with your crew just before the sun rises."

"I will not," I told him, standing taller and dipping my chin slightly to look down into his eyes. *When did I grow taller than him?* I briefly scanned my memories. Perhaps I misremembered his size because of the admiration I used to feel for him. All of that was gone in this moment.

"You are general of the Trovilian warriors. A role I gave you. A role you are lucky to have. Your duty is to carry out my orders. *This* is an order. Disobey me and you will regret it." His tone was dripping with such disdain that I knew to take his threat seriously.

By the many arguments we had in the days prior about his plans to attack the D'Allukans, he was clearly starting to see me less as his son and more as merely an obstacle in his path of destruction. His words were not just words. They were a glimpse into his intentions.

"Is that a threat on my life? You threaten to kill me, Father? Is that where our bond has settled, then?" I threw back.

He said nothing, his silence giving me the answer I needed.

I hung my head in despair. "I would happily join Mother for the final rest than carry out your sickening plans for revenge. I can only imagine the look on her face if she were to see the weak, wretched male you have become." I stormed out of his war room. He yelled something unintelligible as I left, but I did not care to hear what it was.

It was the next eve, when I was supposed to be on a ship with my crew to D'Alluk, that I became violently ill. I could not eat, I could not sleep, and then I could not swallow or breathe without experiencing extreme discomfort. I was drenched in sweat and yet chilled to the bone. I summoned the castle healers to my quarters, but none showed to treat me. It was then that I knew my father had poisoned me and left me to die.

I contacted Ahlvo, and he and his father came to my quarters to retrieve me. They carried me back to their home, far outside the castle walls, and Kaiva, Ahlvo's mother, got to work on treating me. She was the healer for her village and had become like a second mother to me after mine had passed.

It was several days later that my fever had broken, the vomiting had ceased, and I was able to remain conscious. She said that my gold skin had faded to a pallid yellow and my lips had been a troubling blue color during my darkest hours. Ahlvo and I decided then to leave

Trovilia and start a new life elsewhere. There was no other way. We knew where we would go and who we would want to come with us, as this was not the first time we had considered leaving. We just needed a cover to escape. And the right time to do so.

I returned to my father's war room the following eve and agreed to follow through with his plans. I apologized for my lack of respect and for delaying the mission.

He was pleased that I had come around to his way of thinking. But he still demoted me, fearing I could not be trusted, and replaced me with a veteran from his war council as crew leader for the mission. I was told to follow General Kuhl's orders explicitly, to not deviate from the plan, or I would be sentenced to death upon return.

I was to stay near the entrance of our ship and guide the captured females on board, cuffing their wrists and locking them into their seats.

We prepared the ship, our largest vessel, the *Striker*, and landed on D'Alluk in two days. General Kuhl's expression turned giddy in anticipation for battle the moment the *Striker*'s door lurched open. He wasted no time. Kuhl and, following close behind, his band of loyal warriors, which he had recruited specifically for this mission, charged into the village and maimed, beat, and killed any male D'Allukans they encountered.

Then they rounded up the females in the center of the village, bagging their heads so their tears and frightened faces could not trigger empathy. Not that General Kuhl had an ounce of that in his body anyway.

Once they were satisfied with the number of females captured, they brought them to the ship. I did as I was ordered and guided the females aboard. I even let General Kuhl report back to my father and the council that the mission had been successful.

The moment the *Striker*'s door closed, and our crew plus the females were accounted for, one of my warriors, Bruvix, hacked into the ship's data system and rigged the health monitors to record continuous scans for our crew of thirty-two male warriors and for the eighty D'Allukan females we'd captured.

Then we executed General Kuhl and his crew of thirteen. We let the females go, apologizing profusely and giving them each some credits, food, and medicinal supplies to take with them back to their village.

We wanted to assist them in returning to their village. We wanted to help them clean up the carnage General Kuhl and his males had left behind and give their fallen males proper burials. But there was no time. Any delay in the *Striker's* return route would rouse suspicion, and we needed to complete the second part of our carefully crafted plan.

The only justice we had the power to provide was knowing that we murdered the murderers and set the females free.

Before we had left Trovilia, Ahlvo and I prepped a separate, smaller ship for his family and a select group of friends and their families to take with us. None that were within my father's royal circle or who had close ties to his war council, as our escape and future location would need to remain a secret.

We entered the route to return home on the *Striker's* nav system so it could fly without us. Ahlvo's father manned the smaller ship and met us just outside D'Alluk's atmosphere. My crew and I climbed aboard the other ship, leaving the corpses of General Kuhl and his warriors on board the *Striker*, and we continued on our way to Oluura, our new home. When the *Striker* was about halfway back to Trovilia, we remote detonated the bombs we had strategically placed all over the massive ship.

We appeared to be dead, his most formidable and skilled warriors, including his only son, plus the females he planned to force into the breeding program. His largest vessel was destroyed. He would have to abandon his plan. He would have no choice.

I felt relief wash over me the moment the ship exploded. I would be free of him, no longer his target or his pawn, and the females of D'Alluk could live their lives peacefully—well...somewhat peacefully —and blissfully unaware of the dark fate that had almost awaited them on Trovilia.

* * *

ALTHOUGH THERE IS STILL TRIUMPH in my heart at protecting the D'Allukan females, three images continue to haunt my mind.

My father's chilling gaze as he so easily justified something he would have passionately fought against in his earlier days. The realization as my vision blurred and my stomach rejected anything that entered it that my father, my very own father, had tried to kill me for refusing to kidnap a group of females. And finally, the faces of the females on D'Alluk the moment we removed the bags from their heads. The way their mouths twisted in horror at the sight of us and the sight of their males, slaughtered and their bodies covering the ground. The agony in their screams as they were dragged toward our ship.

My males and I did not hurt them, of course. But it didn't matter. General Kuhl had already taken care of that, causing them a lifetime of mental anguish to overcome. They didn't understand what was happening. Why some of our warriors attempted to kidnap them and why the rest of us set them free. They shook with fear and confusion as we led them safely off the ship.

I see that same fear in the faces of these human females. In my female. My inara. I never want her to fear me. The thought of that sickens me.

But shouldn't she fear me? I am my father's son. I did not know he was capable of such hatred and cruelty when my mother was alive. Perhaps it was purely because of her that the madness did not set in earlier. But if it lived inside of him, somewhere deep and buried, then surely it lives within me as well?

I must protect her from this, as I must protect her from all things that may harm her. I must get her away from this place. The males in this room will not give her a better life. Of that I am certain. The way they leer at her confirms this.

I may not be a worthy mate for her, but I will ensure that she has food in her belly, warm furs, and a comfortable shelter. These things I can give her. I will be honored to give her.

Ahlvo slaps his palm on the table to regain my attention.

"Varrek, you must look at me." He points to his eyes. "I know that you struggle with your memories. But it is all in the past. You are not your father."

I nod, still struggling to breathe.

"Now," he says, turning back to the screen pad, "the bidding has begun. Do you wish to participate?"

I lean forward, my forearms resting on the cold table. I touch the screen pad to awaken it. "Yes. Yes, I do."

CHAPTER 4

CHLOE

e sit there—Ava, Kate, and I—on the floor of the cage, shivering as we cling to each other behind the drawn curtain. Strange music plays, and it sounds like if EDM and jazz had a baby. A really obnoxious baby. It's hard to focus on how ear-piercing the music is, though, when we don't know what our future holds.

There are two additional curtains along the edges of the main curtain that block our view from the sides of the cage. I hear footsteps and what I assume is alien chatter on the other side of the curtains, clicking and chirping and words being formed in other languages I've never heard.

We know that the room was set up for some kind of event before the curtains closed around us, but we have no idea what kind of event it'll be.

Ava looks at me and swallows. "I wish it was still dark and silent in here."

I nod. Me too, girl. Me too. Whatever is about to happen here, it won't be good for us.

We stiffen simultaneously as we hear footsteps on either side of the cage. We can't see who the feet belong to, but their steps are loud, like a coordinated march set to the beat of the music.

The footsteps soften a bit as they make their way out onto the floor and then quicken as the routine changes.

"Dancers?" Kate whispers.

"Yeah, I think so," Ava replies. "What the fuck is happening?"

"I…think they're warming up the crowd?" I theorize.

"Lovely," Kate sighs.

After a few minutes of dancing, we hear the footsteps pass by us once again in the other direction and disappear somewhere behind us. Then the music changes and we hear a single dancer stepping and scuttling on the other side of the curtain in front of us. Then he speaks, with a low and deep voice that sounds like he's attempting to whistle while gargling rocks.

"Oh god. Tha-That's the voice. The alien that wheeled me in here on the first day. It's him." Kate's eyes widen with fear as her body hunches inward.

I rub her shoulder to comfort her even though I'm equally as frightened. "Maybe we shou—"

I freeze as the curtains part. Not really knowing why, I rise to stand, like maybe I'll get a better view of the room if I'm on my feet. Ava and Kate mirror me and continue to huddle close once we're upright and against the back wall of glass.

I look to the right corner of the cage, and I see a hideous creature that looks like a slimy bird dressed in a red velvet suit. He's still talking. He's the one Kate must've seen. I look at her, and she nods, answering the question in my head.

Under normal circumstances, I would think a bird in a red suit is the most adorable thing ever, but since this *thing* is responsible for us being trapped in a cage, I see zero cuteness. Plus, he looks like he's sweating in that suit, or maybe his scales just look slippery all the time? Blech. When he speaks, his long reptilian tongue rolls and snaps out of his beak with every garbled word, and it makes my stomach turn.

I snap my eyes shut in an attempt to erase the mental image of the bird man. When I reopen them, I notice the audience. It seems we've drawn a crowd comprised of several different alien species. Then it really hits me that we're no longer on Earth. Aliens are real. They're all around us right this second.

I wish I could enjoy the fact that Mulder of *The X-Files* was right, but since I can feel the hungry gazes from the aliens slither up and down my body—as if I'm a slab of meat stuffed under the glass at the deli—I decide to save the celebrating for later.

I notice two of the tall tables are empty, and four of the tables have two aliens standing close together. All the creatures appear to be male, I think? I tried not to make assumptions about gender on Earth, and that was just among one species. This is uncharted territory. This is Whothefuckknowswhereville in some random galaxy. None of them look alike, so I have no idea.

Jesus, Chloe, FOCUS, I chide myself. *If you're some sort of prize to be won, figure out who you could take down with a swift kick to the balls.*

Most of the aliens I see are definitely scary. Some have massive horns jutting out of their heads. Some are covered in fur. Some have sharp fins going down their backs. And I'm pretty sure the guy in the back corner has wings.

My eyes finally settle on the table in the front of the room, and centered, with two aliens standing behind it. I'm surprised I didn't notice them right away because these two are huge and their table is the closest one to us. They might be the biggest aliens in the room and are at least seven feet tall.

They have shimmering gold skin that catches the light. The one with long, thick black hair pulled back into tight braids looks like you wouldn't want to fuck with him, but the eyes that look back at me—wait, is he looking at me? No, he's looking to my right, at Ava. The expression on his face as he looks at her is soft. It's appreciative, but not creepy. There's some compassion there too. So maybe he wouldn't immediately chop her into a hundred pieces and eat her for dinner.

Is that the best we can hope for here? The bar is depressingly low.

My eyes dart to the other male at the table, and his gaze is holding me so intensely that I feel completely naked and not wearing the billowy nightgown I have on now.

For a split second, I'm embarrassed that I look like a sloppy spinster. Part of me wishes I was wearing something cuter and that my hair wasn't dirty and tangled. Then I remind myself that I have bigger things to worry about than how I look while locked in a glass cage, post-kidnapping, in front of a bunch of aliens.

But those eyes. Goddamn. They're a striking emerald green. It's such a bold, inhuman color that I can't look away. I'm not sure I've ever seen anything as breathtaking as those eyes. Why does he seem familiar to me? Why can't I look away?

He has ridges on his forehead and down his nose and long silver hair, the top half pulled back and off his face as the rest hangs loose over his shoulders. His skin is gold too, but brighter. Richer. He's wearing a navy-blue jumpsuit with sleeves down to his wrists, and his pants disappear into black boots with zippers on the sides.

The jumpsuit appears to be two sizes too small…everywhere. His biceps bulge under the strained fabric, his thighs practically hulking out of the seams. His chest is extremely thick too, almost like he's wearing a bulletproof vest beneath the jumpsuit. Is he? Or is that just how he's built? What is he? And why is he still staring at me like that?

I snap myself out of my bizarre string of thoughts because I cannot be thirsting over the golden god over there.

Suddenly, his face contorts and scrunches up, almost like he's in pain. His breathing seems to change, and while his eyes remain on mine, they look unfocused now, like he's spacing out. The black-haired one leans in front of him, clearly concerned, and says something to him.

What's happening? Why do they both look so worried?

The bird man says something that sounds like a string of consonants that ends in a burp, then points a long, claw-tipped finger in my direction. Every alien in the room starts tapping incessantly on the screens in front of them.

Shit, shit, shit. "Uhhhhm. I don't…"

"I think they're bidding on you?" Ava guesses.

I hear a grinding sound, like metal against metal, before I see the source. When I look down, the floor directly under my feet is separating from the rest of the floor into a triangular shape, skimming dangerously close to the tips of my toes. I gasp and pull the girls tighter to me in a death grip as it starts to rise.

A set of steel cuffs locks around my ankles, keeping them together and immovable, and as I'm raised above the floor, I'm ripped from Ava and Kate's grasp. When I look down, I see that their ankles are now cuffed too, but instead of being raised out of the floor on a platform like I am, they are being pulled away from me, Ava to the right and Kate to the left.

We are being deliberately separated, probably in an effort to let our potential buyers scrutinize our bodies more easily.

I reach down to tug on the cuffs around my ankles, and then another set of cuffs appears from under the raised platform. Before I can stand back up, they lock around my wrists.

I am completely bound now, and utterly helpless.

Not that I had any kind of physical advantage before, but now I can't even kick an alien predator in the balls if I need to protect myself. I can't protect myself at all. I can't protect Kate and Ava either. Tears run down my cheeks, tears I didn't even realize I shed, as I look down at Ava, seeing matching waves of panic in her eyes.

I look at Kate and see her frozen in place. She's staring down at the cuffs on her wrists, barely blinking, her whole body frighteningly still despite the mayhem around her.

The tears continue to fall, and I let them. Hiding my emotions is pointless now because I feel like I'm about to die. Maybe not right here, but once I'm taken from this cage, what will happen? And there's nothing I can do about it because I'm trapped.

My eyes meet the golden god's again, and he looks as tortured as I feel. But why? Why does he care? He's out there and I'm in here. He breaks our eye contact when he starts yelling at the bird man, picking up the tablet and pointing at the screen in his large golden hand.

Bing, bing, bing.

The bings continue to sound, and from what I can guess, each one indicates a new bid has been made.

Bird Man seems to be having trouble keeping up with all the incoming bids as he rushes around the floor on three legs, whispering to the bidders that keep pointing at a yellow triangle on their tablets.

I have no idea what that symbol means in the context of this auction, but it seems strange for the auctioneer to be running around the room. Don't they stay in place and rattle off the current highest bid in a comically fast-paced voice? Why isn't Bird Man doing that? That triangle must signal something else.

Bing.

The toothy gray-skinned guy holding a tablet against his ear yells something at Golden God and his buddy and then frantically taps the other tablet on the table.

Bing, bing, bing.

Golden God responds with a snarl and by hitting his tablet so many times I'm surprised it doesn't shatter.

Bing, bing.

My eyes dart between the two bidders as a chill ripples up my spine. There is part of me, though, that is rooting for the golden god to outbid the toothy guy. There's this...pull I feel toward the golden god. It's instinctual, and not at all logical, but I feel like I can maybe, possibly trust him.

Bingbingbingbing.

Bird Man shouts something I can't understand, and I see the toothy guy slam his hand on the table in frustration.

A low-pitched buzzer sounds, and my raised platform starts to sink back toward the floor of the cage. My hands and ankles remain cuffed, the rough steel edges scraping against the thin skin of my wrists. My platform settles back into the floor with a final jerk, just as Ava's platform begins to rise.

I was just purchased. My auction is over. Now it's Ava's turn.

No, no, no. No, we cannot be separated. We have to stay together if we want to survive this and get back home. I can't do this alone. I can't.

Ava looks from her bound feet to me, and her mouth falls open.

She knows what's coming, and she's terrified too. I can't let them take her. But what can I do?

My breath quickens, and I start pulling against the steel. I let out a grunt of frustration as I yank each elbow in opposite directions. Nothing. These cuffs are no joke. I wasn't expecting them to magically snap under the upper-body strength of someone who still can't do a single pull-up, but I keep tugging anyway. It's the only thing I can do. I pull and pull as the cuffs bite into my skin and my wrists become red and raw as layers of skin are torn away.

I look up to see the aliens eagerly pressing their tablets again, and I scream. As long as I can keep the focus on me and away from Ava, maybe she won't be sold. I know it won't work forever, but I don't care. I need to do something. Anything. So I scream, and scream, and I let the tears pour out of me as I awkwardly yank against my restraints. My wrists and ankles begin to bleed, but I keep going. I shuffle my feet together and move an inch toward Ava. I can't get much space between my ankles, but if I keep hopping, I think I can make my way over to her.

I reach my hands toward her, stretching my fingers as much as I can as I get closer and hop another inch to the right, but my top half is pitched too far forward, and I fall. My knees hit the hard floor with a *crack*, and I yelp as I throw up my forearms to keep my face from connecting with the floor.

Pain shoots through my shins, and I curl in on my side to wrap my arms around my knees. I hope the worst thing that happens to me is that I leave here with bruises all over my legs from my fall, but somehow I doubt I'll be that lucky.

I'm on my side facing the crowd, and I release the breath I didn't know I was holding as a flurry of activity unfolds before me.

Yelling. Aliens getting in each other's faces and the bird man trying to reclaim their attention. The golden god lifting the guy with fins by the shirt and throwing him across the room. More yelling. Golden God grabbing his table and using it to knock down the two aliens approaching him from the next table. The bird man running over and whispering into Golden God's ear as his black-haired buddy holds a sword toward the rest of crowd, keeping them back. Golden God handing something to Bird Man. Something I cannot see.

Another low-pitched buzzer sounds. And then another. Two back-to-back. What does that mean? Has Ava been sold? Has Kate?

I see the golden god pointing at me.

I don't know what the hell just happened, but I think I belong to him now.

CHAPTER 5

VARREK

My precious inara. I must get her out of that cage and examine her wounds. To see her deliberately hurt herself in order to reach the other human female almost sent me to my knees.

I follow close behind Bzzsil as he leads us to the back of the glass cage containing my mate—o fah, the female. I must stop seeing her as my mate because she can never be mine. This exquisite female deserves a male at her side who is steady and stable and who can remain as such for the rest of his days. My father's madness still looms above me, a possible fate that awaits me as well. So for now, I will keep her safe. I will give her shelter and food. And someday, when she finds a male who is worthy of her smiles, I shall take comfort in knowing that she is happy, and that I helped ensure her happiness.

My heart thunders in my chest at the knowledge that I will be taking her back to Oluura, my home, along with the other two human females.

It was clear that those females were important to her, with the way she thrashed and screamed when they were pulled apart. Perhaps they are siblings? Or were part of the same clan on her planet of origin?

Whatever the reason, I did what I had to do in order to win all three of them.

Under normal circumstances, nothing would cause me to hand over the ruby pendant from my mother's favorite necklace. My father gave it to her the day she birthed me, and she wore it each day that followed until her death.

But these were not normal circumstances. I had used all of my credits to win my mate. I had nothing left of value to offer Bzzsil and had to fight off several other males in order to put an end to the bidding on the other two. Trading my mother's ruby to keep the other human females by my mate's side was a worthy sacrifice if it means I put her heart at ease, however briefly.

"That was not wise, Varrek," Ahlvo murmurs behind me. "And it is worse that *I* must be the one to scold *you*. This does not feel natural."

He is right. It was not wise to hand over the ruby to someone like Bzzsil, especially since it could link me to my past if it ends up in the wrong hands. That cannot happen.

"Perhaps not. But it had to be done," I reply over my shoulder, eager to end this discussion. I am about to see my female up close. Nothing will distract me from this.

Bzzsil has drawn the curtains shut on all four sides of the glass cage after asking the other males to leave once the auction ended. The exterior doors have been locked to ensure the safety of myself, Ahlvo, and the human females as the transaction is completed.

"Remain here while I chain the females together. It will be easier to transport them if they stay in their restraints," Bzzsil says in a delighted tone. He is clearly pleased at his newfound wealth.

At the back of the cage, he holds a screen pad in his hand and presses a button, causing the glass walls that meet at the corner to separate from the top of the cage, all the way down to the floor. Bzzsil waddles into the cage, where my mate still lies on the floor curled in on herself, the other two human females—their hands and feet still bound—bent down by her side, concern etched on their faces.

He stalks toward them as they scramble to help my mate to her feet. But she does not move from her place on the floor. Taking a step into the cage, I notice just how filthy it is. It smells of sweat and bodily waste, and there are strange clusters of fabric all over the floor—their purpose I cannot make sense of. Bzzsil slows as he gets near my mate and tells her to rise.

She groans. "Min paen n ey kennut onderrstendewe."

The closer he gets to her, the stronger my instinct becomes to attack him. My hand goes to the blade tucked into my belt. If he lays his greasy hands on her, I will slice his neck down to his cock and let his innards spill onto this dirty floor without a second thought.

Ahlvo puts a hand on my shoulder and in a barely audible voice says, "Do not, brother. Where is your head? He is no threat to us."

I shake my head to clear my rage. My mind must remain sharp right now. "You will not touch them, Bzzsil," I tell him. "They are my property now, yes? I will handle them." I gesture to Ahlvo to collect the other two humans as I approach my frightened mate.

"They do not need to be chained together. We will take them out of here as they are," I say, a clear warning in my tone.

"Very well." His eyes narrow as he backs away from the females and puts his hands up in surrender.

"How did you acquire these females? If the planet of origin is a restricted place?" Ahlvo asks.

Bzzsil chuckles. "I do not ask questions of my suppliers. They do what they do, and for the right price, I get what I want."

His laughter retriggers my urge to cause him irreparable bodily harm. No part of this black-market human trade is humorous.

I look down at my mate, her face twisted in agony. Her scent still cloaked with fear. It stings my eyes, and I want it gone. I murmur soft, calming sounds to her as I gather her in my arms, like I would with a fussy child. She is so light and soft that I lift her easily and clutch her tight to my chest. I know she cannot understand me, and I cannot understand her, so as long as my tone is soothing, I hope that her fear dissipates.

I hear Ahlvo doing the same to the other two human females as he carefully drapes them over each of his shoulders.

"You will be able to make it back to the ship like that?" I ask, heading out of the cage.

Ahlvo scoffs. "You wish to question my strength? In this moment when you need my help *and* my guidance?"

His tone is teasing, and it lightens my mood. "Make it back to the ship and I shall never question your strength again."

Ahlvo, ever the charmer, bows his head and thanks Bzzsil for inviting us to the auction as he passes him. We exit out the back of the soundproof room, which quickly takes us outside. The moment we make it outside, we move quickly through the crowds of people between the tavern and brothel.

My mate asks something I can't understand. "Werrre ewe tekkin mea?"

I hold her tighter against me and make more soft noises at her. Ahlvo and I keep our heads down and our feet swift. Once we arrive back at the port, we weave through the section reserved for ships in various states of repair. Then we make it to where the smaller ships are stationed and race to enter ours.

As I approach, the ship recognizes my heat scan and the door lifts open. I stop in the entryway of the ship and turn to Ahlvo. "Take them to the sleep quarters. Keep those two together. I will take this one to mine to check her wounds."

"Very well. Do you need a language update?"

"Yes, I will meet you on the bridge for the update once I have her safely deposited," I tell him.

Ahlvo nods, and we begin walking toward the sleep quarters. There are only three on this ship. It is a small junker vessel that we acquired after our second year on Oluura. We saved all the credits we earned on Nu'Piix and bought the ship at the port. We use it solely for these short trips. Usually it is just myself and Ahlvo, but sometimes Bruvix comes along.

Ahlvo takes them into one of the sleep quarters, and I take my inara into mine, directly across the hall.

As I place her small body on the edge of my bed, her fear scent gets stronger and she begins to shake, her hands and feet still bound. She looks around the room with bewildered eyes, then inches her body as far away from me as she can without getting up. She does not know me, does not trust me, and does not understand what is happening. I must fix this.

I rush over to my closet and pull a thick fur blanket from it and gently drape it around her shoulders. She does not move, and now she gives me a strange look, as if she does not know what to make of me.

I feel as if I am coming out of my skin in desperation to speak with her. There is so much I wish to tell her. So much to explain. "All will be well, inara. Your wounds will be healed soon. And we will speak," I tell her, backing away from her slowly with my hands up. I exit the room, and the door slides shut behind me as I run down the hall toward the bridge.

I arrive in seconds to see that Ahlvo is not here. He must be trying to calm the other females. I understand this, but it does nothing to settle my frayed nerves. I am impatient to get back to my mate. She is hurting and confused, and I can make everything better once we are able to communicate.

I begin to pace and hear Ahlvo snicker behind me as he approaches. "You look quite flustered, brother. Perhaps you are not in the right mind to speak with that frightened female. I could have a talk with her instead if you prefer?"

"You take a step anywhere near my quarters and I will cut your feet from your body," I bite back.

Ahlvo laughs. "I joke, of course." He gestures to the main command chair. "Sit and I will assist with your update."

"I have not required an update in quite some time. Will it take long?" I ask.

"No, this will take but a moment. Let me see if the ship's monitoring systems can do a scan to determine the native tongue of the females. They have been babbling to each other since the moment we stepped aboard." I watch as Ahlvo's fingers make quick swipes across the screen pad.

"Ah, yes. It is called Ah-meer-ikahn Anng-lahsh. I have it ready to import into your chip." He pauses.

I pull my mane away from my left ear, exposing the chip hidden behind it. It is not something we are born with but implanted with via a necessary procedure as young children—especially for those who will later enter warrior training. If we were to be faced with an enemy we could not understand, we would be at an immediate disadvantage.

Ahlvo holds the screen pad close to my ear, and I close my eyes. A dull pain grows behind my eyelids before subsiding a few moments later.

"It is done," Ahlvo says.

"I thank you, brother. You as well?" He nods as we switch places, and he sinks heavily into the chair.

His chip is already exposed, as the tight braids in his mane are pulled down the center of his back. O fah, Ahlvo and his mane. He is surprisingly finicky about how often he needs to groom and braid it.

"Are the other females settled?" I ask him as he closes his eyes and the upload begins.

His lip curves up on one side, showing his amusement. "Yes, they seem well. I assured them they were safe, though I know they could not understand me. But when I pointed to the wash box and showed them how to turn it on, they seemed quite elated. I will go back and show them the food hall once we are done here."

"Completed," I tell him. "Are you able to determine how far we are from planet Earth? I am assuming the females will ask if we can take them there."

Ahlvo types "Earth" into the ship nav's destination and several error messages pop onto the screen. We both read them silently and nod.

"I must return to my—the female. I thank you for your help this day. For everything. I owe you a great debt."

Ahlvo grins at the slip of my tongue and lightly slaps me on the back. "Go. I will ready the ship for departure."

I sprint back to my quarters with excitement in each step. I press my palm on the screen pad outside the door. It opens just as a large metal pole swings in the direction of my face. My inara has been attempting to escape, it seems.

I block the pole before it can make contact and knock it out of her hands. It falls to the floor with a piercing clatter, and my mate is so startled by it that she stumbles backward, slipping on the corner of the fur blanket that lies in a heap at the foot of the bed.

She lets out a yelp and flails her bound arms as her body gets closer to the floor. Instinctively, I bend forward and sweep my hands behind her back and pull her up toward me.

Her breath comes out in short gasps against my chest as I keep my hand cradled behind her head, my other hand on her lower back. Holding her like this, it feels as if her body was made for mine. It is the most exquisite torture.

Her tiny hands ball into fists, and she pushes against my chest a moment later while grunting in irritation. "Get off me, asshole!"

Her chest heaves, and I cannot keep my eyes from drifting down to her hardened nipples. They strain against the strange fabric of her dress, and my mouth waters at the thought of tasting them. Slowly tracing them with my tongue.

Her fear scent reaches my nose, and she covers her chest with her arms.

"I would choose death before hurting you, female. You need not fear me."

She looks at me, stunned, and her soft pink lips open wide. "You... you speak English? How?"

Her voice is as melodic and hypnotizing as I imagined when I first laid my eyes upon her, especially with her strange accent. "I received a language update so that we could communicate. I am sure you have many questions, and I will answer all that I can," I tell her, my mind growing hazy at her nearness.

Her large brown eyes study mine with great intensity as I wait for her to speak. She says nothing.

Her eyes dip to my lips and back up to my eyes before I clear my throat. I take a step closer to her. "Are you well, inara?"

She blinks hard and shakes her head before speaking. "Oh, um, yeah. I'm fine. Sorry. My name is Chloe, by the way."

CHAPTER 6

CHLOE

I was prepared to scream at the golden god the moment he returned, and possibly bash him bloody with the pole I yanked from his closet. I was in the middle of hitting the door over and over in an effort to open it. Or cause its settings to malfunction enough that I could open it manually. I would've been fine with either outcome.

But that was before he stormed into the room, knocking the pole out of my hands and literally sweeping me off my feet. I don't know what it is about this guy that keeps causing me to lose my balance in his presence, but I'm going to blame those goddamn beautiful eyes of his, at least in part.

The cuffs that still scrape against my cut skin aren't helping either, but those eyes, *whew*. Our bodies are inches apart, if that, and I'm finding it hard to form complete thoughts.

Amazingly, I was able to tell him my name, because he called me "in-ah-rah," whatever that means. I wonder briefly if he thinks I'm someone else.

"Cloy-yee." His low voice is gravelly and has a slight growl to it as he attempts my name, and even though he gets it wrong, it might be the sexiest thing I've ever heard.

"Uh, good try," I say encouragingly. "It's more like, 'Cloh-ee.' Not 'Cloy.' It has a hard 'O' sound."

He stares at my mouth like it's a puzzle he's trying to solve, and then he swallows, hard. I watch as his Adam's apple bobs up and down and his strong jaw ticks.

"Cloh-ee," he rumbles, and the sound goes straight to my core. I squeeze my thighs together, slightly embarrassed that I can get turned on by the sound of my own name. Although, I suspect anything he says would sound equally hot. He could say, "Your minimum payment is past due," and I would probably moan in response.

"I am called Varrek," he says as he places his four-fingered hand on his massive chest.

"Vare-ik?" I repeat back to him, slowly, hoping I got it right.

He closes his eyes and smiles, like he's been waiting a century to hear me say his name. "Yes."

It's then that I notice the fangs. He has *fangs*. Actual fangs. It reminds me just how alien he is.

"Allow me to remove these restraints so I may clean your wounds?" he asks as he leads me over to the bed. His gentle tone does not fit the wild, rage-filled creature I saw while in the glass cage. The way he tossed that other alien across the room, the way he fought with others that came close. He was terrifying, and efficient. And if I'm being honest with myself, his strength was impressive.

I sit down on the corner, where he plopped me down before, and wait patiently as he heads into what looks like a compact little bathroom. "Oh my god, you have a shower?" I ask.

He looks behind him. "Ah, the wash box. Yes. I will show you how to use it," he says with a grin.

Varrek places several items on the bed and lowers himself to his knees in front of me. Even kneeling, I have to look up at his face he's so tall. I suddenly feel tiny compared to him, and it's an entirely new feeling. I've never felt small next to anyone before. I decide it's a good feeling, and I silently pray that he's not about to murder me because I'd really like to spend more time gazing up at those pretty eyes of his.

He grabs a thick, two-pronged metal wire and uses it to open the cuffs around my ankles first, then my wrists before tossing them aside in disgust.

A whimper escapes my lips the second the cuffs are off, and Varrek's body stiffens in response.

"I am sorry you were treated in such a way. You will not spend another moment imprisoned. This I vow." His words hold so much conviction that I want to believe him.

"Thank you. It wasn't a lot of fun being in there," I reply, trying not to remember the hopelessness I felt.

He picks up the medical supplies as he explains how they work. "These strips will clean your wounds. Then I will replace them with the healing wraps. It may sting at first, but the pain will pass." He gestures for my foot and pats his thigh. "May I?"

I nod and place my right foot in his hand, resting my calf on top of his thigh. His thighs are like tree trunks, like the only soft thing about him is his tone of voice. Though I know he can sound just as menacing as he looks when he wants to. Every other inch is hard lines and pure muscle.

"Cloh-ee?" he mutters, and I realize he's been talking to me while I ogled his body. "Hmm?" I ask.

He smirks, and I can feel my cheeks redden at being caught. "You may ask me questions, if you'd like," he reminds me.

"Oh! Oh, right. Sorry. I just…it's been a long day. Or a long couple of days, rather. The whole kidnapping thing, ya know…" I trail off. "Okay. Are you going to kill or rape me? Let's start there."

He flinches like he's been struck and then after a brief pause, continues applying the cleaning strips. "You have no reason to see my words as truth. I understand this. But I meant what I said. It would be easier for me to run straight into an enemy's sharpened blade than lay a finger on you in anger." His eyes lock on mine. "So no, I have no plans to kill or rape you."

A simple no would've sufficed, but that works too. "Where are we going? I need to go home. Can you take me there? Back to Earth?"

The cleaning strips are now on my wrists and ankles, and the sting

Varrek warned me about is starting to set in. I hiss and pinch my eyes closed while I ride it out.

"I am sorry. For your discomfort and that you were taken from your planet. Unfortunately, I cannot return you to Earth. This ship would never be able to travel that far. It is also forbidden to venture into that galactic region." His voice is solemn as his fingers skim the tips of my toes.

"How far are we from Earth?" I ask as the pain subsides.

He gives me a sympathetic look. "There are many, many galaxies between my home and yours, so it is quite far, I am afraid."

Multiple galaxies? I remember watching a documentary on space travel a while ago, and it said it takes about seven months to travel from Earth to Mars, and that's within the same galaxy. How long would it take me to cross several goddamn galaxies?

I decide to put a pin in that for now.

"I am taking you and the other human females to my home, a planet called Oluura," Varrek continues. "You will be safe there."

"Kate and Ava! Can you take me to them?" I saw the other alien carrying them onto the ship and remember feeling relieved that we were heading to the same destination. But why did he buy all three of us? He says he has no plans to kill or rape me, and presumably them, so what's the plan? Uncertainty grows in my belly.

Varrek nods as he continues checking my wounds and then applying the healing wraps. The way he touches me so gently, it's like he thinks I'm made of glass and will shatter at the slightest amount of pressure. His big fingers are calloused, so clearly he works a lot with his hands, but the rest of him is smooth, like leather.

The wraps stick onto my skin like tape and encircle my wrists and ankles completely. There's some kind of cooling gel on the inside, though, that feels incredible, and I swear I could fall asleep sitting up straight.

"The females are in the sleep quarters across from us. I will take you to them if you wish," Varrek says, leaning back on his heels. "But if you would like to wash first..."

"Yes, please." I hop off the bed, fresh energy coursing through me at the prospect of washing off the last handful of days. I swing my arms as I approach the bathroom, just because I can. "I haven't bathed in, well, I don't even know. Do you have something I can change into?"

He opens a drawer that disappears into the wall next to the bathroom and pulls out a pale-gray, long-sleeve thermal shirt that has a slight V-neck. The fabric looks like it would be scratchy, but it's soft, unbelievably soft, like cashmere.

He chuckles as I rub the shirt against my cheek and sigh. "This way, little human."

"Wait, can these get wet?" I ask, pointing to the healing wraps on my wrist.

"Yes, they stick even in water. I will change them tomorrow," he says as he leads me to the shower.

The bathroom looked tiny before, and that was when it was empty. Now that Varrek and I are both in here? It feels like we're stuffed into a casket, face-to-face. We're squished together, our bodies touching and our faces close as we stand next to the upright shower that's enclosed by a sliding glass door. He radiates warmth, and I want it wrapped around me like a blanket. Varrek opens the shower door without dropping his gaze from mine.

I should hate this. I should feel unsafe, uncomfortable, or at the very least, claustrophobic in a room this small with an alien who bought me at an auction. But I don't. He feels familiar and trustworthy, and it makes no sense, but I find I don't care.

"You turn on the water here." He points to the top button with a strange symbol on it that I don't recognize. "Press this button to make the water hot."

There's a jar of navy-blue cubes on a ledge in the corner. "What are those for?" I ask.

"That is soap for your body and mane." His voice drops to a husky whisper as our faces inch closer to each other.

"Uh, thank you, Varrek, for all of your help." My throat suddenly feels dry.

He lifts his giant hand and lightly brushes a lock of hair behind my ear. "It is my pleasure to provide for you, Cloh-ee."

His eyes drop to my lips, and I can't resist anymore, nor do I want to. I tug at the collar of his jumpsuit as I pull him toward me and close my mouth over his.

He doesn't move at first, shocked at my boldness, perhaps? Then his lips move gently against my own. His lips are so soft and lush that I whimper against them. That elicits a growl deep within Varrek's throat. His mouth becomes demanding as he swipes at the seam of my mouth with his tongue, seeking entry.

I pull him closer. He can't get any closer than he is, really, but I need him everywhere. All around me. I open for him and slide my tongue against his. My pussy flutters at the feel of the rough texture of his tongue compared to mine, and I nip at his lower lip playfully as I moan into his mouth.

Varrek's hands begin to wander my body before settling just above my ass. I'm eager to explore him too, but I can't seem to move away from his biceps. I let myself learn every dip and curve of his strong arms and shoulders as his kisses grow hungrier.

Then in a flash, he rotates our bodies so my back is pressed against the wall next to the shower, and he pushes away from me, out of the bathroom entirely, his chest heaving and his emerald eyes now completely black.

"I-I'm sorry if…I mean…that was completely unlike me. I'm sorry, Varrek." I have no idea what changed between us or why he looks so freaked out, but kissing him was clearly a big mistake. "We just met and here I am attacking you. You could be a total psycho, for all I know," I laugh nervously, trying to play it cool.

He turns, with his back to me, shaking his head. When he faces me again, his eyes have returned to that striking emerald, but now they look troubled.

"It is fine, Cloh-ee. Do not give it a second thought." He takes a step toward me and then stops. "I-I enjoyed the feel of your lips on mine."

My stomach drops, and I can see where this is heading. "But…?"

Just out with it already, big guy.

"It is just that, this tether between us will not lead to anything good. I wish to protect you, and I am not certain I can do that if we go further." He looks at the floor. "I will not make a worthy mate for you."

Well, isn't that a bucket of cold water thrown in my face. The sting of rejection is all too familiar. Apparently I'm not even attractive to fucking *aliens*. All I wanted was a casual little make-out session and now he's trying to get rid of me? "Are you seriously blowing me off right now?"

"Cloh-ee, that is not..."

"Nope, it's fine." My voice raises as I turn the shower on. "I'm not looking for a boyfriend in space, okay? My partner on Earth cheated on me, then I got kidnapped, then sold, and now it seems I can't ever go home, so I've got my own shit to deal with at the moment. And you might be hot, and clearly you're very aware of that, but it's not like I was looking to get married simply because I kissed you."

"Are you saying you do not feel the—" Varrek adds, but I've heard enough.

"I'm just going to take a shower and then I'd like to see my friends, if that's okay."

"Certainly. I will wait outside until you are finished. Call for me and I will take you over. I will give you access to the door panel so you can come and go as you please." He looks like he feels guilty, but humiliation hangs over me like a dark cloud so there's no space in my head to worry about him right now. "The bed is yours."

I was planning on going over to the girls' room and bunking over there, but a big bed all to myself sure sounds nice right about now. "Okay, thanks," I say as I shut the door to the bathroom.

If only a shower could erase the last ten minutes...

CHAPTER 7

VARREK

My claws remain extended with my frustration, and they dig into my palms until I draw blood. I am not sure what just happened between Cloh-ee and me, but I do know that I am furious at myself for how it ended. It takes all the willpower I can summon to keep from ripping out my mane.

My first kiss with my mate, with her soft pink lips and breathy moans. The way she used her square, blunt teeth to nip at my lips. My cock throbs at the thought of those lips exploring other parts of my body, sucking and nibbling as they go. Or those lips parted wide as my name falls from them in a scream of ecstasy.

I was not expecting her to kiss me, though the closer her face got to mine, I wanted it to happen. Badly. The way she sought my lips with such boldness, it makes me want to thank the goddess for blessing me with such a fearless mate.

Then I recall the hurt in her eyes when I pulled away from her and my anger returns tenfold. Hurting her is the last thing I ever wish to do.

I had to stop the kiss from going any further though. I *had* to. Otherwise, I would be kneeling in front of Cloh-ee this very moment, my tongue lapping at the sweet juices of her cunt. I would make her back arch, and her hands would clutch at my mane as her first orgasm rips through her body from head to toe.

Then we would fuck. I would pound into her relentlessly until she came again. And again. And again. Only until her body was fully sated after several orgasms would I allow myself to come, releasing my seed deep inside her.

I adjust the pants of my jumpsuit to hide my still-aching cock. I reckon I will be in this amount of discomfort for many days to come as long as my mate is near, so I should get used to it.

I continue to pace outside of my quarters, trying not to picture her pale, voluptuous body under the stream of hot water in the wash box. The drops of water falling off her heavy breasts.

I growl at my inability to escape my heated thoughts and slam my fist into the wall.

Immediately, Ahlvo pops his head out from the door to his quarters and gives me a curious stare. "Is all well, Varrek?"

"I am fine," I bark back. He laughs as his door shuts behind him, leaving me alone in the hallway with only thoughts of my mate to accompany me.

Why did she make it seem like she was unaware of our mate bond? Does she truly not feel it? She is pleased with the way I look—she did admit that, and her desire was apparent in the way her body reacted to my touch. But she also made it clear that she had no intention of anything beyond a possible pleasure mating with me, and that knowledge feels like a deep cut in my side.

Perhaps I should be grateful for that, however, since I have no business making her my inara anyway. If she did want to be my mate, it would be nearly impossible to deny her. I am convinced I could not deny my Cloh-ee anything.

So I am glad, I decide, that her attraction to me is nothing more than a female seeking pleasure. It will be easier to fight the growing urge to make her mine in every possible way. I will provide for her, as I planned, and protect her. That is all.

"Varrek?" Cloh-ee's soft voice calls from inside.

I rush through the door, and my heart stops in my chest at the sight of her in my tunic. It is much too big for this little human, the bottom hem of it falling below her knees and her small hands peeking out of the loose, bunched fabric of the arms. Her wet mane hangs close to her cheeks and down to her breasts, leaving wet marks on my tunic where the ends meet the cloth.

"How do you feel, Cloh-ee?" I ask, my voice a dry croak.

"Much better now." She smiles brilliantly. "Um, may I see my friends?" she asks as she takes a step toward me.

"Yes. I will take you to them." I hold my hand out to her.

She looks at it for a moment, unsure, before placing her palm against mine.

"First…," I say as I place her palm against the screen pad next to the door. The screen lights up after scanning her print and goes through the standard permissions prompts, through which I allow her full access to any area on the ship.

"There. You may move freely throughout this ship." I reluctantly let her hand go.

"Thank you, Varrek. I really appreciate that." She looks up at me, her eyes shining with gratitude.

Ahlvo would surely call me a fool for giving this female full access to the ship, but if I am to get Cloh-ee to trust me, I must place my trust in her as well.

I open the door to my quarters and lead her across the hall to where the other females are staying. I knock twice on the door, with no answer.

Cloh-ee and I exchange a perplexed glance, and she knocks next. "Hey, guys. It's me. I'm coming in."

We enter, and as soon as we realize it's empty, we hear faint, feminine giggles coming from down the hall.

"Ah, it seems they are in the food hall. Would you like something to eat?" I barely get the question out before Cloh-ee is sprinting in the direction of the laughter.

I jog after her and enter the food hall a step behind. Ahlvo and the two females are gathered around the lone table in the middle of the hall, chuckling and snacking on plates of junasii loaf and viiki.

"Girl, they have bread. Get your ass over here!" the female with the brown skin yells to Cloh-ee.

"Are you serious?" Cloh-ee takes two large strides over to the table and grabs the slice of junasii loaf from the female's hand and shoves it into her mouth.

"Mmmmmmmygod. So good." She moans with pleasure as she chews, forcing me to turn away and adjust the straining cock beneath my jumpsuit.

It is unsettling, to realize that my body is no longer completely mine but so in tune with hers that even a simple sound she makes can elicit a physical reaction from me. It is not unpleasant. Not in the least. It is a reminder of the tether that connects us. Or the tether I feel and she does not.

"Try it with the dip," the female with the fire-colored hair tells Cloh-ee.

"Ooh, there's dip? Don't mind if I do." She folds the rest of the slice in two and submerges it into the viiki. I watch her bite into the viiki-covered loaf, and I'm completely entranced by the way her jaw moves as she chews and the delicate lines of her throat as she swallows. And when she licks a small dot of viiki from the corner of her mouth, I have to stifle a groan.

"Varrek…" I hear Ahlvo calling me, as if this is not the first time he has tried to gain my attention.

I turn to face him. "Yes?"

"This is Aye-vah and Kay-teh," he says as he points to the female with the brown skin and then the fire-haired one. "Females, this is Varrek. He is our clan leader."

"Hi, Varrek," Aye-vah says with a smile and a small wave.

The fire-haired female nods a greeting. "Varrek. It's actually Kayt. Just one syllable, but it doesn't seem like you guys can do one-syllable names."

I try it out on my tongue and admittedly, I do find it difficult. "Kay-teh, yes?" I ask.

She grins politely. "Sure."

"This is Ahlvo. Have you met him yet?" Aye-vah asks Cloh-ee. "Ahlvo, this is Chloe."

"Not officially. Pleased to meet you, Ahlvo." Cloh-ee's smile reaches her eyes, and for a moment I am so filled with jealousy that I fantasize about grabbing my oldest friend by the neck and slamming him into the floor.

"It is an honor to meet you as well, Cloh-ee." Ahlvo leans on the table with his elbows and gives her a wink.

How does Ahlvo put every being he meets at ease? How does he win their smiles with no effort?

I grunt in frustration as I walk over to the food dispenser and punch in two more plates of junasii loaf and viiki. Junasii loaf is a staple on Oluura, and we have it with most meals. It is white and soft, and because of the syrup from the da'koi tree used to make it, it's also quite sweet. Paired with the savory viiki spread, it's a rich, decadent treat. Once I have the plates, I take the last empty chair across the table from my Cloh-ee and put both plates in front of her.

"Isn't one of these for you?" she asks.

"I cannot imagine you were fed well in the cage. Eat what you wish and I will finish whatever you do not," I tell her. Cloh-ee's needs will always come before my own. That is simply how Trovilians take care of their females.

"Well, if you insist," she mutters before taking another large bite.

"So, fellas. Now that we're showered up and full of bread, let's get real, shall we?" Aye-vah says as she folds her hands underneath her chin. "What is it that you want with us? What's your plan? I mean, to buy three human women, you must have a plan, right?" She looks at Ahlvo and then back at me. "I think we have a right to know if we're about to become sex slaves."

I take a long sip of water from the cup in front of me and hold her gaze. Aye-vah wants honesty, so I will give it to her with my eyes and then follow with my words.

"That is a fair question, Aye-vah. And you are right to wonder, as that is the reason Bzzsil Chi acquired you. He has heard human females are quite popular in other galaxies," I tell her.

"Buzzil—wha? The bird in the red suit? That guy?" Cloh-ee asks.

"Yes, he sold you as pets. Playthings. I am certain any other male in that room would have treated you as such if they had won you." I turn to Cloh-ee. "But I would not have let them take you. Whether through bribery or force, I would have gotten you out of that cage and safely aboard this ship."

"But why all three of us? You bought one human. Why did you buy us too?" Aye-vah asks, pointing to herself and Kay-teh.

How do I tell Aye-vah and Kay-teh I only bought them because Cloh-ee is my mate and they seemed important to her? That I couldn't bear to watch her injure herself in order to stop the bidding? That her anguish boiled my insides and I came dangerously close to slaughtering that entire room of males to keep them from looking at her for another moment?

I say none of this, though, because doing so would expose a desire that I cannot pursue. "I was sickened by the entire event. On our homeland, the way we were raised…females are revered. They are not forced to do anything they do not wish to do. To force a female into a mating would result in death for the male. It was evident that every male around us had those exact plans for all of you and would likely not face the same punishment."

Ahlvo's head dips in agreement. "We could not let that happen," he says in a low voice.

"On Oluura, you will be given shelter, food, clothing, and you may contribute to our clan in any way that suits you." I briefly look each female in the eyes so they can feel my sincerity. "You will be safe."

"Thank you, Varrek," Cloh-ee says with a grateful nod. "It sounds like a nice place to stay until we can figure out how to get home."

Kay-teh throws her head back in laughter. "Oh, you haven't heard? There are several galaxies between this one and ours, babe. Pretty sure Earth is no longer an option."

Cloh-ee drops her final scrap of junasii loaf onto her plate. "I know. Varrek told me. It's far, yeah, but not impossible."

"Aren't you the optimist?" Aye-vah smiles while nudging Cloh-ee with her elbow. "I once had a flight canceled three times on my way home from Miami and I just started looking for an apartment there."

"I know it's a long shot, but we shouldn't just give up on this, you guys," Cloh-ee pleads, picking at the stray crumbs on her plate.

It feels like a moment that belongs to the three of them, so I nod at Ahlvo, and we get up from the table. "We shall return, little humans," he says over his shoulder.

We exit the food hall and walk a few steps toward the bridge. "We will not speak of my past on Trovilia, Ahlvo. Give me your word," I plead.

"Of course. But does it not seem like a topic that will eventually rise to the surface?"

"Yes, and I will share it in time. The females have been through severe trauma, and they will have to adapt to our lifestyle on Oluura. I do not wish to add to their stress at this time," I tell him.

"What will you tell our clan of Cloh-ee?" Ahlvo asks with a grin.

"I will tell them to treat her with respect, the same as Aye-vah and Kay-teh." I keep my face straight and emotionless, but Ahlvo knows me too well.

"She is your mate, is she not? Your inara? I see the tether between you. It is like a thick rope."

I am reminded of the things Cloh-ee said after the kiss we shared, and my heart sinks. "She does not feel the tether. She said as much. It does not matter anyway. I have a duty to protect her, and I shall."

Ahlvo stares at me for a long time and then nods. "Very well."

I turn to walk toward the food hall before Ahlvo stops me. "Bruvix knows about the females. I sent him a comm. He wishes to speak with you."

I turn on my heel and begin walking toward the bridge. "How did he react when you told him? Unhappily, I assume?"

Ahlvo barks a laugh. "Bruvix happy is a sight I have never seen."

"I will return the moment Bruvix is finished croaking at me. Make sure Cloh-ee eats the rest of her junasii. Have her try some of the gu'tuu tea as well," I tell Ahlvo.

"Certainly, brother."

I sigh as I make my way onto the bridge and lower myself into the command chair. I tap the comm screen in the center of the grid and touch the picture of Bruvix's ugly mug. The real thing pops up within seconds, a deep scowl plastered on his scarred face. "Varrek, you meddling fool."

"Always a joy to see you too, cousin," I snicker.

"Ahlvo told me. You used our credits to buy humans? We are in need of supplies, not pets," he spits back.

The term makes me see red, as does hearing it from my cousin's mouth. "They are *not* pets, and you will not refer to them as such ever again. Understood?"

He shakes his head and looks down. "Yes, I apologize. But why? Surely you could see how I would find this purchase to be a reckless one."

"It is hard to explain. These females, Bruvix…they were locked in a glass cage. They were forced to use a bucket to relieve themselves. The other males who attended this auction, all personally invited by Bzzsil Chi—"

"Bzzsil Chi? That wretched pus bag," Bruvix growls. Bruvix has met the auctioneer as well and instantly hated him even more than I do.

"Exactly. Think about the kind of scum Bzzsil Chi would select to bid on human females."

"You are on that list. You realize that, yes?" Bruvix laughs.

"Actually, Ahlvo was invited by Bzzsil, not me," I clarify.

"Ah, that makes more sense indeed."

"Listen, cousin, our supplies are fine, and we have plenty of herbs we can sell in the meantime if we run low," I reason. "I will not allow females of any species to be sold into slavery if I have the power and resources to stop it."

Bruvix rubs his face, looking sleep deprived. "Very well. You are a noble male."

After a long pause, Bruvix asks, "So, these females. Are we able to pleasure mate with them?"

"How quickly you come around, cousin," I tease. "If they are willing and eager to return your affections, then it is no business of mine. But they have been through much trauma and treated like animals. I would not expect them to be actively seeking a pleasure mate upon arrival. Give them time and space."

"Certainly. Do you wish for me to alert the clan?" he asks.

"No need. We will arrive in less than one day, probably close to mealtime. Once we enter Oluura's atmosphere, you may gather the clan at the hall. I will address them as soon as we arrive with the females."

Bruvix swallows, shifting uncomfortably in his seat. "Has it happened, for you...or Ahlvo? With any of the females?"

He refers to the mate bond. The tether.

I trust Bruvix. I do. He is family. He is also a brilliant strategic mind on the battlefield and can hack into any data system undetected to acquire what he needs or sabotage an enemy's server. But I cannot tell him of my tether to Cloh-ee. It would plant a seed of hope in his chest that the same could happen for him, when it is not even a realistic possibility for me.

"No, it has not," I tell him.

"That is a shame. Goddess knows we could use the gift of an inara around here. Even just one." He shakes his head.

"I shall see you soon," I tell him before ending the comm.

I confirm on the nav screen that the rest of our journey is free of traffic and asteroids, and then I lean back in the command chair, wondering what it will be like when I introduce the females to my clan. Will my clan be kind and welcoming? Will they be able to see how addicted I already am to the nearness of Cloh-ee?

The thought of her makes me rise from the chair and walk toward the food hall. When I enter, it is just Cloh-ee, dropping her cup and plate into the dish cleanser. "All alone?" I ask.

She jumps at the sound of my voice and turns in my direction. "You scared the shit out of me! Yes, they just left. The girls are tired. As am I."

"I understand." I follow her out of the hall, desperate to touch her, but I resist.

She uses her palm scan to open the door, and when we're both inside, she looks back at me, nervously. "Um, where will you sleep?"

"I will sleep on the floor. If that is all right with you, of course." I grab the blanket from the floor and gesture to the spot next to the bed.

"I mean…yeah. That's fine." She stares hard at the bed, seemingly trying to work something out inside her mind.

"It's a really big bed," she says quietly as she scratches at her mane. "You're a big guy, and it seems like more than enough room for both of us to fit. You don't need to sleep on the floor."

To have her next to me, my inara, her lush body within inches of mine while we sleep… The thought of her soft mane spread against my chest as I hold her…I cannot imagine a greater joy in this moment.

But will I be able to give her the space that she needs? If she kisses me again, will I have the strength to stop it and keep us from strengthening the tether? I do not know. For that reason, I must refrain.

"I do not mind the floor, Cloh-ee. I think it may be best if we do not share the bed. It is…safer, wiser, for both of us, if I am down here," I tell her.

The hurt I saw in her eyes from before returns, but briefly. She shrugs her shoulders with a smile as if unaffected by the thought of my nearness.

"Your call," she says as she climbs under the blankets and pulls them in a heap on top of her body.

I get myself situated on the floor, directly beneath the bed. "Sleep well, little human."

"Good night, Varrek," she mumbles.

I listen to her breathing until it evens out and I can tell she's asleep. Only then do I let the weight of my exhaustion pull me under.

CHAPTER 8

CHLOE

’m dragged from a magnificent dream and awakened by the sound of my own half snort. Then I'm instantly aware that I've probably been snoring like a freight train the entire night. I hope I wasn't loud enough for Varrek to hear.

God, it was such a good dream too. I wish I could pinch my eyes closed and return to it. It may or may not have starred a certain gold hunk with silver hair who begged to eat my pussy. Varrek actually *begged*. On his damn knees. But that's how I know it was just a dream. No guy has ever begged me to do that.

I roll onto my side and look down, hoping I can catch a glimpse of him in a deep sleep. But he's not there. His blanket is gone too. I've spent every moment since we met being extremely aware of him, and to not know where he is leaves me feeling unsettled.

It's a new feeling. A strange feeling.

A moment later, the bathroom door opens and out strolls a freshly showered Varrek. Steam floats out of the room all around him like he's a superhero emerging from an ominous fog to save the day.

His hair hangs in damp wavy tendrils around his face and sticks to his chest. His very naked chest. He also has these bright-blue markings around his bicep that loop and layer in exquisite, intricate lines. I wonder what they mean.

He's wearing a pair of loose pants that hang low on his hips, showing off the glorious V shape of his lower abs that I'm dying to trace with my tongue. And if the outline against his upper thigh is any indication, he is extremely well endowed. I tell myself to look away. *Stop staring, perv.* But I just can't.

"Ah, you rise, sweet Cloh-ee. How was your slumber?" Varrek's voice is thick and husky this morning but also chipper.

"It was wonderful. Thank you. Probably the best night's sleep I've had since I was taken," I tell him, trying to keep my eyes focused on his.

Keep those eyes up. Don't let them dip. You go below those magnificent pecs and you'll never get them back up again, I scold myself.

He turns and bends down to shake the wet out of his hair, and my gaze has nowhere to go but the perfect ass in front of me. I think he asks me something as he runs his fingers through the silver strands, but I have no idea what. The curve of his ass, the thickness of it...I want nothing more than to bite right into it.

He straightens and turns to face me. "Cloh-ee?"

"Di-Did you say something?" I stutter.

He grins shyly and scratches the tip of his nose in a nervous gesture that just about kills me. He doesn't blush like a human when he's shy; it's just this look in his eyes and his adorable nervous tic that makes it obvious. How can a specimen like him *possibly* feel shy? Does he have any idea what he looks like? My throat suddenly feels dry and my lips chapped.

"Would you like something to eat?" he asks, his eyes straying to my lips as I lick them.

I slide the covers off my bare legs and stand. His gaze drops to my breasts, and I feel my nipples harden against his shirt, as if completely under his command. I step toward him, slowly, with caution, because even though I can feel the searing heat between us, he did reject me last night, and I'm not eager to go through that again.

Varrek's eyes continue to travel down my body with every step I take, as if he's entranced. His actions and body language do not match his words, because even though he said nothing can happen between us, he looks desperate for my touch. Aching for it.

But until he tells me with his words *and* his body that he wants to take this sexual tension between us to the next level, I'm not putting myself out there again. My ego is a bit too fragile for that.

Besides, there's still so much I don't know about him.

"Yeah, I could eat." I mutter as I attempt to tame my bedhead with my fingers. "Can I ask you something?"

"Of course."

"How old are you?"

We go back and forth for a bit on the differences in time on our planets. A day is roughly twenty-six hours, and there are twenty-nine days in one moon cycle and 382 days in a year. I also learn that weeks do not exist on Oluura. They count days within each moon cycle, and that's it.

Based on this, I estimate that Varrek is roughly thirty-nine in Earth years.

"Our people live over two hundred years, for the most part," he says.

Well, shit. "You've got us beat there. Humans tend to live about eighty to eighty-five years."

"That is all?" Varrek asks, his tone thick with worry as he pulls me against his still-wet chest. "*No.* No, that cannot be all the time we have."

I'm stunned into silence as I listen to his ragged breaths, wondering why he seems so scared. "Hey, it's okay. I'm not going anywhere anytime soon, big guy."

I rub his back, eager to comfort him, and I feel him press his mouth against my hair. "Cloh-ee," he groans.

Just then, I notice his cock jutting between us and pressing against my belly. So much for cutting down the tension. I wonder what it would be like to have him inside me. Would he even fit?

We both pull back to look at each other, and once again I get lost in his eyes. So green. He lowers his head and presses his forehead against mine. I'm breathless at the intimacy of it. He whispers something in his language that I'd never be able to repeat, but it sounds something like, "Heehcuvaliia ere toroh, cive inara."

"What does that mean?" I ask softly, not wanting to break the moment but dying to know what he said.

Varrek's forehead separates from mine, and he places a gentle kiss to the tip of my nose before straightening to his full height and taking a step back. "It means, you honor me."

Was that another rejection? He's so hard to read. It felt like he wanted me. The evidence of that was clear in the hardness of his cock. But he still moved away and didn't let things go further.

I want to scream at him for sending me mixed signals, but something about the look of agony in his eyes when he stops touching me, like it physically hurts him to let me go, gives me pause.

He looks down at my bandaged wrists, lifts them in front of his face. "Let me check your wounds before we eat." He unwraps them slowly, examining the tender pink skin beneath. I watch his lips curve into a smile as he points to my wrists. "They are nearly healed. This is a joyous discovery, Cloh-ee."

He throws a clean shirt on over his head and reaches for my hand as he leads me toward the door. "Come, let us feed you, little human."

A laugh escapes my lips at that. "No one has ever referred to me as 'little.' I'm not considered small on Earth by any means."

"Most human females are smaller than you? That is hard to imagine." He chuckles. "You are so delicate." He holds up my hand and studies my fingers, looking over my knuckles and then fingernails. "If these fingers were any smaller, I might not be able to see them at all."

"Yeah, well, by most standards on Earth, I'm too big. Too soft. And not even a little bit delicate," I counter, failing to hide the bitterness in my voice.

He abruptly stops walking, and I stumble to avoid running into his back. "There is much I still must learn about your planet, Cloh-ee, but if you were made to feel unwelcome among your people because of your body, then I am glad you are no longer there." He looks down at me and lifts my chin with his index finger. "Every speck of skin that I see looks exactly how it should. I could not imagine a more perfect version of you."

I swallow, not knowing how to respond to such a compliment.

He nods in the direction of the hallway. "This way. There is much to do before we land."

Oh, right.

I completely forgot that we're landing on Oluura today. I'll get to see his home and meet his clan. Will they like me?

We enter the food hall and find Ahlvo, Kate, and Ava giggling around the table, just like the previous night. "What are you guys laughing at?" I ask.

Ava nudges Ahlvo's bulky arm. "Say it again," she urges.

Ahlvo looks at Ava and then at me with a wide smirk. Ahlvo's accent is much thicker than Varrek's, so when he speaks, it sounds like, "How mush wud wud a wudchuckle chuckle?"

"Is that it? Did I say I right?" he asks, beaming.

Ava and Kate are laughing so hard they're clutching their stomachs, and I can't help but join in. I know he's reciting that old woodchuck tongue twister, but he butchered it so adorably that I'll treasure the memory for many years to come.

"That was delightful. Well done, Ahlvo," I praise him.

"Your native tongue confuses me. I did not understand any of that," Varrek mutters as he fills a plate with more junasii bread and something else that looks like giant blueberries. My stomach growls in response. "What is this wudchuckle?"

I take the plate he offers me. "It's just this funny thing we used to say on Earth as kids."

I take my seat between Kate and Ava and begin nibbling on the sweet bread. Varrek places a mug of steaming brown liquid in front of me. "This is gu'tuu tea. It is sweet like the junasii. I think you will like it," he says.

I bring the mug to my nose and inhale. It definitely smells sweet, like a faint cinnamon with something else. Citrus, maybe? "Mmm, thank you."

He sends another shy smile in my direction, and I melt.

Kate clears her throat and shifts her gaze to Varrek and Ahlvo. "Something is eating at me."

Ahlvo and Varrek share a confused look, and Ahlvo looks under the table at Kate's feet. "Eating you? An insect on your skin? Or a sickness inside your belly?"

"Not literally eating me," Kate says. "I'm perplexed. I-I don't understand how the bird man or whoever it was took us from Earth and brought us to this side of the universe, since Earth is so far away."

"Ah, I understand now." Ahlvo smiles, his posture loosening in relief.

"We did not get much information from Bzzsil Chi on how you were taken from Earth," Varrek says with a disgusted look on his face, and I'm delighted to see how much he hates the bird man too. "He only indicated that he does not question the methods his suppliers use to acquire their goods."

Ahlvo's brows lift, as if he is remembering something. "He stated at the auction that humans are illegal because your kind does not communicate outside of your planet. Which means Earth is restricted from interplanetary relations."

"But when has a prohibitive law ever stopped a black-market trade from becoming profitable?" Varrek asks dryly.

Varrek rubs a hand down his face, clearly frustrated that he doesn't have much to offer us, and looks at Kate. "We do not have additional information regarding your abduction. But that does not mean we plan to stop looking into this abhorrent system."

I'm disappointed, obviously, as is Kate, but I believe Varrek when he says he doesn't have all the answers. I just can't help but wonder how many human women are currently lost in space, about to be auctioned off to the highest bidder. The thought makes me queasy.

Varrek nods and looks at Ahlvo. "Come, Ahlvo. Let us ready the ship for the final leg of our journey."

"Certainly, brother," Ahlvo replies as he hops up from his chair with cat-like agility. It's impressive for someone with such a hulking frame.

Varrek is slightly taller than Ahlvo, maybe only by a couple inches, but Ahlvo is wider and thicker. Definitely more imposing. Varrek is more lean and cut muscle, with about sixteen abs, but seeing them next to each other, there's no doubt which one is the leader. Varrek's presence is commanding, with his chin held high and that penetrating gaze. I can imagine him entering any room and the crowd falling silent around him. He has that vibe.

A low growl interrupts my thoughts, and I look up to see Varrek watching me with an intensity that makes me shiver. Why is he growling though?

Then I realize I was watching Ahlvo a moment earlier. Is he…jealous?

I look to see Kate and Ava staring at me. Ahlvo is too. But he must sense the tension in the room because he claps Varrek on the back. "Shall we go, then?"

The second the two golden boys leave, Kate and Ava start hammering me with questions.

"Okay, what was that? Between you two?" Ava asks with a smirk.

"Yeah, maaaaaaajor tension in here," Kate adds while swiping at the air, as if the aforementioned tension is tangible.

"Nothing. Seriously, nothing. I'm just staying in his room. He slept on the floor. Totally innocent," I tell them, waving my hands away in dismissal.

Ava leans back in her chair. "Okay, fine. Nothing's happened yet. But he bought you first. Then us. He wanted you from the moment he saw you. You get that, right?"

"And the way he looks at you?" Kate dramatically mimics fanning herself. "It's like he's lost in the desert and your pussy contains his only source of water."

"Jesus, Kate." I will never get used to her bluntness, I'm sure of it.

I place my elbows on either side of my plate and take a big swig of tea before continuing. It's as sweet and citrusy as it smells, and I wish I could sit here and enjoy it quietly, but the girls want details, so details I shall provide.

"Fine, fine, fine. So obviously it feels like there's this heat between us. It came out of nowhere. I wasn't expecting to be attracted to anyone ever again, let alone an *alien* who bought me at an auction. But when he was showing me how to use the shower, I just couldn't take it anymore," I tell them, Kate's and Ava's eyes rapt with interest. "I kissed him, and it was amazing. I mean, I almost came from a kiss. I've never felt anything like it."

Kate's brow lifts to a curve. "So…?"

"So nothing. He pulled away and gave me some bullshit line about it not being safe for us to go further. I felt like an idiot."

Ava tilts her head thoughtfully. "Not safe…hmm. Maybe his sperm is poisonous? Or his alien dick is too big for a human to take?" Her eyes widen. "I mean, have you seen the bulge Ahlvo is packing? I'm pretty sure that thing would kill me."

Kate and I snicker. "Can't say I've noticed Ahlvo's bulge. Interesting that you have though," Kate teases Ava as she tosses a berry into her mouth.

Ava's cheeks turn pink. "Come on. It's impossible to miss!"

"Death by dicking. What a tombstone that would make," Kate says.

We laugh together for a moment longer, and I sigh at how nice it is to sit here with these two and not feel like we're in imminent danger. But we can't let our guards down, not yet anyway. The last twenty-four hours might have been better than being trapped in a glass cage, but we're still lost in space with no conceivable way to get home, and these alien males, whom we don't really know, are in control of our safety. I feel defenseless, and I hate it.

"I think we need to talk strategy," I whisper, hoping Varrek and Ahlvo are on the bridge and can't hear me.

Kate leans in, giving me her full attention. "Right, I'm thinking we bludgeon Varrek and Ahlvo in the heads, take control of the ship once they're out, and then it's just a hop, skip, and a jump to travel the dozen or so galaxies back home." She swipes her palms against each other. "No problem."

"So that's it? You're giving up hope of ever getting home, then?" I ask, looking between Kate and Ava, increasingly frustrated.

"Look, I'm just trying to take this one day at a time. If I don't, I'm going to lose my shit," Ava says, looking emotionally exhausted. "I don't think we've fully processed everything we've gone through. Right now, we're alive. We're safe. We're being fed normal food and treated like human beings. I count today as a win."

"And tomorrow? When we're on a strange planet? Surrounded by aliens? What then?" I ask.

"If something happens, we'll deal with it." Ava gives my hand a light squeeze. "I haven't given up on the idea of going home, but right now, it seems unlikely, so I'm not pinning all of my hopes on it."

"I don't know about you guys, but my life on Earth was pretty terrible," Kate mutters, fidgeting with the hem of her tunic, or presumably Ahlvo's. "As long as I'm not a slave, and can eat more bread, I don't mind not going back."

Out of the corner of my eye, I see Ava's chin dip in silent agreement.

In truth, my life wasn't the best either. My job was fine. I was good at it, and I got to work from home in my pajamas. My love life had recently turned to shit, but I had Jenn and frequent visits from Reggie to keep my spirits up. Things were...okay. Doable. Perfectly adequate.

"Fair enough," I concede. "Okay, so we'll see if the guys know anyone with a bigger ship that could make the journey home. But if we have to stay, we'll make it work."

"Yeah, that sounds like a solid plan," Ava says warmly.

We chat about nothing and everything for the next hour or so. I relay Varrek's age and how time seems similar enough to how we count it on Earth that we should count it the same way on Oluura, just with an "ish" at the end. We wonder aloud why we were specifically targeted, out of everyone they could've possibly taken from Earth, and if other thirtysomething thick girls are next.

When Varrek and Ahlvo return, the three of us are shoveling the last remaining giant blueberry things into our mouths. They're the size of strawberries but the same round shape and deep-blue color of blueberries. The taste is slightly sour though, like a Granny Smith apple, but they pop like bubbles on the tongue and it's an explosion of tangy juice.

"Fellas." Kate mumbles with a full mouth.

"Liking the b'fiko berries, are we?" Ahlvo says, clearly amused at our lack of table manners.

"Mm-hmm," I reply, letting another berry pop under my canine tooth.

Varrek approaches the table, with Ahlvo close behind, and both of them sit down. A serious look crosses Varrek's face, and unease starts to grow in my gut.

"We will arrive on Oluura later this day. Our course is clear, and our landing will be smooth. There are a few things we should share with you first, however." Varrek leans forward, raking his long fingers through this silver hair. "You see, on our planet of origin, Trovilia, not long before my clan and I left, many of our females died from a virus. Thousands of females. It took the elderly and the young first, but when it killed our females, our population—and really, our soul as a people—died with them."

My god. What a devastating loss. "I'm so sorry, Varrek. Did you lose anyone close to you?"

He sighs, his eyes downcast. "Yes, my mother."

Varrek clears his throat, seemingly shaking himself out of the memory. "I share this because you will notice, when you meet my clan, that there are not many females. We arrived on Oluura with our closest friends and allies from Trovilia. Most are males."

Ava stiffens. "Are we in danger on your planet? Is that what you're trying to tell us?"

"Never," Ahlvo says fiercely.

"Our males are honorable. They will not harm you in any way," Varrek adds adamantly. "But it has been five years since our females were taken from us, and four since we fled and came to Oluura. Our males have not seen a new, unmated female in a long while. They will be...fascinated by you."

We sit there, the girls and I, taking all this in, exchanging apprehensive looks.

"Nothing will happen without your consent. This I vow," Varrek says as he places his fist over his heart. "You will not be made to feel unsafe or uncomfortable. I merely…I did not want you to be surprised to find that you may soon have many admirers."

If I hadn't just been kidnapped and so nervous about what my future held, the idea of having all kinds of male attention might be thrilling. It's certainly not how men on Earth treated me. But I feel overwhelmed and slightly wary.

The air in the room starts to feel stale and thick. My palms begin to sweat, and my heart feels like it's about to explode inside my chest. I need to pinch my eyes shut and focus on my breathing without any interruptions. I can't do it here though. I need to be alone. I stand, too suddenly, if the concerned looks from everyone at the table are any indication. "Sorry, I just feel a little tired. Guess I don't have my space legs yet," I joke, downplaying how I feel. "I'm going back to the room for a bit to lie down."

Ava's eyes are filled with concern. "You sure you're all right?"

"Yeah, yeah, I'm fine. Just sleepy," I promise while patting her shoulder to reassure her.

Before I turn and head in the direction of Varrek's room, I notice his fists are clenched on the table and he's looking down at them with intense focus. Almost like he's intentionally avoiding my gaze.

Ooookay, then.

I get to Varrek's room and head straight for the tiny bathroom before shutting the door behind me. I splash some water from the shower on my face, since there's no sink, and take a few deep breaths.

I'm realizing for the first time that my anxiety meds are still back on Earth and I've been without them since I was taken.

Generally, I've felt fine, or as fine as one can feel given the bizarre circumstances. But I think the combination of having no concrete plan and no way to get home plus "by the way, you're about to become *The Bachelorette* on an alien planet" is a bit too much for my brain to reconcile.

I open the door to the bathroom and find Varrek standing in the middle of the bedroom, his shoulders slumped. "Are you well, Clohee?" he asks as his eyes search my face.

I walk toward the bed and step around him to climb under the covers. "Super. Just wanted to rest a bit before we land."

He lowers his big body into a crouch beside the bed and tucks the blanket in around my body. "I brought you some of the tea you like." He points to the mug on the nightstand.

"Thank you," I reply, wanting to say more but not knowing what.

He reaches for my face before pausing and pulling his hand back. There is so much longing in his gaze that it breaks my heart a little.

He heads for the door, and as much as I want to sleep, I don't want him to go. The words leave my mouth before I can stop them. "Varrek, do your people ever engage in casual sex?"

He stills, and when he faces me, the longing is gone from his eyes and is replaced with something else. Something...darker. My skin tightens with goose bumps at that look, but not in fear. It's more feral, and it makes me feel like he's going to pounce on me at any moment. I would welcome it, to be honest. If only to calm my nerves.

"Why do you ask such things, Cloh-ee?" Varrek's voice lowers to a husky growl as he takes slow, graceful steps toward the bed.

My mind is telling me to scramble away, move back, get out of his path, but it's like my body is being pulled toward him like a magnet. I keep him in my sights and try to remain as still as I can. "I was just curious about your customs. If such a thing happens. Or if sex is reserved for married couples only or something."

"Married? This is your people's form of mating, yes?" he asks, his posture still tense as he sits down on the edge of the bed.

"Yeah. I think so. Two people fall in love and decide they want to remain together for the rest of their lives. Then they have a ceremony to make their union official," I tell him. "There are lots of couples who do stay together forever, but most of the time, it doesn't work out and they decide to eventually part ways."

"Mating is different," Varrek says as his eyes bore into mine. "Mated pairs among our people are eternal. It is a bond that is unbreakable once it is made."

We sit there, staring at each other, letting the silence stretch on between us.

"But yes, there are pleasure mates among my people. It is not an eternal or emotional bond. It is merely physical." Varrek places his arm on the other side of my body, caging me in. "You wish to find such a mate upon meeting my clan, Cloh-ee?"

I blink at him, confused. He thinks I want to find a fuck buddy out of a group of guys I haven't even met? How can he jump to that assumption when I've made it clear how badly I want him? And he has the audacity to look mad about it? "What? No! Why would you think that?"

"Why else would you be asking about such things?" He leans forward, his hands moving to either side of my head as he hovers above me, putting his weight on his forearms. "No one in my clan shall touch you, Cloh-ee. Know this. Because you"—his head lowers, and he moves his lips to my ear—"are mine." I feel his tongue lightly trace the shell of my ear, and a whimper escapes me.

His fangs brush against my earlobe, not in a bite, or even a nibble, merely a scrape to remind me of their presence. I start thinking of all the ways I want him to use that wicked mouth of his on me, and my pussy gushes like a river.

"I-I thought it wasn't safe for us to be together," I mumble as his hot breath dances across my neck. I turn my head and arch my back, seeking contact with his body wherever I can get it.

My breasts brush against him, and he plants small kisses along my collarbone. "That has not changed, I am afraid. But you are still mine. Only mine, inara."

My eyes shoot open, and I freeze. "You're joking, right?"

He lifts his head and scrunches his nose in confusion. "Of course not."

Fuck this.

I sit up, and Varrek moves to let me. "Is something wrong?" he asks.

"Uh, yeah," I bark, covering my chest with crossed arms and leaning my back against the wall behind the bed. "So...you don't want me, but no one else is allowed to want me either? What kind of possessive nonsense is that? And my name is Chloe, in case you forgot."

He sighs as he rises from the bed. "It is not that I don't want you, Cloh-ee. I want you more than I have ever wanted anything in my existence. But I cannot have you. It is safer this way. Trust me."

"You keep saying that, but you won't tell me why. Why is it safer for us not to be together?"

Then I remember what Ava said. "Is your sperm poisonous?"

"*Bikar?*" By his tone, I assume this means, "What?"

"No, my seed is not poisonous," he says, perplexed.

I wait for him to continue, but he doesn't, and the weariness I felt before returns tenfold. "Okay, fine. If you're not planning on telling me the truth, then I think we're done here." I flop back down in bed, yanking the covers up to my neck. "I'm not your property. If I want to have sex with someone else, I have every right to. I don't need your blessing or permission. Like you said, we can't be together."

Varrek bristles, every muscle in his golden body appearing to grow slightly bigger at my words. Admittedly, it's hard to stay mad at such a beautiful creature. I feel compelled to comfort him when he seems so distressed, but this is a boundary that needs to be established. I'm not interested in playing games.

Varrek heads toward the door, and before it closes behind him, he mumbles over his shoulder, "I will wake you when we are close to landing. Sleep well, Cloh-ee."

Sleep, right.

Never go to bed angry. That's the saying, isn't it? Well, at the moment I'm incredibly angry…and crazy turned on.

I roll onto my side and stare at the wall, inches from my face. I wipe away the tears of frustration that trickle down my cheeks. I don't want to want him, but my body doesn't give a shit about what I want, apparently.

I hate feeling anything at all right now. How much easier would it be to feel nothing? To live inside a cocoon of numbness that often comes after experiencing traumatic events.

Instead I feel like my skin can barely contain the emotions and sensations swirling within me.

CHAPTER 9

VARREK

"If you keep fiddling with that acceleration lever, you will break it off and we will crash into the sea, Varrek," Ahlvo says, half teasing, half scolding.

I release the lever in front of me. I wasn't actually moving it, rather mindlessly wiggling it in its current position, possibly loosening the base. Still not wise but would not cause us to crash.

It is just Ahlvo and myself on the bridge, doing the final checks as we get closer to Oluura's atmosphere. The females are in their quarters—Cloh-ee still in mine and Kay-teh and Aye-vah in theirs.

My knuckles fade to a pale yellow under my tightening fists. It seems I cannot enjoy the scent and feel of my Cloh-ee without doing something to ruin the moment. Now she is angry with me and thinking about taking a pleasure mate on Oluura.

I consider this.

What it would be like to see her with Bruvix or Waldric, or anyone else with their hands grasping her soft flesh. Or Cloh-ee pulling their face closer to hers so she can kiss them with her glorious, soft pink mouth. I envision her back arched and her head thrown back as she screams, riding out the intense orgasm given to her by someone other than me.

The metal arm of my chair crunches and collapses under the pressure of my grip, earning me a stern glare from Ahlvo before he resumes scanning through the local nav logs of nearby planets. From time to time, he checks to see if any mention of my father or Trovilia comes up.

"Might I remind you that our credits were spent on three human females, so we will not be able to afford all the parts you seek to damage this day," Ahlvo mutters without shifting his gaze from the screen pad in his hands. "Do you wish to speak on it?"

"It?" I reply, playing the fool.

"Whatever it is that causes your obvious distress," Ahlvo says. "Although, I am certain the source is the human female currently in your bed."

I break off a small piece of metal from the arm of the chair and begin folding and shaping the weakened sides of it. "She asked about pleasure mates." I try to keep my voice measured despite the fury I feel at the memory. "She told me she will take one if she wants and I cannot stop her."

"She said this?" Ahlvo looks at me, aghast.

I do not tell Ahlvo that Cloh-ee said these things after I told her, again, that we cannot be together. He would not understand my hesitation. He would tell me that my father and I are not the same and that I should not fear the madness that warped his mind. That my mind is strong and my heart is good and that I deserve my inara. That I am blessed by the goddess to be given one at all and the only foolish act would be to squander this opportunity to make Cloh-ee my mate.

There is no way for Ahlvo to know this for certain, though, and that is why I must resist the desire that threatens to bring me to my knees each moment. The madness could set in at any time, and if Cloh-ee is my mate, she would be in the direct path of my destruction. I will not allow that. She deserves much more. She deserves all.

"Let us go through the plan again, Ahlvo," I suggest.

Ahlvo groans. "We discussed this at length already. But fine. As you wish."

Ahlvo sighs and looks to the ceiling. "When we introduce the females to the clan, we will mention the trauma they endured before we freed them. We will then say that this is what connects us, the clan and the human females—our traumatic pasts and our pursuit for a better existence. A new beginning."

I nod, adding, "Then I will remind the clan that we do not dwell on the past. We rise each day with our focus on the present and working together to safeguard our future. This should send a clear message to the clan not to mention my former role and title on Trovilia or why we chose to flee."

"I do not fully understand why we must hide the fact that you were once a prince, or the king's madness, but I shall do as you ask. Always." Ahlvo shrugs, returning to the nav logs.

Ahlvo and I look up simultaneously to take in the exquisite beauty of Oluura as we near the edge of its atmosphere. My shoulders loosen knowing we will soon be home.

"She is lovely," I mutter.

"That she is," Ahlvo replies, pride thick in his voice. "I shall send a comm to Bruvix to let him know we will soon breach."

I stand, excitement and nervousness fluttering inside me. "I shall alert the females."

I find myself in my quarters, not remembering the steps I took to get here, simply letting my desperation to be near Cloh-ee again carry me. I look down at her face, completely relaxed in sleep, her pink lips slightly parted and her dark hair spread around her on my pillow.

For what feels like the hundredth time since I first laid eyes on her, I question, briefly, whether she is real. She smacks her lips and rolls slightly onto her side, burrowing deeper into the blankets and making a groggy "mmm" sound.

I lower into a crouch at her side and softly stroke the hand that peeks out from under the blanket. Her eyes blink open, and she smiles at me, and the breath is stolen from my lungs.

In the next moment, it seems she recalls our last conversation and her smile flattens to a grim line.

"Oh, hi," she mumbles while rubbing her eyes. "Were you... watching me sleep?"

"Only for a moment. You looked so peaceful I did not want to wake you."

"So why did you?" she grumbles mid-yawn.

"We are about to enter Oluura's atmosphere. I wanted you to see my home," I say, giving her room to stand.

"Oh. Oh, okay. We're gonna be there soon, huh?" She stares at her bare feet as she shuffles across the floor in a tight pace.

"Do I have time to shower before we land? I'd like to be more"—she runs her fingers through her wild mane—"presentable, when I meet your clan."

"You have no reason to be nervous, Cloh-ee. I assure you that you will be welcomed by my people," I tell her. "They will be entranced by you."

She chuckles softly. "That's a very generous term when I look like a gargoyle."

"You have time to wash, if you wish. Just come here first." I offer her my hand, afraid she will not take it.

She places her hand in mine with a shy smile. The feel of her small hand in mine sends a jolt down my spine, and I wonder if she feels it too. We exit my quarters, and I lead her in the opposite direction of the bridge, to the back section of the ship. The bridge has the best and clearest view of Oluura, but Ahlvo is there. I wish to experience my inara's reaction to seeing her new home in private.

I lead her to the storage room with various tools and parts scattered on the floor and shelves. I forgot how cluttered it was in here. I huff as I kick things out of the way, clearing a path for her. "I am sorry about the mess."

"It's fine. But what are we doing in a closet?" she asks, her voice slightly shaky.

I reach the far wall of the closet and slide the light screen back to reveal the large window. "This." I hold up my hand.

She gasps and slowly steps in front of me, getting as close to the glass as her body will allow. "My—oh my god. That's Oluura? Your home?"

I interpret her reaction as one of awe. "It is. Lovely, isn't it?"

"I've never seen anything like it. So many pinks and blues," she murmurs.

"Yes, that is the seaside, the pink part. We have yet to explore that section of our world. We live on the other side. You can't see it from here. It is the Ga'Nvi Forest. Much greener," I tell her, quietly breathing in the floral scent of her mane as it floats into my nose.

"You live in a forest?" she asks as she looks up at me.

"Yes, we built our dwellings among the tall Ga'Nvi trees." I nod.

"How fun. I can't wait to see it." Her smile is so big that it lights up her eyes.

I return her smile and allow myself to enjoy this moment of her nearness, her sweet scent, and how her joy fills me with warmth.

"Come, Cloh-ee. Use the wash box quickly, as you will need to be strapped in soon. It will become bumpier the closer we get to landing," I tell her as I guide her out of the storage room and back to my quarters. "Meet me on the bridge once you finish."

"Oh, okay. I'll be fast." She hustles into the bathroom and closes the door behind her.

I leave the room and knock on the door to the females' quarters. "Come in," I hear one of them call.

I poke my head in as the door slides open, and I see the fire-haired female standing in front of the mirror, combing her mane with her fingers. "Morivikka, Kay-teh." I look around for Aye-vah, but she is not here. "Where is Aye-vah?"

"What does that mean? That thing you just said...," Kay-teh says, turning to look at me.

"Ah, I am struggling to find the right word in your language. Perhaps there is not one that is a match. It means, 'May the goddess give you all the things you desire this day.' Something like that."

"Well isn't that as cute as a corgi's butt," she says, straight-faced, turning back to look at her reflection. "I think she's still flirting with Ahlvo on the bridge."

I am taken aback by so many things in this moment it is hard to pick one. "I...ah," I stutter.

"Oh, it's just a human saying." Kay-teh waves her hand away casually.

"It…is?" I ask.

"Well, I'm a human, and I say it, so…yeah," she says, twisting her mane into a tight knot atop her head.

She puzzles me, this one. "Very well. I came to say that we will be landing soon and you will need to be strapped in. Please come to the bridge."

"It's about time!" she shouts. "I feel like you two have been saying, 'We'll be landing soon, we promise,' since we got on the ship. I was beginning to think it was all a ruse and we were destined to float through space forever."

"Right. Come to the bridge as soon as you are able." I turn to leave, but Kay-teh touches my shoulder, stopping me.

"You know, Varrek, I grew up with three brothers. They taught me all kinds of handy techniques to survive." Her eyes turn dark as she glares at me. "I know how to field dress a deer, for example. Do you know how to do that?"

"What is a deer?" I ask.

"It's an animal that humans often hunt on Earth. Doesn't matter." She steps back a bit and puts her hands on her hips. "My point is that I'm not squeamish. I know how to hunt, kill, and skin another creature."

"Well, that is good," I tell her, curious as to where this is going. "A valuable skill set."

"It is indeed." She nods, an ominous grin stretching across her face. "I want to believe that you and Ahlvo are good dudes, that we're safe with you, but I don't know for sure. The way Chloe looks at you, and the way Ava looks at Ahlvo…you better not hurt them." She pushes the blunt nail of her index finger into my chest. "Or I'll gut you, if I have to."

I fight back a grin. I do not wish to insult Kay-teh, and I have no doubt she is capable of such things, odd little human, but her threats do not worry me. If anything, I am grateful my Cloh-ee has others who look out for her.

"I thank you for the warning, Kay-teh. I shall keep this in mind," I tell her as I head to the bridge.

As I enter, I watch as Aye-vah stands behind a seated Ahlvo, fixing one of his many braids. *Is this flirting?* I wonder.

I would like to play with Cloh-ee's mane this way. Combing it out, braiding it, petting it, anything where I feel the silkiness of it in my hands.

I clear my throat to make them aware of my presence.

Aye-vah turns with a bright smile. "Oh, hey, Varrek. How's it going?"

"I had an unsettling conversation with Kay-teh, but apart from that, all is well," I tell her as I take a seat in my chair.

Aye-vah chuckles loudly. "Yeah, she's...unique. But she means well."

I hear a contented moan from behind me and immediately swivel my chair around. It is my Cloh-ee, cloaked in my too-large tunic, her mane hanging in wet strands down her shoulders.

"I feel so much better now," she says, her tone dreamy.

"I am glad, Cloh-ee," I say, staring at her like a lovesick fool.

"Where should I sit and strap in? I only see three chairs."

"You may sit here, in my chair," I say as I stand and gesture for her to take my place.

"But where are you going to sit?" she asks.

Kay-teh enters and plops down into the third chair.

"I will stand here, behind you. I will be fine," I assure her.

"Finished! Gotta say, this is the best-looking braid on your head," Aye-vah tells Ahlvo.

He rises, stroking the finished braid. "Then you shall have to tend to my braids from now on, little noodle."

I go to ask about the strange nickname he has given Aye-vah, but I am too focused on making sure Cloh-ee is strapped in correctly.

Ahlvo taps his seat twice. "Sit, Aye-vah. I shall stand like Varrek, behind the seat."

We strap the females in one at a time. I have never landed the ship without being strapped in, but Cloh-ee's safety matters more to me in this moment, so I will brace myself and hold onto the chair.

"Landing in thirty blinks. Hold on," Ahlvo warns. I lean over Cloh-ee and pull back on the acceleration levers as Ahlvo plugs in the coordinates to the clearing just outside of the Ga'Nvi forest. Ahlvo sets the ship to auto touch down.

We wrap our arms around the backs of our chairs and curl our bodies around them, leaning our heads down next to the females in front of us.

"Are you sure this is safe?" Cloh-ee whispers as the chairs start to rattle and everything shakes around us.

"Do not worry, Cloh-ee. All will be well," I vow, bracing my body with my legs.

Cloh-ee gasps as the ship dips downward suddenly, and when it rights itself, she wraps her hands around my forearms, her knuckles turning white, pulling them closer to her. "Varrek, hold on to me."

We are close to the ground, and our landing will be smooth, but I will not pass up the opportunity to have Cloh-ee in my arms, especially since she demands it.

I do as she asks and cross my forearms around her chest, just above her breasts, resting them there. I do not want to crush her, so I let them drape around her lightly, hoping the landing is extremely smooth, as I am no longer anchored to the chair like I was.

We experience a few bumps as the ship touches down, and Cloh-ee turns her face toward mine, huddling as close as she can. Her scent is all around me, a dizzying cloud I never want to clear. "You are safe. I promise."

The ship drops into shutdown mode with a final jerk, and a grunt escapes my lips as my chest knocks into the back of the chair. Then the final beeps of the ship begin their sequence as everything stills.

I hear a collective sigh of relief from all of us, and I give Cloh-ee's delicate shoulders a light squeeze before letting go. "We are home."

CHAPTER 10

CHLOE

 e wait to leave the ship so Kaiva, the healer, can come onboard and give us health scans to determine how our bodies will react to our new environment, and the necessary vaccines to keep us from dropping dead as soon as we step outside.

Kaiva, pronounced *Ky-vah*, is about six feet tall and wide and thick, like her son Ahlvo. She's extremely muscular, but whereas Ahlvo is all bulky muscle, Kaiva is softer and more round. Her golden skin has a darker hue, and she has slightly crinkled skin around the corners of her eyes and mouth, as well as subtle white stripes running through her black hair.

After she gives the guys big hugs and kisses their cheeks, she stares at us for what feels like five straight minutes, saying nothing. Varrek speaks to her, presumably telling her all about us. Then she smiles a big fangy grin and rushes toward us with arms extended. Instead of a hug, she takes the time to clasp both of my hands in hers and welcome me in her native language, starting with me and ending with Kate. I don't need to know what she's saying to know that she's thrilled to meet us.

The feeling is mutual.

She speaks to Ahlvo in a low voice and gestures to the back of her head, right behind her pointed ear. He tells us she wants the language implant immediately, and a moment later, he pulls out his tablet and holds it against her head. Then Varrek says everyone in his clan will get their language chips updated with English within the next few days.

Once she gets the update, she conducts health scans on all three of us. Ahlvo and Varrek stand on either side of her, concern etched on their faces and hands extended for us to squeeze as she gives us each three vaccines. The needles are so tiny I barely feel them, just a little pinch, like a mosquito bite, and then it's over.

We follow Varrek, Ahlvo, and Kaiva down the ramp of the ship and are greeted halfway down by another male. Facing us with his hands clasped behind his back is a scarred and extremely surly-looking golden man. He's got silver hair, just like Varrek, but his is shorter, with shaggy waves that frame his face. I try not to stare at the scars on his face, because it's rude, but the way the healed gashes run from his chin up to his left eye, and the other going straight through his lips, makes me wince internally at the pain he must've suffered.

His navy-blue eyes scan each of us humans warily. "Varrek. Ahlvo." He nods in greeting. "I am called Bruvix, and I welcome you to Oluura, females." His tone is cold and clipped, like he was forced to say it. Or perhaps he always sounds this unhappy.

Ava and Kate are both looking at me expectantly, like I'm the unofficial greeter. Okay, then. I step forward and hold a hand out to Bruvix. "Pleased to meet you. I'm Chloe." I point behind me. "And that's Ava and Kate."

He stares at my hand but doesn't take it. "You have too many fingers."

I laugh nervously. "Maybe you have too few."

"That is enough, Bruvix. I did not ask that you get the language update so you could make the females feel uncomfortable," Varrek mutters crankily. "Let us head home."

"Come. This way," Bruvix says to us, waving his hand to indicate we should follow him.

"Um...are we walking? Because we don't have shoes," Kate says.

Kaiva turns and looks down at our bare feet. "Ah! I shall get boots for your feet once we get to the village. Until then…" Kaiva smirks. "These strapping males shall carry you."

Bruvix takes a step toward me, arms outstretched, before Varrek slides in front of me and blocks Bruvix from getting any closer. "No. I will carry Cloh-ee," he says as he hauls me up into his arms with minimal effort. I worry for a moment that the tunic I'm wearing is riding up and my butt is exposed, so I tug on the hem until it's pinned between my thighs and Varrek's arm.

Ahlvo approaches Ava and holds his arms out to her in question. "May I, little noodle?" he asks with a dazzling grin.

Ava giggles and steps forward with a nod as Ahlvo lifts her.

Bruvix sighs and approaches Kate with curious eyes. "Your hair looks like fire," he says as he holds his arms out.

"That's because it is. Try anything and you're gonna get scorched," Kate replies sarcastically.

Bruvix grunts and holds Kate in his arms stiffly. He looks at Varrek. "She is frail. Are you certain I will not break her?"

"I'm not made of glass, you bozo," Kate quips.

Then we're on our way down the rest of the ramp.

The moment we step outside, I suck in a breath. I don't know what I expected an alien planet to look like, but it definitely wasn't this. It's so…Earth-like and somehow not, all at once.

The ground is covered in a layer of something that looks mushy, not unlike moss, but is cobalt blue. It looks damp and like it won't bear much weight, and I'm glad I'm not walking on it with bare feet.

In front of us, about forty yards away, is a grove of massively tall trees. They're wide and thick like redwoods but even taller, with longer, bushier branches shooting out every which way. They look to be centuries old. There's a beaten path leading into the forest, and it disappears far beyond my gaze. The sky is filled with the same pinks and bluish purples of Earth at sunset, but with fluffy clouds the color of lavender adding ripples across it.

A crisp breeze moves over my skin, and I shiver. "You are cold?" Varrek asks in a low voice.

"Yeah, it's a bit chilly, but I'll be fine." I wrap my arms tighter around Varrek's neck and lean closer to him for warmth. "Is it always like this here?" I gesture to the sky. "It's beautiful."

"This is a lovely time of day. But no, it is not always like this. We have the wet season, the warm season, and the cold season," Varrek tells me, his thumb rubbing against my ribcage.

"What season are we in now?" I ask.

"This is the warm season."

"Yikes. Okay, I'm gonna need some pants, then," I tell him.

"I will ensure you have all that you need, Cloh-ee."

It's not the first time he's said this, and I find the promise comforting and more believable the more I hear it.

We enter the forest, and the sky disappears almost entirely. The coverage of the trees blocks the breeze, but it also blocks the remaining light of day, so the deeper we go, the colder it gets.

"Man, it's dark as fuck in here," Kate blurts out.

Bruvix stops in his tracks, looking annoyed. "Kaiva, can you grab the douku orbs from my pouch?"

Kaiva reaches into the pouch strapped to Bruvix's hip and pulls out several balls the size of marbles. They have a thick milky-white fluid in them and look squishy. She tosses them to the ground one at a time, about a foot apart, and the moment they hit the blue moss, a soft glow emanates from them, lighting our path like in some kind of fairy tale.

"Can your human eyes see better now?" Bruvix huffs at Kate.

Before she can reply, Ava yells, "That is so cool! What are those?"

Ahlvo laughs like he's completely charmed by Ava's enthusiasm. "They are douku orbs. They provide light once they touch the ground, then their liquid absorbs into the soil once the light fades. The nutrients in the liquid then feed the plants and trees. Nalba created them. She is our inventor."

"How long does it take for the light to fade?" I ask.

"They will be absorbed by sunup," Varrek says.

The three of us go quiet, collectively mystified by such a unique and handy source of light.

It takes another thirty minutes of trudging deeper into the forest before we see any signs of life. I assume it's intentional, but man, these guys are thoroughly hidden from the outside world.

I see structures in the distance and hear muffled conversations and laughter among the constant buzz of nature all around us. I'm not sure if I'm hearing bugs or birds or both, but there's a consistent hum coming from the trees and bushes.

"Holy shiiiiiiiit," I mumble once we arrive.

It's...a neighborhood. In the middle of the forest. There's a wide path between several houses that looks like an unpaved road, even though I don't see any kind of vehicles that would have flattened the ground like this. The blue moss from the clearing is here too, but a little sparser.

The houses themselves are tall and narrow. They're made of gray stone and dark-brown wood and look slightly primitive in the way the stone and wood are connected to hold the structure up. Rather than taking the place once occupied by trees, the houses were built around the trees, preserving them. I see steps carved into some trees, and trees used as supportive pillars to hold up walls and roofs.

A village of treehouses. My eyes want to gobble this place up and keep the colors and details intact so I never forget that this is a real place I once saw. Because it feels straight out of a dream.

None of the houses look alike. Because of the denseness of the forest, in order to preserve the trees, Varrek's clan clearly had to get creative in how their homes were built. Some houses are round and almost wrap around the nearby trees in a circle. Some are square, not unlike Earth houses, and look as if they're wedged in between two trees. There's even one that looks to have a triangular shape, with the biggest point facing toward us and windows lining the walls that meet.

The one thing they all have in common is how tall they are. I would guess that in order to achieve the desired amount of space needed to live in one of these houses, you need to build up, since you can't build out.

In the center of the cluster of houses on the left side of the path is a wide, one-level structure with a pointed roof and three walls. The front of the building is completely open, and I can see several tables filling the space and five firepits lining the front opening.

Several gold-skinned beings putter around the tables while a few tend to the food cooking over the fire.

I point at the structure. "What's that?"

"That is our food hall," Varrek says. "Everyone should be gathering there shortly."

"Wait here. I shall get boots for you," Kaiva hollers as she runs toward one of the treehouses. She enters the triangle house, and I can see her through the windows on the first level as she rustles through her things.

She comes back about five minutes later with three pairs of the same boots all of them are wearing. They're black, made of what I assume is a type of leather, with gold zippers up the side.

"They shall be too big for your tiny feet, but they will do for now. I can adjust them after the meal," she promises.

The guys place us gently on our feet atop a moss-free patch of black dirt, and we lean down to put the boots on. Varrek immediately crouches at my feet to pull the zipper up the side like I'm a clueless child. "It's okay. I know how to work a zipper," I say with a smile.

He finishes zipping them up and does that shy nose-scratch thing that makes my heart skip.

We wiggle our toes, take a few steps, and shake out our feet for a moment like we're shoe shopping. "They're big, but it's nice not to be barefoot anymore," Kate says to Kaiva.

She places a gentle hand on Kate's shoulder. "I am glad."

"Shall we go, then?" Bruvix asks. "The clan has gathered."

Varrek nods and steps out in front of us to lead the way. As I follow behind, I cross my arms over my chest for warmth, and maybe to hide my nerves. Even though I'm determined to find a way back to Earth, I still want Varrek's clan to like me, no matter how short our time is here.

I step on a clump of the blue moss, and it's not as mushy as I expected it to be. It's like stepping on a piece of bread. Or maybe it's not at all like that and I'm just hungry.

The scents of the food hall waft into my nose, and I decide I'm definitely hungry. I smell meats being grilled, the signature warm sweetness of the junasii bread, and several other scents I don't recognize.

We follow Varrek into the hall and stop as he faces the members of his clan from the back wall. We stand behind him, and a hush falls over the crowd of gold faces. I'm not sure of the exact number, but I would guess there are almost forty members of Varrek's clan.

Most of them have black hair, some have silver, and I see a small group huddled together at one table with maroonish red hair. Not like Kate's at all, as hers is a coppery red. Their hair is striking, and I wonder why it's only them with hair like that. They also have bright golden eyes, like light beams, and bigger ears. Where Varrek's and the rest of the clan's ears are similar to human ears, just with a pointy top, theirs are larger and wider. Theirs are also pointy, but they stick out really far and are loaded with piercings between the earlobe and the point at the top.

Varrek addresses the crowd in his native language, his rough voice even sexier with the volume and timbre of a leader. I wish I knew what he was saying, but I find I'm just as captivated by him as his clansmates.

Ahlvo stands slightly behind Varrek and to the right, with Bruvix to the left of him and farther back than Ahlvo, making the hierarchy clear through their positioning. Varrek points to each of us, saying our names slowly and gesturing for us to come forward and stand next to him.

A young boy with wild black hair yells something at Varrek, and the crowd snickers as his mother scolds him in hushed tones.

"What did he say?" I lean back and ask Bruvix.

"Nothing, Cloh-ee," Varrek replies.

"He asked why your faces are so flat. And why your skin is different colors," Bruvix says bluntly.

Kate, Ava, and I look at each other, exchanging similar glances that say, "Well, this is fun."

Varrek's chest puffs out a bit, and his voice takes on a biting tone as he says something to the boy and the rest of his clan. He looks at me, longing in his gaze, and his tone softens as he continues to speak.

I have no idea what to do, so I smile up at him and give him a reassuring nod to let him know I'm not offended by the boy's comment.

He says a few more statements and ends on something that sounds hopeful and triumphant as he raises a fist above his head. Ahlvo, Bruvix, and Kaiva mimic this gesture, and the crowd does the same. It feels inappropriate to join, since I have no idea what the significance or history of that gesture is, so I keep my hands down and smile. Kate and Ava follow my lead.

Then everyone turns back around to face the bowls of food in front of them and resume their dinnertime chatter. There's a long wooden table along the back wall with bench seats on either side, and Varrek plops down in the middle of one bench with his back to the wall.

"Come, females. We shall feast this eve," Ahlvo says eagerly and gestures for us to sit on the bench across from Varrek.

The moment we sit down, steaming bowls of food are placed in front of us, along with giant mugs of something pale orange and frothy on top. "What's this?" I point to the mug.

"Ah, that is my signature ale. It is delicious, Cloh-ee. You will love it," Ahlvo boasts. "Of this I am certain."

"*Your* signature ale? You lie!" Bruvix pounds on the table. "I make this ale myself. I lose sleep to brew this ale for the entire clan."

"But it is *I* that told you to add the shilmashi petals to the brew. Before that, *your* ale tasted like piss," Ahlvo mumbles with a mouth full of bread.

Bruvix frowns while shoveling a spoonful of what looks like shredded meat into his mouth. "My ale has always been adored by the clan, you beast."

"O fah." Ahlvo waves a hand dismissively.

I've come to learn this expression is their version of "whatever." I continue to watch their banter as I use my spoon and knife to break apart the meat in my bowl. It's a large chunk of reddish meat submerged in a brownish broth, not unlike beef stew, and surrounded by black leaves, which I assume are herbs.

I don't bother asking what kind of meat it is, because we're on an alien planet and I probably won't recognize the animal anyway.

Juices explode on my tongue when I take a bite of the meat, and I find myself trying to chew slowly so I don't miss out on the array of flavors. I'm certain there's no Earth equivalent to this meat, in taste or texture. It's the best I've ever had.

"Wow, if all your food tastes like this, I'm never going to leave," I say between slurps of the broth.

Varrek's eyes lock on mine, and I wonder if I said something wrong.

"Yeah, this is extremely delicious," Ava says as she dips her bread into the broth.

Everyone is quiet during the rest of dinner, just "mmm" sounds and spoons clanking against the sides of bowls fill the air.

"When should we get the language update?" I ask.

"Based on my initial scans, your human heads do not seem to have language chips implanted," Kaiva replies. "This is not a procedure I am able to do safely, as I lack certain tools."

Bruvix takes a big swig of ale and adds, "I shall look to see if I have any of the old translation plugs that you can put into your ear canal."

"Do not fret, Cloh-ee," Varrek says warmly. "The clan will get their updates and will be able to communicate in your native tongue."

I nod, slightly bummed that I don't get to learn a new language and embarrassed that Varrek's clan will be speaking American English on their home planet just so we feel comfortable.

Each member of the clan cleans up their spot at the table and drops their dirty dishes into a bin next to the first firepit. I ask Varrek if we can help wash the dishes, and he tells me not to worry about it yet. That we should get settled in first and offer our help tomorrow.

I don't put up a fight, because getting settled into a bed of my own and passing out sounds heavenly right about now.

Varrek leads us to a circular treehouse with four levels just behind his house. This one is empty, as the former occupant died on a hunting trip about a year ago, he tells us.

The first level of the house has a tiny kitchen and bathroom, as is the case with all the houses, apparently, since the plumbing pipes can only go so high.

The kitchen is sparse, as most of the meals are made in the food hall, so it just has a small firepit and a deep basin with a connected spigot. The bathroom has a shower about the size of the one on Varrek's ship, but this one is round. Eggplant-purple branches that remind of me bamboo are lined up like poles, tied together with a wire of some sort, and formed into a rounded shape all around the strange shower head to block the water from leaking onto the rest of the floor.

The toilet is a large cylinder made of smooth black stone, with a flat lid that flips up, not unlike a human toilet. The cylinder sits atop a deep hole, and when you pull the cord hanging next to the cylinder on the wall to "flush" it, you hear a rush of air, indicating that the waste is gone. It sort of reminds me of an airplane toilet in that way.

The second, third, and fourth levels are bedrooms. Varrek tells us that the previous owner wanted enough rooms in case he was "lucky enough to have a family of his own someday," and my heart breaks at the happy memories he'll never get to make here. The rooms are cozy and all about the same size, with a full-size bed in each that's made up of large, soft cushions piled up high and then covered with multiple blankets and pillows. There's a wooden shelf next to the bed, a lantern, and a chest for clothing in each room, along with a single large window, peering out into the forest.

A layer of dust covers the surfaces in every room due to the home's prolonged vacancy, but we each get our own bed, so that feels like a great trade-off to me.

I let the girls claim the rooms they want first, and I'm left with the bedroom on the fourth level. As I look out my window, I notice it faces Varrek's house, with the long thick branch of the tree our house is built around leading right from my bedroom to his.

Interesting.

The three of us come back downstairs to thank Varrek for letting us stay here as Kaiva arrives. She drops off several tunics and some leggings we can wear. She also gives us each a pair of boots that she resized to fit our feet.

"It was easy!" she reassures us as we shower her with thank-yous. "All of the boots can be resized with little effort. We make them that way."

We each give her a hug, and she leaves. Varrek shows us how to use the wash box in this bathroom, which is slightly different compared to the one on the ship, and then says good night to each of us with a gentlemanly bow.

I resist the urge to curtsy, even though I'm seriously tempted, and give him a small wave before he leaves.

Kate, Ava, and I look at each other and smile. "Finally," Ava says.

"It's not *home* home, but it's cute," I say as I look around.

"Yeah, beats the hell out of a glass cage. I'm going to bed," Kate sighs as she starts climbing the stairs to her room on the second floor.

"Ditto," I say, following close behind.

When I get to my room, I change into one of the several shirts in the pile left by Kaiva and crawl under my mountain of blankets. Even with the window closed, it's chilly in here, so I'm grateful for the extra layers. But I also like the breeze, so I crack the window open. I'm most comfortable when I can burrow under layers and layers of blankets and feel the cold distantly, on just my face and fingers.

I reach over to turn off my lantern and catch a glimpse of Varrek out my window, wandering around his bedroom, shirtless.

I gasp, and then I turn out the light so he can't see my eyes.

Just a look. Just one look. And then I'll stop.

I pinch my eyes closed. *No. Don't look at all, you creep!*

I'll lie down and go to sleep and I'll never look again, I tell myself unconvincingly.

His wide chest gleams in the soft light of his lantern, and it makes the tattoo band on his bicep stand out even more. It's stunning in this light. I want to learn what it means.

Varrek turns away from me, and I'm hypnotized by the muscles in his back, bunching and expanding as he reaches for something on a high shelf. Then I see him tug at the strings on his pants right before they fall to the floor, exposing his perfectly sculpted ass to my prying eyes.

I stifle a squeal and throw myself down onto the bed. *He didn't hear me. He didn't see me.* I put a hand over my mouth to keep another sound from slipping out and revealing myself as a Peeping Tom as I try to steady my breathing.

I stare at the ceiling, counting each breath as it enters and exits my body.

Seems like this man is determined to keep me from getting a good night's sleep.

CHAPTER 11

CHLOE

After about a week on Oluura, we get into a comfortable routine. Well, as comfortable as you can get when the eyes of more than twenty-five alien males are glued to you whenever you pass by.

Ava and I help out by washing the dishes for the clan after each meal at the hall. Ava is spending most of her days with Kaiva and is interested in learning how to become a healer, or at least help out by cleaning Kaiva's tools and organizing her herbs to start. Back on Earth, Ava was in the process of getting her master's degree to become a therapist, but since the clan doesn't seem to rank mental health as a dire need, she wants to help by contributing this way.

Between breakfast and lunch, I've been trying my hand at sewing with the small group of sewers that make clothing and blankets for the clan, but it's not as easy as I thought it would be to learn. The thread the clan uses is thick and wiry, and it takes me several tries to create a single loop and pull the entire thread through. I'm tempted to scream and throw the soft fabric and needle into the nearby firepit several times a day, but I don't because I just met these people and they don't need to know how obnoxiously impatient I am. Yet.

I have no idea what Kate has been up to. She washed dishes with us on the first day but hasn't assisted with that task since. Varrek asked me where she was on the third day as Ava and I were washing dishes, and I told him I didn't know. I mentioned how we hadn't seen her much in between meals, and he brushed it off like it was no big deal. "She will find her strength here. Do not worry. For some it takes time," he said.

I appreciate the reassurance, but I worry that if one of us is seen as dead weight around here, we'll all be seen that way. I don't want that. If we can't find a way back to Earth, we'll need to stay here, and I refuse to be perceived as a burden. I don't want Kate to be seen that way either.

In the afternoons, since Ava is busy with Kaiva and Kate is nowhere to be found, I walk. I like to do a loop around the treehouses and then continue out in larger circles through the surrounding forest. Once the trees start to get really dense, I turn back because I do not want to be the stranded human found screaming for help in the woods.

It's on the eighth day that I run into Nalba on my afternoon walk. She's the clan's inventor, and...she can be hard to read. Sometimes she's friendly, and sometimes she's cold as ice. I think maybe she's one of those eccentric geniuses, but it's hard to tell, since our cultures are so different.

"Hi, Nalba." I smile as I approach. "Nice day, isn't it?"

She's on her hands and knees, studying the bark of a tree so intently that I wonder if she heard me.

"It is not raining, so I may continue my work. That is all I require from the weather," she says flatly without looking up.

"Ah, that makes sense." I swallow, hating this attempt at small talk I'm making. "I actually love the rain. It makes lying in bed so cozy, ya know?"

She stops and looks up at me briefly before lowering her eyes back to the tree bark, following the path of some kind of beetle. "Do humans require ample rest time because of your fragile bones? Is that why lying in bed is such a pleasurable activity for you?"

Normally, I'd be extremely offended by the implication that we're a weak species. But coming from Nalba, the words don't hit like a condescending remark. She sounds genuinely curious about how humans are biologically different.

"Uh, no. We don't require additional rest." I fidget with the sleeve of my shirt, giving me something to do with my hands. "I just find the sound of rain relaxing. That's all I meant."

She stares up at me for a long moment and then stands. "I suppose the sound is quite pleasant." Her lips curl up on one corner and it almost passes for a smile.

"So…what's it like being one of the only unmated females here? Among all these males who seem to be eager to settle down." I scoop up a thin fallen branch and roll it between my fingers.

"You are asking why I am not mated?" she clarifies.

"Yeah. When I walk around here, I feel like the eyes of every male in the clan are on me. Is it like that for you too?"

Nalba tilts her head to the side, considering my question. "It is not that I do not wish for a mate. I simply have not found my own." She bends down, grabbing a chunk of blue moss and rolling it into a ball, then sniffing it. "I had a pleasure mate for a time, back on our planet of origin, but he was not my eternal mate, so it ended."

"Oh, I'm sorry. Breakups are the worst." I feel for Nalba. That's a pain I know all too well. "Who was your pleasure mate, if you don't mind me asking?"

"Varrek," she says, tossing the moss back onto the ground with a plop.

The branch in my hand snaps unexpectedly under the pressure of my grip. I stare at the splintered pieces, not knowing what to do or say. A hot ball of jealousy grows in my stomach, and I'm both surprised and annoyed by it. I don't have any right to be jealous. It's not like Varrek is even mine. But the thought of him with someone else, anyone else, irritates me.

And Nalba, of all people, with her long, lithe body, her shimmering golden skin, her shiny black hair that goes down to her perfectly sculpted butt, and her mesmerizing blue-gray eyes. Then there's her brilliant mind. No wonder Varrek wanted her. I can't compete with any of that.

"Our males are good. Honest. Whether you take a pleasure mate or find your eternal mate among them, they will place your happiness and safety above their own," she says reverently.

She looks up at the sky through the treetops and starts to gather her things. "Come. The sky grows dark, and the predators will soon emerge. If I let you get eaten by the tr'gorys, the males in the clan will never forgive me."

"Tr'gorys? What is a tr'gory?" I step quickly into the footprints she leaves behind, struggling to match her longer strides.

"It is a bloodthirsty beast that attacks when it smells fear," she says flatly. "One of our clansmates was killed by a tr'gory during our first year here. We have not roamed the depths of the forest at night since then."

I pick up the pace and leap into her footprints the moment she lifts her feet from the ground. "Yeah, I don't want to tango with a tr'gory."

We emerge from the forest a few minutes later through a tight space between two houses and run into Varrek and a large group of men walking toward the food hall together, drenched in sweat, dirt, and blood splattered on their bare chests.

"Well, what have you been up to?" I ask, admiring the sharp angle of his jaw as a bead of sweat trickles down it.

"Warrior training." He looks between me and Nalba warily. "Nalba." He nods. "Have you been giving Cloh-ee a tour of the village?"

I watch them closely as they interact, searching for some sign of lingering feelings, I suppose. Silently praying for a lack thereof.

"I do not have time to give tours, Varrek," she states. "I was merely leading this human back before the skies turn dark and the tr'gorys make their rounds."

His features tighten in fear, and he takes a step closer to me, almost instinctively. His hand hovers near mine, not touching it. "You should not be walking alone in the forest, Cloh-ee. It is not safe."

"Oh, I don't go very far. Just trying to get the lay of the land," I reassure him. "There are only so many dishes to wash at the hall."

Varrek's lips form a warm smile.

"Ah, you are bored," Nalba says. "You may help me in my shop. Your tiny hands and many fingers will be of great use to me."

Varrek looks conflicted for a moment before masking his emotions. "This is a grand idea," he says unconvincingly.

"Um…okay. That sounds fun," I add.

"So you will begin tomorrow, then, yes?" Nalba asks.

"Yes. I'll come by after breakfast," I tell her. I'm slightly relieved to have an excuse not to sew anymore, since I suck at it, but I'm also not thrilled to become Varrek's ex's assistant.

"Good. Farewell, human." She gives me a nod and then turns to Varrek. "Your Majesty," she mutters before heading in the direction of her home.

I chuckle at the barb, but when I look at Varrek, his body is rigid and he seems to be frozen in fear. "Are you okay?"

"Uh, fine. Yes."

I'm suddenly feeling a little shy now that we're alone. I haven't seen much of him since we landed, outside of mealtime. I've also tried very, *very* hard not to peep on him from my bedroom window each night.

For the most part, I've kept my eyes to myself.

"Do you train with your warriors often? It doesn't seem like there's much of a war to fight around here." I gesture to the tranquil setting around us.

He wipes the sweat from his brow. "A good warrior must always be ready for battle. Any day that we do not train, we put our clan at risk."

We walk side by side in the direction of our homes as people pass by, nodding and waving as they go. "That seems like a lot of pressure to put on yourselves, especially when you live in a quiet place like this," I say. "Although, I will say, I'm a bit jealous that all of you are so skilled at fighting and handling weapons."

"My crew does not carry this burden. It is mine alone as leader," he says solemnly. "I merely guide them during our trainings to ensure they are physically ready to handle any threat that comes our way."

"I guess a little cardio never hurt anybody." I shrug. "It's not any of my business anyway, obviously."

"That is not true, Cloh-ee." He turns to face me. "Everything about this village is your business. I wish for it to feel like home to you."

"That reminds me, were you able to speak to any of your contacts? The ones that you said might be able to find us a ship back to Earth?" I ask, remembering his words from a few days ago.

He looks down at his feet and continues walking. I follow his lead. "No, I was not able to reach them yet."

I sigh. "That's okay. We'll keep trying, right?"

It's hard to tell with just a view of his profile, but he looks suddenly crestfallen. "Yes, we will keep trying."

We arrive at the front of Varrek's treehouse, but before I can start walking down the narrow path toward mine, he gently touches my upper arm. "Cloh-ee, I…" He trails off as his gaze lowers to my lips.

His fingers glide down from my elbow to my wrist in a featherlight caress. I close my eyes as my entire body starts to tingle. "Yes?" I ask, almost breathless at the contact.

He opens his mouth to say something and then in an instant, snaps it shut. "I…shall see you at the food hall," he mutters as he turns and heads to his front door, roughly raking his fingers through this hair as he goes.

* * *

AFTER A DINNER FILLED with awkward pauses and angst-filled looks between me and Varrek, I'm actually eager to do the dishes for the entire clan. I even tell Ava that she can head home after washing the mugs and I'll take care of the rest.

Having something to do with my hands takes me out of my head a bit, even if it's a mindless activity. I can space out as my hands scrub and wipe each bowl, and think of nothing at all. Which is infinitely better than thinking of Varrek, I must admit.

I cannot figure him out, and it's driving me up a wall.

I finish putting the freshly dried mugs away and wave to the few elder clan members still standing around the firepits, drinking the rest of their ales.

"Pl'zuu," they say with a nod. It's their version of "have a good night."

I say it back and head in the direction of home. I walk slowly so I can take in the soft glow of the douku orbs, large and small, scattered all over the ground and dangling in the trees above. It's like an ethereal woodland paradise, utterly Instagrammable. I sigh at the magic of it and at the absence of social media on this world. It's nice to be away from all that nonsense and the way it made me feel like my life wasn't interesting enough.

I open the front door to our little house and find Kate standing in the kitchen with a large mug of water in her hand. "She lives!" I say jokingly. "Where have you been all week? I've barely seen you."

"Oh, you know. Just been exploring a bit," she says with her eyes darting around the room, avoiding mine, almost.

"Is everything okay?" I grab a mug and pour myself some water as well from the spigot.

"Yeah, I, uh, I'm just taking a little longer to adjust to all this, I think," Kate says as she wipes away a drop of water running down the outside of her mug.

"Personally, getting to know the clan a little better has helped minimize my anxiety," I hint. "And now that I'll be helping Nalba in her shop, there's room in the sewing circle for another helper."

"Oh, okay. I'll give that a try." She forces a smile. "Thanks. I'm gonna head to bed."

"Okay. Good night, Kate," I tell her as she climbs the steps.

"'Night."

I turn out the lights, save for the dim douku orb that sits atop some kind of plant near the window, and I head up to my room on the top floor. I take off my leggings, which Kaiva told me were hand-me-downs from the children of the clan who grew out of them, and change into a tunic that I cut the sleeves off of so it feels more like a nightgown.

I turn off the lantern in my room and burrow under the blankets.

It's a perfect night for sleeping, chilly and mild but not freezing, and I realize that I'm actually happy here. Perhaps happier than I've been in a long time. I have tasks to fill the time, I don't have any bills to stress over, I'm getting to know my neighbors, and there are lots of deliciously hunky men who stroll around in minimal clothing each day.

Most importantly, I feel safe here.

My mental list of things I'm grateful for is interrupted by a shadow falling over my face in the darkness. I gasp, slowly moving to the edge of the bed, feeling for something to grab and use as a weapon.

Varrek pops his head through my window a moment later, and I let out a sigh of relief. "Varrek!" I whisper-scream so as not to wake the others. "What the hell? You scared me!"

He's standing on the branch that stretches between our bedrooms, bare-chested, his hand extended in my direction.

"Do not fear me, sweet Cloh-ee," he says soothingly. "I have something to show you. Come."

"Now?" I ask. "It's getting late. I was about to crash."

His face glitters, his eyes swirling with heat. "I am aware of the time. But I have found the optimal weapon for you. I wish to show you how to use it."

Oh.

I grab his hand, letting him pull me onto the branch outside my window. "Hell yes."

CHAPTER 12

VARREK

I take my inara's delicate hand in mine and pull her onto the branch just outside her bedroom window. She takes a single step forward before I pull her up into my arms. The branch beneath us is wide enough for Cloh-ee's feet to step comfortably, but I cannot bear the thought of her slipping and falling to the ground below. It is easier this way.

She squeaks as I lift her and protests briefly in my arms, saying she can walk on her own, but I take the four strides to my window, and then we are inside.

I have fantasized about making this short trek on the branch between our rooms every eve since I realized she chose the bedroom on the top floor of her dwelling, right across from mine. Being this close to her, it has been…difficult. I find it nearly impossible to tear my eyes away from her when she walks around her bedroom, when she slumbers, and even harder when she strips away her layers at the end of the day.

Despite my overwhelming desire for her, though, I have looked away when she removes her clothing. I do not want her to feel unsafe here, and I will not violate her trust in me. I will not look upon her soft pale skin until she reveals it to me.

But I have noticed her occasionally watching me when I undress, and I find that I am pleased by it. Trovilians are not shy when it comes to baring our bodies. When the weather is warm, it is not unheard of to see my clansmates shed their layers and enjoy the feel of the sun on their bare skin. It does not seem that humans are the same.

Besides, knowing Cloh-ee finds my body appealing fills me with great pride. When I feel her eyes on me, I find myself flexing my muscles and puffing out my chest to give her the show she craves, all while pretending that I don't know she is watching.

I heard her muffled gasp that first night when she watched me from her room. Not only do I have exceptional hearing, but because she is my mate, my senses are attuned to her body. I assume she does not realize this. I could even smell the sweetness of her arousal the moment my pants hit the floor. It was heaven, breathing in her scent, and I wanted nothing more than to bury my face between her thick thighs and see if her taste matched the sweetness of her scent.

Seeing her now, standing in my room, I feel in my bones that she belongs right here. This dwelling should be hers as well. But I brush that thought away before it takes hold in my mind, because she cannot be mine. She can never be mine.

"Your room is really cozy," she says as her eyes scan her surroundings.

Cloh-ee is correct about the coziness. I appreciate a thick blanket and a soft pillow to sleep on, and in the years since we came here, I have acquired several. Beyond the bed, there is a plush shag carpet made from h'rom fur that I purchased on Nu'Piix, as well as a few overstuffed cushions for seating.

"I am glad you find it to your liking," I tell her, delighted by her approval.

"So what kind of weapon am I getting?" She claps and rubs her palms together with excitement gleaming in her eyes.

"Come. I will show you." I lead her down the steps to the second floor, which includes my training room. Separate from the training grounds I use with my warriors, I wanted a private space for me to hone my skills in hand-to-hand combat and practice with any new weapons I may come across. Training tends to quiet my mind when it becomes flooded with painful memories.

In here, a wide array of weapons hangs on the walls. Everything from guns, to bows and arrows, to imposing swords can be found in here, and I have spent many moons practicing with each of them.

"Wow," Cloh-ee says in awe. "Quite the fortress you've got here. You have a treasure hidden somewhere that you're trying to protect?"

I chuckle. "They are just weapons I have collected over time. But I suppose I do find comfort in knowing that I will be able to protect my mate and child, eventually."

When I say the words, the image in my mind is Cloh-ee, her hand resting on her belly, heavy with my child, while another small one runs around her slim ankles. The small one is a perfect mix of her and me, with my silver hair and retractable claws, and Cloh-ee's light skin, her pink cheeks, and dark eyes.

Cloh-ee grows quiet at this, and I wonder if the image in her mind matches mine. "Right," is all she says.

She turns to me, pointing at the wall of swords. "Which one is mine?"

I open the glass case on the wall filled with smaller yet extremely lethal battle tools and pull out the one I had in mind for her. I place it in her open palm.

"Throwing knives?" she asks.

"Yes. They are lightweight, easy to conceal, and you can throw them from a distance, or if you are faced with an enemy close-up, you can use it as you would a regular blade," I tell her as I pull out the dispenser armbands Nalba designed.

"Once you have learned how to properly rotate the blade in your throws, and then master the accuracy, I will give you these to wear." I strap the dispenser band onto my forearm and show her how it works.

The exterior fabric of the band is leather, but Nalba also included metal wiring, additional pockets, and technological elements I do not fully understand to make it easy to conceal and use in an emergency.

"This loop here"—I point to the curved piece of leather that sticks up slightly on the inside of the wrist—"you pull it using a finger on the same hand, and a blade will pop out." I show her how to do it, and the blade's handle ejects from the hidden compartment on the band and extends into my palm. "Each band has five blades at all times. If you pull a blade, there will be another behind it until you pull all five."

Cloh-ee's eyes light up like a child's, all curiosity and pure joy. I marvel at the sight. I vow to find new ways to make her glow like this.

"You are not ready for the armbands yet, however." I smirk at her slight frown and put the bands away.

I walk to the opposite side of the room and pull back a cloth to reveal the wall of targets. The wall has scattered large shapes that contain small circles in the center, and it's made of several layers of pliable, slowly rotting wood. Healthy wood from our Ga'Nvi trees is too tough a target, and we need the blades to penetrate the exterior and then sink into the softer layers beneath the surface, to mimic an attack against an enemy.

"What's that smell?" Cloh-ee's nose is scrunched up tight, her lips flattening.

I lift my nose into the air and smell nothing, but I know the source of the strong scent anyway. "It is the wood from the target wall." Despite my senses being stronger than my Cloh-ee's, my nose has gotten used to the bitter, heavy scent of the rotting wood.

"First, you must put boots on. You do not want a blade to chop off one of those tiny toes of yours." I grab a pair of boots from the drawer under the glass case and hand them to her.

She examines them closely, her brows pulling together in confusion. "You have boots here in my size? Are these...someone else's?"

No, I had them made for you. I wanted to make sure you have the things you need when you are here. I have asked the sewing circle to make you an entire wardrobe. Some of the pieces are here already, in a chest I have designated just for you upstairs in my bedroom. The bedroom I hope we will share someday.

I do not tell Cloh-ee any of these thoughts swirling around my mind though. "No, they are an extra pair I meant to give you earlier."

"Oh. Okay." She seems satisfied with my response and tugs the boots onto her feet.

I show Cloh-ee where to stand and how to position her body. I nudge her left leg forward with my foot and direct her to put her right leg back, slightly behind it.

"Wait, I'm right-handed. Shouldn't I stand the other way?" she asks, looking down at her feet.

"Right-handed? What does this mean?" I have never heard this phrase, so I assume it's an issue with the translation.

"I use my right hand more than my left, so it's stronger and I'm more skilled with it, basically," she tells me.

I am puzzled by this. "Your hands are not equally strong? Why would you allow one of your limbs to become stronger than the other?"

She giggles, and the sound goes straight to my cock. Everything she does seems to strengthen our tether, even though I know the tether is not something she feels. I feel it though. My need for her consumes me more and more each day.

"Where I'm from, everyone is either right-handed or left-handed. Some are ambidextrous, but it's rare," she says.

I do not like the idea of my already fragile mate being unable to defend herself simply because an attacker approached her on her weaker side, but that is a problem for another time.

"Very well." I take a step back. "Let us begin with your stronger side for now."

She alternates her feet, and I walk in a slow circle around her, examining her form. I stop when I am behind her, and the floral scent of her mane wafts into my nose. I breathe it in, enjoying her closeness.

I gently tug her shoulders back a bit so she is almost pressed against my chest, straightening her spine. "You must stand tall when you throw." I feel her skin tighten, and tiny bumps appear all over her arms. "But you must also remain relaxed in your posture, or you could overthrow the blade."

She takes a deep breath. "It's hard to focus, uh, when your hands are on me."

I search the air for her fear scent, but I do not smell it. Still, I remove my hands from her upper back in an instant.

"Maybe we save the touching for another time, when I'm not trying to concentrate on hurling a knife across the room, hm?" Her tone is playful, and she is smirking at me over her shoulder. I get a slight hint of her arousal scent, and I can feel the blood rush to the head of my cock in response. But I must focus on teaching her this skill, so I let my heart hang on the words *another time.*

"I look forward to that," I tease back.

Pink floods her cheeks, and I have come to learn that it signals her bashfulness.

I walk to her side and hand her the small blade. I hold one in my hand as well to show her the proper grip. "You can grip it this way." I hold the knife sideways, with the blade facing out. "Or like this." I pivot the blade and adjust my hand placement so that the width of the blade is facing out. "That one is better for closer distances. But always make sure your thumb is on top."

I stare at her hand, concerned. "Will you be able to manage this with all of those fingers?"

She scoffs. "I've seen humans throw knives before. I think I can figure it out."

I show her how to bring her arm back and then release the knife, using the right amount of force upon release. My blade lands with a thunk into the center of the square target.

Cloh-ee copies my form and flings the blade forward. It clanks against the top of the wall, nowhere near her circle target, and falls to the ground. She huffs in disappointment.

I hand her another blade. "That was good form, but your throw looked too hard. You don't want to throw it as hard as you can, or you will not connect with precision." I point to the circle on the wall with the dot in the center. "Again."

"Why are you helping me? Why teach me how to use this?" She turns to me, holding the knife tightly and pointing it toward my chest. "What if I decide to use this knife on you?"

She takes a step closer, lifting her chin in defiance. She uses the edge of the blade to give my chest a single tap. "Aren't you worried about that?"

Normally, when someone pulls a knife on me, my body buzzes with adrenaline, poised to defend and attack. But this time, the one holding the knife is my mate, and I am merely in awe of her bravery.

I lean into the knife so that it cuts into my skin and draws a drop of blood on my chest. I watch as Cloh-ee's eyes widen at the blood and she pulls the blade back. "You are not my captive, sweet Cloh-ee. You may leave here anytime you wish."

I take the blade from her hand and wipe the blood on my pants before handing it back to her. "I help you because I can see how much you long for independence. You wish to be able to defend yourself if you are ever in danger." I pick up a blade from the pile and do a sidearm twist throw, nailing the center of another target painted on the wall. "I can make that wish come true for you, by teaching you this. It is the least I can do."

"Thank you," she says in a low voice. Doing things for her, kind things, simple things, it seems to take her by surprise. Every time. Are decent males on Earth that scarce?

She takes a deep breath and shakes out her shoulders. This time, she doesn't let her body tense up before releasing the knife, which is good, but her toss is too light, and the blade falls short of the target wall. "Better. Somewhere in between the first throw and your second. That is what you must strive for."

After four more throws, none of which hit the target, I tell Cloh-ee that her shoulders remain too tense. She seems frustrated with herself.

"It will take time to master this skill, Cloh-ee, do not worry," I reassure her. "You must have patience."

"Yeah, I think I was born without the patient part of my brain." She turns to me. "I need a distraction, or something, when I throw. I'm in my head too much."

I can think of many ways to distract my inara, but none of them will improve her accuracy. "What kind of distraction?"

She taps her small foot, thinking. "Let's do questions. I ask you one, you ask me one, and we go back and forth. We'll get to know each other."

"Very well. I may ask you…anything?" I smirk.

"Sure. If I don't like the question, I won't answer." She winks at me and gets back into her throwing stance.

Her cleverness makes my heart swell. She continues to impress me, this human.

She releases the blade, and it sticks this time but well below the circle. She is improving.

Her eyes gleam at the sight of the blade sticking into the wood. "Okay. Favorite food. Go," she says.

My answer comes easily. "Wa'vix spread on qit crisps. Wa'vix is a fruit that is native to Trovilia, and my mother would turn it into a spread. Qit crisps are similar to our junasii bread but made with a different powder. And it was cooked for longer, into crisps. She always used to feed me wa'vix spread on crisps when I was ill, and I came to enjoy it even when I felt well."

I look up and find that Cloh-ee's gaze is intense yet warm. "I love that. And I totally get it. Comforts from home or childhood are the best."

"What about you?" I ask as Cloh-ee releases her next knife. It bounces off the target wall. "Your shoulders were slumped a bit. Make sure to straighten."

"Right." She pulls her shoulders back. "Favorite food…definitely cheese. I ate cheese with everything back on Earth. Didn't matter if it was pasta or a salad, or just a block of cheese on its own. Cheese was always the central ingredient." Her stomach rumbles at her words, and she pats it lightly.

"What does this 'cheh-eese' consist of?" The translation is coming through, but I do not understand exactly what it is.

"It's a dairy product. So it's made from the milk of an animal on my planet called a 'cow,'" she tells me.

I file the information away for later. I will speak to Waldric about this food and see if he has any ideas on how to recreate it. "My turn, yes?" I ask.

Cloh-ee nods.

"What was your favorite place on Earth?" I walk behind her before she raises her arm to throw the next knife. "Chin up, and release the tension in your back."

She does as I command, and this time, when she releases the blade, it lands in the outer rim of the circle target. She turns to me with her mouth wide, and she lets out a squeal of excitement. "Oh my god. I did it!"

"That you did." I beam at her. "Now keep doing it. Hit the target five more times."

"Okay, okay." She takes her next blade in hand and resumes position.

She closes her eyes, deep in thought. "My favorite place is probably the pond near the house I grew up in," she sighs. "It was in the middle of the woods, and I'd walk out to it sometimes when I couldn't sleep and just lie in the grass and look up at the stars. It was so quiet and peaceful. Not unlike here, actually." Her lips curl up into a soft smile. "I found it comforting to look at the stars—something so big, so unknown. It helped me put things into perspective."

"I understand what you say. I have done the same." I rub the handle of the blade in my hand absently. "Whenever I am on my ship, it does not matter if I am coming or going. When I look at the sky before me, I am reminded of how small I am. It is important to gain that kind of humility."

She hits the circle target again, but this time the blade sinks into the wood just to the left of the central circle. She shoots a proud grin in my direction. "Yeah, exactly."

Cloh-ee's next eight hits are mixed, some slightly high, some low, but all close or within the circle. In our question game, I learn that her father died in an accident, and his laughter is what she misses the most.

She also misses something called "tee-vee," which is apparently where her video stories are kept, and in particular, she misses a story she used to watch about a group of workers whose duty it was to sell flattened sheets made from trees. They were led by a buffoonish male who constantly engaged in ridiculous antics.

"Why was this male in charge, then? If he was always getting into trouble?" I ask, puzzled by this.

She giggles. "Because that's what made the show funny. He probably should've been fired though. Hundreds of times."

I also learn that her favorite color is a deep, rich green. She says this as her eyes linger on mine, and my stomach twists in response.

I tell her about a game I used to play as a child called "block down," but when I explain the rules, she laughs and tells me it makes no sense. I speak of my mother some more, to which Cloh-ee says, "She sounds like she was the epitome of a badass queen." I panic for a moment before I realize that her use of the word *queen* is general and not literal and she has not learned of my past on Trovilia.

Then it is her turn once again for a question. "Are you and Nalba still a thing?"

I almost drop the knife that sits in my palm. Then I decide to feign ignorance. "A thing?"

"You know what I mean. Are there still feelings there?" she clarifies.

"Did Nalba tell you this?" I don't want to discuss my past pleasure mates, so I'm stalling a bit.

"Yeah, she shared a little." She grunts as her ninth hit lands perfectly center, with the handle of the blade jiggling briefly at the force of it.

"Look at that! Perfect hit, Cloh-ee," I marvel.

She turns to me, reaching for another blade on the stand between us. Even though she has hit the target well past the five additional times I asked for, she shows no signs of stopping. "Don't distract me with praise, Varrek." She wags her finger at me. "Answer the question."

I release a deep breath I did not realize I was holding. "Nalba was my pleasure mate for a time. She is not anymore. She has not been for years. I am not pleased that she shared this with you."

"Why?" Cloh-ee asks, pinning me in place with her glare. "It's her story to tell as much as it is yours. And she didn't do it in a gossipy way." She steps back into her throwing stance. "Are you ashamed of it?"

"No. Nalba is a good female. A close friend." I kick at nothing on the floor, not knowing what to say. "I suppose I am not comfortable discussing my past mates with you. That is all. I certainly do not wish to hear about yours..." I trail off.

She nods, hitting the target with her blade perfectly once again. "That makes sense."

I am not sure what response would've soothed my mind, or if any such response exists, but implying that she does, in fact, have previous pleasure mates certainly does not calm my nerves. It makes me wonder if there is a male on her home planet waiting for her return. Fear fills my heart as I ask, "Did you have a mate on Earth that you left behind?"

She gives me a teasing look over her shoulder. "I thought you said you didn't want to hear about my sexual past?"

When I say nothing in response, she stares hard at the target wall and the many blades inside the circle. "No, I didn't leave a mate behind on Earth." Her voice lowers to a sorrowful whisper. "I was all alone."

There are many things I wish to tell Cloh-ee in this moment. I wish to tell her she is no longer alone. That I am here for her and will always be. That my time with Nalba means nothing compared to the short time I have spent in her presence. That she is my mate, my inara, and nothing will ever matter more to me than her happiness. But as I open my mouth, the words die in my throat.

We stand there, Cloh-ee and I, for what feels like several minutes, the silence between us hanging heavy, like the air just before it rains.

In the next moment, I hear several knocks on my front door.

"Who could that be?" Cloh-ee asks.

"I do not know," I tell her. But for interrupting my time with my mate, they will pay dearly.

CHAPTER 13

CHLOE

*V*arrek's back tightens, and I swear I see a ripple across his skin as he stomps down the stairs toward the front door. I've always found him a little intimidating. At over seven feet tall, it'd be impossible not to. But right now, he's downright scary. He's all clenched fists and bunched muscles as a growl constantly rumbles in his throat.

I know he won't hurt me, or at least I'm pretty sure? But whoever is on the other side of that door should be very, very afraid. I don't even understand why he's mad. It's not like we were naked and in the middle of sexy, fun times or anything. We were just talking while I practiced throwing knives.

He yanks the thin wooden door open, and it creaks on its hinges. "Bikar!" he shouts. I can't see who is here because his massive back fills the door frame. What I can see, though, is the morning light peeking through the trees and streaming through the doorway around his body.

We stayed up all night? It feels like I just got here.

"Uhh...hi, Varrek. Sorry to bother you," I hear Ava say in a shaky voice. "We can't find Chloe. She never came home. Have you seen her?"

I put my hand on Varrek's side, and I feel his body relax at my touch. Then I gently nudge him out of the way so Ava can see that I am, in fact, alive and well. Kate stands beside her, their hair mussed and flattened from sleep. They look so worried, and immediately I feel like an asshole for not telling them where I was.

"Heeeey, guys." I peek out from behind Varrek, smiling sheepishly.

Ava throws her hands up in the air. "The hell? We were worried sick, Chloe!"

"I'm so sorry. Varrek was just showing me how to throw knives." I grin up at him. "I guess we lost track of time."

Kate just smirks. "You are *so* grounded, young lady. No phone and no TV for a month. Go to your room." She stomps her foot and points in the direction of our house.

Ava pins Kate with a hard stare. "Girl, are you broken?" she asks as she knocks on Kate's forehead like it's a door.

"I thought we were using the whole good cop / bad cop parental approach?" Kate asks genuinely.

"Uh, no. We never discussed—*Kate*, we don't have time for this." Ava rubs her temples, clearly over this whole situation.

Kate huffs a breath. "Okay, whatever you say, dear."

Ava rolls her eyes at Kate and then lets out a long, labored exhale. "Well, now that we know you're alive, come on, Chlo. Let's get dressed so we can get to the hall."

I hand Varrek the blade clutched tightly in my palm. "Thanks for the lessons. And the questions. I had fun." I touch his forearm and turn to leave.

"There is much more practicing to be done. I shall see you later, Cloh-ee." His eyes hold so much adoration that my body doesn't want to walk away.

But I let Ava and Kate pull me back toward our house, since we have to get this day started.

We get inside, and I jog up the steps to my room. "Be down in two seconds!" I yell.

I quickly pull my sleep shirt over my head and kick off my boots. I waste no time as I tug on a fresh shirt and leggings and shove my feet back into my boots and zip the sides. Then I'm racing downstairs and quickly checking my hair in the small mirror of the bathroom.

Kate and Ava were already changed for the day, but now their hair is smoothed down and tied back neatly. They wear matching scowls as we begin to trudge toward the food hall.

"Guys, I really am sorry," I grovel. "I hate that you were worried about me."

"Throwing knives, eh?" Kate says sarcastically. "Is that what the kids are calling it these days?"

"I have no idea what the kids are calling it. That's how long it's been since I've done it. Throwing knives is all we were doing. Truly." I remember the proud look on Varrek's face the first time I landed a blade inside the circle, and butterflies fill my stomach. I can't believe we stayed up all night.

Ava tugs on my wrist, and we stop in the middle of the main path. "Look, I don't care if you're getting a little alien dick, okay? I really don't. I'm not your mom. But we promised to stick together," she says, gesturing to the three of us. "So let's agree to keep each other in the loop. Details can be shared if we want to, but generally, we need to be aware of each other's whereabouts. Got it?"

Kate lets out a big yawn and leans her head on Ava's shoulder. "Yes, dear," she mutters.

I nod. "Deal."

We get to the hall and stand in line to load up our plates. It's a buffet-style setup, and the girls and I stick with the lighter fare on most days, just some junasii bread and berries and a cup of tea.

As I reach for a thick slice of bread, one of the cooks, Waldric, comes lumbering over. "Morivikka, Cloh-ee," he says with a grin that stretches from ear to ear, exposing his sharp fangs.

He makes a point to say hi to me at each meal. He acknowledges the other girls with a nod, but he puts on a bit of a show to greet me. He also tries to sneak me extra portions at breakfast, for some reason. I think he might have a crush on me. Generally, I'd be flattered, but since I'm one of the only unmated females on this entire planet, I don't take it too seriously.

"Morivikka, Waldric," I say back. "Bread looks delicious today."

This is how all of our interactions go. I know he and the other cook, whose name I can never remember, bust their asses cooking for the whole clan, so I try to show my appreciation without being overly flirtatious back.

Not that it would be a hardship to flirt with him. He's just as big and bulky as Ahlvo, but maybe a little less cut. I've heard that Waldric used to be a warrior, but when he came here with the clan, he wanted to put his skills in the kitchen to use, so he became one of their cooks. It's clear that he's still covered in layers and layers of muscle, but instead of an eight-pack, I would guess Waldric has six. He's slightly softer than the rest of the warriors, which makes me trust his cooking even more.

He also has kind eyes and a gentle energy. So I never mind when he hangs around after the meals when I'm washing dishes and nervously chats with me. And I certainly never refuse an extra slice of sweet bread. I'm not a monster.

"I added ah, the juice from the b'fiko berries into your tea. I hope you find it to be…enjoyable." His accent is so thick that he struggles with English. But he speaks slowly, sometimes with long pauses in between words like he's patiently waiting for the perfect word to come to him, and I find it absolutely charming.

"I'm sure I'll love it. Thank you, Waldric." I beam at him. He nods a few times with that big, goofy grin of his as I walk away and sit down with Kate and Ava at our table.

I turn to Ava. "How are things going at Kaiva's?"

She takes a sip of tea, and then her faces scrunches up in discomfort. Clearly it's still too hot to drink. She puffs out short breaths while waving a hand in front of her tongue.

"Too hot?"

"Oh yeah, my taste buds are decimated," she says before gulping down some water. After a moment, she sighs in relief. "Kaiva is great. I love working with her. She has such a generous spirit, don't you think?"

Kate and I nod in unison.

"I mean, obviously it's a new environment for me. But Kaiva's approach to medicine seems to be completely different from the way it's practiced on Earth."

"How do you mean?" I ask.

"It's not just hard science." Ava looks up at the treetops, thinking. "There's a holistic approach to start, then she cross-references it with scientific research, but then…they're also way more advanced here, technologically and medicinally, than we were back home. It's fascinating. All of it."

"She seems like she'd be a good teacher," Kate adds.

"Oh, absolutely. She's been so patient with me," Ava says.

Kate turns to me. "Are you excited about working with Nalba?"

"Uh, yeah. She's brilliant, obviously. I love that the clan's inventor is female. It's just…" I trail off.

"Just…what?" Kate prods.

"She and Varrek used to be a thing," I reply.

Kate and Ava give me the same knowing look, a mix of pity and "yikes," and I instantly regret sharing that bit of gossip. I didn't want to think about it, and now here I am thinking about it. About them. Together.

We finish our breakfast and deposit our plates into the bin before we get to work on washing them. My eyes wandered the hall the entire meal, waiting for Varrek to appear. He never did. I couldn't help but notice that neither did Nalba.

The paranoid, jealous thoughts creep into my mind before I can head them off. *They're probably together right now. I bet he's got her bent over the main table in her shop, telling her how brilliant she is while he fucks her just the way she likes.*

Then logic inserts itself while I separate the mugs from the plates in the bin. *Who cares if he's fucking her? That's his business. It's not like he's yours. Let it go.*

Kate starts humming a popular song from the '90s while she fills up an empty bin with water, and my sour mood dissipates. I'd much rather have this song stuck in my head than the image of Nalba and Varrek together.

After about thirty minutes of me scrubbing plates, Ava scrubbing mugs, and Kate drying, the pile in the dirty dish bin starts to shrink. We wait for the last remaining clan members to finish up their meals, and wash and dry those dishes as they're handed to us.

"Thanks for the help today, Kate," I tell her before we head off in separate directions for the day. "It went so much faster than it usually does with just me and Ava."

"Yeah. No problem," she says as she studies her pruney fingers closely.

"Okay, off to Kaiva's." Ava gives us a wave and heads in the direction of Kaiva's med room.

"Good luck in the sewing circle," I tell Kate. "I was basically useless, so I'm sure they'll be excited to see a new face."

Kate squints up at the trees. "I used to sew my clothes back together all the time as a kid. Should be fine.

"What are you going to help Nalba with?" she asks.

I shake my head. "No clue, honestly. She said my small hands and extra fingers will be of use to her."

Kate chuckles quietly. "Lucky you." Before I turn to leave, she touches my arm. "Thanks for getting me a spot in the sewing circle. It'll be nice to have something to do during the day. I don't know, I think I've just felt lost since we arrived."

"Don't worry about it." I hold her gaze. This is a side of Kate I haven't seen before. She rarely lets anyone in.

"Right. Later tater," she hollers over her shoulder as she jogs away. And just like that, her wall is back up.

* * *

NALBA'S HOUSE is located on the far right corner of the row of houses at the end of the main path, and it takes me about four minutes of walking to get there. Her house is very different from the rest in that it's technically three separate houses, connected by an outdoor staircase that wraps around two trees supporting all three floors. Each level sits on a square platform of flat beams with a lantern placed at the corners to provide outside light.

The bottom level is much larger and wider than the two levels above, and it's where her shop is located. I've never seen the second and third levels, but from the outside, they look like portable storage sheds raised onto platforms and tucked between the thick trunks of the trees holding them up.

The front door to the shop is open, along with the windows. I hear scraping of metal and what sounds like a hammer *thwap*-ing away on a hard surface.

As I approach Nalba's front door, Varrek storms out. He stops suddenly when he sees me, clearly caught off guard. "Cloh-ee. Hello." He forces a smile.

"Hi," I say in a clipped tone, trying to mask my suspicions about his presence here. *None of your business,* I remind myself silently.

He lowers his chin to his chest and continues on, and I try to shake off the interaction like it never happened.

I step inside, and Nalba's beautiful, angular face has a lingering scowl, but it fades to a neutral expression when she sees me. "Ah, Cloh-ee. Come, come." She waves me over to where she's working.

In her shop, there are several long wooden tables that are covered in clutter. Scraps of metal here, piles of kindling there, and lots of dirty dishes with crumbs from what used to be food stuck to the insides. Now I know why I never see her at the food hall. Clearly, she eats her meals here. My stomach turns queasy at the mess.

Nalba sits at the end of one of the tables, surrounded by tools that look vaguely familiar, like magnifying glasses, screwdrivers, and so on, but with curves and loops and other add-ons that make them distinctly alien. In front of her is a flat slab of stone, and on it sit two blobs of something I don't recognize. One is white and thick, and one is brown and clearly in a state of decay.

"What's all this?" I ask as I sidle up to her. She brushes a stray hair that has come loose from her topknots out of her face and grabs a small vial. She squeezes a drop of thick, milky liquid onto the brown blob. It takes a few minutes, but soon the brown blob grows in size and the brown starts to fade into white before my eyes. Then it looks exactly like the white blob next to it.

"What just happened, Nalba?" My eyes are still wide as I try to make sense of the sorcery I witnessed.

"This is a grain bar. It is a food ration we make for our hunters and for when Varrek travels on his ship." She holds up the white blob. "This was made this day. This one…"—she reaches for the one that was brown just seconds ago—"was made before the last moon."

"Did you just…reverse the rot and extend the shelf life of that bar?" My voice squeaks as it raises to a bewildered pitch.

She smiles at me, exposing her dazzling white fangs. "That I did, Cloh-ee." She hands me the resurrected snack food, and I examine it closely. It looks exactly like the fresh one, with its fluffy white grains, not unlike rice, formed into a squishy ball using a spicy-smelling sauce that holds the grains together.

"Is it safe to eat like this?" I ask, gently poking it with my finger.

"Not yet," she replies with a frustrated sigh. In the next moment, the white blob sucks in on itself, deflating and fading back to the brown.

She grabs the shriveled blob from me and crushes it in her large four-fingered hand before letting the crumbs fall onto the floor beneath her. "The elixir does not hold the reversal long enough. I am trying to figure out how to extend it."

"Well, I've never seen anything quite like that. You've done amazing work, Nalba," I offer as I use my hand to sweep the crumbs together on the floor before scooping them up into a dirty mug.

"Your kind is quite primitive, yes?" she asks me. "I have not been able to do much research because the resources on your people are limited, as you are from a restricted region."

I find a shallow, empty bin tucked in the far corner of the room and start putting dirty dishes into it as I come across them. "I mean, I guess? Certainly compared to you guys. We've dabbled in space travel but only within our galaxy. And we haven't found alien life on other planets yet. Many people on my planet don't believe it even exists."

Nalba drops the tool in her hands and throws her head back in laughter. "What arrogance."

"Can't argue with you there," I giggle.

We ease into a comfortable chatter as Nalba works and I tidy. We share tidbits about our cultures, comparing the differences and the similarities, but always with genuine curiosity and respect. Every once in a while, Nalba will scold me for throwing away what looks like trash but is a key part of an ongoing experiment she's working on. After I get all the dirty dishes and rotting food scraps out of the way, it looks a lot better in here.

She tells me about life on Oluura compared to Trovilia, although she's strangely hesitant to share much about the latter. I assume it's because she's homesick and it's painful to talk about.

She also tells me about Maevstra, the upcoming feast to honor their goddess and welcome the new season. "We will be cloaked in our finest garb, the cooks will have endless platters of meat prepared, and Bruvix always makes extra ale so that all our mugs remain full," Nalba says, smiling.

"That sounds fun. When is this feast? I guess I need to find something to wear," I mutter, making a mental note to ask the sewing circle if they have any dresses that will fit a round human woman.

"It is in nine days," she says as she strides toward me. "You may borrow an old garment of mine, if you wish." She lifts my arms and does a circle around me, scrutinizing my frame. "We will have to get it adjusted to your size, however, tiny Cloh-ee."

Having a breathtaking, statuesque woman like Nalba refer to me as "tiny" feels so odd and at the same time, fills me with glee. I am small compared to her, height-wise at least. "That's really kind of you, Nalba."

"O fah." She waves her hand dismissively. "I shall have it for you in the next day."

I finish stacking the plates in the dirty dish bin so they don't topple over and shatter, and I begin to feel my lack of sleep weigh me down. Yawning, I rub my eyes and notice that the sun is no longer peeking through the trees. In fact, the sun is all but gone from the sky, and the shadows outside seem to be getting longer. With the constant cover of thick trees, it gets dark pretty early here, but I'm either still not quite used to it or I keep losing track of time. Most likely, I'm running on empty and need to go to bed.

"You do not look well. Is it time to rest your weak bones, Cloh-ee?" Nalba asks teasingly.

"Actually, yeah, I think so." I yawn again, my body offering additional confirmation. "I'm going to drop off these dishes and head home. I'll see you tomorrow."

"Pl'zuu." Nalba waves to me as I walk out the front door.

I take a few steps before placing the heavy bin down on the ground and looking up. The few clouds I can see through the trees have gone from lavender to deep violet, so I'm guessing it's late afternoon, getting close to dinner. I skipped right through lunch, apparently, which is something I never do.

Sleep. That's what I need. Just sleep.

I haul the bin back into my arms, balancing it on my knee for a second to adjust my grip, and trudge toward the hall. The breeze lifts the ends of my hair as I walk, and I welcome it, as carrying all these dishes is causing me to work up a bit of a sweat.

When I make it to the hall, Waldric is the only one here, chopping pieces of meat into cubes and dropping them into a deep pot over the center firepit.

"Ah, Cloh-ee! There is your face." Waldric beams. "I did not see it at middle meal."

"Yeah, I'm afraid my face was with the rest of me over at Nalba's." I lower the bin of dishes to the ground near the washing section. "Which is where all these nasty dishes were, by the way."

He nods knowingly. "Yes, Nalba does not eat here often. She likes to take her meals while she works. She is different. Special."

His words hold immense admiration for Nalba, and I wonder if I've been reading him all wrong. Maybe he isn't crushing on me at all. Maybe he's just incredibly sweet to everyone. Either way, he's quickly becoming one of my favorite people here.

"She certainly is," I agree as my eyes wander the hall for a quick snack. "Hey, is there a piece of junasii bread I can snag? I'm going to head to bed early, but I'd love a quick bite of something."

He puts his large knife down and wipes his hands on a rag. "Of course, Cloh-ee. You shall not go hungry here," he says as he points to a storage box tucked under the shelf along the back wall. "Additional rations are kept in there. The hunters pull all their travel rations from it before they leave. You may take some anytime you need to."

"Oh, thank you. This is perfect!" I pick through the box and find small bags of cured meat that's been turned into jerky, dried fruits, some kind of olive-green pebbles, and cubes of junasii bread. I take one bag of the bread cubes and one bag of jerky with me.

The spicy scent of jerky fills my nose and makes my mouth water. "Ah, man, I owe you big time, Waldric." I thank him again and clutch the bags of food to my chest as I leave and head back to my house.

When I arrive at my front door a few minutes later, Varrek saunters out from the side of the house with a mischievous grin on his face.

"Well, well, well. You look like you're up to no good," I tell him.

"I have been waiting for your return. I have a treat for you this eve, sweet Cloh-ee." He holds his hands behind his back and rocks back and forth on the balls of his feet excitedly.

"I appreciate that, Varrek, but I am way too beat for more knife-throwing tonight. Maybe tomorrow?" I ask, another yawn escaping my lips. "I'm running on no sleep right now, as you know, so I was going to have this snack and go to bed early."

"No weapons, Cloh-ee. I have other plans for you." He starts walking down the main path, clearly expecting me to follow, "And these plans will have you feeling very relaxed indeed," he says over his shoulder cockily.

"All right, I'm interested. Where are we going?" I ask, now following close behind him.

"You will see..." He trails off, slowing his pace to walk beside me.

I gaze at Varrek's profile, his proud nose, the prominent ridges lining his forehead, and the jut of his chin, and I'm in awe. He side-eyes me without turning his head, and his soft lips curl up into a slight grin. "You watch me like prey, you know," he says.

"Maybe because you're looking tasty tonight."

He throws his head back and howls with laughter. The sound is low and deep and sends tingles down to my toes. I want to hear it again and again. "You are just hungry. Keep eating your rations. I do not want you to starve."

We take a right off the main path onto a much narrower path, lined with waist-high bushes and thickets that we have to dodge and push away with our hands. As the path shrinks to the width of Varrek's foot, he grabs my hand and keeps me close, and I don't mind at all. It's getting darker by the minute, and I don't know my way around this section of the forest yet.

The deeper we go, the quieter it gets. The sounds of the village die down, and only the sounds of nature remain. The chirp of alien birds I have yet to see up close, the crunch of branches and twigs beneath our heavy footsteps, and the whistle of wind through the large leaves hanging above us, shielding our view of the evening sky.

Eventually, we start seeing boulders in the forest. We pass a big black boulder the size of a Toyota Prius when I hear the burble of flowing water up ahead. "What's that?" I ask.

"Your treat," Varrek mutters with a sly grin. A few steps farther, he pulls back the unruly branches of a tree that's my height and covered in azure-blue leaves that look like lily pads, and that's when I see it. A massive waterfall spilling into a pond surrounded by rocks and flowers below.

"Oh god, Varrek. It's so beautiful here," I say, stunned. I step toward it slowly, cautiously, like I'm skeptical this place exists outside of my daydreams. "Is it safe to go in the water? Is it cold?"

"The water is safe. I have been in it many times. And it is quite cold, but I have brought this," he says, holding up a pale-gray block the size of his large hand.

"What's that?"

"It is a powder that dissolves and heats the body of water in which it's placed. It also adds natural nutritional elements to the water for the animals that lurk around our territory," he explains as he tosses it into the pond.

Nalba's handiwork, I assume. I shake my head at how gifted she is. A teeny, tiny part of me is still threatened by her past with Varrek, but the more time I spend with her, the more I want to forget the past and just be her friend.

I unzip my boots and climb up the stones that line the pond. I dip my bare toes in and sigh at the warmth of the water. Our shower at the house hits a lukewarm temperature, and that's as hot as it gets, so we never spend too much time in there. But this, this is like bathwater. It's perfect.

As I wiggle my toes in the cloudy water, I notice Varrek off to my left stripping all the way down. He turns around, and my jaw falls open at the sight of his huge, glimmering gold cock. Scratch that, his huge, glimmering, *erect* gold cock, bobbing in the air, like it's pointing at me.

When he places his pants in a neat pile atop his boots, I clear my throat. "Um, I didn't realize we were wearing our birthday suits for this adventure."

He tilts his head at me, puzzled.

"I wasn't expecting to get naked with you," I clarify, covering my cheeks with my hands, trying to hide the crimson shade they're turning.

He nods with something that looks like a mix of amusement and sympathy swirling in his gaze as he steps into the pond. "I have come to understand that your kind is…bashful…when nudity is involved. But it is natural, Cloh-ee." His brows furrow, and he looks worried suddenly. "Do you fear me?"

"No, no. It's not that. I feel safe with you. I guess I'm just shy," I admit. He's not wrong about humans having hang-ups when it comes to nudity. We don't stroll around naked in public, mostly because it's illegal but also because unless you're fit as a fiddle, your shape is deemed "wrong."

Varrek lowers his body into the pond, that glorious cock and eight-pack disappearing from sight. I swallow a groan of disappointment so he doesn't know how addicted I am to his body.

"Okay," I mumble as I pull my tunic over my head. "When in space, I suppose."

I stand up on the ledge of the pond to remove my pants next. I drop them on the ground next to my boots and straighten, looking down into Varrek's heated gaze.

He opens his mouth and traces one of his sharp fangs with his tongue. I remember the feel of that rough tongue against my own, and I shudder, my nipples pebbling.

Instinctually, I cross my arms over my chest, and immediately Varrek huffs in protest. "Do not hide yourself from me, Cloh-ee." He reaches for my hand and slowly guides me down into the water, his eyes never leaving mine. "You glow like the sun. Sometimes I do not believe you are real."

I realize in that moment that I've never felt so desired in my life.

I sink into the water, letting the warmth envelop my body from my shoulders down, and I moan at how good it feels. I quickly dunk my head under the water to wet my hair and resurface a second later. "This is heaven."

"I am glad you enjoy it." Varrek shoots me a cocky grin, and I splash him.

"Yeah, yeah, yeah, you know me so well," I tease back.

"Not yet, but I intend to," he says, his emerald eyes darkening a bit.

He closes the distance between us and takes a slow, deliberate step around me to stand at my back. I can feel his breath on my neck as he gently lifts my wet hair off my shoulders and gathers it in his large hands. "Your mane is so soft. My fingers ache to touch it each time I see you," he whispers.

My breathing turns erratic at his closeness. "Well, it's wet right now. That certainly helps...with the, um, softness...I mean." I want to punch myself in the face the moment the words leave my mouth. *Ugh. That was officially the least sexy innuendo ever.*

His fingers skate across my bare shoulders and trace the lines of my collarbones. "Is it the only thing that's wet?" he asks, his voice a husky rasp against my ear.

I whimper as his hands run down my arms and rest at my waist. He growls in response and turns my body to face him. He lightly traces the line of my jaw as his eyes shine with tenderness. "I am tired of fighting what I feel for you, Cloh-ee." His gaze drops, and I can almost feel a slight sadness emanating from him.

"Why have you been fighting it? I don't understand, Varrek. Help me understand," I tell him as I raise his chin back up so I can look him in the eyes.

"It is complicated. I know that you cannot feel the tether, and I know that there are better males for you, who are worthy of you. I am not." His voice turns a bit shaky.

I stop him before he can continue with whatever excuse he's got teed up. "Listen. I think I'm capable of determining who is worthy of my time and who isn't. And so far? You are."

His mouth curls into a brief smile before it falls back into a thin line.

I continue, "Obviously I feel the connection between us. I mean, I can't keep myself away from you. I've tried."

His eyes light up at that, though I'm not sure why. This can't be news to him.

"I feel safe with you, Varrek. I want to spend time with you." I wrap my arms around his neck and pull him down toward me. "I want...you."

I close my mouth over his and softly smack at his lips with my own. Just quick, chaste kisses. I pull back, briefly, to make sure he's into this, and a growl erupts from his throat at the severed connection.

His chest heaves with each breath, and he looks about as dizzy as I feel. "Cloh-ee, tell me you want this. I do not want to scare you, but I fear that if you put your lips on me again, *nothing* will be able to tear me away from you."

My pussy squeezes at the intensity in his voice, and I'm relieved that we're finally on the same page. I pull him down so we're almost the same height in the water, and I lean toward his lips once again.

Just before I get there, he stops me and whispers, "Tell me. Say it."

"Touch me, Varrek."

He groans and then slams his mouth onto mine. He grips the back of my head with one hand, his fingers lost in my hair, while the other caresses my hip. I moan into his mouth as I flick my tongue against the seam of his lips. He lets me in, and our teeth clash as we try to consume each other. His tongue glides against mine, and I suck on the tip of it, causing his hips to buck against me. I feel his cock against my belly, getting harder, and I want nothing more than for it to fill me up. Varrek lifts me, and I wrap my legs around his waist, pushing my core closer to the thick, velvety head of him.

Closer. Closer. Get him closer, my mind chants as our hands clumsily explore each other.

I reach my hand down between us and stroke up and down his shaft, admiring the feel of him. He's so big and thick that my fingers don't wrap around him completely, and for a moment, I'm worried he won't fit inside me. My thoughts dissipate at Varrek's growl of pleasure, and I can't form any complete thoughts at all. I'm drunk on that sound. I want to hear it again. And again and again.

He grips my ass in his hands, massaging me, as he pulls my body into his and drags his tongue against my neck, drawing circles with the tip of it over my pulse. "Your taste," he murmurs in between licks. "It is better, sweeter than anything I have tasted before."

In the next second, I'm lifted out of the water completely like I weigh nothing, and the water cascades down my legs. I shriek at the feel of the cold air against my skin and the sudden space between our bodies. I hate it. I need him pressed against me. I need it more than air.

I reach for Varrek, to pull him back toward me, when he stops my grasp. "Lie back for me, inara. I must taste you. I cannot wait another moment," he says as he gently leads me onto my back against the stone ledge.

"Ah, you have a mane here too?" he asks, mystified and amused, as he lightly pets the curls between my legs.

A nervous giggle escapes me. "Uh, yeah. I haven't had a wax in a while. Sorry."

"Why do you apologize?" He leans in and rubs his cheek against it. "It is soft, like the rest of you. And it holds your scent. I enjoy this tiny mane."

I mentally file that under "things I never expected to hear in bed" and smile as he continues to gaze at my pussy like he's just been served his favorite meal.

Then I pause. "Are-Are you sure you want to?" I ask, insecurities flooding my brain. "I mean, you don't have to. It's okay, really."

Varrek furrows his brow, confused. "Why would I demand to taste you if I was not desperate to do so?"

"I just…I want you to know you don't have to."

"I know this, sweet Cloh-ee." He dips his head and slowly licks my inner thigh, his eyes clouded with desire. He groans with delight as his eyes roll back in his head. "Divine. Do you still doubt my hunger for you?"

I shake my head and lean back. "No," I whimper.

I close my eyes and listen to the buzz of the insects in the bushes and the gentle lap of the water against the stone ledge. It's peaceful here. And quiet.

My feet still dangle in the warm water of the pond, on either side of Varrek's imposing body. That's not wide enough, though, because he pushes his body closer to me and nudges my knees apart as far as they can go. The muscles in my thighs welcome the stretch as I gaze up at the beautiful canopy of trees that cover us.

I lift my head just in time to see him descend on my mound and attack it with his eager tongue.

CHAPTER 14

VARREK

*H*ow many times have I fantasized about this moment? The chance to part her soft pink folds, glistening with her juices, and taste her. The sight of it—it is better than I ever could have imagined. And imagined it I have. Stroked my cock to the thought of it I have. Many times.

Now she is here, spread before me, her thick pale thighs brushing against my ears, her soft dark curls—that I was not expecting to find, as our females are bare here—surrounding her wet cunt. I find them interesting, in the way they hold her intoxicating scent. A scent so feminine and sweet and so...*her.*

I lean in and inhale, letting her scent fill my nose. Letting it seep into my lungs and brand me from the inside. I will never get enough of her. Of that I am certain. I look up into her hooded dark eyes that still hold a timidness I do not understand. I make it my goal to remove it entirely, to make it abundantly clear that I am exactly where I want to be.

I flatten my tongue and let it glide up from the end of her seam to the top. I give the swollen pink bud near the top a single flick of my tongue, and Cloh-ee's hips buck in response.

"What do you call this? This here?" I circle the bud with my finger so she knows what I speak of.

"Clit. Muh-my clit." A moan escapes her lips as she drops her head back onto the stone ledge of the pond. So responsive, my inara.

Goddess, her taste. It is the sweetest honey. I let the flavor explode on my tongue before I dive back in, lapping at her as if I could drink her down. She cries out as her body writhes, and her back arches for me. "Varrek, more."

I do not hesitate. I explore every dip and fold of her cunt with my tongue as her wetness slowly spills out of her and covers my nose and chin. I alternate sucking on her folds and clit, and then I fuck her with my tongue, surging in and out of her core, showing her what I plan to do with my cock at a later time.

She reaches down and fists my mane in her small hands, tugging harder each time my tongue darts in and out of her. It is a pain I welcome. I hope she tears my mane out by the root. The surge of male pride I feel at giving her pleasure makes me want to pound my chest with my fists.

She is glorious, this female.

I could come just watching her face twist up in erotic agony, her large breasts bouncing with each jerk of her hips. I think about gripping my cock and pumping until my seed spills out of me, but this is not about me. I have too much beauty before my eyes to feast on. Too many places to rub and caress and taste. I can think of many ways, better ways, to use my hands right now.

I replace my tongue with my finger as I focus my tongue on her clit, slowing down my pace to make languid circles around it. I listen for her moans to guide me, to show me the exact amount of pressure and where to apply it. I am desperate to learn her body, to master it.

She screams my name again, demanding more, and I add a second finger. She is so wet that I slide in and out easily as she fucks my hand. I curl my lips over her clit, and the walls of her cunt clench around my fingers like a vise. *Ah, this is how she wants it.* My smile widens against her core, and I groan.

Her thighs close in around my head and begin to shake, and I think she is close. Her breaths come in shallow bursts, and I look up to see her eyes dancing behind her closed lids. Seeing her so far gone like this, it is my favorite sight of all. I could die in this moment, with her creamy thighs suffocating me, and I would count myself lucky.

Another hard suck on her clit and she cries out, "Yes! Varrek, oh fuuuuck!" and it's so loud that I wonder if my entire clan heard it. I would not mind if they did.

Her cunt spasms around me as she comes, clenching my fingers so tight I wonder if she'll ever let me go. Her feet kick up in the air as her juices flood my tongue. The feel of her molten heat and her sweet taste is too much for me to bear. I grip my cock in my hand and pump, hard and fast, and within three strokes, I am coming too. I empty myself into the pond as I continue to lick and kiss her folds.

Cloh-ee's breathing evens out, her chest rising and falling less erratically, and I can tell she is sated. I crawl up her body, leaving a trail of soft kisses along her hips and stomach, lingering on the fascinating pale, silver stripes that run down the tops of her thighs and the lower part of her belly. I wrap my hand around the nape of her neck, grasp her lower back with the other, and lift her easily, bringing her boneless body back into the warmth of the pond, her head cradled against my chest.

I continue to kiss her mane, which is almost dry now, having been exposed to the crisp evening air. She rests her soft hands against my chest and looks up at me with her sleepy eyes. "That was...incredible, Varrek." She smiles, and it cracks something inside of me. I continue to glide my hand along the length of her spine, enjoying the feel of her.

She pushes back so there's space between us and reaches down for my cock. "Your turn," she murmurs as she kisses my chest.

But I stop her. I take her hand in mine and press her delicate knuckles against my lips. "That was for you, Cloh-ee. Just for you."

Her delicate brows furrow in disbelief. "But I want to," she assures me. "Don't you need release?"

"I came after you did." I run a finger down her cheek, outlining the portion that grows pink so often. "You are exquisite." I press my fore-head against her smooth one and close my eyes.

We remain like this, pressed against each other, letting the warm water slowly cool around us as the sky above grows darker. I know we must head back soon, but pulling myself away from Cloh-ee does not seem physically possible.

"Mmmm," Cloh-ee hums. "I could fall asleep right here."

Before I can agree, I hear the crack of branches breaking in the distance. Someone is coming. Or maybe they have been here the whole time. Watching us.

Fury fills my chest at the thought of someone else's eyes gazing upon my inara, vulnerable and in the throes of passion. I will not have it.

Cloh-ee gasps and tucks her head under my chin. "Di-Did you hear that?" she whispers. "What was it?"

"I do not know. But I will find out," I vow. I untangle our bodies and carefully step onto the ledge of the pond. I turn to look at my Cloh-ee, her body visibly shaking like a leaf. "Do not move."

My warrior training kicks in, and I glide down the stone steps of the pond, silently, as I approach my clothes piled on top of my boots. I redress swiftly and gather Cloh-ee's clothes before placing them on the ledge. I lean in so I can whisper as low as possible. "Here. Dress. Be as quiet as you can. I will keep watch."

My Cloh-ee tries to be quiet, but her human limbs are not as agile as my own, and I hear the rustle of her clothing, the thump of her boot as she drops it, and the curses she utters under her breath upon doing so.

Luckily, her sounds do not cover the sounds of the forest, and with my heightened senses, I hear them all. Except for more branches cracking under the weight of footsteps. Those have ceased. But my guard remains up as I lift a fully dressed Cloh-ee off the ledge and place her on the soft ground.

Both of her hands clutch onto my forearm, and I feel her shivers vibrate through her entire body. Her fear scent surrounds us like a cloud, and I give her hand a reassuring squeeze to calm her. "I do not see anything in the forest, and the rustling has stopped," I lean down and whisper in her ear. "But that doesn't mean the threat is gone."

I pull my dagger from the sheath on the inside of my vest and ready it in my grasp. As soon as my fingers curl around the hilt, I feel at peace. The blade of the knife was forged in klosicahl steel, the hilt made of bone, specifically the rib of a deadly vushk. It belonged to my grandfather, was passed down to my mother, and then was given to me when I was a young warrior. I have used it in battle, and the enemies I have defeated with it number in the hundreds. It has not failed me yet, and it will not fail me now.

I move Cloh-ee behind me and place her hand on the bottom loops of my vest in the back. "Hold onto me. Stay close. Step lightly," I tell her.

"Shouldn't I have a weapon too? Just in case?" she asks.

I was so focused on protecting her that I failed to consider her desire to protect herself. It is an embarrassing oversight. "Of course," I tell her as I hand her a small throwing blade from my pocket. She has practiced this. She knows how to use it.

She returns my smile and thanks me before we begin a slow, steady pace away from the pond where we shared so much pleasure and into darkness of night, where we could be facing a predator, poised to attack.

We exit the clearing and back into the trees and thickets, following a narrow path with Cloh-ee on my heels and gripping my vest in a tight fist. I still hear nothing. I see nothing. But part of me knows we are not alone. On an instinctual level, I know the threat remains. As much as I have grown accustomed to these woods since we landed here, I do not know what would be lurking in this part of the forest. Animals do not cross into our territory very often anymore. Even the nocturnal tr'gorys do not wander into the parts we have claimed. It is only when we enter the wild, untamed parts of the forest that we encounter other creatures.

I do not suspect it is a member of my clan either. As awestruck as the males have become around the human females, this is a boundary they would not cross.

What could be out here with us?

Cloh-ee and I stop to lean against a tree, and we press our backs against it to scan our surroundings. I look up and notice that the tree is tall, with several thick branches I can reach from where I stand. Perhaps I need a different vantage point to find this interloper.

"I am going to climb up to locate the safest path back to the clan." I point to the meaty branch that extends above us, about halfway up the tree. "Stay here. This will take but a moment."

"You're just going to leave me here?" Cloh-ee whispers, aghast.

I hate that she is frightened, but I would rather leave her side momentarily and lead her safely back home than unknowingly bring us both face-to-face with a creature that is hunting us.

"Do not worry, inara. I will take a look and will return to your side in a blink." I rub her arms to comfort her.

She bites the thickest part of her bottom lip, and I feel it in my groin. "Fine," she says. "But when you get back, you're going to tell me what that word means. That 'inara' word. Deal?"

"I shall. I promise." I kiss the tip of her tiny human nose and reach for the branch just above my head. I pull myself up onto the branch in a crouched position so as not to smack my head on the next branch above. The weight of my body causes the branch beneath me to bow slightly and creak, and I worry the noise I am making will expose us.

With the agility and grace that took many years of warrior training to hone, I swing myself up the next five branches to get to the one I know will support my weight with ease. Once there, I creep farther out onto the branch, sliding my feet away from the wide trunk of the tree to the spot that will give me the best view of our surroundings.

Even in the darkness, my eyes can see far. I see billows of smoke coming from the firepits at our food hall. I see members of my clan strolling along the main path of our village. I see the gleaming steel of my ship off in the distance, just on the outskirts of the forest. I search the narrow paths from where we stand back to our village and notice that all are clear.

I look down to let Cloh-ee know it is safe to head back when I see the black speckled fur of a colossal tr'gory, emerging from a nearby cluster of bushes and slinking toward her. My heart stops as I watch Cloh-ee's delicate features frozen in horror. I hear a quiet gasp escape her mouth. The tr'gory is not curling up its lips to expose its fangs, a typical sign of aggression, but wagging its bushy tail in a rapid motion with its front legs stretched out in front of it, its chest resting on the ground. And that does not comfort me either.

We do not know enough about the tr'gorys to understand the full scope of their body language, but we have learned through the tragic loss of one of our own to stay far away from them. The one below has set its sights on my fragile Cloh-ee. My inara. My everything.

It takes another step toward her and tilts its horned head to the side, perhaps sizing her up as an opponent, or even worse, a meal.

I could craft a mental list of all the ways I have failed her, but we do not have time for such things. I must get between her and the beast that threatens her life. If it should end mine in the process, so be it.

I bend down to place my hands between my feet, readying my body to leap down onto the creature's back, my dagger still in my grip. A leaf slides out from under my palm and floats to the ground below. The tr'gory hears this, looks up past the falling leaf, and locks its red eyes onto mine. A growl erupts from its chest, and I know there's not another moment to spare.

As the tr'gory peels back its thin lips with a snarl, I leap down, just as it looks back at Cloh-ee and lunges for her throat.

CHAPTER 15

CHLOE

In the movies, the end of someone's life tends to happen in slow motion, providing enough time for that person's entire life to flash before their eyes. I've always found this rather silly because in reality, how could your brain possibly flip through every important moment you experienced in a matter of seconds?

But now that I'm about to be mauled to death by a wolf the size of a minivan with curled white horns jutting out of its head, I can confirm that this actually does happen.

With each menacing step the beast takes toward me, my mind throws me back in time. I see my dad raising his voice to a comedic pitch while reading me bedtime stories, and that time I fell through the ice while learning to ice skate and my parents pulling me out and holding me so tightly I almost couldn't breathe. I see my parents' divorce when I was in middle school.

Step.

I see my mom stress-eating banana bread every night after the divorce was finalized, and me joining her while we watched reality dating shows. I see my first boyfriend in high school trying to finger me in the cab of his beat-up pickup truck and asking if it was normal for me to be "that wet," causing me to wonder if my vagina was broken.

Another step.

I remember Mom calling to tell me my dad's car hit a patch of black ice on the road and fishtailed into oncoming traffic. My mom getting drunk at his funeral and telling me she wished she could kiss him one more time.

Another step.

The day I left my awful job as a receptionist at a startup and began working for myself as a graphic designer. My first date with Drew. My last date with Drew. Reggie. Sweet little Reggie and his wide, furry face.

It's interesting because the moment I saw the tr'gory creep out of the bushes, I was scared, sure, but only because of the way the clan has spoken of them. I know I'm in danger when it fully emerges, looking at me with those blood-red eyes, but it also kind of looks like a big dog with horns. And when it starts wagging its tail, I have no idea what to do or what I should be feeling.

Dogs wag their tails when they're happy and sometimes when nervous or agitated, but it's mostly a sign of happiness. Are these creatures similar in that way? Plus, the tr'gory has its butt in the air and front paws stretched out, which, for a dog, is typically an invitation to play.

If I hadn't been warned about how deadly these tr'gorys are, I'd be calling this one a "good pupper" and trying to scratch behind its ears. But doing that seems like a monumentally stupid move. I like having hands, and I don't want to lose them.

The tr'gory tilts its black head at me, and I sense that it's as curious about me as I am in return. It stands back up and is now less than a foot away.

Okay, no more fucking around or pretending it's a big puppy. You need to do something.

I clench my fists and realize I still have the throwing knife in my hand. A gasp escapes me at the realization. I'm not totally defenseless. Thank god.

The tr'gory's ears perk up at the sound, and then a rustle from above causes the creature to look at Varrek, still perched on the branch halfway up the tree.

At the sight of him, the creature's body tenses and takes on an aggressive stance as a snarl rips through its throat.

Instinctively, I take a step back, and as my shoulders bump into the tree behind me, the knife slips from my grasp and falls to the ground.

Then there's movement all around me. The tr'gory lunges as Varrek leaps down what must be forty or fifty feet from the branch. He sticks the landing, miraculously, and becomes a blur as he blocks the tr'gory's attack. He throws his shoulder into the stomach of the animal, and the ground shakes beneath my feet when they slam into the soil in a ball of snapping fangs and claws.

It's in this moment that I realize just how dangerous and wild Varrek can be. When we're chatting about our favorite foods, he seems almost human, just with gold skin. But now, I see how much power he's been holding back. It excites me. Probably more than it should right now.

I reach down and pick up my small blade, never letting my eyes stray from Varrek.

I take a few steps closer to them, searching for a vulnerable spot on the tr'gory to use as my target, but they keep rolling and I'm worried I'll throw the knife and hit Varrek instead.

The tr'gory's sharp fangs snap close to Varrek's face, and my heart stops. He's pinned under the monster, and I've done nothing to help him. I dropped my knife right when he needed me to use it.

I see the creature's head dip, and Varrek bellows through gritted teeth as the tr'gory's fangs sink into his shoulder.

"Nooo!" I scream, feeling utterly helpless.

I try to keep my steps light as I head toward them, the knife clutched in my fist. Just as I hover over their flailing bodies, a branch snaps under my foot, and the tr'gory's head snaps back to look at me with fangs bared and drool flying in my direction. I stumble back in fear and fall on my butt with a grunt.

A flash of steel catches my eye as Varrek lifts his dagger in a tight fist above the tr'gory and draws it down swiftly, leaving a deep slash in its wake on the side of the tr'gory's face. Blood pours out diagonally from eye to jaw, and it scrambles off him, yelping in pain. It continues to howl as it speeds through the forest, away from us and into the night.

I crawl to Varrek's side as he rolls toward me, his hands reaching for me. "Cloh-ee"—his voice cracks as he searches my face—"are you hurt?"

I choke out a sob. "Me? You're worried about *me* right now?" I lean over his chest to get a better look at the bite on his shoulder. There's too much blood seeping out for me to see how deep it is, but the wound is wide, so I'm nervous. I don't see bone, which is a good sign, but the mangled flesh looks like raw hamburger, and now I want to throw up. "I'm fine," I tell him. "You're the one bleeding."

I use my throwing knife to cut a scrap of fabric from the bottom of my shirt and fold it twice before I place it over the wound on Varrek's shoulder, pressing on it to stop the bleeding. I replace my hand with Varrek's and tell him to put pressure on the wound. I'm sure he knows all this already, being an experienced warrior, but it feels good to be helping him, so I say it anyhow.

Then the tears come. And they run down my cheeks like rain. "If anything...if that *thing* had...fuck, Varrek..." I babble as my heart thunders in my chest.

Varrek sits up and traces my jaw with a light caress. "This? This is nothing. I will heal. I heal fast. Please do not cry, Cloh-ee."

I smile through the tears and help him stand up. "Let's get you home and all fixed up, okay?"

Varrek nods as I plaster myself to his good side, and we walk back to the village. He walks at a normal pace despite his injury and I have to run-walk in order to keep up. But I don't tell him to slow down because I want us to get to Kaiva's as quickly as possible.

We break through the clearing to the main path, and I start yelling Kaiva's name as we jog toward her house. She steps outside before we arrive, her face filled with worry. "What has happened, Cloh-ee?" she asks as she guides us inside.

Much like the first floor of Nalba's house, Kaiva's is her work area. But unlike Nalba's house, Kaiva's is perfectly clean. There are three steel tables lining the walls of her triangular home. All of them have medical supplies perfectly organized in stacks or kept in clear containers. There are also shelves occupying every speck of wall space in this room. On the wooden shelves are glass jars filled with herbs and other medicinal ingredients.

It reminds me of what a witch's cottage might look like, with a modern spin. It's sterile, and packed with steel appliances, but it's also cozy, with books stacked high in every corner and soft lighting. It puts me at ease.

In the middle of the room, there are four beds, with tall wooden room separators between each bed to provide privacy and metal trays with tools lined up neatly on them.

I hear thundering steps coming down the stairs and turn to see Ahlvo rush into the room. "What is it?"

Kaiva points to one of the beds as Varrek recalls the attack. "It was a tr'gory. It lunged at Cloh-ee at the falls," he tells them as he lies down on the first bed.

Kaiva gently pulls back the makeshift bandage and studies the wound. "The falls? That is strange, is it not?" she asks as she adjusts the light hanging over the bed to a brighter setting.

"It is," Varrek mutters as his eyes go unfocused. "I do not like that they creep into our territory. It puts the entire clan in danger."

Ahlvo nods in agreement. "We must alert everyone to be back in the center of the village before the sun goes down."

I know the conversation they're having about tr'gorys is important, but I can't think about anything other than the blood covering Varrek's shoulder. "Is he going to be all right, Kaiva?"

Varrek gives me a soft smile and starts rubbing my palm.

"O fah, this is a little scrape. Do not fret. I will apply the healing salve and place a new bandage on it. It will close up soon." She pours a clear liquid on his wound, cleaning it, and wipes away the dried blood on the outer edges.

"Should we be worried about infection? Do tr'gorys have venom or anything?" I continue firing questions at Kaiva. I don't know how advanced their medicine is here, but I don't plan on leaving Varrek's side until he's fully healed, so I want to know what I should look for.

"Tr'gorys do not have venom. The salve has antibacterial elements and will prevent infection," she says, her eyes focused on the task in front of her.

"Doesn't he need stitches?" I ask, trying to peer into the wide gash.

Kaiva follows my eyes and takes another long glance at it. "No, I do not think stitches are needed. It is long, but it is not deep enough to require that."

Ahlvo looks amused at my distress. "I have seen this one through many battles, Cloh-ee. He has been stabbed, shot, and poisoned, and he has survived it all. He will be just fine." Ahlvo pats Varrek on the head, like he's a child.

"All will be well, Cloh-ee." Varrek pulls me down so he can place a kiss on my cheek. "He is right. I have survived far worse."

"She is merely fussing over her mate. Let her be, you two," Kaiva teases.

Varrek stills.

Part of me wants to correct Kaiva and tell her we're not mates. That we're just...having a little fun. But it seems unimportant compared to everything else that has happened tonight, so I let it slide.

Varrek grips my hand tighter as sadness fills his gaze. "I never should have brought you out there under the darkened sky. That tr'gory could've ripped you apart. I am deeply sorry."

I hate that he's wallowing in guilt right now. Especially after that orgasm he gave me? Next to a beautiful waterfall, of all places? He has been completely focused on putting my needs above his own all night. And then he saved my life. There's no way I'm going to let him take the blame for a wild animal attacking us. I lift his chin back up so his eyes are locked on mine. "That was not your fault. You saved me, Varrek. I owe you my life."

"You owe me nothing. I will always protect you."

Kaiva puts pressure on the edges of the bandage, making sure the adhesive corners stay put. "You should be healed in three days. Come back to me then and I will make sure."

Varrek pulls himself up off the bed and gives Kaiva a quick, tight hug.

"Thank you, Kaiva." I take her hands in mine and give them a squeeze.

She waves her hand dismissively. "It is nothing. It is like I have two sons."

Ahlvo gives me a high five and beams as he tells me that Ava taught him how to do it. Then he and Varrek exchange a couple brotherly shoves as we say good night. We leave Kaiva's and head to my house first. I need to tell the girls I'll be staying with Varrek for a bit.

Now that the adrenaline is starting to wear off, I notice how cold it is. I'm grateful to have Varrek's warm body to snuggle up to, because I did not dress appropriately for the chilly weather.

When we get inside, the kitchen area is empty, but I hear the shower on in the bathroom. I yell for Kate and Ava to come down, and Kate runs down the steps, skipping the last three and landing hard on the wood floor. "You raaaaang?" she says with an exaggerated bow.

"Hey, Kate. Is that Ava in the shower?"

"I certainly hope so. Otherwise we have a very boring ghost." She looks between me and Varrek, and her eyes zero in on his bandaged shoulder. She rushes over to us with concern swirling in her eyes. "What's going on? What the hell happened?"

Just then, Ava steps out of the bathroom in a cloud of steam and jumps slightly at all of us huddled in the kitchen. "What are you all doing in here? And what's with the grim vibe?"

I take a deep breath. "Well, Varrek and I were attacked in the woods by a tr'gory."

"Oh shit, a tr'gory?" Kate's eyes widen with fear. "You could've died!"

"Jesus. That's terrifying." Ava scrunches the ends of her wet hair up to the root. "What do they look like?"

"They are not pleasant to look at," Varrek mutters.

"Kind of like a giant dog with white curly horns and fangs. And they have red eyes. Blood red." I shudder at the memory. Then I recall the events of the evening. "He's going to be fine, Kaiva assured me. But I'm going to keep an eye on him until his wound heals."

"The clan will be told to stay within the main path of the village once the sun sets. No venturing outside of that, for now," Varrek says as he rubs his eyes, looking defeated.

I turn to Varrek. "Oh, I'm just now realizing you never actually invited me to stay at your place. I invited myself," I giggle. "Are you... okay with that?"

His eyes sparkle, and I am mesmerized. "You may stay with me as long as you like."

Kate shudders, her eyes pinched shut. Then she shakes her head and straightens. "Well. Good. Glad you didn't die. That would've been...a bummer." She gives me a playful punch in the shoulder and awkwardly nods at Varrek before turning and rushing back up the stairs. "G'night!" she calls over her shoulder.

Ava throws her hands up in an "I don't even know" gesture at Kate's exit and gives Varrek and me one-armed hugs while holding her towel with the other. "I'm glad you're okay. Both of you."

"Thanks. Come get me for breakfast in the morning?" I ask.

"Sure thing. Get some sleep."

Varrek and I head back into the brisk night air as we take the few steps to his house. Varrek holds the door open for me and stops in the kitchen to fill two mugs with water from the spigot before we walk silently upstairs to his bedroom. I take the mugs from him and place one on either side of the bed as he hands me one of his soft gray shirts. I quickly pull off the one I'm wearing that's now dirty and covered in his blood and tug the clean one over my head with a relieved sigh. I toe off my boots and then pull my leggings down and step out of them.

Varrek pulls off his boots and pants as well, and before I can fully appreciate his magnificent body, he pulls on a clean pair.

I shouldn't be ogling him. I know that. He's injured and probably exhausted, but the way his abs contract with each breath—the way his

of my hair away from my face, and when I meet his eyes, I'm
y how much adoration they hold.

reathing increases, hissing through his lips. His cock vibrates
dy hum that almost tickles my tongue. Then it speeds up, and
 he's getting close. I suck harder, deeper, as close to his base
et, and use my free hand to massage his tightening sac.

outs my name at the ceiling along with a string of Trovilian
at sound like, "civuzz burgh yalkvib inara" as his come floods
ue. His cock continues to pulsate inside my mouth, and his
arm as it slides down my throat. I gulp it down. It doesn't
ow much I swallow, though, or how fast; he keeps coming,
escapes my lips, dripping down my chin.

feel the tension leave his body as he takes slower, deeper
 and out. He stops vibrating, but he's still unbelievably hard
d, and I wonder if he needs time to recover or he's ready for
und so soon.

y finger to wipe the dribble of come off my chin and lick it
ely with a moan.

ches, enraptured.

grunt, he hauls me back up his body using his good arm.
nks my shirt over my head so I'm completely bare before
ks hungry for me. Desperate to reciprocate.

stop him, to tell him I don't need anything. That this was
t then he cups my face in his hands, and I fall silent at the
of it.

feel you against me. Your skin to mine," he begs.

nd press my lips to his. A slow, loving kiss. Then I lie
uggle into his arms. He lets out a contented sigh.

Was that good?"

my Cloh-ee. I do not know if the words exist in either of
s to describe how 'good' that was." He kisses my hair and
p and down my side. "I am the luckiest of males."

r been particularly into giving head, maybe because it felt
 was giving more of myself than I was ever going to get
 I find I actually enjoyed it with Varrek.

back muscles pull and flex with each subtle movement—I can't help
but admire his beauty.

We move around each other easily, silently, in Varrek's room, as
we get ready for bed, without the need to fill the silence. It's comfortable. Like we're a couple and have been for years.

Varrek flips off the lights, and we climb under the blankets on his
gargantuan bed. I might not know exactly what I feel for Varrek yet,
but I do know that I'm madly in love with his bed. It's so cozy and
plush, and I sink right into it. Staying here for the next few nights will
not be a hardship, that's for sure.

Once Varrek is settled next to me, he lies on his back, and his arms
wrap around me, gently pulling me onto his expansive chest. I look up
to make sure my head isn't pressed up against his wound and catch
him gazing down at me with that same despair I saw earlier.

"What is it?"

"I am just thinking. I could have lost you out there." His voice
cracks on the words as he plays with my hair.

"But you didn't." I squeeze him tighter so he knows that in every
way possible, I'm right here with him and I'm not going anywhere.

Then I have an idea.

I trace a finger over his pecs, circling a nipple slowly before
moving to the other and doing the same. I draw my finger down,
caressing his stomach with light touches. I look up to see his eyes
hooded and already swirling with lust.

"What you do to me, female…" His whisper is guttural and raw.

I lean down to press a kiss to his ribs. "Should I stop?"

"Never. Never stop." His trembling hand rests against my hair, and
I can tell he's using every ounce of strength he has to hold himself
back. To keep from tangling his fingers in my hair and pulling. Part of
me wants him to do just that.

I crawl over him and spread his humongous thighs apart, just as he
did mine at the pond. I continue to kiss down his stomach, and I
admire how solid he is. Even the fittest human would be doughy
compared to Varrek. It's like his body truly is carved from stone. The
surface of his skin is soft to the touch, but under it is all hardness.

Layers and layers of corded muscle. I love touching him. I don't need to put a hand between my thighs to know I'm wet.

My mouth reaches the top of his pants, and I look up at him. "May I?"

He doesn't answer, not verbally anyway. He lifts his hips as I pull his pants down past his thighs and knees, and once they're off completely, I toss them behind me.

I kiss the tops of his smooth, hairless thighs, and then I remember that he's injured. I panic at the thought of his medication making him loopy in this moment. I don't want that. I want him here. Present. "Are you sure you're up for this? I can stop…"

"I do not know what you are planning, but no, do not stop." He clasps his good hand behind his head and props up the pillow so he can watch me. "I am yours. Do what you wish."

I smirk at him in disbelief. "You really don't know what I'm planning?" My mouth is hovering just above his throbbing erection. He must have *some* idea. Unless… "Have you never received a blow job before?" I ask.

He looks confused at the words, so I assume there's a translation issue. Or maybe he hasn't? I'm about to clarify, but he did say I could do what I want with him, so I decide to show him what I mean instead.

I take his cock in my hand, and I'm shocked at the weight of it. The girth. It's smooth but heavy and hard like steel, just like the rest of him. I notice a bead of silver liquid form along the seam at the tip. My mouth goes dry suddenly, and I long to taste it.

I run my tongue along the side of his cock, all the way to the tip, lapping around the head slowly and letting his precome hit my tongue. He tastes like salt and musk and something else. Something uniquely him.

I want more.

His hips buck, and he releases a hard breath through gritted teeth. "What…Cloh-ee, I…" I assume the ends of these sentences are good, so I keep going.

I give his shaft another long lick before closing my lips around the

head, swirling my tongue around the tip u
pumps up and down. He groans loudly, a
thrown back against the pillow, fangs ful
beneath him clenched in his fists.

I chuckle at the sight of my big, feroci
vulnerable beneath my mouth. I feel p
new feeling. I suck him deeper, but I ca
big. My tongue laves at the underside
taking him as deep as I can and releasi
again.

Varrek pants and growls as his he
blanket with his claws.

Then something strange starts to
vibrate. He's vibrating. Inside my mo
make sure I'm not imagining it.

His cock quakes rapidly right befo
Varrek lifts his head, panting heav
Cloh-ee?"

"I'm fine. I just…I didn't realize y
He sits up, his eyes widened in ala
"God no," I interrupt. "It's amaz
was surprised is all." I continue
fascination.

"If you do not wish to continue,
Now that I know what to expe
Varrek utter another word about st

He wants this. And more impor
I swirl my tongue around the
mouth, releasing it with a pop. H
upper body back down on the bed

I take him in deep, as deep as
lips up and down, increasing in
isn't, my hand is, stroking and m

I feel his hand resting agains
doesn't shred my scalp like he

"Was that your first time? For that, I mean?" I know Varrek isn't a virgin, but having my mouth on him seemed like something he's never experienced before.

"Yes. It is not something our females do, but now I do not understand why," he laughs.

"Seriously?" I can't seem to wrap my head around that.

He takes my hand in his and pulls it toward his mouth, placing small kisses all over my palm, fingers, and wrist. "Females already do so much. They fight in our battles. They create life within their bodies, they have a heightened empathic skill set that our males do not have, anchoring us to the emotions of others." He pauses, lacing his fingers through mine. "We are to protect them, care for them, support them, and satisfy all their needs. It is how we give back."

I ponder his response. "Damn. Clearly I was born on the wrong planet."

He nods, amusement dancing in his eyes. "Perhaps this is true." He rubs the tip of his nose against mine before playfully nipping at it with his teeth. "But you are here now."

He gave me an opening. I could ask him if he'd like me to stay forever. I think I know the answer, but I'm not totally sure. And would I want to? Part of me, a big part, wants to say yes. Living in a treehouse in the middle of the forest with a hunky alien who puts my pleasure before his own? I'd be an idiot to turn that down.

But am I really ready to give up on returning home? Forget my whole life on Earth? Everything I've worked for? Just because of a few mind-blowing orgasms?

As if sensing my distress, Varrek interrupts my thoughts. "It gets better once a pair goes through the mating ceremony. They are inside each other's minds, which eliminates the need for verbal communication and guidance in order to learn each other's bodies."

Whoa, what? "A mated pair can read each other's minds?"

"Yes."

"Just from sex? Or is the mating ceremony something else?" I ask, extremely glad I'm getting this information now.

"It is sex, but upon a shared orgasm, a bite is exchanged. The sharing of blood between mates as their bodies are also physically joined triggers the mating bond. They are able to hear each other's thoughts." He holds my hand tighter. He might not even realize he's doing it, but his grip tells me he's worried I'm about to make a run for it. "Once minds are connected, there is never any doubt as to what your mate wants or needs sexually, or otherwise. You would know instantly."

It's hard not to picture what it would be like to have Varrek inside my head. It seems like such an overwhelming and intrusive existence. All my privacy would be gone.

"What would that be like?" I mutter. "How would it feel?"

"I do not know, personally. It only happens once in a lifetime for our kind, and for some it never happens at all. But I have heard that the bond is"—he stops, as if searching for the right word—"comforting, soothing. Less lonely, I suppose."

"Huh. I can see that," I yawn, my eyelids beginning to droop with exhaustion.

Then I remember the tr'gory attack, and there's something about it that still puzzles me. "Varrek, were you watching the tr'gory the whole time? Did you see it as soon as it came out of the bushes?"

"Yes, why?" He sounds perplexed.

I lift my head. "I don't know. You know more about them than I do, obviously, but when it first started walking toward me...I wasn't as scared, I guess, as I thought I'd be."

Confusion swirls in his eyes. "I have no doubt you are courageous, Cloh-ee."

"No, no, I'm not fishing for compliments here." I chuckle. "I didn't feel threatened by the tr'gory. At least, not until it saw you on the branch. Then its whole demeanor changed and it became aggressive, and I was terrified, for you and for me. Up until that point, though, it looked at me with curiosity. Not hunger." Varrek still looks somewhat baffled by my words, so I start to second-guess myself. "But what do I know? It could be because it reminded me of a type of animal back home and I wanted to believe I wasn't about to be mauled to death."

I rest my cheek against his chest again and snuggle into him a little back muscles pull and flex with each subtle movement—I can't help but admire his beauty.

We move around each other easily, silently, in Varrek's room, as we get ready for bed, without the need to fill the silence. It's comfortable. Like we're a couple and have been for years.

Varrek flips off the lights, and we climb under the blankets on his gargantuan bed. I might not know exactly what I feel for Varrek yet, but I do know that I'm madly in love with his bed. It's so cozy and plush, and I sink right into it. Staying here for the next few nights will not be a hardship, that's for sure.

Once Varrek is settled next to me, he lies on his back, and his arms wrap around me, gently pulling me onto his expansive chest. I look up to make sure my head isn't pressed up against his wound and catch him gazing down at me with that same despair I saw earlier.

"What is it?"

"I am just thinking. I could have lost you out there." His voice cracks on the words as he plays with my hair.

"But you didn't." I squeeze him tighter so he knows that in every way possible, I'm right here with him and I'm not going anywhere.

Then I have an idea.

I trace a finger over his pecs, circling a nipple slowly before moving to the other and doing the same. I draw my finger down, caressing his stomach with light touches. I look up to see his eyes hooded and already swirling with lust.

"What you do to me, female..." His whisper is guttural and raw.

I lean down to press a kiss to his ribs. "Should I stop?"

"Never. Never stop." His trembling hand rests against my hair, and I can tell he's using every ounce of strength he has to hold himself back. To keep from tangling his fingers in my hair and pulling. Part of me wants him to do just that.

I crawl over him and spread his humongous thighs apart, just as he did mine at the pond. I continue to kiss down his stomach, and I admire how solid he is. Even the fittest human would be doughy compared to Varrek. It's like his body truly is carved from stone. The surface of his skin is soft to the touch, but under it is all hardness.

Layers and layers of corded muscle. I love touching him. I don't need to put a hand between my thighs to know I'm wet.

My mouth reaches the top of his pants, and I look up at him. "May I?"

He doesn't answer, not verbally anyway. He lifts his hips as I pull his pants down past his thighs and knees, and once they're off completely, I toss them behind me.

I kiss the tops of his smooth, hairless thighs, and then I remember that he's injured. I panic at the thought of his medication making him loopy in this moment. I don't want that. I want him here. Present. "Are you sure you're up for this? I can stop…"

"I do not know what you are planning, but no, do not stop." He clasps his good hand behind his head and props up the pillow so he can watch me. "I am yours. Do what you wish."

I smirk at him in disbelief. "You really don't know what I'm planning?" My mouth is hovering just above his throbbing erection. He must have *some* idea. Unless… "Have you never received a blow job before?" I ask.

He looks confused at the words, so I assume there's a translation issue. Or maybe he hasn't? I'm about to clarify, but he did say I could do what I want with him, so I decide to show him what I mean instead.

I take his cock in my hand, and I'm shocked at the weight of it. The girth. It's smooth but heavy and hard like steel, just like the rest of him. I notice a bead of silver liquid form along the seam at the tip. My mouth goes dry suddenly, and I long to taste it.

I run my tongue along the side of his cock, all the way to the tip, lapping around the head slowly and letting his precome hit my tongue. He tastes like salt and musk and something else. Something uniquely him.

I want more.

His hips buck, and he releases a hard breath through gritted teeth. "What…Cloh-ee, I…" I assume the ends of these sentences are good, so I keep going.

I give his shaft another long lick before closing my lips around the head, swirling my tongue around the tip under closed lips as my hand pumps up and down. He groans loudly, and I look up to see his head thrown back against the pillow, fangs fully extended, and the blanket beneath him clenched in his fists.

I chuckle at the sight of my big, ferocious alien warrior, completely vulnerable beneath my mouth. I feel powerful, which is an entirely new feeling. I suck him deeper, but I can't take all of him; he's far too big. My tongue laves at the underside of his shaft as I bob my head, taking him as deep as I can and releasing almost to the tip and back again.

Varrek pants and growls as his head thrashes, and he shreds the blanket with his claws.

Then something strange starts to happen. His cock starts to... vibrate. He's vibrating. Inside my mouth. What the—? I pull back to make sure I'm not imagining it.

His cock quakes rapidly right before my eyes. Then it stops.

Varrek lifts his head, panting heavily. "What is it? Are you all right, Cloh-ee?"

"I'm fine. I just...I didn't realize you vibrate. Down here."

He sits up, his eyes widened in alarm. "Did I hurt you? I'm sor—"

"God no," I interrupt. "It's amazing. Human men don't do that. I was surprised is all." I continue to gaze at his swollen cock in fascination.

"If you do not wish to continue, I under—"

Now that I know what to expect, I dive right back in, not letting Varrek utter another word about stopping.

He wants this. And more importantly, I want to give it to him.

I swirl my tongue around the velvety head and suck it into my mouth, releasing it with a pop. He groans in approval and throws his upper body back down on the bed.

I take him in deep, as deep as I can without gagging, and slide my lips up and down, increasing in speed as I go. Wherever my mouth isn't, my hand is, stroking and massaging.

I feel his hand resting against my hair, and I pray silently that he doesn't shred my scalp like he did the blankets. He merely pulls the curtain of my hair away from my face, and when I meet his eyes, I'm struck by how much adoration they hold.

His breathing increases, hissing through his lips. His cock vibrates in a steady hum that almost tickles my tongue. Then it speeds up, and I can tell he's getting close. I suck harder, deeper, as close to his base as I can get, and use my free hand to massage his tightening sac.

He shouts my name at the ceiling along with a string of Trovilian words that sound like, "civuzz burgh yalkvib inara" as his come floods my tongue. His cock continues to pulsate inside my mouth, and his seed is warm as it slides down my throat. I gulp it down. It doesn't matter how much I swallow, though, or how fast; he keeps coming, and some escapes my lips, dripping down my chin.

I can feel the tension leave his body as he takes slower, deeper breaths in and out. He stops vibrating, but he's still unbelievably hard in my hand, and I wonder if he needs time to recover or he's ready for another round so soon.

I use my finger to wipe the dribble of come off my chin and lick it off obscenely with a moan.

He watches, enraptured.

With a grunt, he hauls me back up his body using his good arm. Then he yanks my shirt over my head so I'm completely bare before him. He looks hungry for me. Desperate to reciprocate.

I go to stop him, to tell him I don't need anything. That this was for him, but then he cups my face in his hands, and I fall silent at the tenderness of it.

"Need to feel you against me. Your skin to mine," he begs.

I smile and press my lips to his. A slow, loving kiss. Then I lie down and snuggle into his arms. He lets out a contented sigh.

I giggle. "Was that good?"

"Mmm, my Cloh-ee. I do not know if the words exist in either of our languages to describe how 'good' that was." He kisses my hair and gently rubs up and down my side. "I am the luckiest of males."

I've never been particularly into giving head, maybe because it felt like I already was giving more of myself than I was ever going to get in return, but I find I actually enjoyed it with Varrek.

"Was that your first time? For that, I mean?" I know Varrek isn't a virgin, but having my mouth on him seemed like something he's never experienced before.

"Yes. It is not something our females do, but now I do not understand why," he laughs.

"Seriously?" I can't seem to wrap my head around that.

He takes my hand in his and pulls it toward his mouth, placing small kisses all over my palm, fingers, and wrist. "Females already do so much. They fight in our battles. They create life within their bodies, they have a heightened empathic skill set that our males do not have, anchoring us to the emotions of others." He pauses, lacing his fingers through mine. "We are to protect them, care for them, support them, and satisfy all their needs. It is how we give back."

I ponder his response. "Damn. Clearly I was born on the wrong planet."

He nods, amusement dancing in his eyes. "Perhaps this is true." He rubs the tip of his nose against mine before playfully nipping at it with his teeth. "But you are here now."

He gave me an opening. I could ask him if he'd like me to stay forever. I think I know the answer, but I'm not totally sure. And would I want to? Part of me, a big part, wants to say yes. Living in a treehouse in the middle of the forest with a hunky alien who puts my pleasure before his own? I'd be an idiot to turn that down.

But am I really ready to give up on returning home? Forget my whole life on Earth? Everything I've worked for? Just because of a few mind-blowing orgasms?

As if sensing my distress, Varrek interrupts my thoughts. "It gets better once a pair goes through the mating ceremony. They are inside each other's minds, which eliminates the need for verbal communication and guidance in order to learn each other's bodies."

Whoa, what? "A mated pair can read each other's minds?"

"Yes."

"Just from sex? Or is the mating ceremony something else?" I ask, extremely glad I'm getting this information now.

"It is sex, but upon a shared orgasm, a bite is exchanged. The sharing of blood between mates as their bodies are also physically joined triggers the mating bond. They are able to hear each other's thoughts." He holds my hand tighter. He might not even realize he's doing it, but his grip tells me he's worried I'm about to make a run for it. "Once minds are connected, there is never any doubt as to what your mate wants or needs sexually, or otherwise. You would know instantly."

It's hard not to picture what it would be like to have Varrek inside my head. It seems like such an overwhelming and intrusive existence. All my privacy would be gone.

"What would that be like?" I mutter. "How would it feel?"

"I do not know, personally. It only happens once in a lifetime for our kind, and for some it never happens at all. But I have heard that the bond is"—he stops, as if searching for the right word—"comforting, soothing. Less lonely, I suppose."

"Huh. I can see that," I yawn, my eyelids beginning to droop with exhaustion.

Then I remember the tr'gory attack, and there's something about it that still puzzles me. "Varrek, were you watching the tr'gory the whole time? Did you see it as soon as it came out of the bushes?"

"Yes, why?" He sounds perplexed.

I lift my head. "I don't know. You know more about them than I do, obviously, but when it first started walking toward me...I wasn't as scared, I guess, as I thought I'd be."

Confusion swirls in his eyes. "I have no doubt you are courageous, Cloh-ee."

"No, no, I'm not fishing for compliments here." I chuckle. "I didn't feel threatened by the tr'gory. At least, not until it saw you on the branch. Then its whole demeanor changed and it became aggressive, and I was terrified, for you and for me. Up until that point, though, it looked at me with curiosity. Not hunger." Varrek still looks somewhat baffled by my words, so I start to second-guess myself. "But what do I know? It could be because it reminded me of a type of animal back home and I wanted to believe I wasn't about to be mauled to death."

I rest my cheek against his chest again and snuggle into him a little deeper. Ultimately, it doesn't really matter what I saw in the tr'gory, or what I thought I saw. I don't plan on being out in the forest at night again anytime soon.

"The mind can do strange things during moments of extreme horror. But I believe you saw what you saw, Cloh-ee." Varrek runs his fingers through my hair, and it feels so good that my eyes start to close.

"Thank you."

"Always, inara. Always," he murmurs into my hair.

I remember our deal and how he was going to tell me what that word meant the moment he got down from the tree. *Tomorrow*, I think to myself as another yawn escapes my lips. *I'll ask him about it tomorrow.*

CHAPTER 16

CHLOE

I wake up pressed against a hard, warm surface. My lips feel chapped, despite the small puddle of drool slowly crusting down my chin. When I look down with a squinty eye, I notice that the hard, warm surface is Varrek. He emits heat like a furnace, and even though he's all solid, rippling muscle, he's also the perfect pillow. I didn't wake up once during the night.

I feel my cheeks turn red as I quickly wipe away my drool from his chest. Then I hear a low rumble. Varrek's looking at me with those sparkling green eyes and laughing.

"Your efforts are futile, little human. I have been admiring your pool of saliva for some time now." His voice is throaty and deep from sleep, and I'd be lost in it if it weren't for the crushing embarrassment I'm feeling right now.

I use the sleeve of my shirt to wipe away the dried slobber on my face as Varrek rolls us over so that I'm beneath his massive, imposing body. He rubs the tip of his nose against mine. "You have never looked so radiant."

He's still got that smirk on his face, so I know he's teasing me.

"Shut up." I playfully shove against his heavy chest as his chuckle deepens. Then my eyes stray to his bandaged shoulder, and I can see blood seeping through the center of it. "How does this feel today? Any better?" I point at the wound without touching it.

"Better," he mutters as he looks down. "It feels better than it looks, I assure you."

"That's good. But you're going to take it easy today, right? Let that healing salve do its thing?"

"I train with my warriors each day. This little cut will not change that," he says dismissively.

"Seriously? What if you fall and land on your shoulder? Or what if it gets cut in the same spot, making it even deeper? And it gets infected?" I ask, my voice pleading. "Can't you take one day off?"

He brushes a lock of hair off my forehead. "You worry for me."

"Of course I do!"

"I suppose that depends." His grin turns downright devilish. He lowers his head to my neck and presses a kiss to my pulse. "Are you taking this day off as well?"

A shiver races down my spine, and my toes curl. I'm tempted to play hooky and spend the day in bed with Varrek, I really am, but the fear of being seen as lazy by the clan is too strong. It doesn't matter that I'm in bed with the leader of the clan. I want to be accepted by all of them, and that means earning my place here. On my own. Without his help.

"I wish I could. But Nalba's letting me borrow one of her gowns for Maevstra, and she was going to let me try it on today." I twirl his silver hair in my fingers, and I'm still amazed by the feel of it. It's like silk. Thick, lustrous silk.

He bristles at the mention of her name, but then his features soften. "You will look lovely in whatever you choose to wear to Maevstra."

"Is that so? Well, why bother with anything at all? Maybe I should just go naked," I say as I kiss along his sharp cheekbones.

He pulls back and pins me with his gaze. "No. If another male lays his eyes upon your soft skin, I will end him. You are *mine*."

I should firmly remind him that my body belongs to *me* and if I want others to see it, that's my choice. I should. I know I should. But there's something about the slight growl in his tone and the way his muscles flex as he holds himself above me that makes me want to let it slide. Or even encourage it. Just a tad. Because the idea of being *his* isn't the worst thing. In fact, I kind of love it.

I mirror his heated gaze as he leans down and kisses me. At first it's soft and slow, but then it gets hungrier, more frenzied, and soon we're just clawing at each other's skin as our tongues glide against each other.

"I need to taste you again. Now," he commands against my lips.

Varrek peels back the blankets and spreads my legs to fit himself between them. The moment he licks my inner thigh, there's a knock at the front door. Varrek groans, his crankiness abundantly clear as he rolls off of me, taking care to avoid pressing his wounded shoulder against the bed. "That was a human knock."

Kate and Ava. It has to be. They're here to collect me for breakfast, which will be immediately followed by dish duty. I release a groan of my own, as the thought of scrubbing food scraps from a million plates pales in comparison to Varrek licking my pussy until I see stars.

I climb out of bed and tug on my leggings and boots that are still piled on the floor. I turn to Varrek, looking all delicious with his naked torso and his hulking biceps exposed for only my eyes to see. "I wish I could stay," I mumble with a sigh.

"As do I." He puts his hands behind his head and flexes. He smiles at me, knowing I'm drawn to this view, and wiggles his brows.

My body goes to take a step back toward him, instinctively, like a moth to a flame, when a second knock sounds from downstairs. I toss a pillow at his head for the distraction, and he throws his head back in laughter.

"I will see you at breakfast shortly," he says.

I lean down to give him one last kiss and skip down the stairs to meet the girls. I swing open the front door, smiling like a lovesick teenager. "Good morning, beauties."

Ava smirks knowingly. "Well, hello there."

"For almost becoming dog food last night, you're in an awfully good mood," Kate adds.

"Perhaps I'm carpe diem-ing after my near-death experience. Is that so wrong?" I throw my arm around Kate's shoulder and squeeze. Her face scrunches up in disgust, but I know this is just Kate's cold front and really her heart is as big as the moon and as soft as marshmallows.

"You're 'seizing the day-ing'? Did y'all not learn Latin?" Ava scoffs.

"No," I reply. "It's a dead language."

"Dead but lovely," Ava hollers over her shoulder.

"Aw just like me," Kate says with a dreamy sigh.

We take turns trying to remember the foreign languages we learned in school. Ava is fluent in Latin and Spanish and spouts off several sentences in each. But Kate and I can only come up with a handful of terms in Spanish and French. We remember the curse words, naturally, and how to ask where the library is, but that's about it.

I pile my plate high as we go through the buffet line at breakfast because I'm now realizing how little I've eaten in the last twenty-four hours. My stomach growls in agreement once I reach the white grain bars, and I grab two of those as well.

"How's Varrek's shoulder?" Ava asks once we're seated.

"It seems okay, I guess." I take a deep breath. "If that thing had bitten my shoulder, I'm pretty sure it would've ripped my arm clean off. But I think the Trovilians have thicker skin."

"They do. Kaiva has been doing medical scans on me to determine all our biological differences," Ava says between bites. "And the Trovilians do have thicker skin. About seventeen times thicker. They also heal quicker than we do."

"You're cool with being her lab rat?" Kate asks.

"Absolutely. It's not like I'm taking a bunch of experimental drugs and bedridden because of side effects. Kaiva takes samples of my DNA and compares the cellular data to that of a Trovilian female," Ava says thoughtfully. "It helps her determine which medicines are safe for us to take, which diseases humans have not eradicated but their race has, that sort of thing. She's already been able to confirm that we can't pass diseases to each other. Sexual...or otherwise."

"Plus, I'm sure she's hoping to confirm that humans and Trovilians can procreate," Kate says as she chews on her last chunk of bread.

Ava nods. "Yeah, that's definitely part of it."

I consider this. Could I see myself pregnant with an alien baby? I've sort of given up on the whole idea of becoming a mom because I figured Drew was my last real shot at it unless I wanted to raise a kid on my own, which I do not.

"And what's the verdict? Are Trovilians and humans compatible?" I ask.

"She's not sure yet," Ava replies. "We're similar species in many ways, but we're also very different. I think she's skeptical."

Kate stares off into the distance. "I suppose we are their only hope, huh? From keeping their race from dying out."

"Yep, you're probably right," I mutter.

Then I picture a little gold-skinned toddler running into Varrek's ginormous arms and him spinning the child around as he or she squeals happily. A deep sense of longing strikes me in the chest at the thought.

Varrek, with his protective instincts and his unflappable sense of honor. He would make an incredible father. He's taken such great care of his clan since they landed here. I have no doubt he'd take good care of me and all our hypothetical babies.

But making that daydream a reality would mean that we stay here. Forever.

I don't know how I feel about that concept yet. Even if I were ready to make that commitment, I can't ask Ava and Kate to spend the rest of their lives on an alien planet if by some miracle we could go home. This is about more than just what I want.

So far, the odds that we can find a way home seem to be pretty slim, and getting slimmer by the day, but I haven't let that hope fade away yet. Not completely.

The girls and I seem to be lost in our own thoughts as we finish our meals. We wash and dry the dishes in silence, and even when Varrek swings by and grabs a few bites, I find it difficult to return his lingering gazes.

I'm still in a daze when I make my way over to Nalba's, but once I'm inside, the sounds of laughter and the native Trovilian language fill the air and clear my head.

Zohma, one of the females from the sewing circle, is here chatting with Nalba as she fiddles with a flowy gown that's laid out on one of the tables.

"Ah, Cloh-ee! You have met Zohma, I trust." Nalba gestures to Zohma.

"Yes, I have. Morivikka, Zohma." I give her a small wave. She nods and returns the greeting.

I don't know much about Zohma, but I do know she's the best seamstress in the sewing circle. Not only is she quick with clothing repairs, but she also has a knack for design. Most of the clothing the clan wears is limited to functional long-sleeve shirts and fitted leggings in shades of black and gray. But I remember seeing Zohma add little details to sleeve cuffs, necklines, and seams using the thick thread I couldn't seem to handle.

She's also mated to Grotahk, one of Varrek's warriors. They make an adorable, equally soft-spoken couple.

Nalba gets up from her seat at the corner of the long table and guides me over to the gown in front of Zohma.

It's long-sleeve, floor-length, and looks like it has layers of flowing, drapey satin in a variety of rich green shades. It's breathtaking.

"This is the gown you shall wear to Maevstra. I have not worn this for many years. It is yours." Nalba holds it up and hands it to me.

"Oh, Nalba." I marvel at it, speechless. "It's gorgeous. Are you sure?"

"Am I sure of the words I just spoke?" She stares at me, thoroughly baffled. "Yes, I am sure."

I laugh because Nalba's confidence is refreshing and give her a hug. Her body stiffens, and her arms hang at her sides. "Humans are an affectionate race, it seems?"

"Yes, I suppose we are." I release Nalba and lift the gown to hold it against my body.

I frown at the sight of the small waist of the gown, knowing there's no way that part of it will fit. Thank goodness Zohma is here. I pull that part taut across my ribs and show her the lack of room for my thicker middle.

"Ah!" She beams, then looks at Nalba and says something in Trovilian.

Nalba mumbles something back that I can't understand as Zohma uses a sewing tool to rip the original seams that hold the waist together, and the gown falls open.

Zohma indicates that I should undress so I can try it on and she can make alterations.

"Here? In front of Nalba?" I ask, mildly horrified at the idea of being naked in front of Varrek's ex.

"O fah, it is just skin, Cloh-ee," Nalba grumbles. "Zohma and I have seen each other's skin many times."

That doesn't reassure me all that much, since Nalba and Zohma are both stunners, but whatever. I strip down quickly and put the dress on like a coat, wrapping it in front of me.

"Like this," Zohma orders, in her extremely thick accent, holding her arms out straight from her sides.

I do as she says, and her hands are fast and efficient, pinning and tucking the layers of fabric around me to accentuate my curves.

Zohma and Nalba continue to chat in Trovilian while I stand there quietly.

I wonder if they're talking about me. Meh, it's none of my business, even if they are. I stare at a knot in the wood on the wall while the movie *Clueless* starts to play in my head.

Zohma looks up at me at one point, and I worry I missed something she said. "What?"

She smiles as she lifts the foot or so of fabric that still drags on the ground well past my feet. Then she giggles and holds her hands up, close together, indicating the shortness of my legs.

"Oh, yeah," I laugh. "You're going to have to bring the hem way up."

After she makes her final tucks, she steps back and gestures for me to give her a spin. I do, and she and Nalba reward me with the biggest smiles I've ever seen. I feel like a bride-to-be in a dress shop.

"You like?" I ask.

Nalba steps forward and places both of her hands on my shoulders. "I knew this gown would suit you well, Cloh-ee."

Wow, genuine praise. From Nalba, of all people. I reach out to hug her again, but she holds her hands up, blocking me. Fair enough. Some people don't like to be hugged. I get that, and I respect her boundaries.

"Thank you, Nalba." I do another twirl in the gown and love the way the satin feels against my skin. So soft. And how the bottom of the gown flows out around me like a bell with subtle ruffles.

I don't want to take it off, but if I help Nalba with anything, I'm sure to stain it. Plus, it's held together with pins at the moment, so I change back quickly, and Zohma takes it from my hands and wraps it in a bag.

"Varrek will not be able to look anywhere else during Maevstra," Nalba says as she takes her seat and starts fiddling with something in her hands.

I freeze. "Varrek?" I scoff. "Oh, we're, you know, we're nothing."

She looks up at me and blinks several times without breaking the silence. I can feel my palms start to sweat.

"Why do you lie?" she asks. There's no venom in her words. Just curiosity. "Because I have seen you two together. I have seen the way he looks at you. The way he speaks of you. And I know that you do not speak truth."

"I just—"

"Is it because he and I were pleasure mates?" she asks.

"I mean, yeah," I answer, my voice quiet. "I didn't know how you would feel about it—he and I being together."

She stares at me for another moment before releasing a roar of laughter. "You are worried I am jealous?"

I don't know how to respond, so I just stand there, forcing a smile.

"Oh, little human. How precious you are." She slaps the table with another giggle as Zohma joins in. "Varrek and I could never be more than pleasure mates. We were only compatible in that one way. In every other way, we are not."

I have noticed some tension between them the few times I've seen them interact. I assumed it was the lingering sexual tension of former lovers. But now, looking back, it could also be that they get on each other's nerves.

I didn't realize how much anxiety I was holding at the thought of Nalba and Varrek still possibly having feelings for each other. I'm so relieved right now I feel like I could fly.

Nalba's been a friend to me. She's a bit aloof, and downright gruff at times, but she has a fascinating mind and I like helping her with all her projects.

She waves me over to her side and tells me that she needs help adding the fluid inside the douku orbs and that my tiny hands will be able to funnel the liquid into the hollow balls and seal the tops. I pull up a chair next to her and begin my task. She has a box full of these balls, easily over one hundred, so I certainly have my work cut out for me. But the task is somewhat mindless, so I enjoy it.

We work quietly for a few minutes before Nalba starts telling me what to expect of Maevstra. Apparently there's a clan band that plays drums and a string instrument, the name of which I cannot pronounce. They will play all night, until the sun rises, and that's how long the ale will be flowing, apparently.

She also briefly mentions "the Hexrins" and how "they will probably be engaging in some kind of sorcery," like they are collectively seen as obnoxious outcasts among the clan.

"Who are 'the Hexrins'?" I ask. I don't want to get caught up in clan gossip, but the mention of sorcery has certainly piqued my interest.

"They have the red hair. Have you not seen them around the village?" Nalba asks, surprised.

"Oh!" I exclaim. Now I know who she's talking about. "They have the big ears with the piercings. Yes, I've seen them."

"They are quite peculiar. You will see," she says as she drops some preservative liquid onto a grain bar, and when it turns brown after about twenty seconds, she shouts in frustration and hurls it out the window.

"Peculiar. Right." I go outside and retrieve the bar, since leaving food on the ground seems like a bad idea when tr'gorys are creeping around at night, and toss it in the trash bin.

I remain at Nalba's side for the rest of the morning until she dismisses me for the day in a huff. She's frustrated with the lack of progress on a few of her inventions and wants to tinker with them alone.

I head to lunch at the tail end of it and snack on the few remaining fruits and slices of smoked meat before I get started on the dishes. Kate and Ava aren't here, which I don't mind, since I've skipped dish duty a couple times now. It's only fair that I do the scrubbing and drying solo.

Waldric keeps me company and tells me all about his menu for Maevstra. It mostly consists of meat with a variety of sauces and spices he's been perfecting. I try to describe barbecue sauce, but I have trouble comparing the flavor to anything he might recognize. "I'm sure I'll love all of them, Waldric. The whole clan will."

I'm drying the final mug with a rag when he leans down and whispers, "Do you think Nalba will enjoy them as well?"

There it is.

Confirmation of Waldric's true intentions. He was never crushing on me. He's had his eyes on Nalba this whole time. I'm so relieved that he and I are just buddies that I could kiss him. But that would obviously destroy our friendship, so I don't.

"I think she will, Waldric. I really do," I tell him.

"She is complex, that female," he mutters, his tone filled with awe.

"That she is." I laugh. "But I'm with her every day, so maybe I can help you? You know, provide a little insight into her likes and dislikes and all that."

Waldric gives me a big, toothy smile. "I thank you, Cloh-ee, for your assistance." Then he pauses. "Will you...refrain from sharing this with others? Until I am certain Nalba could return my feelings?"

Poor, sweet Waldric. "Of course. Your secret's safe with me, big guy."

I'm about to give him a few flirting tips when I see Ahlvo laughing as he walks back from the training grounds alongside Bruvix. I look for Varrek, but I don't see him anywhere.

Ahlvo sees me, and his mouth stretches into an even wider grin. "Ah, Cloh-ee!"

"Hi, guys. How'd training go?" I ask, my eyes still searching for Varrek.

Bruvix grunts, and I notice he looks crankier than usual.

"'Twas a victorious session, little human. Especially once Varrek left. Then we were able to have fun." He elbows Bruvix in the chest, and that quickly transforms into a wrestling match in the middle of the main path between the two of them.

"Wait, Varrek left?" I shout, trying to regain their attention.

It doesn't work though, so I walk over to where Ahlvo crouches over Bruvix holding him in a headlock. "Ahlvo! Varrek left? Where did he go?" I try again.

Ahlvo smiles up at me as Bruvix gasps for breath and kicks his back leg in the direction of Ahlvo's crotch. "He went to see my mother shortly after our session started."

"Why did he need to see her? Is he okay? Did his cut open back up?" Panic rises in my throat like bile. Kaiva told him he didn't need to come back for three days. That he would probably be healed by then.

But what if his cut is infected? I think about the moment in the woods when I froze and dropped my knife. If his injury gets worse, it's all my fault. I could've done something, anything to help him in that moment and I choked.

I take a deep breath, and even that is a struggle. I don't understand why I'm so worried. He's fine. He has to be. Their medicine is more advanced than ours. Plus, they can heal quicker than we can. He'll be fine. Just fine.

Bruvix flings himself backward, pinning Ahlvo beneath him and catching him off guard enough for the arm around Bruvix's neck to loosen and let go.

"Okay, thanks for your help," I mutter dryly. I put the clean mug I didn't realize I was still holding on the nearest surface and run toward

Kaiva's as my mind continues to race. Why would he have to return so soon unless something was wrong?

CHAPTER 17

VARREK

$\mathcal{M}$y focus is not where I need it to be, and I grow more agitated with each breath. It is not the wound on my shoulder that distracts me. It aches, but it is a dull ache and does not prohibit me from training.

It is Cloh-ee. It is the tether between us that intensifies each time she touches me. It is her nearness, without touching me at all. It is her scent. It is everything I have not told her, about my past, my father, and the pain that lingers in my mind. It is the fact I still do not know whether she will remain on Oluura or if she will continue trying to find a way back to Earth.

My heart is hers. Wholly and completely hers.

I long to be inside her mind. To know how she feels about me. I imagine her mind to be a warm place. Warm and soft, like her heart.

But my obsession with the curvaceous little human is starting to affect my ability to lead my clan and train with my crew.

Today we train with swords, as I prefer to alternate our use of certain weapons. If we use a different weapon each day and rotate them in and out, we will master them all, making us the most formidable crew in the galaxy.

Everything is fine until I think I catch a whiff of Cloh-ee's scent and Grotahk sees it as an opportunity to strike. His sword clashes against mine as he knocks it out of my hands and points his blade to my throat.

I dust myself off and try again. And again I am defeated. When it happens a third time—against Ahlvo, no less—I throw my sword to the ground in frustration. Ahlvo leans in, and I think he is going to mock my poor performance, but instead he expresses genuine concern. "It is not your wound, is it, brother? It is the tether. Your inara."

I am not ashamed to feel the mating bond for Cloh-ee, but I am embarrassed that she does not feel it for me, or...not in the same way. I worry that what she feels is merely attraction, or infatuation at most, and because she is not Trovilian, that is all it will ever be for her.

I brush off Ahlvo's comments. "I am fine, brother. Perhaps I require more medicine for my shoulder." I look out at my crew, paired up and swinging their swords expertly at each other as they practice different maneuvers. They are seasoned. They will be fine without my supervision this day. "Take over for me. I am going to see Kaiva."

Ahlvo nods as I put my sword on the rack and head out of the training grounds.

At times, I think about how much simpler it would be to mate with a Trovilian female. I would not have to wonder how she feels. The tether would be undeniable. She would feel it as strongly as I do. We would not hesitate to proceed with the mating ceremony. And then we would share minds. A simple, straightforward process from courting to eternal happiness.

But there is a reason the tether has not presented itself until now. I was not meant to bond to a Trovilian female. I was meant for Cloh-ee as she was meant for me.

I cannot imagine a life without seeing her delicate eyelashes flutter open to reveal her big brown eyes as the sun rises. I cannot imagine not seeing her smile, with those small blunt teeth and the amusing space between the two in front. Seeing her wide hips sway with each step she takes. Or holding her generous, soft flesh in my palms, up against my body.

Feeling this way for her comes with many challenges. And I cannot navigate this alone. That much has become clear. I must speak with someone who has experienced the mating bond before. Someone who understands the intensity of it. Someone who knows who I was and who I have become. Someone who will be discreet with the questions I ask.

That person is Kaiva.

I enter Kaiva's med room and find her huddled over a glass jar filled with herbs and explaining something to Aye-vah.

"Morivikka, females." I smile broadly, trying to conceal my jumbled mental state.

Kaiva strides over, her brow furrowed in concern. "Ah, my son. Is this a friendly visit? Or is your wound bothering you?"

Out of the corner of my eye, I see Aye-vah stealing glances at us. I cannot discuss my problem while she is here, but I also do not want to make it clear that she is not allowed to listen. I give Kaiva a panicked look and whisper, "I wish to discuss a health concern, not my shoulder. Something…else."

She nods, and then her eyes light up knowingly. "Yes, yes, very well." She turns to Aye-vah. "Aye-vah, can you—"

"Totally fine, doctor-patient confidentiality. I get it," Aye-vah says as she scurries toward the other side of the room. "I'll, um, go upstairs and organize your medical books by color."

"Ah, very well." Kaiva smiles and then faces me. "I do not know what any of that means. Do you?"

"I do not." I laugh. "Human thing, I suppose." I shrug and lower myself onto the same bed as the previous night.

Kaiva pulls back the bandage and decides to redress the wound, just to be safe. "Tell me what ails you, Varrek."

I sigh, so grateful to have her ear. This is the same closeness I had with my mother. A pang of sadness strikes me in the gut, and I wish more than anything that she were still alive to guide me through this. "I am consumed by the tether that bonds me to Cloh-ee. It gets harder to resist. Each day, I find it more difficult to be away from her, even for a moment."

"It is an unstoppable force, the mating bond." Kaiva cleans the gash on my shoulder, reapplying the healing salve.

"Is it always this way? Did you feel this for Rumo before your mating ceremony?"

Ahlvo is very much his father's son, their jovial energy cleansing the air of every room they enter. Rumo is a hunter and is often away with the other hunters gathering meat and vegetables for us from the surrounding areas outside the forest.

After the virus took my mother, I would spend as much time as I could at Ahlvo's home, just so I could watch the happiness and love that flowed freely between Rumo and Kaiva. Even after many years of being mated, they still show each other the same abundant affection as newly mated pairs.

It was a welcome escape from the rage that radiated from my father.

"I felt it then, and I feel it now. It never fades."

I find I am somewhat disappointed to hear this. If it is always this powerful, how does one focus on anything else? "Why does it feel like it gets stronger? You say that it will continue to get stronger for… forever? I cannot lead the clan like this." I rub my chest, trying to silence the blaring ache in my heart.

Kaiva chuckles as she presses against the adhesive edges of the new bandage. "You are a young male who has found your mate. It is bound to make you feel many new things. Overwhelming things."

"But to this severity? Perhaps it is me. Something is wrong with me. This we know to be true already."

Kaiva tilts her head, puzzled. "There is nothing wrong with you, Varrek. Why would you say such things?"

I mirror her puzzlement. How can she not understand? "Because there is madness in my bloodline. My father was not right. Surely there is part of me that is wrong as well."

Her eyes shine with sadness, and the silence hangs over us, so I continue, ensuring she has the information she needs for a diagnosis. "Perhaps that broken part of my mind is causing the intensity of the mating bond. Or the mating bond itself. Perhaps it is all in my mind.

Cloh-ee does not feel the tether because she is human, but perhaps there is no tether at all and I am imagining it. Just like my father created the idea that the people of D'Alluk were to blame for the virus."

It is only when I am finished speaking that I realize I have not taken a breath in some time. Then my breathing starts to come in quick, shallow bursts, and I struggle to keep up with it. It is like I am a step behind each inhale and exhale, and I am pleading with my body to catch up.

"Varrek, my son." Kaiva turns the dial on the side of the bed so I am in a seated position and puts her hands on my shoulders in an effort to comfort me. "Look at me. Do not look away from my eyes. Breathe."

She draws in a deep breath, and I am watching her do it, but as much as I try, I cannot match it. I am trapped. I am trapped in this body. My heart jumps in a way I do not recognize. I do not like it. It feels wrong. I am wrong. My body is wrong. Or it is my mind. Perhaps both. I need to get out. But since I cannot leave my body, I must get out of this space. This room. Air. I need fresh air.

I go to stand, and Kaiva pushes her hands down so that I plop back into the seat. "Do not go. I can help you," she vows as she runs over to the wall of jars and pulls one down. She takes out three small, pointy brown leaves and puts a drop of liquid on them before crumpling them into a ball of mush and rolling it between her palms.

When she opens her hands, the leaves have turned into a paste, and she wipes some on my chest and on the edges of my nostrils. The scent of it fills my nose instantly, and it is pleasant, crisp, calming. My breathing slows, and she resumes her place in front of me, breathing in and out slowly while holding my gaze. I find it easier to match her breaths, and soon I am breathing with her, in and out.

We do this several times. Slightly longer than it feels necessary, but she is scared for me, I can tell, so she is making sure I am okay.

Her next breath is a heavy sigh, one of secondhand exhaustion and pity. "You hold much pain within you. It suffocates you, my son."

I look down at my hands, folding my fingers into clenched fists. I am the leader of this clan. I must act like it. I am filled with shame and anger over my outburst. But I find that when I look back at Kaiva, my anger dissipates. It feels like there is no room for it in this moment. I am tired. Unfathomably tired.

She pulls a stool over so she is seated in front of me. "Varrek, you are not broken. There is no part of you that is broken. You are also *not* your father. I have said this to you many times, and I do not mind saying it over and over throughout your life, but you must listen to me. You are not him. You are you, and your heart is as big and bright as the morning sky." She gives my hand a comforting squeeze.

"As for the tether..." Her eyes scan the room, looking for something. "I recall a pair that refused the mating bond when I was younger. They did not get along at first and did not want to be mated. I believe that their tether strengthened the longer they denied the bond. I will research this."

Okay, that's slightly good news. I release my clenched fists in mild relief. "That would align with some of the things I have been feeling."

Kaiva leans forward, putting her elbows on her knees. "Can you not tell Cloh-ee about the tether? About any of this? The pain you feel? To anyone with eyes, it is clear that she feels strongly for you. Perhaps she does return your feelings. She might even stay here and proceed with the mating ceremony."

"It must be her choice, to stay here." I tell Kaiva the same thing I tell myself thousands of times each eve. "I need it to be because she wishes to remain at my side, not because she prioritizes easing my pain over her own happiness. I have no doubt she would do that if she knew. Her heart is kind. The kindest."

She nods, carefully considering my words. "But if she is truly your mate, should she not know all there is to know about you? Even the parts you consider to be broken?"

She is right. I know this. "It is different for humans though. Their mating customs are different. They choose their mates and then leave them for another. They come together and then break apart as frequently as the seasons change."

"Aye-vah has mentioned this to me," Kaiva says as she cleans up the herb paste and returns the jar of brown leaves to the shelf.

"It is because of this that I cannot tell her. I am bonded to her already." It is the first time I have said the words aloud, though it is not the first time I have thought them. Now hearing them, I am terrified of the power Cloh-ee holds over me. "She is not bonded to me. She could share with me the darkest corners of her soul, and I would not cherish her any less. But she is not like us. She does not feel this same intensity."

Kaiva sits back down and gives me a sympathetic smile. "You are already worried that her feelings for you could evaporate like mist on the wind so sharing your pain would drive her away, and you cannot bear this. Yes?"

"Yes," I choke out.

"I wish I could help you, my son. Seeing you in such agony…it is awful."

"Please, Kaiva, you cannot tell her, or Aye-vah, or anyone, what have I told you. Promise me," I plead.

"Kaiva! Varrek?" Cloh-ee calls our names as she bursts through the front door, her eyes frantic. "Oh my god. Varrek! I was so worried. Are you okay? Kaiva, is he okay? Is his shoulder infected?"

I stand and reach for Cloh-ee, pulling her into my arms and crushing her against my chest. "I am fine, Cloh-ee. Do not worry."

She pulls back to look at me, her big eyes filled with fear for me. "I-I saw Ahlvo, and they said you left training early, and I figured you'd never do that unless you were really hurt, and then they said you were here, and then I thought the worst," she rambles, clearly in a rush to get the words out. "But you're okay?"

She looks at Kaiva. "He's okay?"

Kaiva gently pats Cloh-ee's shoulder. "He is well, Cloh-ee," she says, then she grabs my eye. "This I promise," she says with a wink. And I know my embarrassing admission will stay between the two of us.

"Thank fuck!" Cloh-ee exclaims as she buries her head against my chest, and her small arms squeeze me tighter around the waist. "Well wait, why are you here, then? Is something else the matter?"

"I wanted to make sure my shoulder was healing properly. I, uh, got some dirt on the bandage while training, and I needed a new one," I tell her as I kiss her soft mane. It is not entirely a fib, and I find it is all I can offer her in this moment.

She seems satisfied with this, and I am relieved she does not press me on it. "Good. Okay, well, Nalba gave me the rest of the day off. Wanna practice throwing knives?" she asks, beaming at me in excitement.

I can deny her nothing. "A brilliant plan, Cloh-ee." I wrap my arm around her shoulders as we head toward the door.

I turn back to thank Kaiva for her help, and Cloh-ee does the same. Kaiva waves us away with a warm smile, and we head outside.

The air this day is slightly warmer and a bit heavier than usual, but it is most likely due to the lack of wind. There is a stillness that indicates the wet season is upon us, but hopefully it will hold until after Maevstra.

"I should warn you, inara, I will not go easy on you. I still have some training energy that I must expend, and that means you must hit your target twenty times in a row."

"Twenty? Are you insane?" She playfully shoves my chest as I pull her up into my arms.

She wiggles her way down to stand on the tops of my feet, pulling my head down to meet her. I feel her breath against my lips as she leans in. Just before our mouths meet, a bloodcurdling scream fills the air.

CHAPTER 18

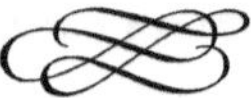

CHLOE

"What the fu—" I run toward the sound, so afraid for the person screaming that I can't even finish dropping the f-bomb. That was a human scream. I know it.

Varrek and I round the corner at the edge of the village to find Kate running toward us at full speed, still screaming at the top of her lungs. She emerges from a narrow path in the woods, her face scrunched in horror, her cheeks streaked with tears.

"Kate, what happened? Are you all right?" I extend my arms as I ask, and she runs straight into them, a blubbering, shivering mess. She doesn't seem to have any obvious injuries, so instead of pushing her to answer that question, I rub her back.

After a few minutes of this, I notice people gathering around us. Ava makes her way through the growing crowd and asks what's going on in a whisper. I shrug, and she wraps her arms around mine, caging Kate between us. Varrek still hovers over my shoulder, and I can see the desperation for answers in his eyes. But I won't push Kate to talk. She will when she's ready.

I hear murmurs and whispers all around me from the clan. Some in English asking what's going on, some in Trovilian, but I ignore them all and keep my focus on Kate. I gesture to Varrek to lean down and ask in a low voice, "Can you get them to back up a bit? Give us a little space?"

He does as I ask, thankfully, and as people back up and give us room, Kate lifts her head, seemingly a bit calmer. "Ready to tell us?" I ask softly.

She nods and wipes the tears from her cheeks. Ava and I release her but remain close.

She looks up at the trees. "It was huge. Like, the size of a fucking plane. Bigger, maybe."

"What was?" Ava asks.

"I-I'm not sure what it was. Not completely. I couldn't really tell. It flew over so fast…" She trails off. Then she pinches her eyes shut. "I think it saw me, because then it swooped down. I felt it. The air as it flew over my head. I ducked down. I didn't see how close it got"—she shudders—"but it felt close."

She narrows her eyes at Varrek in a glare. "Why didn't you tell us there were dragons on this planet?"

"Drag-ohns?" Varrek asks, his eyes filled with confusion.

"You know, big scaly beasts with giant heads and teeth that breathe fire and sleep on gold coins or whatever," Kate replies drily.

Varrek stands silently, his eyes raised to the sky, thinking. After what feels like forever, he speaks. "We were told stories on Trovilia about distant planets ruled by draxilio, creatures that match what you describe, but they were an ancient species that could shift forms. And nowhere in this galaxy."

The quiet murmurs from the clan sound like agreement, and shock that a draxilio could be here on Oluura.

"Where did you see this draxilio, Kay-teh?" Varrek asks.

She rolls her eyes at the drawn-out pronunciation of her name. "I was walking along the edge of the forest, so—"

"Why were you on the edge of the forest? It is dangerous to be outside of our territory, especially alone," Varrek chides. "There are tr'gorys, many tr'gorys, that could have killed you before you even reached the edge of the forest. Have you no sense?"

Kate's features contort with rage. "Okay, first of all, it's not even dark out. Second of all, what does it matter what could've happened when I'm telling you what *did* happen? I saw a motherfucking dragon!"

The crowd gasps at her tone, as if addressing Varrek with such disdain is unheard of. I can't say I blame her though. I don't like the way he's disregarding the severity of what she saw in an effort to blame her for not worrying about a threat she didn't even encounter.

Kate rubs her temples in frustration, and I realize I need to step in here. "Let's forget the tr'gorys for a second, since you didn't even see them today"—I look at Varrek while uttering that last part—"and tell us everything you can remember about the dragon."

"We have been here for years, Cloh-ee, and no one has ever witnessed a draxilio before," Varrek addresses me but faces the crowd as he speaks, as if trying to reassure them that dragons do not exist on this planet, simply because there hasn't been a sighting.

Ava crosses her arms and mumbles quietly, "Unbelievable."

"Are you saying you don't believe me? That I didn't see what I saw?" Kate asks Varrek.

The three of us are staring daggers at him now, and he's silent under our collective scrutiny. He clears his throat and holds up his hands in surrender. "I do not say this, Kay-teh. I simply do not see how a predatory creature as large as a draxilio could go undetected in the time we have been here. We have hunters who spend extended periods of time outside of our territory, and they have never spotted a draxilio."

It's a reasonable response, but I still don't like it. This whole thing feels uncomfortably familiar. Plus, the way Kate and Ava's postures are stiff and defensive like mine, I can tell they feel it too. I can't allow this to go any further. Not here on Oluura. "If Ahlvo had told you that he saw a dragon, what then? Is this how you'd respond? Insisting that he's mistaken? Interrogating him for being somewhere he's not allowed to be?"

Varrek's reaction is subtle, and I wonder if anyone else sees it, but he flinches at my words like he's been slapped. He wasn't expecting that from me. This is the first time I've challenged his authority, and with an audience, his clan. But I don't care. Kate's scared, and she's giving us information that we need to know, and he's dismissing her like she's a hysterical woman causing a scene.

He takes a deep breath and looks from me to Kate. "You are right. Kay-teh, I am sorry. I take the safety of the clan on my shoulders, and the tr'gorys are a true threat to us. This we know for certain." He pauses, turning toward the crowd. "But this draxilio is a new threat, one we must take seriously."

The clan surrounding us seems to calm at that, some dispersing and returning to whatever they were doing before. Many remain, silently waiting to hear Kate's account.

Kate looks annoyed but not as angry, and her stance has relaxed a bit. "I think it was blue. I was, um, looking up at the sky, enjoying the warmth of the sun, when I noticed a shadow blocking it out. Then I saw it. Flying in a wide loop overhead." When her body starts to shake, Ava reaches for her hand and holds it tight. "I gasped. That's all I did. I didn't even mean to; it just came out. And I-I made no other movements or sounds. But it was like it heard me."

"Is that when it swooped down?" I ask, finding it difficult to accept that dragons not only exist but are also on this planet.

"Yeah, the thing peered down at me with its giant head, and I saw it take a sharp downward turn. I dove to the ground and rolled back into the trees. I didn't see it after that. I just felt the whoosh of air over me."

"Then what did you do, Kay-teh?" Bruvix asks in a tone so gentle and sincere I didn't recognize it was him. I didn't even realize he was here. His eyes are locked on her though. He looks so worried about her and fascinated by her tale at the same time. I didn't know his cranky face was capable of showing either of those things.

"I ran. I screamed and ran. I didn't stop until I got here," she says, her eyes downcast.

Ava and I exchange knowing glances. "Okay, I think it's time to get this girl some rest," Ava says with a finality in her tone that I very much appreciate.

Varrek nods and straightens his spine. "Ahlvo, Bruvix, alert the clan at the evening meal to stay within the forest and not to venture outside of it." He looks up at the trees that are blocking the sky entirely. "I am thinking we have not yet seen a draxilio because of the tree cover. It could also be the reason we have been protected from them until now."

He looks at Bruvix. "Bruvix, message the hunters and tell them to return. They need to know about this and should alter their routes accordingly to stay beneath the cover of the trees as much as they can."

Bruvix nods in response.

"Ahlvo, tell the crew we will be paired up on patrols for the foreseeable future."

"Done," Ahlvo says, as serious as I've ever seen him.

Bruvix gives Kate a comforting yet slightly awkward pat on the arm before heading off with his new task. Ahlvo gives her a high five.

The crowd splits, and then it's just me, Kate, Ava, and Varrek. His looks remorseful, and I'm compelled to comfort him. But I think maybe letting him sit with this anguish is a good thing. Plus, all my compassion needs to be directed at Kate right now.

"Let's go home, eh? Have a girls' night?" I look at Varrek, "See you tomorrow?"

He opens his mouth and then closes it. Then he gives me a tight smile. "Yes, indeed." He bows his head at Kate. "Rest well, Kay-teh. We will not let this draxilio hurt you or anyone else. This I vow."

"'Kay," she says in a clipped tone.

Ava and I walk on either side of her back toward our house. Before we get there, Bruvix jogs up to us with a bottle in his hand. It's his signature ale. "To keep the monsters away." He smiles and hands it to Kate.

"Thank you, Bruvix." Kate takes the bottle and holds it against her chest as if it's the most precious gift she's ever received.

He dips his chin and trots off toward the center of the village.

Once we get inside, we kick off our boots by the door. Ava uses the bathroom while I pull our only three mugs down from the shelf. Kate leans against the wall while I pour the ale, her eyes glazed.

Each with a full mug in hand, the girls and I head up to Kate's bedroom on the second floor and climb onto her bed, piling the blankets and pillows around us like a cozy, protective fort.

We sit there, staring at the frothy orange contents of our mugs, letting the events of the day sink in.

"So…dragons. Didn't have that on my alien kidnapping bingo card. Did y'all?" Ava asks with a grin.

I giggle at the absurdity of it all, and Kate cracks a smile.

I take a swig, letting the bitter liquid awaken my taste buds and tingle down my throat. "I guess we shouldn't be too surprised that they're real."

Kate shakes her head. "Hey, remember when aliens weren't real?"

"And dragons were just efficient modes of transportation on *Game of Thrones*?" I add.

"Simpler times," Ava retorts as she props a thick cushion behind her back and leans against the wall.

"They don't believe me," Kate says sullenly. "They think I'm lying. The weird human with the fire hair, who's just…weird." She takes a long pull of her ale and grimaces at the aftertaste. "You guys are so lucky."

Ava plays with a stray thread on the blanket draped over her legs. "Well, we're three humans among an alien race. Of course they think we're weird."

"No, it's not a human thing. They don't think *you* are weird. They think *I* am," Kate says while clenching her jaw. "It's like"—she points her mug at me—"you're the nice one, Ava's the smart one, and I'm the weird one, but not in a charming way. In a *there she is again, that freak. Let's cross to the other side of the path so we don't even have to make eye contact* way."

"Ugh, the 'nice' one? That's what the clan thinks of me?" I find I'm thoroughly disgusted by that label.

"You *are* nice though," Kate says as if it's obvious.

I think back to all the times I've been referred to as "nice." For the most part, the people who have described me as such also walked all over me. They benefited from my politeness, or rather, my inability to call out their shitty, selfish behavior. Ex-boyfriends, toxic bosses, and bad friends. I gave, and they took.

What does "nice" even mean, anyway? Because "kind" and "nice" are not the same. A kind person is someone who follows through on their word and helps others. A nice person tells you you look gorgeous even when there's an entire salad stuck in your teeth. A kind person is honest, even when it might make you uncomfortable. A nice person tells you what you want to hear, to ensure you're always comfortable, even when your comfort is harming them or others.

I don't want to be the "nice" one anymore. Sometimes you need to have a bit of a bite in order to protect yourself and the ones you love. And I want to protect my people.

Ava's voice cuts through my revelation. "I thought we, as a society, agreed that women are no longer just one thing. We can be all things —smart, nice, weird, et cetera."

Kate chuckles darkly. "I don't know if society is fully on board with that concept yet."

I empty my mug, drinking much faster than I probably should be. "Then fuck society."

Ava and Kate join me. "Fuck society," they say as we clink our mugs together.

The moment I stand up, I sway on my feet, suddenly realizing how strong this ale is. "Ah, thank you, Bruvix," I mutter to myself as I slowly, carefully make my way down the stairs.

I grab the bottle, which is now half empty, and head back upstairs to refill our mugs. There are about two sips left in the bottle once I refill our glasses, so I hand it to Kate to finish off. With the whole dragon encounter, she's certainly earned extra booze.

The mood in the room is lighter, happier, than when we first came up here, and I don't know whether to credit the ale for that or just the good ol' fashioned girls' night we're having. I find I don't care.

"So is it something in the water here, or...?" Kate asks Ava as I return to my spot on the bed.

"Actually, yeah, I think it might be. Or it was something in the vaccines Kaiva gave us before we got off the ship that are balancing our hormones. But when I asked her, she wasn't sure because she's never heard of cystic acne before." Ava sees the question in my eyes and asks, "What about you, Chlo? Any breakouts since we've been here?"

I think back to my skin before we were taken and wince internally at how bad it was. Whoever said acne disappears when you exit your teenage years is a filthy liar whom I'd love to punch in the throat. I tried everything, from switching birth controls to cutting out dairy, which lasted about a day, to the embarrassing amount of money I spent on skincare products. Nothing worked.

Since we've been here though, I haven't noticed any painful zits along my jawline, which is where they always pop up. The mirrors here are few and far between, so I'm spending less time looking at myself, but when I touch my face, it feels smooth and surprisingly supple.

"No! I can't believe I'm just realizing this now, but no. No zits." I put my mug down on the floor next to the bed so I can caress my face with both hands. "Mmm. Like a baby's ass."

"Oluura: one; Earth: zero," Ava giggles.

I pull up my shirt to expose my stomach and look down with a frown. "Man, I was hoping my stretch marks had disappeared too."

"Are you kidding me? I love mine." Kate pulls down the waistband of her leggings just enough to expose the silvery lines along her hip. "They break up my freckles."

"Yeah, yours are cute," I concur. But so are her freckles. They cover pretty much every patch of skin she has, and paired with her fiery red hair, she looks like a fierce Scottish queen.

We continue to drink, finishing the ale in our mugs as we share the random aspects of Earth life we didn't expect to miss.

I glance out Kate's window and notice how dark it is outside.

Kate lets out a loud yawn and lowers herself an inch more in the bed so she's almost lying down completely. She looks relaxed, and that fills me with relief. Her eyelids droop and close, and after a few minutes of waiting for her breathing to even out, Ava and I tuck her in and turn out the light.

We're still buzzy from the ale, based on the clumsiness of our trek downstairs, but not overly messy.

We rinse out our mugs and dry them in silence, then I fill them both with water from the spigot and throw mine back in three big gulps. I don't want to be hungover tomorrow. Based on the way Ava chugs hers, she doesn't either.

"What are you gonna do now?" I ask as I refill our mugs.

She fusses with her tight curls. "I'll probably crash. You?"

I yawn, surprised by how desperately I want to lie down. "Yeah, same."

We say our good nights and climb the stairs to our rooms, still stumbling as we go.

* * *

ANOTHER WEEK PASSES IN A BLINK, with endless preparations for Maevstra. It's tomorrow, and the clan has spoken of nothing else—apart from the dragon sighting. That's still a hot topic for discussion, mainly because there hasn't been a sighting since Kate's.

I know Kate's frustrated by this. I can feel it every time someone brings it up and notes how odd it is that even though Varrek's crew has been patrolling the path around the forest nonstop for days, zero dragons have been spotted. No one says it accusingly, but she takes it that way nonetheless.

Ava and I have been keeping a close eye on her and her mental state. We take turns walking with Kate to the sewing circle, making sure she shows up for each meal, and spending more time with her at night.

She thinks we're hovering. She acts annoyed, but beneath her deadpan retorts and dark jokes, I can tell she likes having us around more.

When I'm not with Kate or helping Nalba, I'm with Varrek. Every night, he walks across the branch connecting our rooms and either carries me to his or stays in mine. We snuggle, we talk, and we put our mouths and hands all over each other. We haven't had sex yet, and

I'm not sure what we're waiting for. I know that we can have sex without completing the mating bond, that we can just be pleasure mates, but that label doesn't feel right when I think of how we are together.

When he touches me, it's with such reverence that I feel worshipped by him. When he makes me come, with his hand or his mouth, he watches me with such intense desire that I feel like the most beautiful creature he's ever laid eyes on.

There's so much more between us than attraction. Can we truly be nothing more than fuck buddies? Then again, maybe Trovilians are all spectacular in bed. Maybe it would feel like this with Ahlvo, or Bruvix, or any of them. But the thought of being with someone other than Varrek turns my stomach.

It's not just the orgasms that make me feel more connected to him either. Those are incredible, of course, but he's also throwing knives with me each night, helping me improve my form. He wants me to be able to protect myself, and he's so proud of me when I hit the target. I've never had that kind of support from a romantic partner. I assume it's because I've exclusively dated insecure men, who only feel comfortable in their manhood when I depend on them for something, and Varrek isn't like that.

Mastering this skill is something I want, something that will make me happy, and that's what matters to Varrek. Not how it'll make him look or how it'll make him feel when I no longer need his help with it.

There's something ridiculously sexy about that.

I let my eyes linger on his bare back as he stands in front of me, positioning himself to throw the knife in his hand. His taut muscles pulling and contracting with each breath, each step, and the release of each shot. Once again, he hits the target dead center.

But luckily, I do too. Despite the constant distraction of Varrek's chiseled body, I've gotten good. My aim is deadly, and my throws have some speed to them now. Varrek has been a stellar teacher, encouraging me to keep going when I miss and offering constructive feedback to improve my form.

Last night, I earned my armbands. After hitting the target thirty times in a row, Varrek beamed as he put them on my arms. It felt like I was receiving an Olympic gold medal.

I spent the next hour getting used to the weight and feel of them, pulling on the loops at the wrist to make sure the hidden knives ejected properly. I didn't want to take them off, and the only time I did was when I took a shower this morning.

I step into place, straighten my spine, and tug on the loops from both bands at the same time, releasing a blade in each hand. I raise my arms parallel next to my head and throw. Both hit the target, sinking into the sickly-smelling wood. "Boom! Another double bull's-eye," I cheer.

"What will you give me if I hit this next one, Cloh-ee?" Varrek asks, a sly grin on his face.

He's been extra flirty today, touching me and kissing me every chance he gets, even around other members of the clan, which is new for him. "Why should I give you anything?"

He tilts his head and points at the target, the center circle filled with our knives tightly pressed together. "Do you not think my performance has deemed me worthy of a reward?"

"Hmm. I suppose." I tap the handle of the blade against my cheek. "What is it that you want? To play strip knife throwing?"

"This is a game?" Varrek asks, looking nervous suddenly.

"Well, anything can turn into strip game, technically. In this scenario, we'd take off an item of clothing each time we miss a shot. So the first person completely naked loses the game," I explain.

Varrek's eyes swirl with hunger at the mention of nudity. Typical male. "Why should nudity signal a player's loss?"

"I guess because if you are able to get me naked while you remain clothed, you win."

"Ah, and what a victory that would be." He sighs, starry-eyed.

I playfully shove him in the shoulder, which has been fully healed for days, thank goodness.

"As much as I would love to play this game of yours, Cloh-ee, I do not think throwing knives and nudity are a safe combination." He strolls over to the pile of knives we have laid out and grabs another. "However, if I make this next shot, I would like a kiss."

A kiss? That's it? He's kissed me a hundred times at this point. "It's not much of a novel prize, but if that's what you want…" I trail off.

He lowers his head next to my ear and rasps, "This is what I want."

Goose bumps cover my entire body, and I shiver with anticipation. He grins at the visible effect he has on me and turns to face the target. He pulls his forearm back and hurls the blade forward. It hits the center with a metallic clink, knocking two other knives from the circle and sending them clattering to the floor.

He spins around, the soft light accentuating his marble cheekbones and making him look like a god. His emerald eyes now hooded and smoldering. I hear a low rumble deep in his chest as he steps closer, and suddenly I feel like he's hunting me. I want him to catch me, to claim me. I'm desperate to be his.

My stomach clenches, and a rush of heat floods my core. He towers above me and lowers his head until his lips hover over mine. I feel his breath fan my face, and he's close, so close.

I close my eyes as his lips brush against my own, soft and gentle. Covering my mouth in light caresses.

Then he tangles his fingers in my hair and pulls, not hard enough to hurt me, just a tug to pull my head back, lifting my chin. Reminding me of his strength and how he could use it to pleasure me, if I allow him to. A moan escapes me at the sensation. It feels like a bolt of lightning travels up my spine.

I want more.

He grunts and crushes his mouth to mine, diving into my parted lips with his tongue, exploring every corner. My arms wrap around his neck as his lips roam my cheek, my jawline, and I gasp as they reach my neck. He tastes my skin there, and his tongue traces slow, tantalizing shapes over my throbbing pulse. "More, Varrek. More," I whimper.

He moves his hand to my breast, cradling it at first and then rubbing my nipple to a sharp point through the fabric of my shirt. There are too many layers separating us, I decide, as I push his body away from mine just long enough to tug my shirt over my head and toss it to the floor. Once it's off, I pull him against me, rubbing my hardened nipples against his mouthwatering chest.

He groans as he lifts me up, his big hands gripping my ass while I wrap my legs around his middle. His hands are so big that they completely cover each cheek as he continues to grip and massage the soft globes. I pull myself up so I can kiss his neck. "I smell your arousal, inara. It is dizzying," he mutters against my skin.

I feel his hot breath on my chest, just above my nipple. I push his head lower as I climb him like a tree. I need his mouth on me.

As his lips close around my nipple, he sucks, hard, and I scream. I throw my head back, and the world blurs. Every part of him is so big and rough and sexy, and I can't take it anymore. I lick the shell of his ear and then bite on his earlobe before whispering, "I want you to fuck me, Varrek."

He pulls back, his face a mix of shock and longing. "You are sure?" he asks, his chest heaving with each breath. "This is what you want?"

I let my fingers trace the intricate band that wraps around his bicep. "This is what I want," I whisper.

He moans into my mouth as he gives me another toe-curling kiss before shifting me in his arms. I giggle at how easily he lifts and tosses me so that I'm now draped across his arms, bridal style.

"I will not fuck you here, inara. Not the first time, anyway," he grins as he carries me upstairs to his bedroom. *I need to ask him what that word means*, I remind myself. Later though. My arms are wrapped tightly around his neck as he climbs the stairs, so much confidence, so much swagger in each step. I'm in awe of him.

He sets me down on my feet, and we both kick off our boots and pants in a flash. I lower myself atop his bed and scoot backward so my head is closer to the pillows. I prop myself up on my elbows, and when I look up at him, standing at the foot of the bed, my heart thunders against my chest as if it's about to burst through my skin. I wonder if he can hear it.

His eyes shine with matching admiration as his hand goes to his hard cock, stroking it slowly. "You are beautiful, Cloh-ee. So beautiful."

I gasp at the sight and chew on my lower lip. I never realized watching a guy touch himself would be so hot. But Varrek isn't just any guy. He's Varrek.

He leans down, putting his hands on the bed between my feet. "Spread your legs for me. Let me see how wet I make you."

I do as he commands, my eyes never leaving his. His eyes go wide at my pussy on full display, and he licks his lips as he runs a light touch up my calf. He crawls up the bed, pressing a kiss up my leg as he goes. I'm spread as wide as I can by the time he settles his wide frame between my thighs. He leans in, closing his eyes and taking a deep inhale of my sex. He sighs, "Ah, your scent. I will never get enough."

"Oh fuck," I mutter as his tongue drags along my inner thigh and goose bumps cover my skin from head to toe.

He chuckles darkly. "So very responsive."

He grips my hips and swipes his tongue along the seam of my swollen pussy. I arch my back, and my hips buck into his face. "Ahhh!" I cry out.

I suck in a sharp breath the moment he spreads my lips and laps at my sex with an eager tongue. "You will always be my favorite meal," he growls. He circles my clit with his tongue in just the way I like, adding more pressure to the left side and alternating between slow and quick swipes. Then he inserts a finger, and then two, stretching me to make sure I'm ready. His thick digits surge in and out as he sucks on my clit. I feel like I may pass out.

"Varrek, so close. I n-need you." My breath hitches as I tug on his silver hair and claw at his shoulders. I can't wait anymore. I need him inside me. *Now.*

He growls in protest but climbs up my body and settles himself between my quivering legs. "I could deny you nothing," he croons.

I gasp as he rubs the head of his swollen cock against my entrance. Varrek slides himself inside me at a painfully slow pace. *Too slow. Need him now.* With my mind and body in full agreement, my limbs shaking with desire, I reach between us and wrap my hand around his cock, guiding him deeper. "Now, Varrek, please," I beg.

A strangled gasp wrenches from his throat as his hips surge forward. He's only about halfway in, but already I feel stretched wider than ever before.

I grip the blankets beneath me, my knuckles going white as my breath hisses through my teeth. "More, more," I plead with Varrek.

Sweat forms on his ridged brow as his jaw clenches, and I can tell he's holding on to every shred of restraint he has left. "So tight," he rasps. Sweet male. He's so worried about hurting me that he looks ready to climb out of his own skin. I decide to make it easier on him and arch my back, sinking deeper onto his hard cock.

Varrek pulls out, almost all the way, before slamming back into me, and this time, we're hip to hip. I scream, maybe forming words, I don't know, and claw at Varrek's back as my heels dig into his tight, sculpted ass, pulling him closer. I feel my pussy grip his hardness as it starts to shake inside me. "Ahh! I forgot that you vibrate," I mumble when he starts to move.

"Feels good?" he asks, his voice strained and his muscles bunching while he holds himself above me.

"Yes. Yesss!" I shout as he slams into me again, the vibration hitting me just right deep inside while providing the perfect amount of friction against my clit.

"Look at me," Varrek grits out, and I can tell he's close. I am too.

The slap of his skin against my own fills the air, and my body tightens all over, like a bowstring about to snap. He rocks into me again, and again, and I raise my hips to meet him each time.

Then I go over the edge, my nails digging into his shoulders as my mouth falls open in a silent scream, the walls of my pussy holding him tight. I keep my eyes fixed on his, and a moment later, he's coming too, my name tumbling from his lips in a low growl, his fangs catching the light. Or maybe they're glowing? I can't look away from them though, and a deep craving builds within me to have them sink into my neck as he releases his seed into my body.

Well, that's new. I've never wanted to be bitten during sex before.

But this isn't just regular sex. This is sex with Varrek. Everything with him is different. More intense. But I can't let that happen, since a bite will solidify the mating bond.

He collapses onto me, and even though he's heavy, his body doesn't crush mine. It's nice. Like a weighted blanket. I feel completely protected beneath him.

Our breathing is ragged, and we say nothing. We just cling to each other as we come back down to reality.

After a few moments, Varrek rolls off of me, and I whimper at the loss of him. He lies on his back, chest still heaving, as he wraps his arms around me and pulls my head to his chest. I let my eyes close, and an "mmm" escapes me.

Panic floods my mind when I realize we didn't use any sort of protection. I hate that I forgot to bring it up. *Stupid!*

But it passes when I remember that we can't pass diseases to each other and that Kaiva still hasn't been able to confirm whether humans and Trovilians can procreate. Besides, I'm thirty-five, so I know I have *some* eggs left in my metaphorical basket, but I'm probably no longer a fertile myrtle.

Varrek presses a kiss to my hair as he gently cups my breast. I look down at his hand and chuckle at the possessive way he holds me. Rubbing a thumb back and forth over my nipple. "Is that one your favorite?"

His eyes are sleepy and full of tenderness. "Yes, I think that it is. But so is this one," he says in a playful tone as he reaches for my other breast.

"They can't both be your favorite."

"Nonsense. They can. And they are." He gives my nipple a light pinch that makes every inch of my flesh tingle. I giggle and roll slightly away before Varrek grabs my hand and pulls me back, draping half of my body atop his.

Normally, I prefer space to sleep. I'm not much of a cuddler, but with Varrek, it's like every nerve in my body revolts the moment we break contact.

I burrow against him, our breaths synchronized and slowly returning to normal while we bask in the glow of our sated bodies.

* * *

I WAKE up with the light of the sun shining in my eyes. It peeks through the thick trees, warming my bare skin just as the breeze wafts through the room and cools it. I'm still pressed against Varrek, my leg thrown over his, and I wonder how this is comfortable for him. Clearly it is, since he's still fast asleep.

A smile spreads across my lips when images of our night together fill my mind. The way his cock vibrated inside me, the delicious way he filled and stretched me, and the way he held me afterward.

How can someone be so intense and so gentle all at once? I wonder as my eyes trace the strong lines of his cheekbones and jaw. His beauty is almost unfair. My eyes travel down, to his brawny shoulders and arms. I lick my lips, and I can feel the wetness pool between my thighs.

His lips smack together quietly, and a low rumble from his chest fills the air. "My female needs to come again, does she? Your scent reveals all, inara," he says groggily without opening his eyes.

I can feel my cheeks turn pink at being caught, and I give him a poke him in the ribs. "What does 'inara' mean? You promised to tell me, remember?"

His eyes flutter open suddenly and lock onto mine. His gaze turns serious as he shifts onto his side and props himself up with an elbow. His lips form a tight line before he says, "It means, 'my light, my everything.' My…'mate.'"

The moment the words register in my brain, my heart stops.

CHAPTER 19

VARREK

My mate knows she is my mate. It feels as if I have waited entire lifetimes to share this with her. I thought that I would be relieved once she knew, but the sheer disappointment on her face fills me with regret.

I should have been more careful around her, and called her only by her name, but when it comes to Cloh-ee, I find it nearly impossible to be careful. She makes me do things I would not normally do. She makes me want things I have no business wanting, such as a family, a future, eternal happiness with my mate by my side.

But as her body turns rigid before my eyes, and I wait for her to say something, anything, I realize I can have none of those things. Not even with another. My heart was lost to Cloh-ee the moment I saw her in that cage. Wherever she goes from this point on, she will take it with her.

She clears her throat, and the sound causes me to release a breath I did not know was trapped in my lungs. "So, um, I'm your mate, then? Because you've been using that word 'inara' since you met me." She moves over slightly, putting more space between us. Not much, but enough for my stomach to tighten with dread.

Her eyes dart around nervously. "Is it also an affectionate term pleasure mates use for each other, or more for eternal mates?"

I consider my next words carefully. I do not wish to scare or overwhelm her, but I want her to know the truth of how I feel. I have kept so many parts of myself hidden from her. I do not want this to be one of them. Not for another moment. "You are my mate, Cloh-ee. The center of my world."

She sits up, takes a deep breath, and climbs out of bed. Standing, she looks around the room. Then back at me. Then at the wood slats above. Then she starts to pace.

I wish that I could take a moment to admire her soft curves in the daylight. Her skin is completely bare. She does not hide it from my eyes. It is only because her mind is somewhere else, too distracted by the truth that was just revealed.

I rip the covers away from me and come to stand in front of her. The tether pulls me to her, but I do not touch her. I am desperate to place her small hand in mine and ease the furrow in her smooth brow, but I do not know if that kind of contact would be welcome, so I keep my shaking hands at my sides.

"Cloh-ee, tell me what I can do," I plead.

"I mean, that's crazy, right? How can a human be your mate?" she asks as she clasps her hands together tightly. I cannot breathe, knowing how easily this small human could shatter me with a single word. "I just, this whole time? Why didn't you tell me?"

I dip my head in shame. "I should have. There are many reasons I did not." Now it is my turn to pace. "I did not want to scare you. I did not know if you returned my feelings. I was not sure if you still planned to return to Earth." I pause, turning to her. "These are things I still do not know."

Her hand goes to her throat as she struggles to swallow. She nods, her eyes downcast. "Yeah. No, you're right. That's fair." I wait for her to continue, but she says nothing, just fidgets with her fingers.

"Cloh-ee?" I nudge.

She looks up, as if suddenly remembering where she is, and then down at her naked body. "Clothes," she mutters absently.

"Clothes?" I repeat.

"I need clothes." Cloh-ee pulls on one of my shirts and tugs on her leggings. She avoids my gaze while dressing, and it feels as if this conversation is over, though it has only just begun.

I wait for her to finish, and once she's fully dressed, I inhale a sharp breath. "Cloh-ee, are you leaving? Because I thought—"

She sighs, looking confused and distressed. "The words," she sputters. "I don't have the right words for this. I'm sorry. It's not that I don't want to talk about it, the thing you just told me. I need to do something first." She nods jerkily. "Yeah, I have a thing. So let's just put a pin in this for now, and once the thing is done, we'll talk, okay?"

She's smiling at me as if she has just revealed a brilliant plan that should soothe my soul. In reality, however, she has left me dizzy with vague statements. If I were not so disoriented by all of it, I would be devastated. Because it felt very much like a rejection. She does not want to be my mate, right? That is what she refuses to say to me?

I do not know what to say to Cloh-ee, so I just nod and tell her, "Very well," as she zips up her boots.

She turns toward the window to cross the branch between our homes, but before she goes, she grabs onto my hand. Her eyes hold many things I do not recognize, but beneath it all, there is warmth, which I cling to as a good sign. "Later. We'll talk later, okay?"

I nod, squeezing her tiny hand in mine, afraid to let go. "Later," I repeat, putting all the hope and promise I cannot articulate into that one word.

She smiles, and her long dark mane floats around her in the wind as she turns and climbs out the window. She steps across the branch, and I watch until she disappears inside of her bedroom.

I remain frozen in place, replaying the conversation in my head over and over, wondering if I should have lied and told her "inara" meant something else, something casual and innocent. But then where would we be?

It is better this way, a quiet voice whispers inside my head as I pull on my pants. Now she knows the truth.

I rub my hands over my face and rake my fingers through my hair.

They immediately get stuck in more than one knot, and I pull my pants off once again and head to the wash box. A steady growl hums from my throat as I stomp down the steps.

I slam the door to the wash box behind me and turn the water on at full blast on the highest heat setting, hoping to wash this frustrating morning off my skin.

Once I am dried and dressed, I send a comm alert to my crew to come to my home. We do not communicate using our screen pads often, but for important matters, it is easier to keep everyone informed this way. It is also how we tell the hunters who are far from the village to return home.

Ahlvo and Bruvix are the first to arrive, and we gather in the training room as we wait for the others. My eyes cannot help but stray to the target board, where Cloh-ee's knives still stick in the center of the target. I rub my chest, where a deep ache starts to form as I recall her words from earlier.

I shift so my back is facing the target wall. I do not want to be distracted during this meeting, but with Cloh-ee's scent still thick in this room, I worry that is inevitable.

I ask Ahlvo and Bruvix to fill me in on the tasks I assigned them the previous day.

"Rumo and Ulkii returned late last night. Syrix, Viltress, and Eh'Nd returned but moments ago. We still await the return of Krahn, Mikarya, and Lahkzo," Bruvix counts them off. "They were the greatest distance away but were already returning for Maevstra, so we expect them to arrive soon."

"Good, good. Ahlvo, any draxilio sightings?"

Ahlvo sighs and crosses his arms. "None. Not a trace. There are whispers among the clan that such a thing never occurred at all."

"If Kay-teh says it happened, it happened," Bruvix growls.

"I believe that it happened, Bruvix. Do not get your tunic in a knot," Ahlvo groans wearily. "I am saying that others are skeptical. And with each patrol concluding without a draxilio to report, it is more difficult to convince them."

Grotahk enters, along with the other eight members of my crew, and Ahlvo repeats the updates he and Bruvix just gave me. There are hushed murmurs among the group when Ahlvo says there still hasn't been a draxilio sighting, and I don't need to hear their words clearly to know they are tired of the constant patrols for a threat that has yet to reveal itself a second time.

"Enough!" I shout, silencing them immediately. "The patrols will cease for now. We will reassess after Maevstra. For now, let us enjoy the celebration. The remaining hunters will be back soon, and our clan will be reunited in its entirety. This is all that matters…" I pause. "Besides, what we do know of the draxilio is that we have been safe under the cover of the trees. As long as we stay within the forest, our clan will be fine."

They nod and mutter in agreement.

"We will not train this day. Go home. Rest. Prepare for the feast." I clap each of them on the shoulder as they leave.

Ahlvo and Bruvix linger behind. I tilt my head at them. "Why do you remain here?"

"You do not look well, brother." Ahlvo shakes his head in disapproval. "I expected a healthy flush to your skin and a spring in your step, with all the time you have spent with your inara."

I clench my jaw at the term. "Well, I do not think she wishes to be my inara. I told her what the word meant in our language and she left."

"The tether exists. It is real. How can she possibly deny it?" Bruvix asks, astonished.

"The tether exists for me. She does not feel it. Not the same way. It is different for humans."

"Humans. They are different in many ways. It makes my skull ache," Ahlvo agrees, seemingly distraught.

Bruvix strolls over to face the target wall and picks up a knife from the pile Cloh-ee and I left the previous night. He hurls it into the target with impressive precision. "Perhaps it was a mistake to bring them here. To think they could live among us."

Fury rises in my chest at the very thought of leaving them in that cage, for Bzzsil Chi to sell off to some other male in that room. The audacity of Bruvix to suggest such a thing. He is often in a foul mood, but this kind of thinking is unacceptable. Our lives have been different since their arrival, this is true, but different does not mean bad. In fact, with the way the three of them have pitched in to help members of the clan, our lives have improved.

I think of Cloh-ee's kind heart and how she smiles and greets each member of the clan when she sees them. How worried she was when she thought my injury had gotten worse, how easily she has adapted to life on Oluura despite being ripped from her home planet and ending up in Bzzsil Chi's cage. She has been warm, grateful, and eager to contribute.

I consider what could have happened to Cloh-ee and the females had we not attended that auction, and it twists my insides. Ultimately, they are safer here than they would have been anywhere else, and that is what matters. Conflict or even a disruption in our day-to-day lives as they learn to mesh with our people seems a meager sacrifice if the alternative for them is slavery or death.

"It was the right thing to do. I will never regret it," I say, attempting to rub the exhaustion off my face.

Ahlvo catches Bruvix's eyes and nods his head toward the door. "Perhaps you should follow your own command, brother, and rest up before Maevstra begins."

I let them leave without another word, flinching when I hear the front door slam shut behind them.

Ah, the silence of an empty house. It used to calm my busy mind. I would long for it at the end of a day filled with training alongside my crew. Now all I hear are the echoes of Cloh-ee's tinkling laughter, and it's a painful reminder of the happy life that was never meant for me.

I pick up an empty glass jar from the shelf and throw it against the wall. It shatters, and I smile at the burst of noise. It is not the sound I wanted to hear, but it was better than the crushing silence.

I stare at the scattered shards, too frustrated to clean them up. I grunt and climb the steps to my bedroom.

Perhaps rest is indeed the best use of my time, I decide.

* * *

I MAKE my way toward the hall, the steady beat of the drums hammering in time with my heart. The sky has darkened through the trees, and the smell of seasoned meats fills my nose.

The lilting sound of the mussashk harp being played instantly brightens my mood, and I force myself to focus on the celebration I am about to join.

There are long wooden benches lined up outside of the meal hall, spilling onto the main path of the village. The drummers are seated in a half circle to the left of the meal hall, with the mussashk harpist front and center. People are dancing to the lively song they are playing as others sit and eat. Bruvix's signature ale is spilling over the tops of mugs everywhere I look. Douku orbs of all sizes sit in the low branches of the trees and cover the soft moss on the ground surrounding the hall, making it appear as if the celebration itself is tucked inside a ball of twinkling light.

My chest swells with pride at the sight of my clan laughing and drinking without a care in the world. Each time we welcome a new season, and I get to watch the clan celebrate, I am reminded that leaving Trovilia was the best choice I have ever made. That the effort to rebuild our lives on Oluura, the struggle to adapt, the ache of homesickness—it was all worth it because we are here, alive and together.

My stomach reminds me that I have not eaten today, and I let it lead me toward the platters of seasoned meat and bread. "This is what you have been working on, Waldric? The entire forest smells of heaven. You have done well," I tell him as he fills my plate.

"I thank you, Varrek. It took many days to get the blend of the seasonings just right." He smiles warmly.

Bruvix thrusts a full mug of ale into my hand as he passes by, slurring his words as he mumbles about how "this is the best batch yet."

I hear a loud cackle behind me, and I turn to see it is Nalba. She leans heavily on Lahkzo, one of the hunters we were waiting on to return, as she empties her mug of ale.

209

My eyes scan the crowd, looking for Cloh-ee, and when I see her approaching the feast, I suck in a breath.

Her thick curves are wrapped deliciously in a deep-green dress. It is a green that is the same shade as my eyes, and I wonder if the color choice was intentional. It hugs her body in a way that makes my cock pulse against my pants.

The top of the dress follows the shape of her frame, nipping in at the waist and flowing out, skimming the tops of her small feet. It has long, billowy sleeves that cover her pale skin to the wrist. The front, however, is open wide in a shape that exposes her delicate collar bones and comes to a point between her heavy breasts. Her skin is the color of snow, making the green of her dress look even richer in the soft light.

Her long, silky mane is pulled off her face in matching twists on either side of her head that meet at the nape of her neck and end in a loose ponytail draped over her shoulder.

Cloh-ee's eyes find mine, and she offers me a shy smile, her cheeks turning pink under my visual perusal. I see them swirl with desire, and I wonder if perhaps all is not lost with us. Maybe she has reconsidered her confusing babble from this morning and has decided to stay with me. My body moves in her direction before I realize my feet are in motion, the tether between us growing stronger.

We drift toward each other until we are face-to-face. I do not know what I should say, or not say, to her with this tension still lingering between us, but I blurt, "You are the most ravishing creature I have ever seen," and pray that I did not speak out of turn.

"You don't look so bad yourself, sir," she says, her voice low and husky as she straightens the collar of my shirt and then fiddles with my vest. She pauses, uncertainty flashing in her eyes, and drops her hands to her sides. "Look. About this morning...I want to apologize for the way I reacted. You put yourself out there and I-I froze."

"It is oka—"

"No, it's not," she interjects. "I was an asshole. You were vulnerable and honest, and that's all I've ever wanted from a partner. That's all anybody wants, really. My exes, each one of them lied or cheated, or both." She reaches out to squeeze my hand. "You are the opposite of everyone I've ever been with, and I mean that in the best possible way. The thing is, I need to speak with the girls first. I need to—"

"Attention, clan!" Tibik, the eldest member of the Hexrins, bellows to the crowd. His voice is deep, as if it comes straight from the planet's core, and even silences the chirps and buzzes of the insects in the forest. All who hear it cannot help but obey his commands. I suspect it is part of his power as a Hexrin, but I am still unfamiliar with the scope of their abilities. They keep to themselves for the most part, only leading the clan chants at our three seasonal feasts and assisting in urgent clan business when they can.

Tibik stands on one of the wooden benches with his silver hooded cloak floating in the wind behind him. His arms are raised as he waits for each of us to take a seat. The other members of the Hexrins stand behind him, ready to assist with anything he needs.

Cloh-ee looks back at me and whispers, "We'll talk later?"

"Yes, later," I agree.

She spots Aye-vah taking a seat on a wooden bench a few rows away and sits down next to her. The two huddle close and whisper as the clan settles in around them.

I watch, trying to listen to what they say, but there is too much chatter around them. It seems my mate requires permission, or a blessing of some sort, from her human companions in order to proceed with our mating. It must be a human custom.

Ahlvo sidles up to me and gives me a knowing smile. "The females look lovely this eve, do they not?"

"Shh, I am trying to listen," I hiss, leaning forward a bit in their direction.

"What are you listening for, brother?" he asks, mirroring my stance to do the same.

"Apparently it is custom for a human female to get permission from those closest to her before she is able to take a mate," I explain. "Cloh-ee is asking Aye-vah this now."

He huffs a breath in surprise. "I did not know of this custom."

"Nor I." Do Aye-vah and Kay-teh realize how much power they

hold? My entire future, my reason for existence is in their hands. *Have I been kind enough to them? Could I have done more to make them feel at home here?* A layer of sweat covers my palms as doubts fly through my mind.

Tibik's apprentices stand on either side of him, holding up a massive book, turning to the page he needs as he clears his throat. Ahlvo steers me toward an open seat on one of the benches as we abandon our attempt to eavesdrop on the females.

As Tibik begins with the history of the celebration, and what the coming wet season represents, I only half listen as I look for Kay-teh. Once Cloh-ee gets permission from Aye-vah, she will need to speak to Kay-teh, and once that is done, Cloh-ee will be mine. I find Kay-teh in the very back row of benches, eyes wide and locked on the treetops as she sits alone. She is worried about the draxilio she saw. I shall speak with her after the chant, I decide, to calm her nerves.

Tibik recites the chant in our native tongue once before he gestures for us to repeat it.

We join hands with clan members on either side of us and close our eyes as we chant in our native tongue,

We honor you, Goddess of Maevstra
And all that exists in your light
May you bless this land of Oluura
May you protect us in the darkness of night
We call upon your gracious energy
To bless us with a bountiful harvest
To rid us of painful memories
To remind us of where we started
We honor you now
We honor you always.

To end the chant, we shout, "Aye!" together, as a way of closing the blessing to the goddess.

Tibik does not recite the chant in the human tongue, but I see Kaiva whispering to my Cloh-ee and Aye-vah, so I think she is translating the chant in their language.

As the clan begins to rise from their seats and the music resumes, I go to Kay-teh, who is the only one that remains seated. "Kay-teh, are you enjoying the feast?"

She gives me a look I cannot decipher. "Why isn't anyone on dragon patrol tonight?" she asks, her tone stiff.

I sit down beside her. "I thought it best to cease patrols for the celebration. So that we could be together as a clan." I lightly pat her shoulder, wanting to comfort her but not knowing how best to do that. "We are safe within the forest. *You* are safe, Kay-teh."

Her shoulders slump forward, and I notice the dark circles beneath her eyes. She is worn. The draxilio sighting has been tormenting her mind. "Okay, yeah. Okay," she mutters before making her way toward the food. Sustenance will do her good.

I hope.

Ahlvo is speaking with some of the warriors about…something. I am not listening to their words, but I come to stand among them anyhow. Instead of joining the conversation, I watch as Cloh-ee and Aye-vah are handed mugs of ale from Bruvix and take generous sips as they approach Kay-teh, her plate piled high with food.

This is it. Cloh-ee is going to get Kay-teh's permission, and then she will be mine.

I do not breathe. I do not look away. My gaze is locked on the three tiny humans as they speak. They are too far for me to hear, and I cannot read their mouths as they speak their strange language, so I pay close attention to the expressions they wear on their faces.

Kay-teh's mouth is full as she chews a piece of meat, while Cloh-ee speaks and Aye-vah looks on. Aye-vah nods in agreement with Cloh-ee's words and adds something more. Kay-teh's face remains neutral, and she says nothing.

She takes a swig of ale and then seems to ask a question. Cloh-ee and Aye-vah share a gaze, seemingly mystified, and then it is Cloh-ee who responds. Kay-teh's eyes roll, and she raises her hands, ale in one and plate of food in the other, in defeat before walking away.

I do not know what to make of this.

But in the next moment, Cloh-ee wraps her arms around Aye-vah, her smile bright, before releasing her and strolling toward me.

I hear my name mentioned by Ahlvo, but I do not care to respond. My feet take me toward my inara, my heart in my throat, not knowing what her words will bring: sorrow or elation. She grabs my hand and pulls me away from the noisy crowd to the side of the hall.

"How did it go? Did you get permission from the females?" I ask as I pull her to me and cup her soft face in my hands.

Her eyes narrow in confusion. "Permission? Oh, I was asking if the girls were okay with staying here."

I wait for her to continue, but she just traces the planes of my chest with her finger. "And are they?"

"Yes! Well, Ava is. Kate just said, 'Like we have any other choice?' so I think that's a yes for now." She pulls me down by my vest and rubs her nose against mine. "So…like I was saying befo—"

"Cloh-ee! There you are, you little human baby," Nalba shouts as she stumbles toward us.

"Nalba, not now," I growl. She doesn't hear me though, or she chooses to ignore me, as she trips over her own foot and bumps into us.

"Ah, the pretty, pretty people." Her acidic ale breath fans our faces as she pokes at our cheeks.

She grabs Cloh-ee's hand and pulls her along, back toward the crowd. I follow, frustration boiling my insides at the interruption. Cloh-ee is being kind to Nalba and letting her drunken ramble continue, but the moment it is over, I will be pulling Cloh-ee away from here so we may speak privately.

"How ya feeling, Nalba?" Cloh-ee hollers over the music as she holds Nalba up.

Nalba pulls away to snag a full mug from a nearby table and puts her empty one in its place. "Mmm. I feel like a dunchya bird taking its first flight—invigorated and seeking the crisp air on my bare nethers."

"Wow, okay, then," Cloh-ee chuckles. "I'll have what you're having."

Nalba howls with laughter at Cloh-ee's response and wraps her hands around Cloh-ee's shoulders. "Varrek, did you know this little human is my favorite? She is so clever and silly, and her bones are like feathers." She tickles Cloh-ee as Cloh-ee squirms and tries to pull away, a strained smile on her face. "How easily we could snap her into many bits. The fact that her body carries her around each day and does not crumble is miraculous."

"Nalba, that is enough," I warn through gritted teeth.

"O fah." Nalba waves her hand near my nose dismissively as she takes another big sip of ale.

"Do you see this lovely dress Cloh-ee has on, Varrek? Is it not a vision against her pale skin?" she asks.

"Of course. Cloh-ee is a vision in anything she puts on her body. She glows like starlight." I let my eyes travel over Cloh-ee once more in the green dress.

"You see, Cloh-ee? I told you he would love it," she says, her gaze unfocused.

Nalba has a tendency to do everything with ferocity—whether it be research, innovation, or feasting. And when there is ale in abundance, Nalba does not stop pouring it down her throat until it reemerges with the rest of the contents from her stomach.

She also becomes quite loud and obnoxious. Usually, this behavior is easy to ignore. Sometimes her drunken antics are even humorous. But they are certainly not in this moment. Especially since I am about to find out if my inara has decided to stay with me forever or crush my heart into dust by deciding to leave.

"I am happy to see you enjoying the feast, Nalba. Now, if you will excuse us…" I gesture for her to return to the celebration.

Her eyes narrow at me as she shakes her head back and forth disapprovingly. "Varrek, are you still hiding your past from your pretty mate? Because I do not think Cloh-ee would be bothered by it. You are being a foolish fool, truly."

She tries to pat my shoulder, but I brush her hand away angrily. I do not respond, to avoid drawing additional attention to her comments. I need this moment to pass like a leaf floating in the water.

Cloh-ee giggles. "What is she talking about?"

Nalba sways again and rests her folded arm on Cloh-ee's shoulder for support. "Tell her, Varrek."

"O fah, it is nothing. Just a joke. Nalba does not know what she says," I spit out as a bead of sweat forms and runs down the length of my spine. This is not good.

Please, Nalba. Please do not respond, I silently beg.

"Bikar? No, this is no joke. You wish for me to do it? Fine, I shall do it." She takes a deep breath, and a belch escapes her before she continues. "You see, Varrek was the Prince of Trovilia. And his father, King Muryk, lost his brain to madness. Then Varrek faked his own death to escape Trovilia." She turns to me. "He brought us along with him, and that is the story of how we came to Oluura."

The music has stopped. The feasting has stopped. The drinking, the dancing, the happy chatter from the clan. Everyone is watching us. Silence fills the air, and I feel as if I am drowning in it. She knows. Cloh-ee knows I have lied.

I fear I have just lost her forever.

CHAPTER 20

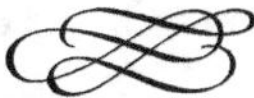

CHLOE

I can practically feel the nervous energy flowing off of Varrek's rigid body. His face is frozen. I haven't even had the chance to ask him if it's all true or not. But his body language does not bode well.

"Um, what? You were a prince?" I'm not sure where I should even begin, but that seems like a good place to start.

Nalba, clearly not taking the hint that she should exit this conversation, responds for him. "Oh, yes. Prince Varrek was beloved throughout all of Trov—"

"Nalba, that is enough!" Varrek bellows, his gaze murderous.

Nalba's buzz seems to shield her from properly sensing Varrek's wrath, so she attempts to take another sip from her empty mug, and upon realizing she's already emptied it, she grunts in disappointment, shrugs her shoulders, and stumbles away.

Varrek's chest heaves for a few more moments until Nalba is completely out of sight, and his fearful expression returns. Still, he says nothing.

"Is it true?" I ask again.

He sighs. "Yes, it is true."

"What about the rest of the stuff she said? Was that all true too?" I can't believe I'm only now finding out that my mate, at least...that's what I thought he was, used to be a prince? And that he hid it from me. "What did she mean about your dad? The madness? What madness?"

Varrek takes a cautious step toward me and lets out a breath. "My father, the king, was not well after the virus took my mother. His mind began to rot as he sought comfort in his rage and focused only on avenging her death. He was convinced that the virus was intentionally sent to poison and kill our people. You remember I told you about the virus that killed our females, yes?"

"Yes, I remember." I think back to the story he told us on the ship and with it the warning that the male members of the clan would be interested in us, not having seen an unmated female since the virus ravaged his planet. My heart broke for him and his clan.

"My father became desperate for revenge against the virus's planet of origin, D'Alluk. He planned an attack—"

"Varrek, would you prefer I tell this tale? I do not mind," Ahlvo interrupts, his brow furrowed in concern.

"It must be me, Ahlvo," Varrek replies before continuing. "I tried, many times I tried, to convince my father that attacking the D'Allukans was absurd and cruel. That it would solve nothing and only cause more pain." He rakes his fingers through his neatly braided hair, snagging a few strands and creating uneven bumps. "He did not listen. Rather, he chose not to, knowing he could get unequivocal support from the veteran warriors who were also grieving their mates. When I refused to lead the attack, he poisoned me."

"Poisoned you? Your father actually poisoned you?" I cannot believe what I'm hearing. I knew the Trovilians were capable of brutality, but not against their own kind. Everyone has been so welcoming to us here. Then again, I've only met the ones who fled.

"Yes, Kaiva nursed me back to health. My father was determined to accomplish his goal, with or without me." Varrek sighs heavily.

I think about what he's endured. It's devastating.

"That is when Ahlvo and I devised our plan to escape Trovilia, as we became certain that staying would lead to war, and ultimately, our deaths." He looks at Ahlvo, respect and appreciation shining in his eyes. "We planned our escape, who we would bring, and where we would go. I apologized to my father for standing in his way. I agreed to join the mission. To attack D'Alluk. I was replaced as general by a veteran warrior on his war council, but my father was pleased that I came around to his way of thinking."

Varrek stops, pinching his eyes closed, as if physically pained by the memories. I hate seeing him distraught, but I need him to keep talking. I need to know the truth. "We arrived on D'Alluk, and my responsibility was to stay by the ship, the *Striker*..." He trails off. "I did, for a while, and then...the veteran warriors. They attacked the village. There were dead bodies all around us."

He drops his face into his hands, his whole body slouching forward in shame.

Then he opens his eyes and straightens. "We stopped them. We let the warriors loyal to my father back on the *Striker*, and we killed them. All of them. The rest of us took over the *Striker*, and we met Ahlvo's father, Rumo, just outside of the D'Alluk atmosphere and boarded that ship, which held the clan. We set the *Striker* to autopilot back to Trovilia and remote detonated the bombs we placed all over it once we were a safe distance away. And we continued here."

"You made it look like you died on the *Striker*," I conclude. "Everyone."

Varrek nods solemnly. "Yes, and in destroying Trovilia's largest vessel, we prevented my father from successfully attacking D'Alluk in the future. At least, that was the hope."

I feel several pairs of eyes burning into my back, but I find it impossible to care while I take in all the information Varrek just threw at me.

I'm feeling so many things at once it's hard to pin down each emotion. Sorrow is probably the most prominent because clearly Varrek is still struggling with the aftermath of battle, leaving his home, and his father's attempt to poison him. Of course he is. I can't imagine living through all that and then leading an entire clan as they struggle to survive on a new planet. He's had to be the strong one, the steady one. He hasn't been given the space to grieve for what he's lost. For the gruesome sights he's seen.

Then right behind sorrow, there's anger. Why did he keep this from me? A lie by omission is still a lie. He chose to hide a huge part of his past from me, his mate, his "inara." How can I really mean that much to him if he won't even tell me who he is? It's not like I couldn't keep his secret. Like I would tell anyone the Prince of Trovilia is alive and well and living on Oluura? I'm just a human lost in space. Who would even listen to me?

I'm also slightly confused. It feels as if there's a part of this story that's missing. Though I don't understand why he would bother sharing such a painful story and leaving parts of it out, but who knows? I'm playing catch-up here as it is.

Confusion leads me right back to anger at the realization that he might still be lying. I would have no way of knowing. It feels like the Varrek I've known up to now is a stranger. Will I ever be able to trust him again? What if I can't? How could we be mates if there's no trust?

My heart rate speeds up, and my breaths become shallow to match it. It feels like the entire clan is standing in a tight circle around me, and there's no opening for me to escape. I know this isn't the case, but it feels like I have no room to breathe, and I need to get out of here or else I'll pass out.

"I, um, I need to take a walk," I mutter, dizziness starting to consume me.

Varrek takes a step toward me. "Cloh-ee, I—"

"Varrek." I put up my hands to stop him. "You shared a lot with me just now. But you also lied. I need time to think. To process." I trudge through the soft moss as I head toward my house. The wind whips through my hair, chilling the exposed skin of my chest, and I wrap my arms around myself as a shield.

Just before I reach the front door, I hear footsteps. I turn to find Varrek jogging toward me, his mouth in a grim line.

"Why? Tell me why," I demand. I asked for space, and now he's here, and I find myself getting increasingly annoyed that my wishes were ignored.

"Why I did not tell you?" he asks.

"Why did you lie?" I correct.

Varrek gulps. "I did not think you would understand. I was afraid that you would no longer see the male you have come to know. In his place, you would see only the traitorous coward who faked his death and abandoned his home."

"I wouldn't understand? You don't get to make that call. You should trust me enough to be honest and to have your back." My eyes are filling with tears, and I take short, slow breaths to stop them from falling. "If you can't do that, then how can this even work—you and I?"

He flinches, like my words are a knife cutting into his side. "You deserve better than me, Cloh-ee. I am not worthy of your heart. I have known this all along."

Tears spill onto my cheeks. I can't hold them back anymore. His heart is breaking in front of me, and his betrayal is breaking mine as well.

Not only that, but he said he "doesn't deserve me," which is exactly what Drew said right before he left. Moments after I caught him in a lie. This is a nightmare. A nightmare I've already lived through. I can't do this again.

"I need to go to bed. I need to sleep on this. We can talk in the morning, okay?" I open the door, my hands shaking.

"May I come and see you later? Across our branch?" Varrek asks, his tone hopeful but uncertain.

The thought sends a flash of excitement through me, but almost immediately, it's replaced with dread. I can't be near him right now. I need to clear my head and figure out how I feel and what I want. "I will come to you when I'm ready to discuss everything."

"Very well, Cloh-ee." His voice is strained. He sounds so disappointed. "I will wait for you."

The list of things I almost say to him is endless. I want to jump into his arms and tell him it's okay. That I forgive him. That we can work through this. There's also part of me that wants to tell him he's a dick for not trusting me.

I end up mumbling, "Okay, thanks," instead and shutting the door.

I muster up every ounce of strength in my body just to climb the steps to my room and throw myself down on the bed. I don't even turn on the lanterns. Darkness matches my mood, so I leave it that way and let it wrap around me.

I was ready to stay. Forever. I had officially let go of the hope of ever returning to Earth. It seemed unlikely anyway, since we hadn't found any safe transportation, or any transportation at all, really. But still. I was ready to make Oluura my home.

I even pulled Kate and Ava aside to make sure they were on board with staying too. I wouldn't have decided to stay unless they also wanted to, because they're all the family I have left. Whatever we do, I want us to do it together.

Ava was happy to stay. Kate just screamed, "Like we have any other options?" with a mouth full of meat, but I wasn't expecting a straight yes from Kate anyway, so that seemed close enough.

I like life on Oluura. I like helping Nalba with her inventions. I like living in a village of treehouses and waking up to a giant sexy alien licking my pussy until I come. It's a hell of a way to start the day. Plus, Varrek taught me how to defend myself. He was sweet and affectionate, and the way he looked at me...it was with so much desire. Almost as if he waited entire lifetimes to find me.

Now all of that is tainted. I don't know what was real and what was part of his web of lies. Was it all bullshit? When we practiced throwing knives and asked each other questions, were his answers real? It's hard to believe he would lie about any of that, but he was a prince and didn't tell me. He faked his own death and didn't tell me.

What if Nalba didn't spill his secret tonight? When was he going to reveal this to me? I think I would've found out once we did the blood bond and our minds became linked, because how would he have hidden anything? But the thought of becoming his eternal mate and then discovering the truth terrifies me. Would Varrek have let that happen?

Suddenly, a wave of homesickness washes over me. I miss coffee. I miss getting pizza delivered to my apartment. I miss scrolling mindlessly on my phone. I miss wearing underwear. I miss Jenn. And Reggie. The only animals around here seem to want to eat me.

My life on Earth wasn't magical. It certainly wasn't a fairytale. There was comfort in the monotony of it all though. In the routines. I was fine with being alone. Well, I was newly heartbroken, but I would've felt fine eventually. Now I'm going through my second heartbreak in a month, and I feel like such an idiot.

I curl into my pillow and scream into it, letting it absorb the noise as I pull my blanket over my head. I toe off my boots and tug the blanket over the rest of my body until I'm covered completely.

I feel a little bad about abandoning the celebration, but if I stayed, I'd be the hot mess in the corner crying into her mug of ale. Nobody likes that girl. Suffering in silence is better.

* * *

I WAKE up some time later to my pillow clutched tightly to my chest. It's still dark outside, but I no longer hear the music or crowd noise from the celebration, so it must be really late.

My mind has a moment of peace before memories of the night before come flooding in. I feel bile rising in my throat and decide I need some fresh air.

Now that the party is over, I can walk around outside without running into anyone. They're probably all passed out and on their way to killer hangovers.

I slink downstairs on bare feet so I don't disturb Kate and Ava as I pass their rooms. I have my boots in hand and slip them on once I reach the main floor.

I slowly pull open the front door, just wide enough for me to slip through, and close it quietly behind me. I look toward the food hall and find it empty, but just in case there are a few clan members still milling about, I go the other way.

Because it's still dark out, I don't dare enter the thick of the forest. I'm not about to become breakfast for a tr'gory simply because I'm sad. So I pass Varrek's house and continue on. I pass two more houses on my right before I take a few steps on a path into the forest. The path is wide, so I'm technically in the forest but still exposed and close enough to the village that I don't feel unsafe.

The air is colder, and foolishly I forgot to grab a blanket to wrap around my shoulders, so I shiver as I lean against a thick tree trunk. I wrap my arms around my middle and take a few breaths. This is all I need, and I'll head back home in a minute. Just a couple more lungfuls of crisp air.

I close my eyes as I breathe in and out. It's the closest I've ever come to successfully meditating as I focus on the breath and try to ignore how cold I am.

Then the hairs on the back of my neck rise, and my skin prickles with alarm. I open my eyes to find a massive gold-skinned man standing in front of me. I don't recognize him. And his armor is thick and encrusted with jewels.

His eyes are pure black, and the grin that spreads across his face is ominous.

"Oh, I—"

His large hand covers my mouth, and I feel a pinch just above my collarbone. I gasp against his palm, and he watches me, waiting for something.

There's a numbness filling my limbs from the bottom up. I feel… tired. A bone-deep exhaustion that I desperately want to fight, but I can't.

I go to scream, but the sound dies in my throat as the ground rises to meet me.

CHAPTER 21

VARREK

My eyes blink open as sunlight streams through the window. It seems I've fallen asleep facedown on the window ledge, waiting for my Cloh-ee to come to me in the darkness. I sat here for hours after she retired to her chambers, hoping for her to visit me, or at least to catch a glimpse of my sweet inara in her room. Neither occurred though. Her room remained dark the entire eve.

She said she would come to me when she was ready, and she has yet to do that. I want to be patient, but I am so filled with guilt and shame at how she discovered my past that I must see her and apologize, again.

Nalba.

I growl at the thought of her name. That devious monk slug. I cannot believe she has ruined everything Cloh-ee and I have built. It felt like she was on the verge of agreeing to be my mate.

My skin tingles with desperation to see Cloh-ee. It has been far too long since I have touched her softness or been wrapped in her sweet scent.

I straighten my rumpled clothing that I have worn since the previous day and slowly climb across the branch to Cloh-ee's room. I step inside and find it completely dark. The blankets are twisted into a messy pile, but Cloh-ee does not slumber beneath them. She is not here.

I pull back the blankets, just to be sure, and when my suspicions are confirmed, I scan the rest of the room, finding her scent to be somewhat weak. She has not been here for perhaps many hours. I find this quite troubling because if she is not here, where could she be?

Unease speeds up my heart, but I tell myself that there must be an explanation. That she slumbers with the other human females, maybe, seeking their comfort. I step gingerly down the stairs, not knowing which room belongs to which female. I open the door to the room on the floor below Cloh-ee's and find one human female asleep in bed.

"Hello? Aye-vah?" I say quietly. I want to wake her, but I do not want to scare her in the process.

She rubs her eyes with her small fists and sits up. "Huh? Varrek? What's going on?" She groans and stretches her arms above her.

I step deeper into the room, looking for signs of my mate, finding none. "Aye-vah, apologies for disturbing your slumber. I cannot find Cloh-ee. Do you know where she is?"

Aye-vah yawns and rises from her bed. "What do you mean? She's not in her room?"

"No, I was hoping she would come to see me, but she did not. And she is not in her room now."

Aye-vah blinks a few times, sleep disappearing from her face, and in its place, concern appears. "That's weird."

She jogs down the steps, and I follow close behind. She swings open the door, calling for Kay-teh. The fire-haired human is already awake and staring out her window at the sky above. She turns at our entrance, dark circles under her eyes.

"What is it?" Kay-teh asks, her tone flat.

Aye-vah runs her fingers through the puff of her tight curls nervously. "Chloe isn't in bed. Did she come by your room at all? To say where she was going, maybe?"

"Nope. Haven't seen her," Kay-teh replies, turning back around to the window to resume her staring. "I'm sure she just went for a walk or something."

Aye-vah puts a hand on my arm. "She's right. Let's head outside."

We walk up and down the main path of the village and do not find my Cloh-ee. We ask everyone we pass if they have seen her. None have.

Fear fills my chest. Cloh-ee knows we are on high alert because of the tr'gorys and the draxilio sighting. She would not wander the forest alone. My Cloh-ee is smart and cautious.

Aye-vah and I are discussing the strangeness of the situation when Ahlvo bursts through the front door of his house and charges toward us.

"Varrek! Varrek, there is a message. You have received a message. On the private comm line." Ahlvo shoves his screen pad in front of me and presses play.

It is fuzzy at first, but as the recording clears, I see Cloh-ee's face. She is asleep on a floor of some kind. A ship, I think. Her lips are parted, and her lovely green dress is slightly torn at the neck. There is a red welt on her cheek, as if she has been struck.

I grip the screen pad tight enough for the screen to crackle briefly before Ahlvo takes it from my hands and holds it in front of me.

The recording cuts away from Cloh-ee's face, and I see...my father. He glares at the screen. At me. His smirk wicked. He has aged significantly since I have been gone. He looks haggard and weak, but the evil remains. It darkens his eyes.

Then he speaks. "I have your human pet. Cease this foolishness and come home, or she dies."

The recording stops. My heart with it.

"How did he find us? When did he take her? How were we unable to detect his ship's approach?" Ahlvo asks more questions I do not have answers to. We need to find these answers, that is certain, but I can think of nothing beyond the fact that Cloh-ee is gone. She has been taken from me. She has been hurt.

"Oh god," Aye-vah gasps. Her breath quickens, and I can hear her soft cries.

I fall to my knees on the mossy ground. I cannot get air into my lungs. I feel it in my mouth, but that is where it stops before it escapes my lips in short huffs.

This cannot be. My mate has been stolen away, by my father. My hands dig into the moss and soil as rage boils the blood within my veins. I tear out the moss and toss the mushy clumps of it to the side as I throw my head back in a primal roar.

I leap to standing. My chest heaving. My fangs and claws extended, poised to shred. "Ahlvo, tell the clan. Ready the speeder ship. Fill it with weapons. I will meet you there shortly."

"Varrek, we need a plan," Ahlvo warns.

I turn to face him. "I have a plan. I will travel to Trovilia. I will kill my father and every warrior who stands in my path. I will retrieve my inara. Then I shall bring her home."

"Where are you going now?" Ahlvo shouts as I storm away.

"Nalba's!" I yell back.

It does not take me long to reach Nalba's house. My mind is so clouded with outrage that it feels as if I floated here. Once I arrive, I kick the front door open, knocking it off the top hinge.

Nalba looks up, her mane wild and her face puffy. "O fah, it is you," she mutters bitterly before dropping her head in her hands.

"How dare you address me in such a way. Do you have any idea of the mess you have caused?" I chide her as I clench my fists at my sides.

"Why do you speak in such a loud manner? Your mate has to listen to this each morning when she wakes?" She rubs her temples, not looking at me. "I pity her."

Her head pops up suddenly. "Speaking of, where is your pretty little human? Death is dancing inside my skull, and Cloh-ee is always such a helpful creature. She would be getting me tea, tidying up my suppli—"

"Silence!" I scream, causing her to flinch. "Cloh-ee is missing! She was taken, and it is because of *you*."

"Wait...she is missing? Taken? What are you saying?" Nalba darts her eyes around, confused.

"My father has found us. He took Cloh-ee in the night and is keeping her on Trovilia until I return. He sent a message. If I do not come for her, he will kill her!"

Nalba sits there, stunned into silence. She looks down at her table, absently rubbing her finger against the grain of the wood.

"Well? Are you not going to apologize?" I demand.

"And…what might I apologize for?" Her eyes narrow at me.

My claws dig into my palms and draw blood. I feel the wetness on my calloused fingers as I glare at Nalba. Does she truly not know? Is she so oblivious to the havoc she wreaks? "For destroying my chance at eternal happiness? Let us begin there, Nalba."

She scoffs, infuriating me even more. "I do admit my recollection of the celebration is murky, but I find it hard to believe I have the power to impact your life in such a way."

My patience, if I had any at all when I entered, is now gone. "You told Cloh-ee of my past. She did not know. You told her just as she was about to agree to stay here, with me. To become my mate. You have ruined us. And now she has been taken!"

Nalba starts laughing, the sound maniacal. "Varrek. Oh, Varrek, you poor fool." She stands and walks toward me but stops to brace her hands on the edge of the table as another fit of laughter overtakes her. "It is *my* fault that Cloh-ee discovered your secret and was kidnapped by your father, the king? This is what you say? Do you joke with me?"

"This is not funny. Not in the least," I grit. "Do you do this because you are jealous? Of what I have with Cloh-ee?"

She straightens, clasping her hands together. "Varrek, your cock was quite fun to play with, and I enjoyed the many orgasms it gave me. But I would never be jealous of you and Cloh-ee. I do not want you as a mate. You annoy me. I believe I annoy you as well. Our compatibility was limited to pleasure. Even if you wanted me as your mate, I am certain I would rip my mane out if I were to spend all of my days by your side. You are not for me."

Her words are biting, but there is no malice in them. She speaks truth, simply in the most brutal of ways. That is Nalba. And she is right. We made exceptional pleasure mates, but whenever we were together, not mating, we drove each other mad.

She pats me on the shoulder. It's an attempt to comfort me, but it is not working. "You are angry with me because I did what you were too cowardly to do. That is the reason for this outburst."

"Excuse me?" I reply, aghast.

She sighs, frustrated. "Varrek, you did not treat your mate as a mate. She did not even know you were a prince. Did not know the people of our homeland think you are dead. You cannot keep such things from someone you plan to spend eternity with. Do you not think this would be important information for Cloh-ee to know when making her decision of whether or not to stay with you?"

Nalba walks back to her seat and plops down, then reaches for a box and begins digging through it. "You acted as if she is too fragile to see your scars. The vulnerable parts of your mind and soul. Perhaps she is physically weak. Fantastically weak. Humans tend to be. But if she is your mate, she will accept the parts you wish to hide from the world. She will cherish those parts as you. All of you."

I consider Nalba's words as I lower myself to sit on one of her stools. "That is…quite wise, Nalba. Simple, but wise."

She does not look up from her box of trinkets. "I know this. I am extremely wise, Varrek."

My mouth quirks up on one side. This is very true. Nalba's mind was the brightest on Trovilia. I did not want her to come to Oluura with us because of the history she and I share. Perhaps in spite of our history, I brought her along. It is because our people need her. She creates marvelous tools and products that make our lives here much easier than they could be. Oluura is much more primitive than Trovilia. But with Nalba's brain and the supplies she demands each time we go to Nu'Piix, she has ensured our survival here with her advanced technological gadgets. I am grateful for the work she does. Endlessly grateful.

"Do you know who else is extremely wise?" she asks, her eyes locked on me now.

I shake my head.

"Your Cloh-ee. She helps me name my creations." Nalba chuckles warmly. "She comes up with the greatest of names." She pulls out a small vial of liquid and holds it up. "Do you know what I named this? 'This Liquid That Extends Food Rations.' Do you know what she named it? 'The Snack Saver.' Is that not so much better?"

I smile, thinking of Cloh-ee and how clever she is. I am not surprised Nalba has enjoyed spending time with her.

Silence hangs heavy for a moment. We are both lost in our thoughts about Cloh-ee.

"Your father. He has found us?" she asks.

"Yes. I do not know how, but he has."

"What will you do?"

I scratch my jaw, imagining all the ways I will make him pay for what he's done. "I will kill him."

"Splendid!" Nalba cheers as she puts the box down and reaches inside another. She pulls out a few small items, rectangular and flat. "These will help with that."

She shows me where to hide these discreet weapons she has just finished making and how to use them. Once I feel confident that I will not accidentally kill myself trying to use them, I thank her. I also apologize for yelling at her, to which she says, "Just bring back little Cloh-ee, Your Majesty."

I race out of the forest at top speed and toward the ship. When I arrive, Kaiva, Rumo, Aye-vah, Kay-teh, Bruvix, and Ahlvo are huddled by the doors.

"Is it ready?" I ask Ahlvo.

He nods, his face solemn. "It is, brother."

"Very well. I shall be back with my mate as soon as it is done," I mumble, not knowing what else to say. I am confident I shall return, but I also know that my father will not simply let me go. Either he will die or I will. I do not care if it is the latter as long as Cloh-ee is safe. That is all that matters. Still, part of me understands that this might be the last time I see these people again, and I find it hard to look in their eyes.

Kay-teh is sobbing loudly, Aye-vah with an arm wrapped around her shoulder, trying to soothe her. Aye-vah is visibly distraught, but she is trying to be strong for Kay-teh. Bruvix, Kaiva, and Rumo look worried but are trying to mask it, for me. Ahlvo stands at the entrance of the door, a bloodthirsty look in his eyes.

He thinks he is coming with me. I will not let him.

"This is a solo mission, Ahlvo. I must go alone," I tell him, clasping his shoulder.

"No, brother. I will go with you. I will not let you face him on your own. Not after everything he's done."

"I cannot let—"

"Varrek, you need him," Bruvix interjects. "If you do not make it back, Ahlvo will make sure that Cloh-ee does."

Bruvix knows exactly what to say to entice me. I sigh, as I cannot argue with that. "Very well." I gesture for Ahlvo to head onto the ship with me.

We turn to face our loved ones.

"Do not fear. We shall return with Cloh-ee," I vow.

Ahlvo gives Kaiva and Rumo tight hugs, then turns to Aye-vah and presses his forehead to hers while giving her a look so full of promise and heat that I remind myself to question him about it when we have the time.

We nod and wave to them before we head onto the ship, the sliding doors hissing shut behind us. We go onto the bridge, which is much smaller than the one on the ship we use to go to Nu'Piix for trading goods. This ship is half the size and built for speed.

We take our seats at the controls and ready the ship for takeoff.

"It will take three days to reach Trovilia," Ahlvo says as he connects his screen pad to the ship's system and checks over our route maps.

"Plenty of time to practice," I mutter while I check our fuel levels.

"Practice what?"

I turn to him, adrenaline filling my insides. "All the ways to kill my father."

CHAPTER 22

CHLOE

I miss the glass cage. I miss the little scraps of fabric all over the floor. I miss the single water bowl. I miss all of it.

These are thoughts I never expected to have, but as I lie on the dirty floor of my new cage in the constant darkness that makes it impossible to tell what time it is—the steady drip, drip of a leaky pipe nearby—I long for that creepy glass box, poop bucket and all.

There's no bucket in here, just a square drainage grate against the back wall. I've learned that it's automatically rinsed once a day to clean out our business.

My bed is a hard metal bench half the length of my body, so I usually end up sleeping on the floor.

I'm pretty sure I'm in a dungeon, with the thick steel bars and slight echo that follows each sound. The cell I'm in is not the only one down here. It's one of many. I'm also not the only occupant. I hear whispers between other prisoners. All in unfamiliar languages I do not understand. Guess I'm the only human here.

Because of the never-ending darkness, it's hard to say how long I've been here. Maybe two days, maybe two weeks. I spent the first several hours screaming for help, then sobbing into the sleeve of my once-beautiful green dress, which is now covered in dirt and torn in several spots.

I can't believe I wasn't wearing my armbands when I was taken. *WTF, Chloe!* I was worried they'd make the arms of my dress bulk out too much and ruin the flattering fit. Now I'm in a cage with no way to defend myself, and my dress is ruined anyway.

What do they want with me? I wonder for the umpteenth time.

Then I replay the final moments before my capture that I can remember. Strangely, I find comfort in this exercise. Maybe because it feels like a puzzle I'm trying to solve, and once I find the missing piece in the deep corners of my mind, I'll be able to escape this nightmare and go back home. Back to Oluura. Back to Kate and Ava. Back to Varrek. Even Nalba. I miss them so much it hurts.

Okay, focus.

It was the middle of the night. I needed fresh air. I went outside and headed toward the forest, away from the hall, because I wanted to be alone, but I didn't go too deep into the forest because of the tr'gorys.

Oh yeah, the tr'gorys.

The encounter I had still lingers. Something about it doesn't make sense. Why did the tr'gory suddenly become aggressive when it saw Varrek? Why did it seem curious and even mildly...playful with me up until then? Could the difference be in the clan's scent, compared to the scent of humans? Could their biology be distantly linked to dogs on Earth? Maybe it's because it couldn't smell my fear at first?

Ugh, I don't know. It's another in a long list of questions I don't have answers to.

My mind drifts back to earlier that night, after the Maevstra celebration ended, when everything turned to shit.

I picture Varrek's face as Nalba drunkenly revealed his past. How pale he looked. Then how devastated he was when I told him I needed time alone to think. He took it as rejection.

I have every right to be angry at him, and a big part of me still is. But now that I'm locked in a prison cell, it's hard to hold on to that rage. There's also a big part of me that might, possibly, maybe love him. And I might never see him again. I could die here. The last thing I said to him was that I wanted to be alone. But I would happily sit on a knife if it meant I could soon be wrapped up in his big, strong arms.

A groan escapes me at the memory of my head pressed against his expansive chest after we made love. Our bodies lightly coated in sweat despite the cool night air blowing in through the open window. I was desperate for the feel of his fangs sinking into my skin. To become his eternal mate. And I almost let him bite me that night. If I had, and we completed the blood bond, he'd be in my head right now. I'd be able to tell him I've been kidnapped and that I'm in some sort of weird dungeon. I wouldn't be able to share many details beyond that, but maybe, just maybe, it'd be easier for him to find me.

An unfamiliar golden face pops into my mind, and I shudder. It's the face of the male who took me that night. He said nothing, but his menacing expression gave his intentions away. He wanted to harm me. I remember his fancy armor, so different from the armor Varrek's warriors wear, with the jewels lining the edges and ornate patterns etched into the center.

He clearly was not a member of the clan. But where did he come from? Was he from Varrek's homeland? Trovilia? Or are there other alien species with golden skin and silver hair?

What value am I to him?

I realize in that moment how out of my depth I am. I have no idea what's going on, or why I'm here, or how to escape. I feel helpless.

I get ready for another round of sobbing in the fetal position when the doors to the dungeon creak open. Since my arrival, I have seen the same guard come down here to deliver what look and taste like dry, stale patties of oatmeal and rubbery bags filled with water to each cell.

He's older. He's dressed in the same regal armor my captor had, but this one walks with a limp, and he has deep creases next to his eyes and mouth.

He opens the narrow food slot on my cell and stuffs my rations inside. I catch them before they fall onto the grimy floor and pour the fresh water into my mouth. My lips have been dry and cracked, so I'm grateful for the hydration.

I hear my cell neighbor whispering something to the guard. The language sounds familiar, possibly Trovilian, but I can't be certain, since I don't understand it. I nibble on my oatmeal patty as I lean my head against the bars, watching their conversation.

A shimmery white cloud forms around the guard, swirling rapidly, and in the next second, he transforms. He's taller, more muscular, and the wrinkles on his face disappear to reveal a much younger male. Then his silver hair turns maroon, and I gasp. A Hexrin. He's a Hexrin!

Hope fills my chest at the sight. Maybe he knows Tibik. Maybe he can get me out of here.

He hands something small to my cell neighbor before looking at me and pointing.

"Heh-llo? Hello, female?" my cell neighbor says in English, her accent thick.

"Hello? Hi! My name is Chloe. Can you help me? I need help," I stammer, silently praying that she can say more than a few words.

She's silent for a beat too long, and I start to wonder if I imagined the whole thing. But then she speaks. "I am called Ekoya. You are a human, yes?"

I introduce myself, and when she stumbles over my name the same way the clan does, I smile at the familiarity of it. "Yes, I'm human. How are you speaking English? Did this guy really transform into a Hexrin right before my eyes?"

The Hexrin gives my neighbor a panicked glance and then points from his head to his feet before turning back into the old male guard and taking a step farther away from me.

"How do you know that he is a Hexrin? How do you know this word?" she asks, her tone wary.

I'm not sure if revealing Tibik's current location is a good idea or a terrible one, but considering that this Hexrin has given my neighbor the ability to communicate with me, I feel like they might be on my side here and willing to help. So I choose honesty. "I've been living on Oluura, with Varrek and his clan. Tibik and a few other Hexrins are there too."

She gasps, and he says something to her that sounds like a question. She speaks in another language to him, presumably Trovilian, and I watch as his face lights up with a brilliant smile. He clasps his hands together and leans heavily against the bars of my neighbor's cell, as if he's unable to stand.

"Is he okay?" I ask, increasingly concerned.

"Oh, Cloh-ee, you do not know the happiness you provide with this information. This is Cruvo, my mate. He feared his Hexrin brothers and sisters were dead. He did not know they escaped with Varrek. He assumed, but he was not certain." Ekoya sighs, and I see her long gold fingers gently caress his cheek through the cell bars.

I rub my temples, trying to piece everything together. "Wait, so you know Varrek escaped? That he's alive? What else do you know? And why are you still locked in here if your mate can just let you out?"

She kisses Cruvo through the bars, and he leaves a moment later. "It appears we have much to tell each other, Cloh-ee."

* * *

I SIT down on the floor of my cell, hours later, trying to process all that Ekoya has told me.

She is one of only four Trovilian females out of thousands that actually survived the virus. The bodies of those who did not survive it were taken to a medical facility so that the healers of Trovilia could run tests and try to find a cure. Every family who lost someone to the virus agreed to their remains being used to find a cure.

Ekoya was one of the last females to contract the virus, by which time the healers had all but given up trying to find a cure. They were inundated with corpses. They were exhausted from working long hours and getting very little sleep. They had done extensive tests and research to find a cure, with nothing to show for it.

Their focus had shifted to the development of a vaccine. They had no use for the bodies at that point, so Ekoya, along with a few other females who appeared to have died, were basically forgotten about.

What the healers didn't realize, though, was that some victims developed a condition in the late stages of the virus that made them appear dead when they were still very much alive. Their vital signs dropped to undetectable levels, the healers theorized, as a way to prevent organ failure and give them time to recover without putting too much strain on the heart.

Ekoya's family thought she had died. They didn't have individual funerals for the victims of this virus. Too many had perished. So they had one big ceremony, honoring everyone they'd lost.

A few weeks after developing this condition, Ekoya woke up. The others did too. They've been kept in this dungeon ever since.

Apparently, King Muryk concluded that their families had already mourned for these females, so why send them back home if they could remain here and be of use? By "of use" he meant becoming lab rats for the healers to study, and ultimately, becoming breeders for Trovilian males, as a way to rebuild their race. The virus wreaked havoc on the bodies of the survivors, and King Muryk wanted to find out whether their fertility could be restored.

Ekoya and the others were taken from their cells every couple days to the medical lab, a few floors above us, to endure painful and invasive tests, tissue extractions, and other procedures that would provide enough data for the healers to determine if their bodies were able to carry a child to term. Based on the results of the experiments, their fertility seemed to be in good shape.

This new breeding program is King Muryk's obsession. Ekoya and the other Trovilian females are his "top choice" breeders, as he wants the bloodlines of any new children born to be "pure."

"Wait, can't your mating bond with Cruvo protect you from being used as a breeder? How can he expect you to mate with other Trovilian males when you're already mated?" I ask.

Ekoya sighs deeply. "The king has been trying to find a way to reverse the bond. He does not want it to hinder my ability to breed."

I shiver. What a vile male he is.

Ekoya continues, telling me that even if all four do get pregnant and carry the babies to term, it would mean only four new children born each year. The king wants more. So he's started scouring the seediest parts of the galaxy for kidnapped females of all species that he could buy and force into the breeding program. Ultimately, he doesn't care if these new children are only half-Trovilian, as long as he can ensure dozens of them are born each year.

Currently, King Muryk has acquired four non-Trovilian females for the breeding program, and Ekoya has confirmed that number includes me.

Upon hearing the grim fate that awaits me, I vomit the contents of my stomach all over the floor, so Ekoya decides to shift the conversation to Varrek and the clan on Oluura.

"Is-Is Nalba there? Is she well?" Ekoya asks, her voice shaking.

"Oh yeah, Nalba's there. She's great. I work with her in her shop, mostly trying to keep her organized, which is nearly impossible."

Ekoya chuckles knowingly. "Yes, that is Nalba. She is my sister. I miss her the most. I am happy she is happy though."

Poor Ekoya. I have a feeling she would've ended up on Oluura if she hadn't gotten sick. Instead, she's been stuck in this dungeon for years. I've only been here a handful of days, I think, and already I feel like my sanity is slipping away.

I tell Ekoya about Varrek, about how he's been calling me his "inara." Ekoya gasps when she hears this and spends the next few minutes gushing about what an honorable male Varrek is. She tells me story after story of times Varrek stood up for the people of Trovilia, the most vulnerable among them, and how everyone knew what a great king he would someday become. She remembers him fondly and was devastated when she heard he was killed in that explosion.

Her mate, Cruvo, is the one who informed her that Varrek didn't die. At some point, King Muryk learned that Varrek survived and was living on a remote planet with several other warriors whom he thought had died in that same explosion. That Varrek had deliberately sabotaged the mission to kidnap a large group of D'Allukan females.

"He saved their lives? The D'Allukan females?" I ask. He didn't say anything about that when I confronted him and demanded he tell me the truth about his past. He just briefly mentioned the carnage he saw on that mission.

"Why, yes. Cruvo told me that the warriors who were loyal to King Muryk slaughtered several D'Allukan males once they landed. That was part of the plan, to eliminate obstacles. Varrek and Ahlvo did not take part in that though. And when they rounded up the females who were to be brought back here, Varrek led them onto the ship, recorded their health scans, and made it look like they remained on the ship, but he let them go instead."

My jaw falls open.

Ekoya continues, and I wish she could see how undivided my attention is. "He killed the warriors who were loyal to King Muryk for the bloodshed they caused on D'Alluk."

My mind is spinning. I can't believe he did that. Actually, I can believe it. He traded his royal title and his relationship with his father in order to keep those innocent females from a life of rape and incarceration. He's honorable, right down to his core. And right now, he's back on Oluura thinking he doesn't deserve me. "How-How do you know all this? How did King Muryk find out?"

"My Cruvo is quite clever. He has the ability to take other faces, as you saw. The face he wore earlier was the face of a veteran warrior who served on King Muryk's war council. Cruvo killed him and has been taking his face to attend council meetings and share all that he learns with me. We mated before the virus, so he tells me through his mind. Do you know about this?" she asks.

"Yes, I'm now regretting not completing the blood bond with Varrek before I was taken." I sigh in frustration.

"Cruvo says that King Muryk discovered Varrek's treachery not long ago. Something about a necklace that Varrek traded at an auction as a form of payment. Once he found out, he reviewed the ship logs and recordings before the explosion and was able to confirm they were false. I do not know how he determined the rest."

My stomach sinks at the mention of the auction. It sounds like Varrek used a necklace to purchase Ava, Kate, and me, and that's how the king found out Varrek survived. This all happened...because Varrek saved me.

Then confusion mangles my thoughts. "Why did they kidnap just me? I mean, if all the king needs is more breeders, why didn't he kidnap Nalba, or even the other humans on Olurra? Is this to get back at Varrek?"

Ekoya hums for a moment before answering. "Cruvo thinks that you are bait to bring Varrek back here. King Muryk has told his war council that once Varrek arrives, he plans to sentence him to death for his crimes. He will be killed, and you will be part of the breeding program."

"Did you just ask Cruvo that?"

"Yes, through the bond," Ekoya replies, her tone slightly dreamy.

To be honest, I'm jealous of their bond. I would love to have that right now. I wish I could tell Varrek not to come back here. That it's a trap.

I find a vomit-free spot on the floor of my cell and sit back down. I can't do anything for him while I'm locked in this cage.

"But you should not fear, Cloh-ee."

My brow furrows. "What do you mean?"

"I have been planning our escape for some time." Ekoya's tone turns wicked. "Cruvo has been helping me. You will not be stuck here for much longer."

"When?" I ask, desperate to do everything in my power to get the fuck out of here.

"Cruvo has given me the keys to the cells. We wait for his signal to leave. It will be this night. Then we shall attack the guards and storm the council room. That is where King Muryk spends all his time, apparently." She pauses. "Cruvo has secured us the weapons we need. Do you have any skills to attack? Can you handle a weapon? Any weapon?"

My lips curl into a smile. "Yes, a knife. I can use a knife."

Ekoya lets out a pleased and excited laugh. Then a moment later, she chokes out a gasp and whispers a string of Trovilian words I don't understand.

"What? What is it?" I demand, worry fraying my nerves as I clutch the cell bars.

"Varrek. He is here. The time has come."

CHAPTER 23

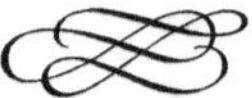

VARREK

I did not know how it would feel to return to my planet of origin. Now that we are here, I am stunned to find that I do not care for it. I was certain I would find beauty in the familiar red skies and inky blue sands. The very sands on which I learned to walk as a child. Only when we first entered Trovilia's atmosphere and viewed it from a distance did my heart swell with affection for this place.

The closer our ship got to the planet's surface, though, and the port just outside of Ahlvo's village, the more my stomach tightened with anxiety and fury. This is now a place of painful memories, of my father abusing his power and his people. It is also a place where my mate is being held against her will. And so I shall rip down every wall that separates us and slice the throats of all who keep me from her.

The moment our ship touches down, Trovilian warriors surround us. We expected this. My father is no fool. He may see me as the cowardly boy who turned his back on his royal title, but he also knows what I am capable of, and as such, he requires protection.

Ahlvo and I spent the three days on the ship going through every possible scenario, practicing with every weapon we packed, and devised a plan. The larger weapons—the swords, the guns, the bows and arrows—we chose to leave on the ship. We knew they would be confiscated the moment we arrived, so we did not bother to strap them on. But the weapons we could safely conceal? We put them all over our bodies and hidden beneath our clothes.

Nalba, though she is often a pebble in my boot, is a very clever female. The small, discreet weapons she has developed during our time on Oluura are not known to the Trovilian warriors. And what they do not recognize, they will not seize. We hope.

After we are searched—none of our concealed weapons taken from us—we are led off the ship and marched by a large group of warriors through the surrounding villages to the castle, their new general leading the way. I do not recognize him. I do not recognize any of them. This does not surprise me, as we killed most of the warriors that did not accompany us to Oluura.

My father had to recruit an entirely new crew, and he has. I wonder why these males fight for my father. Do they have no dignity? No honor? Or are they being forced into it?

"You know who you fight for, yes?" I ask as we walk past the villagers. They stand outside of their homes, eyes narrowed on me and Ahlvo. Sweat begins to cover my skin and seep through my layers, but I don't dare remove anything. I forgot how much warmer it is here year-round.

The warrior directly to my right stiffens and clears his throat before answering. "We fight for Trovilia. To ensure peace for our people."

I scoff. "And yet you point guns and blades at two of your own right this moment."

The warrior to my left shoves the butt end of his gun directly into my ribs, causing me to fall to my knees. "You are not one of us. You are a traitor to your king," he grits above me.

Ahlvo releases a menacing growl behind me, and though I cannot see him, I can hear him shoving the guards.

"No, Ahlvo," I mutter between ragged breaths. "Save your energy. This is not the fight we seek." Then I am hauled to my feet once more, and we continue on. Luckily, with this kind of escort, they do not bother restraining us. But if we get into a scrap with these guards, that will likely change.

When we enter the castle, the vast empty halls fill me with a deep sense of loneliness. After my mother died, I hated living in this place. The laughter, the warmth, the general softness of it all, she took it with her. It became a cold, drafty compound with two miserable, lonely males. It has not changed a bit since I have been gone.

We are taken to the war council room because nothing fills my father's charred lump of a heart with joy quite like vengeance. He assumes he will achieve it this day. I have to stifle a laugh at the thought. He assumes he will get what he wants from me and his leverage is my human "pet." He has no idea he has come between a Trovilian male and his eternal mate and therefore will be surrounded by the bodies of his fallen warriors before I unleash my wrath upon him.

I know I have lost my chance with Cloh-ee. She does not trust me, and for that, I do not blame her. But she is still my mate, whether or not we complete the blood bond, so I will gladly give my life to ensure her safety. She will be freed, and she will return to Oluura. If I do not get to return to Oluura by her side, so be it.

My father does not rise when Ahlvo and I enter the room, flanked by several guards. He does not even lift his gaze to mine. He flicks his wrist, and half of the guards leave without a word.

"Where is she?" I demand.

He sits, silently, looking at a map in front of him spread across the table. "Now, is that any way to address your father?" he murmurs flatly. "Your king?"

"You are not my king," I spit.

He stands before walking slowly toward me. He stops an arm's length away and gives me a cold stare. "I gave you life, you traitorous boy. I gave you riches. I gave you a crucial role that would prepare you to take over my throne one day. I gave you everything, and you ran away like a frightened child."

I laugh, and I do not even try to hold it back this time. "Oh, what a sense of humor you have. I do not remember this about you." I turn to Ahlvo. "Is he not a master of jokes?"

Ahlvo gives me a bloodthirsty smirk and nods.

I shift my gaze back to my once handsome and sophisticated and formidable father, who looks so incredibly weak that I barely recognize him. His hair is still the same silver color as my own, but it is stringy and flat. His upper body is slightly hunched, and he walks as if stiffness and discomfort fill his joints.

"Let us be clear. Mother gave me life. You mated with her and provided your seed. I thank you for your contribution. But she carried me within her body and brought me into this world. She also gave me a soul filled with empathy, a mind filled with enough wisdom to know I will always have things to learn, and an understanding of what is good and right. You? You gave me my fighting spirit. My drive to never quit. You gave me a role to defend my homeland, which I did with unwavering pride. Sadly, all the good in you died with Mother. You expected me to keep fighting your battles even though your vision had changed? Even though your soul had turned to ash from your anger? Even tho—"

The same guard thrusts the end of the same gun into my right side this time, and the words die on my tongue as I struggle to breathe.

My father laughs maniacally at the sight of my pain, and the sound of it reminds me why I am here. I am not here to reason with him or to make him acknowledge his flaws. That is a pointless quest. I am here for Cloh-ee. My precious inara.

"Where is she?" I shout as the warriors haul me back up.

"You are right," my father straightens. "Enough pleasantries. Let us discuss the trade."

"Trade?" I ask, my chest heaving as I rub my aching ribs.

"Why, yes," my father mutters, as if I should know all about this trade he speaks of. "I shall let your little pet go, on one condition: you will stay, reclaim your place, and give me an heir."

An heir? This is what he seeks? As he is clearly nearing the end of his life, and I am his only child, the throne will not remain in the

Daaskano name if he has no heir to pass it to, so his demand is not unexpected. Greed and rage are the only parts of himself he embraces.

But to give him an heir, I must remain here. He will never let me travel back to Oluura, and Oluura has become my home. I do not wish to take the throne or pass it to my child when it is their time to rule. I want nothing here on Trovilia.

However, if remaining here and giving him an heir will ensure Cloh-ee's safe passage to Oluura, I should not hesitate to do so.

Will my father keep his word though? Will he truly let her leave if I agree to stay and give him an heir? Will he forgive all that I have done —killing his warriors, blowing up his largest ship, and sabotaging his mission on D'Alluk? All for the sake of ensuring a Daaskano remains on the throne?

"If I agree to this…staying here and giving you an heir, you will let Cloh-ee go? Back to Olurra? Ahlvo too?"

My father grins, his eyes gleaming. "Why, of course, my son. You may not know the male I have become, but I am true to my word. They shall both return to Oluura, unharmed. I have no need for them anyway." He waves his hand dismissively at Ahlvo.

He has always had a problem with Ahlvo. It is because Ahlvo's family is not of royal blood. We grew up in different social circles, and his family lived in a poorer nearby village. But once we began training together, Ahlvo and I became inseparable. My father preferred I spend my time with other royal males, and he was extremely unhappy when I chose Ahlvo as my second-in-command over Bruvix, my cousin.

I glance at Ahlvo, my closest friend, who has been quietly growling since we entered the room, and I know that no matter what happens here this day, he will be sure to get Cloh-ee home safely. However, when I consider this deal my father proposes, I cannot help but hear my sweet inara's voice saying, "This is the bullshit," or whatever the phrase is.

I will not take this deal because how can I trust him? He is the same male who had me poisoned when I did not agree with him. But I need to pretend a bit longer in order for our plan to work.

I steel my spine and turn to my father. "I cannot agree to this until I am certain Cloh-ee is unharmed. Until I see her for myself."

"Certainly, certainly," he sneers as he leans over to the older guard closest to him and whispers something in his ear.

The guard leaves the room, and we wait.

After a period of uncomfortable silence, I hear several grunts and thuds coming from the open door the guard just left through. I know that it leads to a long stone staircase to the castle's underground dungeon.

To think that my bright-eyed, delicate Cloh-ee has been kept in that dreadful place has my claws and fangs fully extending and adrenaline pumping through my veins.

There are screams, more thuds, choked noises, and what sounds like a lifeless body tumbling down the stone steps. My body hums and readies to attack, and then...females, several females, burst through the door, covered in blood.

I hear the loud thump of my heartbeat in my ears as I hold my breath. My Cloh-ee. She must be all right. She must.

The remaining guards point their guns at us and swivel back and forth to the females that continue to emerge through the door. The guards surround my father, blocking him from sight. He peeks his head above their shoulders to see what is happening but stays in place. Coward.

Cloh-ee enters last, with a long and narrow blade held to the throat of the guard my father told to retrieve her. His nose drips with blood, and there are scratches all over his face. She fights back, my mate. I rub my chest as it swells with pride.

"Where is Varrek?" Cloh-ee shouts. She does not see me yet. "Tell me or I'll cut this fucker's head off!"

My father and the guards look at Cloh-ee, their faces twisted in confusion. She speaks in her human tongue, and they do not understand her threats.

Seeing her this way, vicious and confident while expertly wielding a blade in her hand—it sends a surge of heat straight to my cock.

"Cloh-ee," I gasp as her eyes meet mine. "I am here. They cannot understand your words, sweet inara."

"Inara?" my father mutters in shock. "I thought she was your pet."

"That is what *you* called her. I said no such thing. She is not my pet. She is my mate," I grit.

My father's face is barely visible through the circle of guards that surrounds him, but I can see his brow pinched in disgust. "A human? You mated a human? You would desecrate our name by bonding to a *human?*"

His tongue rolls over the word *human* like it leaves a bitter taste in his mouth. I cease trying to make sense of my father's prejudice against humans, as prejudice is never rooted in coherence.

"You will free us at once, or this *human* will cut out your guard's innards and spill them upon the floor of this very room!" shouts the blood-covered Trovilian female who led the pack.

She turns to face me, and a smile stretches her lips. "Hello, old friend." She gives me a nod, and then I recognize her.

"Ekoya? Ho-How are you here? You were dead." My stomach flips in disbelief. I hear Ahlvo suck in a breath beside me. "We mourned you. The virus, it—"

"Did not kill me," she finishes. "I am still here. I have been locked in your father's dungeon ever since I recovered." She pins my father with a chilling glare. "I am the first breeder he acquired for his program."

I search for my father's gaze, but he is hunched behind his guards, like the weakling he is. "You *dare* lie to our people about one of our own, let her family believe she has died, and then keep her locked in a cell?" I shout. What my father has done to Ekoya, to all of these females, it is unthinkable.

I clench and unclench my fists and shift slightly onto the balls of my feet. My body is ready to attack.

He lifts his head only to grunt a quiet command to his guards. The guards surrounding him split into two groups, with half of them spreading out in front of my father and the other half pinning me and Ahlvo against the wall with swords poking at our bellies. We raise our hands in surrender. "Everything I do, I do for Trovilia," my father says flatly, his tone cold.

I do not know who this male is, or how he was able to erase every shred of dignity inside his soul and turn into this. What I do know is that we are running out of time, as well as opportunities to take out his guards. We must act now.

I tap the claw of my third finger against the claw of my thumb on the same hand. It makes a light clacking noise. Loud enough for Ahlvo to hear it, but not loud enough to draw the attention of the guards. I do it twice more.

After the third clack, I yell to Cloh-ee, "Get down!" in her language, as Ahlvo yells the same to Ekoya in Trovilian. We pull the loops wrapped around our fingers, and the hilts of our daggers ascend from their hidden compartments on the backs of our vests. We reach back and free our blades, bringing them down across the faces, necks, and chests of the guards surrounding us.

Within moments, there is a bloody pile of bodies at our feet. But we do not stop swinging our daggers as all but one of the guards protecting my father surge toward us.

Ahlvo and I end up standing back to back, and I see Ekoya and a few other females joining the fight with their various weapons.

I turn on my heel, and out of nowhere, a fist connects with my jaw. My vision blurs, and one of my daggers is knocked out of my hand. I recover and focus all my attention on that guard, ducking another punch, shoving my blade into his gut, and dragging it up toward his sternum. I'm unable to pull the blade free, so I scramble to grab my fallen dagger from the floor.

We take out four more guards, and the females take out one more, which leaves only three standing. I silently thank the goddess for the females being able to escape the dungeon and help us, as their presence made this entire ordeal much easier.

The scream of a female draws my attention away from the guard I'm fighting off, and I hold my breath as I search for Cloh-ee. I see another Trovilian female fall to her knees, clutching her arm as blood seeps through her fingers from a long knife wound that stretches from her shoulder to elbow. The other females huddle around her, a few blocking her from the remaining guards, the rest offering her aid.

Cloh-ee shouts my name in warning, horror filling her tone as I am shoved to the ground. It is Ahlvo who pushed me down, landing on top of me with a grunt. I look up to see a compact pistol clutched in my father's hand aiming at us, still smoking at the release of the bullet. Then Ahlvo rolls off of me, screaming at the top of his lungs, as his hands go to cover the gaping wound just above his knee that the bullet has created.

My father backs away, suddenly realizing all eyes are on him, and tucks himself behind the three remaining guards. Ekoya snarls wildly and charges toward one of them, their swords colliding like the crash of thunder.

I reach down and roll up my sleeve to reveal the dispenser band wrapped around my forearm. I place the exposed loop around my finger and give it a tug to release the first concealed throwing knife. I use my other hand to pull out the first blade and aim it at the approaching guard's throat. I release before he can raise his sword above my head, and his jaw falls open with a choked scream as the knife sticks into his neck and his body crumples to the floor.

Cloh-ee snaps her fingers and yells a string of strange human words at the guard fighting Ekoya, and when that does not work as a distraction, she huffs, "Fuck it," and hurls her dagger at his lower body. It sinks into his thigh with a meaty, wet sound, and he looks down at it long enough for Ekoya to swing her sword and slice his head clean off his body. It rolls to the wall, eyes still open, and the room fills with an eerie silence.

I pull another blade and yell Cloh-ee's name to get her attention. Then I slide the blade across the floor until it skids to a stop at her feet. She snatches it up and mouths, "Thank you." I know she feels safer when she can defend herself, and she is most comfortable with a small blade that fits in her hand. I do not want her to be forced to defend herself at all—that is my job as her mate—but what she wants is more important than what I think she needs.

I sneak a glance at Ahlvo, his hand wrapped around the angry and deep-looking wound on his leg as he shivers. He seems to be losing consciousness when his body should be entering the healing process. This is not good.

Only one guard stands between us and my father. And that guard appears to be older, surely not a challenge for me to take down by myself, and I have several armed females who are hungry for vengeance.

Ekoya breaks the silence by throwing her head back in laughter. "The time has come to give up, King."

He turns to the guard at his left with panic in his eyes. "Do something, Jolvik!"

The old male smiles, and a blinding cloud swirls around him before disappearing and leaving a young Hexrin male in his place. Ekoya steps toward him and wraps an arm around his neck, pulling down for a quick kiss.

"Cruvo!" my father bellows as his grip tightens on the gun he shot Ahlvo with. "You traitorous cretin!" His eyes dart to each of us, all here to kill him, and he looks...scared. Truly frightened. The only other time I remember seeing this look on his face was when my mother's heart rate was slowing down. It was moments before she passed.

I pity him. But I can process the pity later, once he is no longer a threat to our people or my mate. "Surrender, Father. Put the gun down. It is over," I tell him.

He lowers it slightly, his shoulders slumping in defeat, but then he lifts his chin defiantly, pulls the cloth from his desk, and tosses it in our direction, causing all his maps, writing utensils, and tools that were on top of it a moment ago to fall at our feet. He turns to run.

Just before he reaches the door, the air crackles, and an explosion knocks us to the ground.

I wait, letting the ash and dust fall on me in a thick layer, as my ears pop and I am able to hear again.

I look over my shoulder to find a gaping hole through the door and the wall where my father was attempting to escape. I see rubble, and I cannot decipher what else is scattered there from this distance, but I would assume it is the charred and dismembered remains of my father, since there is no way he could have safely escaped that blast.

A small, soft hand touches my shoulder from behind me, and I instinctively cover that hand with my own. It is Cloh-ee. She is here. She is alive. And she is touching me. It is all I need.

I turn to my right to see Ahlvo snickering quietly as he looks toward the door. "Got him," he chuckles. Resting on the floor, just beyond his open palm, is the trigger box for the weapon Nalba had recently finished making. We brought it with us but were not sure it would be safe for us to use in an enclosed space. She said that Cloh-ee had named it the "Supreme Blaster," as it shoots fireballs that explode at the moment of contact.

Ahlvo just used it to blow up my father.

I find myself searching through my emotions, looking for grief but finding none. I wonder briefly if there is something wrong with me for not being overcome with sadness, or rage directed at Ahlvo for what he has done. But neither takes up space inside my mind.

What I do find, though, is relief. Relief that it is over. That my father is gone. That my Cloh-ee is safe. That I need not spend another day worrying that my father has discovered I am alive. That I have betrayed him. These fears have weighed heavier on my shoulders than I realized.

Now that they are gone, I feel as if I could float home to Oluura using just my body and not my ship.

Ahlvo grunts as he tries to sit up, and my gaze travels back to his leg. It is a mess unlike any I have seen before. The veins surrounding the wound are turning black, and the black is spreading above and below the wound. I pull a rag from the inner pocket of my vest and tear it in half. I wrap it tightly just above the wound, using the other half to cover the open gash from the dust that continues to fall.

Cruvo crouches next to me, looking at the wound, his mouth forming a grim line. "It was a maahtio bullet."

"Bikar?"

"Maahtio. It is a flesh-eating bacteria," Cruvo says solemnly. "King Muryk found an additive that keeps it active but frozen within a serum. He coated the bullets with that serum, and once the bacteria touches an open wound, it spreads. Quickly."

A sheen of sweat covers Ahlvo's brow as his eyes start to close, and his breaths come in labored pants. I hold on to Ahlvo's forearm, letting him know I am by his side, as Cruvo, Ekoya, and Cloh-ee help me lift him and take him out of the war council room. We move into the hall and lay his body on a bench as we wait for the healers to arrive.

Cloh-ee kneels beside me and takes my hand in hers. She gives my hand a single squeeze, and I close my eyes to savor the physical connection between us. I do not have the words to tell Cloh-ee all the things I wish to tell her, and all that she deserves to hear, and breaking the silence to say anything after what we just endured would seem banal and almost...wrong. Words cannot reach this moment we are in, and so we continue to gaze at each other, our eyes both filling with tears, our hands clasped tightly.

Cloh-ee sends me a soft smile, and with a nod, I feel as if she can read my thoughts. That she understands.

Perhaps I have not lost her after all.

CHAPTER 24

CHLOE

I scrunch my wet hair between my fingers and wring the excess drops of water from the ends with a towel. That was quite possibly the best shower I've ever had in my life. Not only because of the waterfall-style shower head with exceptional water pressure, but also because I was able to scrub every drop of blood and dirt and ash from my skin. The past week, the escape, the battle in the war room—all of it washed down the drain in a dark stream that chilled me to the bone.

It's funny...whenever I heard the phrase "wearing the blood of her enemies," I would smile at how completely vicious it sounded. I imagined how satisfying it would feel to have the physical proof on my skin that I defeated someone who sought my demise. But actually wearing the blood of my enemies is not something I ever want to experience again.

I almost gagged several times at that coppery smell. Plus, Trovilian blood is so sticky. Disgustingly sticky. I held my breath as I covered my body with a thick layer of soap and scrubbed my skin almost raw trying to get it off. Then I rinsed and repeated until the water ran cold.

I drape my towel over the bathroom door and pull on the large tunic that was lying on the bed when I came in. I scan the room again and find the lack of decor surprising, and sad. I expected each room of this massive castle to have plush carpets, soft lighting, and tapestries and giant oil paintings covering the walls. Just more stuff. This room has a bed, a side table, and a lantern on that side table. That's it.

Are all the rooms like this?

For a change of scenery, I go to stand at the floor-to-ceiling window in my room. The view is magnificent, certainly an upgrade from the dungeon, and I can see the entire city from here.

King Muryk's black stone castle sits at the top of a sprawling hillside, with the city at the bottom of the hill and stretching out from there. I see several sections of homes clustered together in pockets and spreading for miles. I'm assuming those are separate villages, but it's hard to tell. There's also a set of stalls that appears to be a marketplace, with crowds of people coming in and out.

The most striking part of this city, though, is the flowers. There are flowers everywhere I look. Huge, gargantuan, cartoonish flowers. They sprout up between buildings and homes and sporadically on the paths that connect them. They grow around each structure, looking as if they're a few days from swallowing the buildings whole if someone doesn't trim the heck out of them. The petals come in a variety of shapes and colors, but the stems are all thin and different shades of brown. Despite the flimsy appearance of the stems, some of them are as tall as pine trees, so they must be stronger than they look.

My eyes lift to the small and large ships zipping around the red sky as the sun begins to set.

What a strange but beautiful place. With the gloomy, desolate castle and the contrast of the bright, happy flowers below it, the city reminds me of a neighborhood in a Tim Burton movie.

I see gold bodies scurrying about below in all directions, and I wonder if they know what happened here today. That their king has been killed and their prince has come back from the dead.

A knock sounds on the door, and Varrek pops his head in. "Clohee?" he calls, scanning the room for me.

"Hey, over here." I wave from the window.

I notice his hair is wet and his skin is blood- and dust-free, and I'm happy he was able to wash away the trauma we faced as well.

He enters the room with hesitation, and a hint of fear on his face. He doesn't know where we stand at the moment, and frankly, neither do I.

"Whose room is this?" I ask without turning around.

"It is mine," he says from behind me. "*Was* mine."

I jerk my head around to look at him. "Yours? But there's nothing in here."

"Not anymore, no," he scoffs. "I am sure my father cleared the room of my personal items mere moments after I was pronounced dead."

I hear him take a step closer to me, and goose bumps cover my skin at the proximity of his body to mine. "But my bed is the comfiest in the castle, and I knew that would still be here. It is why I chose this room for you."

I smile at his thoughtfulness.

"The view is just as I remember it." He sighs as he comes to stand next to me.

"What's this city called, by the way?"

"Oovahr, which means 'flower' in your language."

I chuckle at the perfectly chosen name. "Makes sense. Are all the cities on Trovilia named for their most distinctive feature?"

He smirks. "Yes, our first settlers were quite literal."

"How's Ahlvo doing?" I ask him, nervous about the answer. The gunshot wound on his leg was straight out of a nightmare. The gaping hole it left, exposing the bone, and then how it continued to open wider, the flesh surrounding the bullet turning gray and black and almost curling with decay right before my eyes. And the smell…as if an infection was already present. It was awful.

Varrek clears his throat, and his eyes are on his feet. He looks like he's aged ten years in a day. "He is in stasis. They were able to stop the spread of flesh-eating bacteria, but his wound was too large to close surgically. We must wait for his body to heal enough for the healers to close it."

Oh god, poor Ahlvo. That sounds excruciating. "Flesh-eating bacteria? Yikes. Where did that even come from?"

Varrek's face hardens at the question. "My father found a way to add an exterior layer of it onto the bullets in his pistol. When he shot Ahlvo, the bacteria instantly attacked the flesh around the bullet."

I inhale sharply as I back away from the window and sit on the bed. The idea of creating a weapon like that rattles my bones. Especially since the bullet could've killed Ahlvo immediately if the gun were aimed at his head or chest. Why bother adding an additional element to an already deadly weapon? It's a rhetorical question, of course, because I know the answer: suffering. Varrek's father seemed to get a kick out of witnessing it. What a monster he was.

We were able to confirm that King Muryk was killed in the blast after Ekoya discovered half of his head under a scrap of that cloth he pulled from his desk as a distraction before trying to escape. I didn't look. I didn't want to look, as I've accrued enough graphic imagery to give me night terrors for years to come.

Varrek looked though. I tried convincing him not to, that he might never be able to shake that image, but he said he needed to be sure. He needed the peace of mind that his father was truly gone. I don't blame him.

"How are you holding up?" I pat the space on the bed next to me, encouraging him to come sit down. "I'm sorry about your dad."

He walks over slowly and then sits on the bed, about a foot away, facing me. "Do not feel sorry for my father's passing, Cloh-ee. It is what he deserved."

"I don't disagree, but that doesn't mean you're not allowed to feel sad about it. I mean, he was your father."

He scrunches his ridged nose in thought, and I can't help but smile at the sight. It makes him look slightly angry when he does it, but I find it adorable. "It is hard to remember the male he once was, especially knowing the pain he has caused to so many."

I nod. "That makes sense. I'm sure it will take time for you to reconcile the good with the bad. Time heals all wounds though, as they say."

Varrek's eyes glisten with sadness, and I wonder if I've said the wrong thing. "Cloh-ee"—he scoots an inch toward me—"there is still much I must tell you."

"Right," I mutter with a sigh. I'm not looking forward to this conversation, but it has to happen if we're going to move on from this.

He exhales deeply, looking nervous. "I do not think I could offer the adequate number of apologies you deserve to hear for what I have done. I wish I had done everything differently. I wish I had told you about my past from the beginning. I am deeply ashamed that I did not."

"Is it really because you thought I wouldn't understand? That's the part I'm having trouble with." I quickly throw my drying hair up into a bun to get it off my face. "That doesn't make sense to me."

He folds and unfolds the edge of the blanket between his fingers. "Why, of course. What kind of male abandons his people and his birthright? What kind of male allows innocent people to die right in front of him? What kind of—"

I stop him there. "Your father tried to murder you, Varrek."

He stares at me, his expression blank, so I continue. "Based on the story you told me, you tried to stop him from attacking innocent people, and he poisoned you. You could've left Trovilia right then and there, and you would've been justified to do so. But you didn't leave. You stayed and made sure you could be part of the mission to limit the number of casualties and so you could successfully flee the planet with everyone you cared about before your father could hurt them too. Does this all sound correct so far?"

His chin dips bashfully. "Yes, this is true."

"And you didn't kill any D'Allukans, did you? Those deaths were caused by the warriors your father hand selected for the mission? Because he knew they would kill innocent people without batting an eye."

He nods.

"Then you avenged those deaths and protected the female D'Allukans they captured by killing the Trovilian warriors on the ship and freeing the females, saving them from a lifetime of captivity in that awful dungeon and who knows what else?" I remind him. "By the way, why didn't you tell me about that part?"

He clears his throat. "Yes, we freed them, but only after the males of their village were slaughtered. It was hardly a heroic act."

"You prevented them from becoming breeders in your father's twisted little program," I remind him.

He tilts his head thoughtfully but says nothing.

I'm not an expert on war, so I'm in no position to say whether he made the right choice, or if there was a better way to execute that plan that would've saved more lives. What I can say is that he was betrayed by his own father and put in an impossible position. It seems like he did the best he could, given the circumstances. I have no idea what I would've done if I'd been in his shoes.

"What about the madness Nalba mentioned? You told me what it was, but why did it play such a major role in why you hid your past from me?" I ask, still puzzled by the phrasing and the lack of details surrounding "the madness."

Sadness fills Varrek's eyes. "My father was once a good male. An honorable male. A kind male. But after the virus took my mother, it is like all that was good about him died with her. He became sick. Evil. Rot consumed his soul. He became capable of things I could never have imagined."

"Now having met him, it's definitely hard for me to picture the guy he was before," I say, but clearly that version of him existed at one point, because Varrek's a good egg. Though, maybe all the credit goes to his mother for that.

"I did not tell you about my father's madness because clearly it resides deep within me as well. It has yet to emerge, but when it does, those closest to me will be in danger." He avoids my gaze.

Does Varrek truly believe that he's destined to be a monster simply because his father turned into one? I'm suddenly very confused. "Why...why would you assume that?"

"Because he is my sire. I am of his blood." His tone is so resolute, as if this is obvious. "Rumo and Ahlvo are both charming and carefree.

Ahlvo gets this from Rumo. Bruvix is as glum as his father. Do humans not take after their parents in these ways?"

"I mean, we do, but our personalities change and shift based on our experiences." He seems skeptical, so I continue, "Like, you and your father, you both lost your mother and you both handled it in very different ways. You may have some similar characteristics, but you didn't immediately seek revenge on innocent people as a way to cope because that's not who you are. We're all a product of our upbringings, but at a certain point, we can choose to be better versions of ourselves and behave accordingly."

He rubs his chin, lost in thought.

"You wake up each day and you choose how you treat people. Every single day since your mother died, your father could've chosen to be better. To act with empathy. To care for his people. To care for you, his son. He didn't." I immediately feel bad about framing it this way. It's the truth, but perhaps this is not the right time. "Sorry."

He smiles warmly, and I know he's not offended.

"I understand it must be excruciating to watch someone you love abandon all their principles and let their anger and greed guide them, but you did everything you could to help him through his pain." I pull his hand toward me and hold it in both of mine. "We can't choose who we're related to, unfortunately."

His eyes meet mine, and he nods in agreement. "You have had similar experiences with your family on Earth?"

"Well, none of them have tried to poison me," I laugh. "But yeah. I have an uncle that tells racist jokes at our holiday dinners. It's awful. My mom always scolds me for telling him why he shouldn't. She says she just wants to 'avoid the drama.' Last year, it got really heated when he wouldn't apologize, so I told him to get fucked and I left."

He beams with pride. "I would not want to be on the receiving end of your wrath, though I admit it is a lovely sight."

I can feel my cheeks turning pink, and I sit up a little straighter at his compliment. I've never been the tough one. I've had a few moments, but they are extremely rare. Mostly, I've been the pushover, the "nice" girl, and the accommodating one. But Varrek makes me feel like I could walk away from an exploding car in slow motion and not look back. He's never tried to change me or take more than he gives. All he wants is for me to be happy, and in that, I get to be me.

"Yeah, sometimes I dread family gatherings, to be honest. I wonder why I bother going at all."

"Even though it is your family? Your blood?" he asks, surprised.

I sigh, as this is a question I've asked myself a million times. "It's tough. A lot of people will say since it's the only family you've got, you need to love them unconditionally. To a certain extent, I agree.

"However, not everyone is born into a loving, supportive family, and if embracing the family you've got means constantly enduring hateful comments, abuse of any kind, and general unhappiness, then why keep them in your life?" I feel guilty even saying this, but verbalizing the thoughts I've had for so long feels good. "I think everyone deserves to be happy. So if your blood relatives make you feel like trash, then build your own family."

His hand closes around mine, and he lightly strokes my wrist. "Build your own family. I very much like the sound of that."

"You've already done that, Varrek." I lift his chin so he meets my eyes. "You took all the people you love and got them out of this dangerous place and brought them to Oluura. You started fresh on a new planet, and you relied on each other to survive. Your clan is the family you've built. Be proud of that."

His gaze dips to my mouth, and a hunger deep within me shoots across my skin. My body leans toward him before I even realize it, and I wet my lips with my tongue in anticipation of tasting him again. I've missed his lips on mine. I've missed his large hands gripping my waist and ass. I've missed his emerald eyes searing into mine. I've missed all of him.

His hand cups my cheek as he inches closer, our slightly parted lips desperate to reach other like magnets. I close my eyes as his mouth covers mine, my tongue thrusting between his lips, wasting no time to explore all the parts of his mouth I've dreamed about since I was taken. His tongue meets mine and slicks around it, and I moan at the friction.

Varrek pulls away suddenly, leaving me dazed, my mouth already swollen from his kisses. "Does this mean you forgive me, Cloh-ee? That we may start again?" His thumb gently caresses my jaw as his eyes plead with me to give him another chance.

I want to. I really, really do. "You'll never lie to me again, right? From this point on, we tell each other the truth, no matter how scared we are to do so. Promise me."

He lowers his forehead and presses it against mine. "I promise. Honesty. Always."

My heart skips at the devotion in his voice. He's either brilliantly persuasive or he's telling the truth. I choose to believe it's the latter. I tilt my head and press my lips firmly against his. He groans as I nip at his bottom lip, and his hands become frantic as they clutch my back. They settle on the nape of my neck and my lower back as my hands grip his expansive chest.

He lifts me onto his lap so I'm straddling him, and I grind my hips against him, seeking contact between our bodies from head to toe. I feel him, hard and long, beneath me, the fabric of his pants the only thing that separates us.

I mewl at the sensation, certain I could come just like this. I pant against his mouth as I continue to rub myself against his straining cock.

"What you do to me, inara," Varrek rasps. His mouth goes to the base of my neck, and he inhales with a deep groan. "Your scent...I have missed it."

I run my fingers through his silver locks, so silky and thick. His plants feathery kisses all over my neck before running his tongue along the open neckline of my tunic.

"Ahh!" I cry out as he sucks my nipple through my shirt while cupping my breast in his hand. The dampness of the fabric sends a chill through my spine, and my nipples pebble in an instant. He pinches and rubs my other nipple in his hand as I grind harder against his length. The friction of the fabric against my clit is driving me insane.

"Off, now," he whispers huskily as he tugs at the hem of my shirt. I lift my arms over my head so he can pull it off, and once he does, my hands are back on him. It's like I need to touch him everywhere or I'll explode, and I wish I had six other hands so I could.

I yank on his shirt, only separating our bodies long enough so I can toss it behind him and then feel his skin directly on mine.

He pants against my chest as his tongue laves and strokes against each hardened nipple. He continues his ministrations as his hand lowers and brushes against my hip. I shudder, knowing what's coming, and lick his jaw as his fingers part my folds and he dips one inside my already soaked pussy. I feel him smile against my collarbone. "It seems you are ready for me, my mate."

"So ready for you. Always ready for you," I whimper, my nails digging into his bare shoulders. He adds another finger, stretching me, then pressing his thumb into my clit as he moves his fingers in and out of my sex. "God, Varrek!" I shout as I move up and down, impaling myself on him.

"Take what you need, Cloh-ee. Fuck my hand," he breathes, his tone filled with awe as he watches me. He swipes the calloused pad of his thumb across my clit, and I see stars.

"S-So close," I pant as I grip his neck, holding on for dear life.

Then Varrek throws me onto my back, covering my body with his own as a vicious growl is ripped from his throat. For a brief moment, I want to cry at the unfulfilled orgasm, but then my head clears, and I realize we might be in danger.

I hear a timid voice say something from the doorway, and then Varrek shouts a rage-filled response in Trovilian. Even though I know he's covering my naked body completely, I burrow deeper into his chest where I feel the safest. The conversation continues for another minute or so, with the quiet male voice repeating the same thing over and over, what I assume is an apology for interrupting, and Varrek yelling back at him.

When I hear the heavy door close, I look up to see Varrek's fangs still bared and his eyes murderous. I brush a lock of hair behind his pointed ear, and when he looks down at me, his face softens into complete adoration. It makes me feel treasured.

"What was that about?" I ask, still gasping from my almost orgasm.

Varrek huffs in frustration. "I am sorry for that outrageous intrusion. The council has called an urgent meeting to discuss the transition of power. I must attend."

Worry fills my gut. "The war council that your father assembled? That seems dicey. You're not going in there alone." I go to sit up, looking for my clothes and knife, but Varrek nudges my shoulder back down.

"It is not that council, my mate. This is the council of various leaders within our city. It includes healers, historians, scientific researchers, and teachers, among others. A few war council members will be there, but they are not a threat, as they are now outnumbered." He winks.

"When you are concerned for me..." He places a hand over his heart, and his eyes close. "I did not think I would ever find this. Find you."

I cover the hand on his heart with my own. "I'm here now, Varrek. You have my back, and I have yours. We're a team."

His eyes shine with emotion as he leans down and gives me a soft, smacking kiss. He gets up from the bed and grabs his shirt off the floor. Then he turns to me and offers me a hand. I let him pull me up and into his arms.

"Do you wish to attend the meeting?" he asks as his fingers run through my messy sex hair.

"Would the council really allow me to be there?"

"I do not care what the council wants or does not want. You are my mate. If you wish to be there, you will be there." His tone holds such authority that I pity the next person who challenges it.

I know what this meeting is about. Or I think I do, anyway. They want Varrek to take his father's place as King of Trovilia. Of course that's what the council will want. He'd make an excellent king too. He's a born leader. He's also not a murderous psycho, so it'll certainly be an upgrade from their previous king.

"It's okay, I think I'll sit this one out. I'm exhausted." He narrows his gaze, as if he doesn't buy it. "Besides, I won't be able to understand a word of it anyway."

"Do you wish to receive the language implant? It is a much safer procedure here than it is on Oluura. We can get it done tomorrow, if you would like."

"Yes, absolutely." I don't bother hiding my excitement.

I've hated not knowing how to speak Trovilian, especially back on Oluura. I realize the clan didn't take extensive lessons to learn English —they just had it uploaded into their little brain chips or whatever— but seeing them all speaking my language on their planet and not knowing how to speak their language has made me feel like a supreme asshole.

Varrek chuckles at my enthusiasm and pulls me in for a tight hug. He pulls back, and his eyes linger on my still very naked body. "I shall make this meeting as quick as possible. When I return, I vow to finish what I started," he rasps. My nipples harden under his gaze, and a cocky grin spreads across his face. My body reacts in such a primal way to everything he does. He knows this. I want to be annoyed, but I can't muster it. More than anything, I just want to fast-forward to when he's back in bed with me.

"Be safe. You owe me a brain-melting orgasm, okay?" I poke at his chest playfully.

His face turns serious, his eyes smoldering. "On my honor, Clohee, I will give you so many orgasms that you will not remember your name when the sun rises."

I sigh as he leaves. I turn off the lantern next to the bed and crawl under the covers. I close my eyes, waiting for sleep to pull me under, but instead, I find myself worrying about the council offering Varrek the position of King of Trovilia. If he decides to stay, should I stay too? Do I even want that?

CHAPTER 25

VARREK

As I stride angrily toward the meeting room, I see Ekoya round the corner with an equally sour expression on her face. "Coming to the meeting?" I ask, slowing my pace to walk with her.

"Unfortunately," she huffs, straightening her clothes. "I do not know what is urgent enough to interrupt the lovely feast we were having. Could this not wait until morning?"

"Mmm." I nod in agreement, envisioning Cloh-ee coming apart in my arms, calling my name, her blunt nails digging into my skin…right before that pitiful squire walked in and ruined the moment.

I shake the image from my head as I mentally prepare for the meeting we are about to enter. A barrage of questions swirl in my mind as I ponder the reason for this gathering. I must remain neutral and focused for whatever they wish to discuss.

"I admit I have missed Trovilian cuisine. What were you and Cruvo eating?" I ask, deciding a change in subject is an ideal distraction.

Ekoya side-eyes me with a devilish smirk. "Uh, no. *I* was the feast."

"Ah," I reply. So much for a change in subject.

We enter the meeting hall, a few others filing in behind us. Ekoya and I take seats next to each other. I certainly feel like an outcast here, as I am sure Ekoya does.

I have been inside this meeting room many times. It is a small windowless room, with curved tables lining the back wall. Those tables face the seven seats occupied by the council at the front of the room on a dais. They represent scientific researchers, healers, historians, farmers, essential laborers, and teachers. The seventh seat is held by one of the five remaining members of my father's war council. Together, these members use their collective expertise to guide the king or queen in making key decisions that will impact our city, our planet, and our future as a people.

Before my father started relying exclusively on his war council for advice, he would meet with the general council leaders once each moon cycle in this very room. I have heard those meetings have not occurred in years.

Once everyone is seated, the mild-mannered male in the middle council seat clears his throat and addresses the group. His name is Bihluk, and he has been the council's historian for as long as I can remember. I have always been fond of his ability to command attention without raising his voice. He makes his points forcefully and effectively, but without personal attacks on those he disagrees with.

Bihluk briefly recounts our history, all the way through my father's reign, and how our society has shifted under his rule. Ekoya and I sit with our arms crossed as the war council member, Diroh, frequently interrupts Bihluk to justify my father's choices. His proximity to power is disintegrating right before his eyes, and it is clear he is desperate.

I feel out of place in this room. Trovilia no longer feels like my home and, therefore, no longer my responsibility.

After several consecutive outbursts from council members and others in the seats around us, Ekoya gets to her feet and slams her palm on the table in front of us. The sound silences everyone in the room. "It is well past nightfall. I was in the middle of riding my mate's face when I was dragged here for this urgent meeting. And all I have heard thus far are the petty squabbles of males much too old to exhibit this behavior."

She straightens her spine and lifts her chin in a way that makes her look lethal, but also elegant. Then she shoots a glare at each council member at the front of the room before she speaks. "There are only two pieces of information I am interested in getting this eve. The first is where the other female prisoners are. I have not seen them since we were taken to the healers after the explosion. You will tell me where they are and how you intend to make amends for the pain your former king has caused them."

"Was there a second question you had, Ekoya?" Bihluk asks, calmness permeating his tone and energy.

"Yes." She smiles wickedly. "I would like to know how you plan to atone for my years of captivity and torture. And let me say, an apology will not be enough."

Bihluk goes to say something in response but is cut off by Diroh. "What happened to you is unfortunate, Ekoya, but the data we have gathered based on the samples you provided has brought us many steps closer to saving our people. I do not wish to speak for you, but I am certain you would not refuse your people that kind of hope, would you?"

My fists clench at his condescending tone. How dare he speak to Ekoya in such a way after all she has endured. I lean forward to rise and defend her before Ekoya holds up a finger, indicating I should remain seated.

She faces Diroh, and a look of calculated rage flashes across her face.

"If you do not wish to speak for me, then why did you speak for me, Diroh? I find it interesting that you describe my treatment as 'unfortunate,' when in reality, it was more…'shockingly traumatic' or 'unfathomably cruel.'"

She takes a deep breath before continuing. "My family was told I was dead. They mourned for me. Today was the first day I have seen the Trovilian sun in five years. I was kept in a dark cage. I was poked and prodded at more times than I am able to count. The 'samples' you say I provided were not given freely. They were tissues and cells taken from my body painfully and without my consent." Her eyes well up with tears, but she stiffens, fighting them back.

Diroh rolls his eyes at her show of emotion, and a smile stretches my lips as I envision cracking his jaw with my fist. "It was for the greater good of our peo—"

"Diroh, you will cease speaking now," Bihluk says, his tone biting. He turns to face Ekoya. "Ekoya, there will be no attempt to justify what happened to you, because it never should have happened." His brow is furrowed, and his gaze fills with sorrow. "We do not have an answer for how we will right the wrong you endured. There is much to discuss before we reach a solution that we all agree upon, but we do not expect your forgiveness, no matter what we offer.

"As for the other females, we have given them their own quarters here in the castle for now. We will be offering them automatic Trovilian citizenship, should they choose to remain here. If they do not, we will provide them safe transport to their home planets."

Ekoya still looks displeased, but she gives Bihluk a curt nod and takes her seat.

"Part of the reason we have been unable to determine the best form of restitution for you, Ekoya, is that we are now leaderless." Bihluk's eyes go to mine on the last word. "Varrek, your father's death has left Trovilia without a voice, a guide, a spirit. Muryk did not have a chosen successor listed to take the throne. That is why, today, we ask you to claim your birthright and assume your place as King of Trovilia."

Diroh immediately stands, his face scrunched in alarm. "We did not vote on this. I do not agree to this choice."

"Varrek is Muryk's son. A vote is not required for this transition of power. The throne is Varrek's whether you agree to it or not, Diroh." Bihluk's eyes are pleading as he looks at me. "That is, if he wants it."

Diroh pins him with a hateful glare. But just beneath that hate? Fear. Me taking the throne is Diroh's worst nightmare. And even though I know what my answer will be today, tomorrow, and the rest of my tomorrows, I decide to let Diroh suffocate under the weight of his fear, at least for now.

"I shall consider it," I say unceremoniously as I stand from my seat. "I have much to think about. As do you." I shoot Diroh one final icy gaze. "Ekoya and I are done here."

She follows me out of the room as every pair of eyes locks onto our backs. We reach the corridor that will take us to our rooms, and Ekoya speaks, "Should I start bowing down to you, Your Highness?"

"No. I have no interest in claiming the throne." I smirk at her. "I merely wanted to see Diroh suffer for another day."

She grabs my elbow, halting my steps. "You do not want to be king? What is wrong with you?"

"Excuse me?" I am slightly taken aback.

"You could do so much good here. You could change everything. You could fix the damage your father has caused. You could repair the relationship between Trovilia and D'Alluk. You could properly honor all those we lost to the virus." She looks utterly baffled. "Why would you waste that opportunity?"

"Because this is no longer my home to fix," I tell her simply before turning toward my room. I hear her mumble something else, the tone mocking, but I do not care because as I enter my room and find my inara peacefully slumbering in my bed, all other thoughts leave my mind.

I strip off my layers before joining her under the blankets. Then I gently pull her into my arms, her back to my front, as I stroke her mane. I do not wish to wake her, but I cannot refrain from touching her either.

"Mmm, you're back," she whispers sleepily.

"Yes, my mate." I kiss her hair, breathing in her sweet scent. "Go back to sleep."

She grumbles adorably and then burrows backward into my chest, the soft globes of her ass pushing against my aching cock. She giggles at the contact, but a moment later, her breathing evens out, and I hear a hushed sleep snarl fall from her parted lips.

I promised her several orgasms upon my return, but she is clearly exhausted, and I am glad she is able to rest.

I close my eyes as I nuzzle into her neck, and my own exhaustion pulls me under.

* * *

"WAIT, that's it? It's over?" Cloh-ee sits up and climbs out of the med tube, anxiously feeling behind her ear.

"How do you feel?" I ask, relieved her language implant procedure is done. She was not unconscious long, but it still tore at me to see her drugged and operated on. The healer ordered me to leave the room when Cloh-ee first lost consciousness because I began pacing and clawing at her med tube. Apparently, she found that to be a distraction. I could not help it, though, because seeing my mate helpless and vulnerable in such a way drove me mad.

I suspect it also has to do with the fact that Cloh-ee and I have not fulfilled the mating bond and my primal instincts are overpowering my logical thoughts. But that is something I shall worry about later, once we are back on Oluura.

"Say something to me. I want to make sure it works," she says, bouncing on the balls of her feet with excitement.

"Qotahri ni byiio xe'wa cjuo jah. Pokihr neemavi ffu liyoh."

Her eyes dart back and forth as the first translation of her implant registers in her mind. The first one is always slightly delayed as the mind is still adjusting to the onslaught of new information. Then she smiles as she slowly repeats the words I just spoke. "Your sleep snarl is my favorite sound. It makes me feel like I am home?"

She giggles, seemingly confused by the phrasing. "What is a slee—" Then it hits her, and her cheeks turn that bright-pink shade I find so captivating. "Oh my god, my snore?" she yelps. She covers her face with her hands in embarrassment. "Is it loud? Does it keep you up at night?"

I tug on her wrists, trying to pull them away from her face, and she lets me. "Look at me, my mate," I say, laughing at her dramatic reaction. "Did I not say it is my favorite sound?"

She scrunches her nose in disgust. "Ugh, really?" Then she waves her hand as if to push this topic aside. "Anyway, we know the implant works, so that's good."

We thank the healer for her work on Cloh-ee and for the handful of earplug translators to take back to Oluura for the other human females. She shares Ahlvo's status, which is that his leg has healed enough for surgery, and that will take place later this day. If the procedure is a success, we can travel back to Oluura as early as tomorrow.

We step outside the med center and immediately climb into the zip ship waiting at the entrance. It is a small ship that seats only four people and is used for short-distance travel, mainly around the city.

This particular ship was given to us by the council because once the destinations are programmed into the ship's nav system, they cannot be changed. This allows them to track my movements while I remain here. Since I have not yet given them my decision on becoming king, I am treated as a castle guest that needs to be monitored.

The ship takes us back to the castle, and we find Bihluk waiting for us the moment we land. "Are we late?" I ask as I lead Cloh-ee from the ship and up the steps to the side entrance of the castle.

Bihluk smiles warmly. "Not late. I was just enjoying the crisp air for a moment before reentering the chaos of the council."

I introduce him to Cloh-ee as we walk through the narrow hallways in the castle, and she makes small talk with him in Trovilian. She asks him questions about his role as historian, and the passion he has for his work is clear in each enthusiastic response. I can also see the twinkle in his eyes when Cloh-ee speaks. She has charmed him already.

We enter the same meeting room from the previous day to find the rest of the council members shouting over each other.

I cannot tell what they are shouting about, but I pick up various phrases, such as "need Varrek to lead" and "not the Trovilian way" and "stand for honor and dignity." So it seems they are still arguing about me taking the throne.

I look down at Cloh-ee and roll my eyes. She smirks and then gestures to Ekoya and Cruvo, who sit in the corner, looking amused by the buffoonery displayed by the current leaders of Trovilia.

It confirms for me that I am making the right decision. That Trovilia will soon be in the most capable hands.

Cloh-ee goes to take a seat next to Ekoya, but I stop her. I keep her hand in mine as I go to stand in front of the council members.

At my approach, the council members fall silent.

"I shall make this quick." I look around the room and take in the faces of some of my former fellow citizens. Those I have known since birth. "My father's reign, while impressive at the start, resulted in overwhelming tragedy and pain for our people. It also weakened our alliances with neighboring planets."

I pause, looking into my Cloh-ee's dazzling brown eyes. She nods, encouraging me to continue. I am so glad she can understand my native tongue. I do not think I could get through this part without her. "The legacy that King Muryk Daaskano left behind, unfortunately, should serve as a guide on precisely how not to lead the people of Trovilia."

Diroh interjects, "You dare insult all that King Muryk accompl—"

I open my mouth to silence him, but Cloh-ee beats me to it. "*You dare interrupt Prince Varrek when he is speaking?*" Gasps fill the room at my mate's outburst, in perfect Trovilian. "Your beloved King Muryk was a narcissistic and murderous ghoul, so you can take a fucking seat, sir."

Diroh looks utterly stunned. In fact, all the council members do. They did not expect a human to attend this important meeting, let alone take control of it. But while Diroh's eyes swirl with humiliation and rage, the others seem...impressed?

I do not blame them. My Cloh-ee is fierce in all that she does. My heart has chosen well.

Bihluk clears his throat. "Respectfully, Cloh-ee, these are Trovilian matters, so if you could please refrain from stealing focus."

"Respectfully, Bihluk, she might not be Trovilian, but she was kidnapped and locked in that wretched dungeon as well, so she has every right to object to Diroh's pathetic fawning over King Muryk," Ekoya hollers from her seat in the back.

I nod in agreement and shoot Bihluk a hard stare. His chin dips. "Varrek, please continue."

"Right." I straighten and give my mate's hand a grateful squeeze. "While I am honored to be given the opportunity to take the throne and restore Trovilia to a place built on honor and dignity, I simply cannot.

"Trovilia is no longer my home. It stopped being my home the moment I escaped and was presumed dead by all of you. I have built a new life on Oluura, a life that fulfills me. There, I am surrounded by the family I chose, and it is where I shall remain, with my mate. And perhaps, someday, the family she and I will build together."

The council members sit silently, letting my decision sink in. "Very well, if Varrek does not want the throne, we will select a suitable candidate ourselves," Diroh suggests, barely containing the glee in his voice.

"No, Diroh, you will not," I reply with a grin. "As heir to the throne, I have the authority to appoint the candidate whom I find suitable, and a majority vote from the council shall solidify it."

Everyone turns to Bihluk. "This is true," he confirms.

Diroh looks as if he has hundreds of objections to this law, none of which I care to hear.

"I choose Ekoya Nizahno to take the throne as Queen of Trovilia, effective immediately."

Ekoya's mouth falls open. "Varrek, wha—"

"This is insanity! She has been underground for five years!" Diroh sneers. "She has no concept of what it means to lead."

I ignore Diroh and focus my attention on the remaining members of the council. He will never agree to this, but I do not need his vote. I just need theirs.

"The virus that took the lives of so many of our people, our females—Ekoya survived it. Then she was locked in a cage underground. Again, she survived. She brought her fellow prisoners together and found a way to escape." I gesture to Ekoya, who still looks shocked down to her bones. "Now here she sits. A fighter. A survivor. A leader. She has the drive to take charge and repair the damage that my father's reign has caused the people of Trovilia. Remember, this is after years of living in darkness, forgotten and tortured. Trovilia let her down, and she remains passionate to make it a better place for those who live here. Even I am not willing to do such a thing."

I turn to Bihluk. "You wish to find a way to repay Ekoya for all that she suffered? Allow her to lead. Give her the opportunity to lead Trovilia with empathy."

I am not certain any of the council members will agree to this. In fact, I would expect them not to, but the passion in Ekoya's eyes when she talked about all that I could change made me believe that she would be more effective in making those changes than I or anyone else would be.

Bihluk nods, his eyes twinkling as his gaze goes to Ekoya. "Ekoya, you seem surprised by Varrek's proclamation. Is he correct in that you wish to claim this role and the burdens that come with it?"

She turns to Cruvo, and the panic that shone on her face is quickly replaced by determination after he gives her a reassuring wink. She stands. She smiles at me, her eyes bright, and then at Bihluk. "Yes, I would be proud to rule Trovilia."

Diroh scoffs and throws his hands in the air. "What happens if the experiments we conducted have resulted in Ekoya's restored fertility? She is mated. What if she ends up carrying Cruvo's young? We cannot have a pregnant queen!"

Cloh-ee laughs indignantly at Diroh. "Or you'll have someone in charge who can rule an entire planet while growing a new life inside her body at the same time. Maybe look at it as the impressive feat that it is?" Then her cheeks turn pink. "Sorry, I know I'm not supposed to weigh in here. Sorry."

She gives me a sheepish glance, and it takes every shred of

willpower I have to keep from lifting her into my arms and smothering her with kisses for defending Ekoya.

Bihluk smiles warmly at Cloh-ee. "We appreciate you offering that perspective, Cloh-ee."

He turns to his fellow council members. "This calls for a vote. A majority will determine whether Ekoya Nizahno shall be named Queen of Trovilia. If you wish to name her as queen, say 'zai.' If you do not, say 'zik.'"

Cruvo stands at Ekoya's side and takes her hand as the vote begins. Bihluk calls on each council member by their area of expertise.

"Scientific research?"

"Zai."

"Healers?"

"Zai."

"Farmers?"

"Zik."

"War council?"

"Zik," Diroh spits.

The votes are tied. I hold my breath as they continue, trying not to squeeze my mate's delicate hand too tightly.

"Essential laborers?"

"Zai."

"Teachers?"

"Zik."

It is all down to Bihluk's vote now. If he does not vote zai, Ekoya will not be queen, and they will select someone else, since I turned down the role. I suspect the council members who voted against Ekoya have other candidates in mind that influenced their vote. Perhaps they long to take the throne themselves.

Bihluk inhales deeply. "It seems I am the deciding vote."

He clasps his hands together and tilts his head, thinking. "As the council's historian, I have studied the different approaches to leading a society since our people first settled here. I have also studied the leadership methods from many planets, in many galaxies. It does not matter the race, or the species. A leader who instills fear in their people stunts the growth of their society. In some cases, it even causes hatred among neighbors, and violence inflicted upon the most vulnerable."

He rises from his chair and steps off the dais, turning to face the council members. "This is the Trovilia King Muryk built. But it does not have to be the Trovilia of tomorrow." Bihluk swivels to look at Ekoya. "Therefore, I vote zai, to allow Ekoya to instill hope in the hearts of all Trovilians, and to give our society a chance to thrive once more."

Cloh-ee is the first to clap and scream with delight, and the council members that voted for Ekoya quickly follow suit. Ekoya's eyes fill with tears as Cruvo lifts her and twirls her around.

Diroh crosses his arms and pouts like a petulant child.

After a few moments of celebration, Bihluk quiets the room and calls for Ekoya to stand in front of the council. "Ekoya Nizahno, you have been officially named Queen of Trovilia. The crowning ceremony will take place in two days. In the meantime, you will be moved into the royal quarters of the castle. You must also select your chief adviser. This person shall provide thorough, constant guidance and support in your decision-making throughout your reign as queen. There will be—"

Ekoya interrupts, "I already know who I want for chief adviser, Bihluk. You."

"You wish to appoint…me?" Bihluk eyes swirl with astonishment.

"Yes," she says confidently. "Are you able to continue serving as council historian as well as chief adviser?"

He clears his throat, trying to hide his emotions. "Well, yes."

"Grand! You are my chief adviser, then."

"Oh, well, I-I am honored, Queen Ekoya." He bows his head in respect, and she beams at being addressed as queen for the first time.

Ekoya's chin lifts as she surveys the room. She instantly has the air of a queen.

Cloh-ee and I offer our congratulations before we leave, giving her space to discuss logistics with Bihluk and truly step into her new role.

I feel as if a massive weight has been lifted from my shoulders. My father is gone, my mate is safe, Ekoya is alive and now Queen of Trovilia, and I may return to the only home my heart recognizes: Oluura.

There is just one thing left to do.

Cloh-ee touches my elbow. "You ready?"

"Ready," I tell her.

* * *

"Damn, it's windy out here." Cloh-ee pulls her new cloak tightly around her arms. Her long mane whips in the wind behind her as she scans the valley.

I pull her tightly against me as we walk from the zip ship to the Resting Lands, where our loved and lost are buried. This sacred ground is a quick journey from the castle and is located just outside Oovahr City.

I spent much time here before fleeing to Oluura, and the memories of burying the bodies of virus victims come rushing back more intensely the closer we get. There were days when I would be here with many other males, covered in soil, from sunup to sundown because there were so many newly deceased.

"You cold too?" Cloh-ee asks as she feels a deep shiver run through my body. It is not the temperature that has me chilled to the bone, however. It is the reminder of the torment I felt here.

She gives me a knowing look, heavy with sympathy, and rubs my back as we step through the stone arches of the Resting Lands.

"I like the trees. Is the spacing of them intentional?" Cloh-ee asks as we pass by the rows of trees.

"Yes, for each person we lose, we plant a tree at the top of their resting place. The height of the tree indicates how long they have been buried. The taller the tree, the longer they have been gone." I point to the saplings scattered throughout the Resting Lands, indicating new losses. "It is a way to thank the land for accepting the vessels that formerly held the souls of our loved ones."

Cloh-ee tilts her head thoughtfully. "That's lovely. What a great idea."

My mother is buried in the very back, with an unbreakable glass case containing her most prized possessions on the soil to mark her location. It holds her crown, the gold Daaskano armband my father gave her after their mating ceremony, and a vial with my baby fangs.

I tell Cloh-ee the stories behind each item in my mother's resting case, and somehow, she laughs and cries simultaneously through each one.

"Thank you for accompanying me." I kiss the top of her head and breathe in her scent. Even in this blustery weather, her scent is strong enough to calm my soul.

"Of course." She wraps her arms around me and buries her head into my chest. "I wish I got to meet her. She seems like she was supremely cool."

I smile. "You are correct about that."

I wave my hand over the top of the case, and a hologram of my mother pops up to deliver the standard message of all who are buried here. "Opli hu vihlka cial g'ti sehluz," which means, "My soul is at rest now."

Cloh-ee jumps at the initial sight of the holo but soon mutters "wow" as she circles it in awe while my mother speaks.

My mother would have adored Cloh-ee. I know it. With her kind heart and her tireless pursuit of all that is good and just. She radiates a constant warmth that draws people in. I am not surprised that my heart chose her for me. But I am infinitely lucky that she chose me back.

"You could introduce yourself to her if you would like," I tell her.

"Oh, yeah, I guess you're right."

She clears her throat and pulls away from me just enough to stand straight. She nervously pats her cloak and runs her fingers through her mane, tidying the wild strands that have been mussed from the wind. She takes this seriously, and my heart thunders in my chest at the sight.

"Hello, Queen Vahla." She waves hello at my mother's resting place.

"It is such an honor to meet you. I've heard so many wonderful things from Varrek, and I wish you were standing in front of me so I could hug you for bringing such a sensational male into this world."

She pauses, her bottom lip quivering. "I'm sorry your life was cut short. It's not fair, what happened to you, and what happened to the others. But I hope you'll take comfort in knowing that your son has become the kind of leader you knew he'd be one day. He is a symbol of hope for his people. An endless source of generosity. He may not be King of Trovilia, but as the leader of his clan on Oluura, he continues to put their needs above his own."

She takes my hand and meets my gaze, her eyes glistening. "He also saved me. He protected me and my friends from a life of slavery and…probably a lot of other awful things I don't even want to think about. I will love him with every cell in my body for the rest of my days. I promise."

I pull her into my arms and cover her lips with my own. It is a gentle kiss, but full of emotion. My lips move over hers slowly, deepening as we press our bodies together, never getting as close as we need to be.

After a moment, I pull away, and she rewards me with a smile so big and full of adoration my knees almost buckle. "What now?" she asks, her voice cracking with emotion.

I sigh, feeling overwhelming relief at what comes next. "Now, inara, we go home."

CHAPTER 26

CHLOE

A week passes by in a flash. Although, with the long trip back from Oluura and the nonstop sex I've had with Varrek, time was sure to fly.

We still haven't completed the mating bond. Not yet, anyway. Despite the fact that I've been nervous about having Varrek in my head twenty-four seven for the rest of time, my resolve is weakening.

Almost losing him has made me reconsider.

We may have had a rocky start, but I trust him. I believe that he feels bad for lying about his past. And really, he only did it because he was afraid I would judge him for his father's actions. I get that. Especially after the pain he experienced on Trovilia before he left. I'd want to put that whole nightmare behind me too.

After we returned from the Resting Lands, we packed the ship with extra furs, cloaks for the entire clan to wear during the colder months, spices for Waldric, translators for Ava and Kate (along with a few extra), and a video message for Nalba from Ekoya, loaded onto Varrek's screen pad. Ahlvo, still in stasis following his surgery, was loaded up as well inside a med tube.

We said a bittersweet goodbye to Ekoya and Cruvo, wishing the freshly crowned Queen of Trovilia well in her new role and begging her to come visit Oluura the first chance she gets.

And since the moment we landed back on Oluura, life has been a bit chaotic. Between helping Bruvix open comm lines to Trovilia, setting up perimeter tracking devices to announce incoming ships, and overseeing dragon patrols, Varrek has been busy from dawn until dark each day. The only time we get together is at night, and we have certainly been making the most of it.

The dragon patrols have resumed because Kate had another sighting while we were gone. She was at the edge of the forest again, and the big blue dragon swooped down near her, but this time, it dropped the limp corpse of a decapitated tr'gory at her feet. I have no idea why she ventured into dragon territory after that frightening first encounter she had, but at least it seems like the clan believes her now.

I'm worried about her though. When Varrek and I first landed, Ava, Kate, and I jumped on each other in a pile of sobs and hugs, but since then, Kate has been quiet. Despondent. It's like she's haunted by that dragon.

Before I was taken to Trovilia, she was definitely struggling, but it was different. She'd fake her smiles around the clan. Now she doesn't even do that. There's no attempt to mask her fear, or whatever it is that's messing with her mind. I've tried asking her about it, but she brushes it off every time, claiming she's "just having trouble sleeping."

Ava has been spending all her time at Kaiva's, tending to Ahlvo. Sometimes she even sleeps there, on the med bed next to Ahlvo, so she can be there if he needs anything in the middle of the night. His leg is still healing, and it will take a long time for him to make a full recovery, but Kaiva is confident he'll be able to do so, as long as he listens to her and doesn't try to do too much too soon.

That's been the main problem, and why Ava is there so often. Ahlvo, the carefree, charming goofball, is apparently a terribly difficult and stubborn patient. He's been quite the grump about not being able to train with the other warriors and has made several attempts to hobble out of Kaiva's when no one is looking.

We've all offered to take shifts babysitting Ahlvo, but Ava hasn't taken us up on it. She insists she has it covered, but I suspect she has trouble being away from him for even a moment.

So among checking on Ava and Ahlvo, keeping an eye on Kate's mental state, and attacking Varrek with my mouth, I've been spending less time at Nalba's each day, much to her chagrin.

But I don't think she minds all that much, since the comm line to Trovilia has been opened and she can chat with her sister, Ekoya, every chance she gets.

Seeing her face when we told her Ekoya had survived the virus and was now Queen of Trovilia was priceless. It was as if Nalba experienced every extreme emotion possible in the span of three seconds. And then she sobbed so hard I had to hold Varrek's screen pad for her so she could watch Ekoya's message while kneeling in the dirt.

"Cloh-ee? Little human with the strange round ears!" Nalba hollers across her shop.

"Oh, sorry. What were you saying?" I continue trying to scoop a single hair from the milky liquid of a douku orb before sealing it closed. "I'm listening, I promise. I just…can't get the…arghhh."

I put down the curved wire I was using to pull the hair and take a breath.

Nalba chuckles, shaking her head disapprovingly. "If you are this distracted now, you will be insufferable once you complete the mating bond."

Really? I don't want that. "Is it that overwhelming?"

"I cannot say for sure because I have not experienced it myself, but my mother would tell me many stories of tasks she tried to complete when she was first mated to my father and how difficult it was for her to get anything done." Nalba looks disgusted at the idea of not being able to focus on work. "It is much like having a conversation with your mate that never ends, she would say."

Oh. When she puts it like that, it sounds nice. Saying goodbye to Varrek in the mornings is torture. I hate it. If our minds were connected, it'd be like we're always together.

Memories of the moment I was taken from the woods fill my

mind, and I shudder when I think about the dirty cage I woke up in on Trovilia. The thought of never seeing Varrek's face again, or that beautiful smile of his—fangy but sweet at the same time. The long nights I spent wide awake on the floor of that cage, sniffing the tattered sleeve of my dress and trying to hold on to Varrek's faint scent that remained, terrified of the day it would completely fade.

Anxiety fills my gut, causing me to brace my hands on the table in front of me for support. "I, uh…Nalba, I need to go. Is that okay?"

Her eyes widen in alarm. "Cloh-ee, what is it? What is happening?" She looks around and out the windows, searching for the source of my panic.

"No, no. It's nothing. I need to see Varrek right now. I'll be back in the morning, okay?" I push my tools together in a messy pile and grab my cloak as I head toward the door.

"Okay," Nalba calls from her seat, confusion in her tone.

I race out of Nalba's shop and turn toward the training grounds. I pick up my pace with each step as my desperation to be near Varrek, to touch him, threatens to consume me.

No more waiting, I decide. I need to be wholly his, and I want him to be all mine. I want to complete the mating bond, and I want our minds connected.

I hear Waldric call out a cheerful greeting as I pass, but I don't slow to respond. My mind is focused completely on getting to Varrek. Nothing else matters.

I see the clearing in the distance and hear the clashing of sword against sword as I get closer. I should probably slow my pace, as running into a crowd of tall, muscled aliens swinging swords around is certainly a bad idea. But my legs keep pushing.

Varrek sees me approach and steps away from his opponent, dropping his sword to the ground. He opens his arms right before I launch myself into them, wrapping my arms and legs around his big body and squeezing tight.

He rubs my back soothingly as he holds me. "Cloh-ee, what is wrong? Are you well?" He pulls my face back so he can search my eyes. When he sees that I'm smiling, he looks baffled.

I give him a quick kiss and then whisper against his lips, "We need to go home. I want you to fuck me, and then we're completing the mating bond. Right. Now."

He yells at Bruvix to take over the training session and not to bother him with anything until tomorrow.

He walks with purpose out of the training grounds with me still clinging to him. He doesn't put me down. Seeing him carry me through the village like I weigh nothing is making me crazy with need. I run my tongue along the veins in his neck and rub my body against his.

I'm sure people are watching us. It's the middle of the day, and the clan is either going to or coming from lunch. But all I want is Varrek. If he threw me down in the middle of the path and pulled out his long, thick cock, I'm certain I'd spread my legs and beg him to take me.

He groans as I continue to grind against him, and I can feel his steps getting clumsy. I nip at his lip, and that causes him to speed up.

He jogs the rest of the way, throwing open his front door and not even stopping to close it before racing up the stairs. I bounce in his arms, my breasts bob against his chest as he goes, and a low growl erupts from his throat at the contact.

When we finally reach his bedroom on the top floor, he lowers me onto the soft, shaggy rug a few feet short of the bed. He's panting, his chest heaving. "No more. Cannot...wait," he mutters as his hands fly to my shirt and he lifts it over my head.

I look up into his green eyes to find his pupils blown out, making his eyes almost completely black. I love watching him lose control. I'm addicted to it. Because I am the cause. Always so calm and steady, my Varrek. Not now though.

His mouth latches onto my nipple, sucking hard, and I cry out. My hands go to his hair and pull, needing to anchor myself to something. Anything. He loves when I do this. When I get wild with lust and pull his hair or scratch his back. He groans against the hardened peak as his tongue circles it, and I feel a brush of his fang against my nipple. It makes me think of the bite I'll soon endure, and I can't imagine feeling anything but ecstasy when his fangs sink into my skin.

He tears at my leggings, pulling my boots off with my pants. Then I lie back down on the rug, naked and too turned on to feel even a tinge of self-consciousness. Besides, the way Varrek takes me in, gazing down at me like I'm a treasure he's been searching for all his life, it's impossible not to feel beautiful. I squeeze my breasts, pulling on my nipples as he strips down.

"My Cloh-ee," he groans. "I am the luckiest male." He pulls his shirt over his head and tosses it to the side. Then he's standing above me, his body glorious and brutal, both.

I point to the intricate tattoo covering his bicep. "What does that mean? The design. I haven't seen it on anyone else here."

"It is the royal Daaskano band. It signifies my former role on Trovilia," he says with a flex of his arm.

"You mean your secret past has been right in front of my eyes this whole time? In a tattoo?"

He chuckles, the sound low and gritty. "I suppose it has, my mate."

I take him in, from head to toe. This gorgeous alien. His cock hard and standing at attention. My mouth waters at the sight. My pussy clenches around nothing, and I moan.

"Varrek, please." I hold out my hand, and he takes it, letting me pull him down until I roll our bodies and I'm straddling him. He stares down at my pussy and licks his lips. "Need you now," I beg before he can get any ideas about foreplay.

Don't get me wrong, his tongue against my clit is heaven, but there's time for that later.

He spreads my folds and inserts a finger. His eyes close in what appears to be pure bliss as he adds a second finger. "You are ready for me, inara. So wet for me."

"Yes, Varrek. More…give me more," I mumble mindlessly as he crooks his fingers inside me and rubs my G-spot. "Please. Please."

He pulls his fingers from my body and takes his cock in hand. I lift myself high enough to hover above him before slowly sinking down. Then all the air leaves my lungs when he grips my hips and pulls me down, his cock fully sheathed inside me.

He leans up and braces himself on one arm, so he's seated on the rug and we're face to face, and places soft, fluttering kisses along my forehead. He presses his forehead against mine and whispers, "I am yours until the end of time, just as you are mine."

I nod, unable to speak. I kiss him instead, letting my mouth tell him all the things I can't say in this moment.

Then he starts to move. His hips pump upward as I slam mine down in a perfect rhythm. He quickens his pace, and my breasts bounce as I hold on to his shoulders and fuck him hard. His cock is vibrating inside me, driving me mad. The slap of our bodies fills the air.

Varrek's mouth moves to my chin, and then his tongue traces my jawline, and my heart thunders in my chest knowing he's getting close to my neck. He's going to bite me soon, and I'm desperate for it.

"I am close, Cloh-ee. I cannot wait much longer. You feel too good," he says, his voice husky and low in my ear.

He reaches between our bodies, and his thumb circles my clit. "Varrek! Yessss!" I cry as he pushes lightly on the left side of my clit. "Close. So close."

He pulls his hand away as I ride him harder, faster, his vibration spreading out to reach my clit. Then I'm gone. Stars dance behind my eyelids as I come, screaming his name along with several unintelligible sounds.

I barely feel him turn my head to the side before he strikes. His fangs sink into the base of my neck just as I'm starting to come down, and his bite extends my orgasm. I feel like I'm flying, and there's no pain. Or if there is, there's too much pleasure to even notice it.

After a moment, he pulls back and licks my wound, his rough tongue cleaning the blood away.

"Cloh-ee," Varrek says, pulling me out of my haze. "You must return the bite."

I can feel his thrusts getting faster and slightly erratic, so I know he's close. I wait until he roars his release and sink my teeth deep into his chest, on his right pectoral, just above his nipple.

"More!" he grits. "You must draw blood."

It feels wrong to do this, to deliberately hurt him, but this is the mating bond, and this is what must be done to complete it. He holds my head against his chest, keeping me in place as I sink my teeth in deeper.

He grunts as a sticky, coppery liquid hits my tongue. I suck it down and lick at his wound the way he did mine.

Our chests continue to heave against each other as we both come down, and he pulls me down and rolls us so we're on our sides. He's still inside me, and I feel like I never want him to leave. My body is buzzing from his bite, and even though our bodies are pressed against each other, he still feels farther away than I want him to be. Is this the mating bond?

He gently brushes my damp hair off my forehead, and a yawn escapes my lips. "Mmm," I groan, "why am I so tired all of a sudden?"

"It is the bond," he chuckles. "We must sleep now, to let our minds reach each other. When we wake up, we will be connected, mind and spirit."

I smile, putting my head on his chest. "I can't believe I was so worried about the bite. It didn't even hurt."

He kisses my hair, and he strokes up and down my spine. "My mate likes a little pain with her pleasure, I see."

I let out another yawn and let my eyes close. "Guess so."

* * *

I FEEL my lips stretch into a smile before my eyes open. In my mind, I see...me. It's like a mirror, even though I'm not looking at one. I look different. Better. Like a goddess, kind of. My hair is spread out around my head like a halo, my skin is perfectly clear, and my lips are plump and pink. Instead of looking like a sleep-deprived gargoyle, I look like I was professionally styled.

Then I realize, this is Varrek, in my head, showing me what he sees.

Do you see now how lovely you are? My stunning mate.

My eyes shoot open, and I find Varrek propped up on one elbow, looking down at me with a sleepy grin on his face.

At last, she awakens.

"Holy shit!" I shout. It was Varrek's voice, but inside my head. His lips didn't move. That was freaky.

Freaky? This is not a word I know. It is good or bad?

I pause, trying to figure out how to send him my thoughts.

Stop trying, inara. I am already here.

Oh. Okay, then. *Test. Test. Test. Your body is a wonderland.*

I am glad you find my body pleasing.

I chuckle at the lyric he didn't pick up on, and his eyes widen as I play the song in my head.

I shall see your home world this way. I am quite excited for that, Chloe.

Wait! How are you getting my name right here, but it sounds different when you say it?

He tilts his head, thinking. *Have I not been saying your name correctly?* I can feel his anxiety pulse through my brain at the thought.

It's okay. It wasn't totally incorrect; you just say it with a pause in the middle. Maybe it's your accent?

He nods. *Ah, yes, that is probably the case.*

So now that our minds are connected, neither one of us can tell a lie, right? I smirk at him.

This is true...

Good! I've been meaning to ask, did you actually try contacting anyone about taking us back to Earth? Or was that a bluff?

Varrek clears his throat, and his chin dips. Uh-oh. I know that look.

It is not what you think, Chloe. I swear it.

He shows me his memories, of the times he thought about reaching out, and the people he considered contacting. The pattern I find in each memory is a lack of trust. It's a long, long trip from here to Earth, and he didn't feel comfortable handing me off to anyone else for a risky journey like that. Plus, there was no way for him to take me himself, so he stalled.

When I see it from his perspective, it does seem a bit ill-advised. Did I think I could just buy a ticket to board a nearby ship and I'd be back home within a few days? This is space. It's pure chaos. I'm incredibly lucky Varrek outbid everyone else at that auction because I could easily be living a different life right now. I could be someone's slave, or perhaps something worse...

You are safe, inara. You are mine. I never would have let them take you from me.

Varrek's thoughts cut through my own, and he sends a rush of loving images into my head, all of us together and how he felt holding me in his arms the first time, and all the times since, and it instantly calms me.

I audibly sigh and lean back down against his chest. *I can't believe we found each other. How lucky are we?*

Perhaps it is not luck at all.

He takes me back to the day of the auction, and I can feel his heart seize at the sight of me. The undeniable pull he felt to get me out of that cage and take me far away. The tether. I get it now. I can feel it. It's so intense I can barely breathe, and I have no idea how he held out so long without just jumping on top of me and biting my neck.

You were not ready. It was not what you wanted. That mattered more than my own needs. It always will. I would have waited a lifetime for you.

Aww. Sweet male. *Well, you're stuck with me now. For the rest of our lives, buddy. Until death do us part.*

Death will not part us, inara. Wherever it takes us, we shall go together.

EPILOGUE

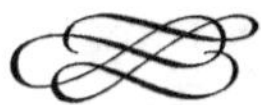

CHLOE

I pull the blankets over my head and burrow deeper into the bed like a sleepy groundhog.

What is a groundhog?

I giggle and send him the clips I remember most clearly from the movie *Groundhog Day*.

I still do not understand.

It's a cute animal that likes to hide in the dirt. He has a day where he predicts the weather, but not really. Don't worry about it, my love, I send back.

He's downstairs in his weapons room, sharpening my throwing knives. We were planning on practicing today, but for the fifth day in a row, I'm beyond exhausted.

We should go to Kaiva's. I do not like how tired you have become. You have been eating less. Your stomach bothers you. It is concerning.

I'm sure it's nothing. The wet season has started, and I just love snoozing when it's raining out. Stop stressing.

I will never stop stressing when it comes to your health and safety!

I pinch my eyes closed to tune out the yelling in my head. *Ugh, okay. I'll be right down.*

Before I can even throw the blanket off of me, Varrek is there, helping me get to my feet. I stumble, and a brief wave of dizziness hits.

He gives me a stern but worried look, and I respond with a nod. He's right. I haven't been feeling well and it's time to see Kaiva.

Varrek kneels to help me put my boots on, and I fall in love with him all over again. Seeing this hulking alien warrior on his knees, delicately holding my ankle as he puts my boot on makes me want to rip off all my clothes and jump on top of him.

Varrek's eyes darken with heat. *There is plenty of time for that later, my mate. Once we know you are healthy.*

I pout like a child as he takes my hand, carefully leading me down the stairs, and pulls my hood up before we step out into the rain.

When we get to Kaiva's, she's putting jars of herbs away on a high shelf, and her smile brightens once we step inside. "Aye, my son and daughter! Come, come." She gestures for us to make our way over to the med tube. It's the one Ahlvo arrived home in, and Kaiva was ecstatic to be able to keep it once he got well enough to move to a bed.

"Any word from Ava or Ahlvo?" Varrek asks.

Kaiva's lips flatten to a grim line. "None since they left." She takes a deep breath and straightens. "Such a stubborn male he is. But I am sure they are well. Aye-vah can handle him."

Because of Ahlvo's ongoing effort to ignore Kaiva's orders and return to training, Varrek has sent him to the small cabin the clan built on the edge of a lake, about four hours away from here. He needed someone to open the comm lines to Trovilia as well as do some fishing during the wet season, and since these are both tasks that require little movement, Varrek ordered Ahlvo to go. He also ordered him to rest in between tasks. Ava went with him to make sure he does just that.

Kaiva looks at us expectantly and clasps her hands together. "Now, what can I do for you?"

I go to tell Kaiva it's nothing, but Varrek beats me to the punch.

When he rattles off my symptoms, his voice is filled with worry, making it seem like I'm dying.

Kaiva pats his arm reassuringly. "Let us see what the med tube has to say about it, yes?"

I climb into the tube and lie back as the top closes over me with a whoosh. Several lights blink, and beeps sound, and I have no idea what any of it means, so I just wait and try not to freak out. Kaiva takes notes on her screen pad, nodding while she does it.

After a few minutes of this, the tube opens, and I climb out as fast as I can. I'm not claustrophobic, but in case I am dying, I don't want to waste another second of this life trapped in a tube.

"Let us sit." Kaiva leads us over to the med beds, and Varrek and I sit down next to each other on the one in the middle.

She takes my hand and Varrek's in hers. "Cloh-ee, you are not sick. You are perfectly healthy."

Varrek and I release matching exhales at the good news.

"As is your child."

Varrek jumps to his feet as my mouth falls open. "Wh-What...did you say? My child?" I stutter.

Kaiva smiles warmly. "Yes, you are carrying Varrek's child. Right now, in your little human belly."

What? How? When? The fuck?

"Child. Right. So that means I'm going to be a mom. Okay," I continue, verbally walking myself through the news as it sets in. Then a loud, unladylike cackle falls out of my mouth.

Varrek and Kaiva laugh along with me, at first. Then they just stare at me, perplexed.

When I feel like I'm no longer possessed by a demon, I explain, "It's just, I thought I was too old to have kids. On Earth, I'm on the older side to become a mom. My eggs were drying up or falling out...or whatever the biological process is. I had given up on the whole mom thing."

I touch my stomach, no longer in disgust at how soft it is—or wishing it were tighter, smaller, without stretch marks, blah, blah,

blah—but in wonder. There's a microscopic half alien, half human growing in there. Wow.

Varrek sits back down beside me, covering my hands with his. Our eyes meet, and his glisten with unshed tears.

You continue to honor me with a life I never thought I deserved. My love for you runs deeper than a thousand seas, my Chloe.

My knees would buckle if I weren't already sitting down. My big alien mate is such a romantic.

Kaiva gives us an armful of teas and herbs for me to start taking and tells us to return each week, or sooner if needed. We put our cloaks back on and head out into the rain. But I barely notice it falling down around us. I'm too stunned with the fact that *I'm pregnant with an alien baby*. And in a place where cheese doesn't exist. How am I going to do this?

I wrap my arm around Varrek's and notice that his face is still plastered with a euphoric smile.

Our lives will never be the same, I send to him.

He leans down and plants a soft kiss on my cheek. *You are right. I cannot wait.*

* * *

THANK you for reading SAVING HIS MATE! I hope you loved Chloe and Varrek's story. Their story might have come to an end, but Ava and Ahlvo's story is just beginning! Find out what happens when Ahlvo returns home from Trovilia with a massive gun shot wound in his leg and Ava takes it upon herself to become his nurse.

CHARMING HIS MATE is available now!

"A wonderful follow-up to book # 1 . Ava & Ahlvo make a great couple. Together they battle their demons , emotional and physical. A mysterious new character appears and now I NEED BOOK #3!" - 5-star reader review

After sustaining a massive injury, Ahlvo has been in a dark place. He can't train with his crew. He can't fulfill his duties as Varrek's second-in-command. And now he's bedridden, stubborn as a mule, and incredibly cranky.

Ava, an Earth native and healer-in-training on Oluura, has been charged with caring for him. Not that she minds. She loves her job, and under normal circumstances, spending this much time with the most charming male in the galaxy would be a treat.

But this is not the Ahlvo she'd come to know.

The longer his leg takes to heal, the more his depression threatens to crush him from the inside. Ava wants to help him, but she knows she can't force him to prioritize his mental health—he has to want to help himself.

Most importantly, she refuses to let her feelings get in the way. No matter how much he flirts with her, no matter how much she trusts him, no matter how many butterflies fill her stomach when his hand brushes against hers, no matter how badly she wants his lips on her.

She feels an intense connection with Ahlvo, but surely he would've told her if she was his fated mate? And in his current mental state, it's not like she can ask.

Will Ava be able to guide Ahlvo through his emotional turmoil? Or will his depression destroy the friendship they've built?

Want to find out what happens next? Start reading Charming His Mate now!

ALSO FROM IVY

<u>ALIENS OF OLUURA</u>

Saving His Mate

Charming His Mate

Stealing His Mate

Keeping His Mate

Healing His Mate

Enchanting Her Mate

(This series isn't finished. There's plenty more to come!)

<u>STRANDED ON EARTH</u>

Her Alien Bodyguard

Her Alien Neighbor

Her Alien Librarian

Her Alien Student

Her Alien Boss

ENJOY THIS BOOK?

If you liked this book, please leave a review. It helps others find my work. Thank you for reading.

Stay up-to-date on bonus chapters, new releases, cover reveals, giveaways, and general smutty shenanigans by subscribing to my newsletter.

FROM IVY

You just finished reading my debut novel and for that, I am endlessly grateful. THANK YOU. I'm currently sending you virtual hugs, or, if you're not a hugger (I respect your boundaries), a virtual fist-bump.

Chloe and Varrek will forever occupy a big chunk of my heart because they're both empathetic, emotional, and bursting with anxiety, which I can very much relate to. You probably noticed that Chloe even takes medication for anxiety, and struggles when she has to go without it.

Chloe and Varrek each experience varying degrees of anxiety and depression, and are brought together by these struggles as often as they are torn apart by them. Honest communication ends up being the key to their Happily Ever After, and now that they can read each other's thoughts, they've got it made in the shade.

Next up is Ava's story. You'll learn about her past, her internal struggles, and how things are going between her and Ahlvo at the cabin by the lake.

You'll also get to know Kate a bit more through Ava's eyes, as they developed a tight bond in the cage before Chloe arrived.

Things are about to get wild on Oluura, y'all. Stay tuned!

Love,
    Ivy

RESOURCES

SAMHSA (Substance Abuse and Mental Health Services
Administration Hotline)
1-800-662-HELP (4357)
TTY: 1-800-487-4889
samhsa.gov

RAINN (Rape, Abuse, & Incest National Network)
1-800-656-4673 (call or chat)
rainn.org

National Suicide Prevention Hotline
1-800-273-8255 (call or chat)
suicideprevention.org

National Domestic Violence Hotline
1-800-799-SAFE (7233) (call or chat)
thehotline.org

ABOUT IVY

Ivy Knox has always been a voracious reader of romance novels, but quickly found her home in sci-fi romance because, frankly, life on Earth can be kind of a drag. When she's not lost on faraway worlds created by her favorite authors, she's creating her own.

Ivy lives with her husband and two neurotic (but very cute) dogs in Chicago. When she's not reading or writing, she's probably watching *The Good Place, What We Do in the Shadows, or Fall of the House of Usher* for the millionth time.